MELT
FOR
YOU

Also by J.T. Geissinger

Slow Burn Series

Burn for You

Bad Habit Series

Sweet as Sin
Make Me Sin
Sin with Me

Wicked Games Series

Wicked Beautiful
Wicked Sexy
Wicked Intentions

Night Prowler Series

Shadow's Edge
Edge of Oblivion
Rapture's Edge
Edge of Darkness
Darkness Bound
Into Darkness

MELT

A SLOW BURN NOVEL

FOR
YOU

J.T. GEISSINGER

Montlake
Romance

Text copyright © 2018 by J.T. Geissinger, Inc.
All rights reserved.

Published by Montlake Romance, Seattle

www.apub.com

ISBN-13: 9781503902138
ISBN-10: 1503902137

Cover design by Letitia Hasser

Printed in the United States of America

To Jay, for teaching me what a real man is, and isn't.

ONE

Top Ten Reasons Why the Holidays Suck

1. I'm fat. As much as I hate to admit it, the point was driven home with brutal clarity by Granny Gums when she saw me at Thanksgiving and said with a cackle, "Looks like somebody already ate the turkey!" I'd blame it on her dementia, but the photos Mom sent me this morning offer irrefutable proof that sometime over the past few years, I have acquired an alarming similarity to a barnyard animal.

2. Snow. Manhattan snow is never white. It's a drab, listless brown, like my hair. (Note to self: call the hairdresser. Red???)

3. Christmas movies. Why is *Home Alone* considered a good holiday family movie? Kevin McCallister and his siblings should be adopted by concerned relatives. And *It's a Wonderful Life*? I'm sorry, but someone has to say it: George Bailey is a dick. There are so many examples of his dickery during that movie, it's another list altogether. One of my favorites quotes: "You call this a happy family? Why do we have to have all these kids?" I can feel the love, Superdad.

4. Christmas shopping. Also known as Standing in Line until You Die, Christmas shopping includes three of my all-time favorite things: screaming children, angry soccer moms, and me aimlessly wandering around a crowded public space until I'm drenched in sweat. December in a mall is like *The Hunger Games* meets *Lord of the Flies*, completed with a reenactment of *Death Race* in the parking lot when you finally try to leave after twelve hours of spending money you don't have. Fun times.

5. Office Christmas parties. Oh, great! Awkward, forced conversations with coworkers I want to unfriend on Facebook!

6. Christmas music. It is awful and depressing. As a perfect example, I offer the lyrics to "Do They Know It's Christmas?" by Band Aid: "There's a world outside your window / And it's a world of dread and fear / Where the only water flowing is the bitter sting of tears / And the Christmas bells that ring there / Are the clanging chimes of doom." Please excuse me while I go jump off a ledge.

7. Santa is a lie.

8. Kiss at midnight on New Year's Eve? The chances of being flattened by a stray asteroid are better.

9. Michael still doesn't love me.

10. See number nine.

"Jocelyn!"

I jerk, startled from my list making by the sound of a voice. It's Portia—blade-thin, elegant, blonde editorial director Portia—looming over my desk, smiling in that way she does that makes me self-conscious and uncomfortable, attacked by her physical perfection and how hideous I feel in comparison.

The woman looks airbrushed. I have back fat, pores a toddler could fall into, and cat hair on my sweater. Normally I wouldn't let her get this close, but the witch snuck up on me.

"Hi, Portia." I peer up at her and nervously adjust my glasses, too weirded out by how she can materialize from thin air like Dracula to be annoyed that's she's called me by the wrong name. Again.

"Would you mind taking a look at this manuscript? Maria called in sick, and we're behind deadline." Without waiting for a response, she drops a thick rubber-banded sheaf of papers on my desk, right on top of the Holidays Suck list I was making on a yellow legal pad. "We need it by Monday."

"Monday?" I stare in horror at the enormous pile of papers.

"Thanks! You're a doll!" Portia turns to leave.

I stand abruptly, knocking over my chair in the process. Because of course I would. It clatters to the floor and makes heads turn in my direction. I sit in the middle of a warren of cubicles on the thirty-third floor of Maddox Publishing, where I've worked for the past ten years. It's four o'clock on a Friday afternoon, and I'm about to make a fool of myself.

So it's situation normal in the world of Joellen Bixby.

I blurt, "Wait!"

Portia stops. She turns slowly, pivoting in a pair of red-soled heels that likely cost more than I make in a paycheck, then props a hand on one bony hip and stares at me with arched brows.

Conscious of the sudden quiet and the field of my coworkers' staring eyeballs, I clear my throat. "Um. I, uh, don't think I can finish it by Monday."

The field of eyeballs eagerly shifts to Portia, who is gazing at me with all the warmth of an iceberg. "You don't *think*?"

She makes it sound as if my cognitive ability is in question. Someone in a cubicle nearby coughs into his hand to hide a laugh.

"I . . . I mean, I'm already so busy with all my other projects, and this one looks like it's fairly substantial . . . I'd have to work all weekend."

Portia sends me a narrow-eyed look that could wither crops. "So you're saying you're incapable of handling your workload. Is that correct?"

Whispers begin to rise all around me. A trickle of cold sweat snakes down between my shoulder blades, and my cheeks flame with heat. "No, I . . . I'm sure I can work it in. Monday it is."

"First thing in the morning," says Portia, in the same tone someone pointing a gun at a cashier would say, "Give me the money."

I swallow. Gulp, actually, like a goldfish. Then I nod, but Portia doesn't see it because she's already turned around and left.

I duck down, avoiding all the smirks and stares aimed in my direction, right my chair, then sit hunched over my desk in misery like Quasimodo. I stay that way for several minutes, silently ordering my hands to stop shaking and my stomach to settle while I gaze at the calendar pinned to the gray felt wall of my cubicle. It features twelve months of Grumpy Cat. December shows the cat in a Santa outfit, complete with a little red hat and black boots.

It's a present from my mother. I must've done some truly awful things in a previous life.

"Why didn't you just say no, Joellen?"

Sue Wong, recent college grad and youngest person to be promoted to the position of acquisitions editor in Maddox Publishing's eighty-year history, stands at the entrance of my cubicle. Sue has shiny black hair that falls to her shoulders, a fringe of bangs so precise it looks like it was sliced with an X-ACTO blade, and an adorable pair of dimples that make her look years younger than her actual age of twenty-three.

I am insanely jealous of those dimples. And of how she can consume approximately five thousand calories per day and never gain an ounce. And of how she is not terrified one bit of Portia, Dragon Queen of the Upper East Side, or of anything else as far as I can tell.

"Because I'll get fired if I say no! I have these little things called bills? Rent? You've heard of them?"

Sue finds my logic faulty and waves a hand dismissively in the air. "Pfft. They'll never fire you. You're a workhorse."

For an unpleasant moment, I imagine myself as a Clydesdale with steam billowing from my nostrils, clumps of dirt flying behind my thick fetlocks as I pull a Budweiser hitch through Central Park.

"And you've been here forever," Sue continues. "Besides, you're in a protected class. Portia wouldn't want to risk a lawsuit."

Genuinely confused, I stare at her. "What protected class is that?"

"Age," she says, as if it's obvious.

"Age?"

"Yeah. You're, like, totally old."

"I'm thirty-six!"

"Oh. Really?" She looks me up and down. "Huh."

I say drily, "Thanks. Are we done with the pep talk? Because I've got a ton of work to do."

"I just wanted to see if you felt like going to that new tapas place after work. A bunch of us are going for happy hour."

She's being nice because I'm so pitiful, which makes me feel even worse. "It's sweet that you always include me, but . . ." I gesture helplessly at the sheaf of papers Portia left on my desk.

"Okay. Maybe next time." Sue departs with a shrug and a smile.

I spend the next few hours at my desk with my nose buried in pages. I keep at it long after everyone else has gone home for the weekend, long after any sane person would've packed it in.

Maybe I ate my sanity with the gallon of ice cream I had for dinner last night.

∞

By the time I get back to my apartment, I've got a headache that feels like a serial killer is drilling a hole into the top of my head with a rusty drill bit soaked in hot sauce. My plan is to eat something, get a few hours of sleep, and get back into the office bright and early to work on the manuscript. Normally I can work on my projects from home using the computer, but paper files aren't allowed to leave the building for security reasons, so I'm stuck going back to my desk.

Thank you, Portia.

As soon as I step off the elevator, I hear the music. It's extremely loud and thumping with bass—some kind of rock. Or maybe rap. I can't tell for sure. All I know is that the lyrics include a few words that would curl my mother's hair.

As I walk down the hall, I'm alarmed to discover the music is coming from the apartment directly across from mine. Judging by all the voices and raucous laughter, my neighbor isn't alone.

Kellen never has parties.

Irritated, I pull up my coat sleeve and look at my watch. I debate whether or not I should knock on his door, but my stomach is making some aggressive rumbling noises that manage to penetrate through the thundering bass, so I decide to eat first and deal with Kellen on a full stomach.

In the event of a nuclear war, the first thing I'd do is eat. I can't handle life when I'm hungry.

As soon as I unlock my door, Mr. Bingley attacks.

"Rr-ow!" He stands on his hind legs and sinks his claws into my skirt.

"I know, baby, I'm sorry I'm so late. Mommy's gonna feed you right now, okay?"

Another howl tells me I better, or there will be hell to pay.

I scratch behind Mr. Bingley's ears, talking baby talk to him the way he likes, which makes him sink his claws deeper into my skirt in pleasure, which in turn makes me wince in pain, keeping the eternal feline/human relationship in balance. He's lucky he's so adorable, or I might . . . do nothing. Never mind.

When it comes to Mr. Bingley, we both know who's in charge.

I close the front door, drop my purse on the table in the foyer, avoid looking at myself in the mirror, and hang my coat in the closet. Then I head to the kitchen, Mr. Bingley trotting at my heels.

He's a bossy, plump ginger tabby cat with amber eyes and a fluffy plume of a tail. He's also totally deaf—the unfortunate side effect of a reaction to antibiotics prescribed for an ear infection. He doesn't seem to mind, however, or even realize he's handicapped. I think he's learned how to read lips.

The only problem is that I can't sneak up behind him. I startled him once, and he ended up hanging by his claws from the living room curtains, wild eyed and hissing.

"You're lucky you can't hear that music," I tell him, removing a can of cat food from the cupboard. "Somebody sounds like they have anger management issues."

Mr. Bingley twines around my ankles, purring and rubbing his head against my legs. I fork the food into his special china dish, put it on the floor, and watch, smiling, as he digs in.

Then I jump at the sound of a woman's scream.

"What the hell?" I rush to the front door. My heart galloping, I flatten myself against the door and peer through the peephole. The hallway is empty. Warily, I ease open the door and poke my head out. Then I hear *another* scream, this one accompanied by the sound of female laughter and a chorus of male hoots.

The noise is coming from the apartment across the hall.

Relieved I'm not dealing with murder, only a house party spiraling out of control, I start to fume. I picture an inflatable kiddie pool filled with Jell-O in the middle of Kellen's living room, a pair of naked girls squirming around in it while a bunch of frat boys gleefully spray them with champagne and dollar bills.

Before I can talk myself out of it, I'm marching across the hall and applying my knuckles with vigor to Kellen's door.

The music doesn't lower, but after a moment, heavy footsteps approach. Then the door opens and I'm rendered speechless.

A man I've never seen before stands in the doorway. He's tall, broad, solid as a mountain and about as large. He has shaggy brown hair, hazel eyes, lots of tattoos, and a devastating smile, which my brain notes at the same time it's trying to process that the man is wearing unlaced combat boots, a kilt, and nothing else.

You could get lost in the canyons between his abs. If he has any body fat at all, it must be hidden beneath the kilt, because his muscles are so defined it's like looking at an anatomical drawing.

Staring open mouthed at his stomach, I say, "Uh . . ."

The Mountain says, "Can I help you, lass?"

Cannae help ye, lass?

Dear God, he's a Scotsman. A huge, half-naked Scotsman in a kilt. Smiling at me like he knows all my secrets, what color my panties are, and that I'm curious what it would be like to have a man pull my hair during sex.

"Uh . . ."

"Ach, sorry, it's the music, innit? Just havin' a wee party. I'll get it sorted." Over his shoulder he thunders, "Turn the bloody music down, you dumb knobdobber, you're disturbin' the neighbors!"

Inside the apartment are people of both sexes, drinking and laughing, in various stages of undress. They lounge on the sofa and sit cross-legged on the floor around the coffee table, where a blonde woman with stupendously large naked breasts is dealing cards.

I start to blink as if I'm trying to signal someone in Morse code.

The music lowers one decibel, and the Mountain turns back to me with a triumphant smile. He's weaving slightly on his feet. And unless he doused himself in malt-and-barley cologne, he's been drinking what smells like an awful lot of beer.

Before I recover the power of speech, he belches loudly, sends me a jaunty salute, then slams the door in my face.

TWO

When the alarm goes off at five o'clock the next morning, I'm jolted from a disturbing dream about Mel Gibson leading a clan of burly kilt-wearing warriors into battle. There's a lot of spears, screaming, and blue face paint, along with copious belching.

I grope for my iPhone on the nightstand, knocking it to the floor in the process.

"Mr. Bingley." I gently poke the slumbering ball of fur on my chest. "Mr. Bingley, wake up."

He lifts his head from his paws and blinks, then yawns cavernously, flattening his ears and displaying his canines. Then he lowers his head and promptly goes back to sleep.

"Mr. *Bingley*," I insist, rubbing his cheek. "I have to get up."

His answer is a gentle snore.

"C'mon, kitty, Mommy has to go to work so she can afford to buy you kibble. You don't want to starve, right?"

Sometimes, like now, I wonder if his hearing is better than he lets on, because in answer to my question I get a tail flicked in my face.

"You leave me no choice." I roll to my side, dislodging the cat. He leaps clear with a little disgruntled chirrup at my bad manners.

I fish my phone off the floor, then hold it an inch from my nose as I fumble to find the "Stop" button on the alarm. I grab my glasses from the nightstand and put them on, bringing the room into view.

Mr. Bingley sits at the end of the bed, giving me a look like I've offended his great ancestors.

"I know, I'm a disobedient slave. Let's go get breakfast."

I shuffle into the kitchen with the cat at my heels. I feed Mr. Bingley, then make myself a cup of coffee while waiting for last night's leftovers to reheat in the microwave. I made meat loaf—my grandmother's recipe, the best comfort food in the world—and listened to the party rage on across the hall. I was tempted to call the police, but that seemed snitchy, so I suffered through hours of screams and laughter until it got quiet around one a.m. because, I assume, everyone passed out.

Or whatever it is people do after a rousing game of strip poker.

I'm shoveling meat loaf into my mouth when a door slams out in the hallway. Curious to see who's doing the walk of shame at quarter past five on a Saturday morning, I head to the front door with my plate and peer out the peephole.

There stands the Mountain across the hall, wearing a gray sweatshirt and matching sweatpants on his massive frame. He's got a pair of earbuds in and is thumbing through his phone, swiping his finger across the screen like he's searching for something. Music?

Is he going jogging?

No. That would be ridiculous. It's December in New York City. The sun isn't even up yet; I'd be surprised if the temperature outside is above freezing. And let's not forget the boobs and beers of last night. He's probably nursing a massive hangover, not to mention considerable chafing in his groin area. And he couldn't have had more than four hours of sleep, tops. He's probably just going to Starbucks.

He finds whatever he was looking for on his phone, tucks it inside his waistband, and starts to do stretching exercises.

You don't need to stretch to go get coffee.

The man is stretching in a hallway at quarter past five on a Saturday morning after a long night of debauchery, in preparation for a predawn run in the freezing cold.

Clearly, he's not human. And he's crazy. He's an insane kilt-wearing alien who enjoys dirty card games, big breasts, alcohol, and early-morning jogs around dangerous urban areas.

Fascinated, I watch as he does this whole elaborate routine of bends and flexes, warming up his muscles. By the time he's done, I'm exhausted. I'm also finished with my meat loaf. Then the Mountain jogs off down the hallway, headed in the opposite direction of the elevators, which means he must be taking the stairs.

We're on the nineteenth floor.

I wish I had Kellen's phone number so I could find out who this psychopath is. But Kellen and I are only friendly neighbors, not friends who do things together, so I'm out of luck.

I shower and dress, then kiss Mr. Bingley good-bye and head to work. The morning air on my face is a freezing slap. It's a half-block walk to the subway station, but it might as well be a half marathon for the way I'm sweating and wheezing when I get there, despite the cold. I've got a treadmill in my bedroom I keep promising myself I'm going to use, but its current main purpose is as a clothes hanger.

It's another half-block walk to the office. I ride the elevator up to the thirty-third floor with Denny, the building's head maintenance guy, who, for the past ten years has been telling me the worst jokes ever invented.

Invariably, they involve farts.

"An old woman goes to the doctor," he says, starting in as always with no preamble. "She says to the doctor, 'I have a really embarrassing problem. You see, I constantly fart, but my farts don't smell, and they don't make any noise, so it hasn't bothered me all these years. I've even farted three times since coming into your office.'"

Denny looks at me to make sure I'm listening. I nod solemnly, wondering if perhaps I died years ago in some terrible accident and I've been living in purgatory ever since. Honestly, it would explain a lot.

Denny continues. "'I see,' says the doctor, and prescribes her some pills. 'Take these three times a day, and come back for a checkup in a week.' A week later, the woman storms into the doctor's office. 'Doctor, what have you done? Ever since I started taking those pills, my farts have become unbearably smelly! You've made it worse!'

"The doctor calmly replies, 'Now that we've cured your sinuses, let's start working on your hearing.'"

My smile is feeble. "Good one."

"You think? I told my wife that joke this morning at breakfast, and she didn't think it was funny."

Denny has been married for about one hundred years to Phyllis, a woman I've never met but for whom I have great sympathy.

"Here's my floor. Have a great day, Denny."

"See you around, kiddo," he calls as the doors open and I step off the elevator.

The reception area is deserted, as is the cubicle field. I take off my coat and scarf, settle into my chair, and have just removed the rubber bands from the manuscript Portia gave me when from the hallway leading to the executive offices a man appears, striding confidently down the hall with a mug in his hand. He's in navy slacks and a crisp white dress shirt, the collar open and the sleeves rolled halfway up his strong forearms.

My heart stops dead in my chest.

It's Michael Maddox, CEO of Maddox Publishing, the most perfect man who's ever lived.

I've been in love with him for a decade. Inconveniently, he's married.

It's a strange fact that no matter his pace, Michael appears to me to be always moving in slow motion, with a gentle breeze stirring his hair, a golden glow around his head. To call him beautiful would be doing him a disservice. The man is glorious. Godlike. He's a Michelangelo sculpture brought to life. Black hair, broad shoulders, a pair of blue eyes that could melt steel but mostly melt panties. He does, in fact, bear a striking resemblance to Superman.

And he's headed right toward me!

My first instinct is to hide. But he's already seen me, so my desire to throw myself under my desk until he passes will just have to suck it.

"Well, hello there." He stops by my desk and smiles at me, and I swear I hear angels singing. "I see I'm not the only unlucky sod working on the weekend. How are you, Joellen?"

He's originally from London, so he has this incredibly suave British accent, which is made even more incredible as it caresses the vowels in my name. That he remembers me at all makes me quiver all over.

"Good morning, Mr. Maddox."

Thank you, God, for allowing me to sound like a human being and not the screaming playground of kindergarten children that I am inside.

He quirks his lips. "How many times do I have to tell you to call me Michael?"

I nearly faint. Not only does he remember my name, *he remembers having talked to me before.* Sweet baby Jesus, Christmas came early this year.

"Michael." I say his name with such reverence I'm surprised tiny confetti hearts aren't spilling off my tongue. *Don't be weird! Stop staring at him! Close your mouth!*

I look down, cheeks flaming, and realize I'm clutching the manuscript so hard my knuckles are white. I force myself to breathe, which is probably the most difficult thing I've done in years.

"I hope we're not working you too hard." Michael frowns at the death grip I've got on the manuscript.

I unglue my tongue from the roof of my mouth. "Just a little catch-up. Trying to get ahead for next week." *Lies, lies, all of it lies. You are one big fat liar. I wonder if his hair is as soft as it looks?*

"Jolly good! I love to see initiative."

His eyes—the blue of summer skies over an undiscovered tropical paradise—smile along with the rest of his face. He has little crinkle lines around them, which somehow only add to his beauty. Unlike mine, which make me look haggard.

"Well, I do love to take the initiative."

As soon as the words are out, I want to stuff my fist into my mouth so I won't say anything else, because I somehow managed to take an innocent expression and make it sound like I was propositioning him for sex. Which is proven beyond a doubt when Michael's perfectly sculpted brows lift.

"Do you now?" he murmurs, sounding amused.

Why am I like this? I silently beg the universe. *Why can't I be a normal person? When are you going to drop a piano on my head and put me out of my misery?*

After an excruciating moment wherein Michael watches my face burn and my hands act like big pale moths fluttering helplessly around the manuscript, he takes pity on me.

"I'll let you get back to it, then. Can I get you a cup of coffee? I'm just on my way to the kitchen for a refill."

I shake my head, too embarrassed to speak or even look at him.

"All right. Cheers." He lifts his mug in farewell, then heads off toward the kitchen.

As soon as he's out of sight, I slump facedown on my desk and groan.

I shouldn't be allowed out in public.

I don't see Michael again for the rest of the day. He might've thrown himself out a window to avoid having to speak to me again for all I know. Not that I'd blame him. I'm such a loser, it's probably hard for someone like him to breathe the same air as me.

When I leave, it's dark and cold, like the inside of my heart. And a few other places in my body. I'm so deep in self-recrimination mode when I get off the elevator on my floor that I walk right past Mrs. Dinwiddle standing in her open doorway.

"Ducky! *Ducky!*" she calls in an excited voice.

I turn around and blink at her. "Oh, hello, Mrs. Dinwiddle. Sorry, I didn't see you there. I'm a little spaced out today."

She makes a sweeping gesture with the hand she's holding her martini in, causing gin to slosh out and spray the wood floor. "I've got *news!*"

Penelope Dinwiddle is a retired stage actress from Yorkshire, England, who found her fame and fortune in a Shakespeare troupe that toured Europe during the fifties and sixties. Now somewhere north of eighty, she hasn't lost a bit of her theatrical nature. She stands in her doorway wearing red lipstick and false eyelashes, a flowing lavender chiffon robe and matching negligee, a white feather boa, and all her jewelry, including the diamond tiara given to her by some minor prince of the Saudi royal family.

She's been married eight times. Kellen and I call her the Elizabeth Taylor of SoHo.

Giddy with excitement, she waves me over. Somewhere in the apartment, her Filipino caretaker, Blessica, shushes the yipping trio of Pomeranians named Fee, Fi, and Fo.

"So you know *Kellen* went to *Scotland* for the *holidays.*" Mrs. Dinwiddle adds emphasis every few words because there's nothing she loathes more than a dull delivery.

"No, I didn't know that. I haven't talked to him in a few—"

"And his *cousin* the *rugby* player is staying in his *apartment!* They traded *off,* you see?" She tries to clap but only manages to spill more of her martini.

I ponder this information. So the Mountain is a rugby player. And he and Kellen have switched apartments for the holidays.

Wonderful. Judging by last night's performance, I'm in for weeks of hell.

"Blessica ran *into* him this *morning* when she went to walk the *dogs*, and he told her the *whole* story! You know how she can get *anyone* to talk. She told me he was this big *handsome* fellow, but her eyesight isn't what it *used* to be, bless the poor dear. Then I saw him just *moments* ago, and my *word*! He isn't simply big—he's gar*gan*tuan!"

From a pocket of her robe, she produces a Chinese silk fan. She snaps it open with a flourish and begins to fan her face, rolling her eyes in ecstasy at the thought of a large, good-looking athlete living on our floor.

"Yes, he's huge. And noisy. I could hardly sleep with all that commotion last night."

The fanning ceases. She peers at me, perplexed. "Commotion?"

This is when I remember that Mrs. Dinwiddle starts drinking at one o'clock in the afternoon every day because that's cocktail hour in London. Her entire life is still run on London time. By nine p.m., she's anesthetized in a snoring dog pile with Fee, Fi, and Fo on her pink satin bed.

"Never mind. Anyway, I was thinking of making lasagna for dinner tonight."

Mrs. Dinwiddle crinkles her nose. "Italian?"

I resist the urge to sigh. Because I'm pathetic and have zero social life, I always cook dinner for Mrs. Dinwiddle on Saturday nights, but unfortunately my first few suggestions are usually met with a distinct lack of enthusiasm. Divas are notoriously picky eaters.

"How about shepherd's pie?"

"Oh, *lovely*!" She brightens, batting me coyly with the fan. "I haven't had that in *ages*. It reminds me of the time I played Lady Macbeth at the Piccadilly and I met this *strapping* stagehand who was studying to be a *chef*—"

"I'll see you in an hour," I interrupt before she can wax poetic about one of her boy toys of yore.

"All right, Ducky! Ta!"

"Ta," I mutter, stomping down the hall, irrationally angered that an eighty-year-old woman has better memories than anything I could possibly conjure in my most prurient fantasies.

My sexual dry spell has been going on so long it's less of a drought and more of a biblical pestilence.

I open the door to find the cat sprawled in the middle of the living room floor like he's been shot by a game hunter. "Hi, Mr. Bingley."

He doesn't lift his head until the door slams shut behind me, then he leaps to his feet like someone poked him with a hot iron and looks wildly around. Spotting me, he then pretends nonchalance and starts to groom his tail.

"You don't fool me, kitty. You're not that cool. C'mon, help me make dinner."

He follows me into the kitchen, but not too quickly, making sure I know it was his idea and not mine.

I feed him, open a bag of salt-and-vinegar potato chips to snack on while I make dinner, then get all the ingredients ready for the shepherd's pie. I preheat the oven, dice the vegetables, and put a pot of salted water to boil on the stove for the potatoes. I'm in the middle of browning lamb, garlic, carrots, and onions when the music starts up across the hall.

It comes on full blast abruptly, like someone's been listening to earphones and yanked the plug out of the receiver—all hard, squealing guitar riffs and thundering drums, loud enough to rattle my windows. Then the chorus kicks in, sung by a man who sounds as if his hobbies are smoking crack and swallowing razor blades.

Got yo BACK, muthafucka
I be WITH ya, muthafucka
We be gangstas, muthafucka, for LIFE!

"He's got to be kidding me," I say to the cat, who blandly slow blinks in response, like, *He's obviously not.*

I turn off the burner, set down the wooden spoon, and, for the second time in twenty-four hours, march my butt across the hall to knock on my new neighbor's door.

THREE

This time when the door opens, I'm prepared. Or I *would've* been, if the Mountain had been wearing his kilt, or his sweats and hoodie, or pretty much anything else but what he's wearing.

An itty-bitty white bath towel, held closed with one meaty fist, and nothing else.

His hair is wet. His broad, tattooed chest glistens with droplets of water. The towel is so small it splits open over one leg like the slit in a skirt, giving a view of bare muscular thigh so provocative it's probably illegal in some countries.

Staring wide eyed at his leg, I say, "Uh . . ."

The Mountain grins at me. "That's the second time I've left you speechless, lass. Imagine what would happen if I dropped the towel. I'd probably have to call you an ambulance."

Okay, I'll give him this: the accent is hot. Those rolling *Rs*—whew! My ovaries are fanning themselves. But he's obviously full of himself. And who answers the door half-naked? *Twice!*

A narcissist with terrible taste in music, that's who.

I square my shoulders and force myself to look into his eyes. "Can you please turn down that music? It's very loud, and I had to listen to it all night last night—"

He puts his hand to his ear and shakes his head, as if he can't hear me.

Grr. I shout, "Can you *please* turn down the *music*?"

But he's lost interest in what I'm saying and is now sniffing the air, leaning forward with his eyebrows furrowed and his nose up, like a hound.

"What's that smell?"

In my haste, I left my apartment door open behind me. The scent of simmering lamb permeates the hall. "Shepherd's pie!" I shout over the din. "Can you *please*—"

He walks right past me, crosses the hall, and waltzes into my apartment like he owns the place.

"Hey!" I start after him but decide to run into Kellen's apartment and switch off the music first. I've been in there a few times, so I know where the stereo is, and I quickly hit the power button. Merciful silence instantly follows. Then I scramble back to my place in a panic, frantic to throw a blanket over the mound of clean laundry I haven't yet folded, which is strewn all over my sofa.

It's a load of socks and underwear, of course.

I find the Mountain standing over my stove, eating out of the pan of lamb and vegetables *with his fingers*.

"Hey! What the heck is wrong with you?" I flutter around him like a butterfly around a lion, slapping feebly at his hands. "Get your paws out of my dinner!"

"They're clean," he says innocently, licking his fingers. "In case you couldn't tell, I just got out of the shower." Then he winks at me.

Winks. The man has obviously had one too many concussions.

I snatch the pan off the stove and stand in the middle of the kitchen, clutching it by the handle and glaring at him. "Could you please leave now? And keep the music to a dull roar? Other people live in this building besides you, you know."

He licks his lips and runs a hand through his wet hair, which makes all the muscles in his arm bulge. I wonder how often he's practiced that move in front of a mirror, the preening peacock.

"You're not gonna invite me over for dinner? I could help you fold your laundry."

I ked help ye fold yer londray.

He says it with a twinkle in his eye, and I enjoy a brief but satisfying fantasy of smashing the pan against his thick, conceited skull. Jamie Fraser from *Outlander*, he's not.

"I'm Cameron, by the way. I'm stayin' at my cousin Kellen's for—"

"I know," I say, cutting him off. Why won't he *leave*?

"And you are . . . ?"

"Joellen. Nice to meet you. Good-bye."

He glances around my apartment. "What, you don't want to introduce me to your boyfriend?"

"What I *want* is to finish my dinner and not have a wet, half-naked stranger with more muscles than manners standing in my kitchen."

Cameron's grin comes on in full, dazzling, I'm-so-irresistible mode. "So you've noticed my muscles. And you don't have a boyfriend."

For a moment, I'm stupefied. *Is he flirting with me?*

Then I realize no, he's not flirting with me. He's *teasing* me. Because obviously a woman like me—big, bespectacled, alone on a Saturday night with her cat and a basket full of granny panties—doesn't have a boyfriend.

Mr. Bingley sits at Cameron's feet, looking up at him like he wants to be picked up and snuggled. Traitor.

With as much dignity as I can muster, I draw myself up and square my shoulders. "If you'll excuse me," I say coolly, "I have a dinner date. You're making me late for it."

"Oh." He looks flummoxed, as if the possibility I'm telling the truth about having a date is so outlandish he doesn't know what to make of it. He probably thinks I've won a bachelor auction or something. "Well. Right, then. Have a good night."

He turns and swaggers away without another word, leaving me staring at his perfect, retreating backside.

Why is life so unfair that it bestows all the beauty on the least deserving beasts?

Except Michael Maddox. *He* is beautiful both inside and out.

I put the pan on the stove and turn the heat back on, then shut the front door. But not before getting another wink from the Mountain, who's closing his own door just as I'm closing mine. With perfect timing, he spins around, pulls off the towel from his hips, and drops it on the floor, so the last thing I see is a peekaboo shot of his naked ass as the door swings shut.

I'm too young for menopause, but boy is this hot flash a doozy.

Dinner with Mrs. Dinwiddle is an hour of listening to stories about her youth as I shovel food into my mouth and she drinks martini after martini and feeds the dogs right from her plate. Blessica, her caretaker, is about sixty but has the energy of a four-year-old. She bustles around the apartment cleaning things that don't need to be cleaned, generally making me feel like a sloth in comparison. *She'd* never leave a pile of unfolded laundry on the sofa.

By the time I leave, Mrs. Dinwiddle is singing a slurred version of "Danny Boy" in honor of a young Irishman she had a scorching affair with when she was a girl, who drowned himself in the sea when his father refused to allow them to marry.

I'm not entirely sure that story is true, but I find it terribly romantic anyway.

Blessica helps Mrs. Dinwiddle to bed, then we do the dinner dishes, then I go home alone to my apartment, with the possibility of bumping into Michael again at work in the future the only thing to look forward to.

I'm unlocking my apartment door when I hear a long, low moan coming from behind me.

I turn and frown at Kellen's closed door. The moan comes again, followed by a thud that shakes the doorframe. Then a man's low voice starts to murmur indistinctly as the moans and thuds increase. I put two and two together when the moans take the shape of a name.

"Cam! Oh God, Cam, yes, yes, *yes!*"

No, no, *no*. He's having sex with someone! *Against the door!*

Not only is this Scot a rude, boozy playboy with questionable exercise habits, he has sex standing up! Who does that?

Thud. Thud. Moan. Thud.

Apparently, he does.

Shocked, I stand with the dish of leftover shepherd's pie and listen until the thuds and moans reach a thundering climax. The woman screams like an air-raid siren. Cam grunts some unintelligible words—something dirty, I'm sure, though I can't make it out—and then makes a sound like a wolf growling. It raises all the hair on the back of my neck.

Then it's quiet, and I feel like I need to take a shower. In bleach.

Ticked off that I'm now a two-time unwilling participant in the Mountain's sexcapades, I holler across the hall, "She totally faked it!"

I go inside and slam the door shut behind me.

What a pig. What an absolute animal! *What a cocky, conceited, self-centered, insufferable man whore!*

From his perch on the back of the sofa, Mr. Bingley watches with interest as I stomp into the kitchen and violently throw the dish of leftovers into the fridge. "I'm complaining to the super first thing in the morning," I tell the cat while slamming the refrigerator door. "We shouldn't have to deal with this idiot and his music and parties and loud vertical hookups! I *work* for a living! I pay my *bills*! I shouldn't be subjected to—"

Boom, boom, boom!

I pull up short. Someone is pounding on my front door. "Who is it?"

The answer is muffled but clear enough. "Stop spyin' on me, you little Peepin' Tom, or I'll call the super!"

I gasp in outrage. It's Cameron. Accusing *me* of peeping!

I march to the door and yank it open. Into the big idiot's face, I shout, "*I'm* going to call the super because you're loud, obnoxious, and *rude*!"

My tirade loses a bit of steam when I realize he's smiling. And—of course—he's barechested and barefoot, wearing only a pair of shiny black athletic shorts that are so tight the bulge in front practically screams *Look at me!*

Holy cow. This beast is packing some serious heat.

"Starin' at my baby maker again, lass," says the Mountain with a low chuckle. "It's becomin' a bad habit of yours, innit?"

Steam pours from my ears. My entire face goes red. I clench my hands to fists to stop them from curling around his throat. "If you wouldn't prance around half-naked all the time—"

"*Prance?*" he repeats, one eyebrow lifted. "Cameron McGregor does *not* prance."

"—people wouldn't have to be subjected to the sight of your body—"

"You make it sound like a punishment."

"—accosted in their own homes while they're trying to mind their own business—"

"When I know for a fact you actually enjoy it."

My mouth hangs open. "*Excuse* me?"

He grins. "You heard me. I know when a woman wants me."

I'm surprised he doesn't explode into a million tiny caveman shards from the thermonuclear look I give him. "For your information, you're the *last* man on the planet I'd ever be attracted to. In spite of your obviously overinflated opinion of yourself, you're not my type."

"Oh, really?" Still grinning his ridiculous, conceited, pearly-white grin, he props his hands on his hips. "Then why're you always starin' at me like I'm lunch and lookin' at me through your peephole?"

"You're insane," I say flatly.

He jerks his chin at the tiny round window in the middle of my door. "It goes dark when your head's there, blockin' the light. I'd say you stared at me for a good five minutes while I was warmin' up this mornin', lass."

Damn. He knew I was watching.

My face flaming, I glare at him. He grins back at me. This lasts for an uncomfortably long time, until a woman's voice floats into the hallway.

"Cam, get back in here! We're not finished!"

Without looking away from me, he says casually over his shoulder, "Aye, we are, sweetheart. I'll call you a cab."

"Wow. What a gentleman."

He shrugs. "She knew the deal. You don't go home with a stranger after one drink if you're interested in a long-term relationship."

This guy is a real piece of work. "Okay, number one? You're disgusting. Number two? This conversation is over. Number three? If you keep up the noise, I'm not only calling the super, I'm calling the cops."

He cocks his head, looks me up and down, then pronounces, "You're tense. Guess your date didn't go as well as mine did, eh?"

I suddenly understand how otherwise rational people can lose their minds and commit murder in a fit of rage. "It's been real, McGregor." I swing the door closed. It slams shut in his face with a loud, satisfying thud.

Through the door, he says, "I'll make you a deal, Joellen."

"If it involves you swallowing a vial of poison, you're on."

"Bake me one of your shepherd's pies, and I'll be quiet as a mouse. Your pie for my silence." A hint of laughter warms his voice.

"Pie. I get it. Hilarious. What are you, ten years old?"

For an answer, I get two short affirmative knocks on my door, as if we have an agreement, though I've agreed to nothing. Then his door closes across the hall, and I'm left standing there glaring at a slab of painted wood like an idiot.

When I turn around, Mr. Bingley is busy lovingly licking the place where his testicles used to be.

"Ugh. Men. Everything you are is between your legs!"

I console myself with the thought of Michael Maddox, who has more class in his pinky finger than that beast across the hall has in his entire body.

When I hear the beast's door open and close again, I refuse to go to the peephole to get a look at the girl he shagged standing up, even though it nearly kills me.

FOUR

"What did the maxi pad say to the fart? You're the wind beneath my wings!"

"Denny, it's eight o'clock on Sunday morning, and I haven't had my coffee yet. I'm not mentally prepared for fart jokes."

I enter the elevator at work with the enthusiasm of someone ascending the steps of the gallows and slump against the wall, bleary eyed. I had approximately two hours of sleep last night, thanks to the rap concert going on in Kellen's apartment.

Twice I picked up the phone to call the police to make a noise complaint, and twice I hung up before going through with it. Despite my threats to Cameron, I really don't like being cast in the role of the grouchy, fun-hating spinster who's out to ruin everyone's good time. Even if they are selfish idiots. So instead I slept with a pillow over my head, promising myself I'd invest in a pair of good earplugs in the morning.

I had more fitful dreams of Scottish warriors in battle, only this time they all wore tiny white bath towels around their hips.

I don't allow myself to consider why all those bath towels had conspicuous bulges in front. I suspect that's a topic for a trained therapist.

"What do you get when you eat refried beans and onions?"

I heave a sigh and close my eyes. "Denny. For the love of God."

"Tear gas!"

Denny cackles like a crone at his own joke, while I stand with my eyes closed, pondering the life choices that have led me to this moment.

"Why don't little girls fart? Because they don't have assholes until they're married!"

"Okay, that one's a *little* funny," I admit grudgingly, but only because I'm in a special man-hating mood.

"Yeah, that's one of my wife's favorites, too."

Poor Phyllis. The woman is a saint.

The elevator spits me out on the thirty-third floor right in the middle of another fart joke, this one involving the pope. I say good-bye to Denny and trudge to my desk, expecting to be the only moron at work at the crack of dawn on a Sunday, but to my great shock, I'm not alone.

Michael Maddox stands at the wall of windows across from the cubicle field, gazing out into the gray December morning with his hands shoved into his trouser pockets and his proud shoulders rounded with an invisible weight.

I stop dead in my tracks. My heart leaps into my throat. All my nerve endings sit up and holler *rr-ow!*, like Mr. Bingley when he wants his dinner.

Michael looks like he might've slept in his clothes. His hair is rumpled, his shirt is wrinkled, his normally crisply pressed trousers are distinctly *un*crisp. A shadow of stubble darkens his square jaw, and holy *hell* the man is beautiful.

I must make a little gurgle of lust, because Michael turns and sees me standing there, staring at him in a hazy, hormone-fueled stupor.

"Oh," he says, startled.

Oh, indeed. How much drool must be coating my chin?

Flustered, I stammer, "I . . . I'm sorry. I didn't mean t-to disturb you. I just . . . just . . ."

My lips aren't working right. My brain is refusing to coordinate with my tongue, which sits inside my mouth like roadkill, trampled to death and gathering flies.

"You're working again today?"

The universe, taking pity on how utterly pathetic I am, finally allows me the power of speech. "Yes."

Michael draws a breath, squares his shoulders, then smiles. It's forced but gorgeous nonetheless. "We can't be paying you enough for this kind of dedication."

Take off all your clothes and I'll consider us even.

I laugh. It sounds unhinged, like I've recently freebased cocaine.

He blinks at me as a wave of heat rises from my neck to my hairline. I send him a pinched smile, wrench my gaze from his, and scurry over to my desk like some nocturnal rodent in search of food. I collapse into my chair. It wheezes in protest and deflates six inches on its pneumatic cylinder, leaving me boob-high to the desk with my bulky handbag shoved up under my chin.

Which is how Michael finds me.

"Oh dear. Are you all right?"

He peers down at me from his godlike height, genuinely concerned by the ridiculous predicament of the silly mortal girl in the puffy down jacket the color of rancid pea soup that her mother gave her when she moved to New York a lifetime ago and she was too cheap to replace.

Ah, hindsight. You are one giant, ruthless bitch.

"Fine," I manage, cheeks blazing. With as much dignity as I can muster—which isn't much—I push the chair back, stand, set my handbag on the desk, and readjust the chair, all the while acutely aware of Michael's presence.

He must think I'm an absolute train wreck of a human being. He must think I'm a stuttering, clumsy fool who doesn't have the coordination God gave a one-legged goat. He must think—

"I think we need to replace that chair." He frowns at the object in question as if it has offended him by refusing to more stoically bear my weight.

I take that as evidence of his chivalry and nearly swoon. I catch myself before my knees give out and try to casually steady myself against the desk, but I'm too far away, so my casual lean turns into a highly awkward sideways stagger until my thigh collides with the edge of the desk with a thunk that topples the jar of pens next to the computer and sets the calendar of Grumpy Cat swinging from side to side.

I would literally kill a small child right now for the power of invisibility.

"You seem as out of sorts as I am," says Michael with a melancholy smile. "I hope your Saturday was better than mine."

I freeze. *Ohmigod. Was that an invitation to talk about his personal life? Is he asking me about* my *personal life? What do I do? What should I say?*

After a few moments, when it becomes clear I'm unable to act like a functioning adult, Michael's smile falters. "Well, I'll let you get to it."

When he turns to leave, I blurt, "Yes!"

Startled again, Michael looks back at me with wide eyes. "Sorry?"

I make myself a promise that if I can just get through the next sixty seconds without acting like an insane asylum escapee, I'll treat myself to dinner at the Italian place down the street from my apartment, a bottle of wine and all.

"I meant, yes, I'm out of sorts." I say this robotically, concentrating on making my lips form the right sounds while my hormones are doing five-hundred-mile-per-hour laps around my nervous system in Formula One racing mode. "I haven't been sleeping well the last few nights. I have a new neighbor who's apparently trying to turn the rest of us in the building deaf with his music. I didn't realize stereos could be used as torture devices."

The tiny lines around Michael's blue eyes crinkle charmingly. My heart palpitations are so extreme, I stand there and try not to die.

"I had a neighbor like that once."

I can't picture anyone inhuman enough to disturb this beautiful creature in his home, which is probably a golden castle in the clouds staffed by cherubs and unicorns. "What did you do?"

A dimple flashes in his cheek, and all my hormones abandon their mad dash around my veins and collapse into a sighing pile at Michael's feet.

"I went over to his house, explained that he was disturbing me, and asked him to stop."

"And that worked?"

"No, that actually made it worse. So then I beat him up." He laughs at my shocked expression. "I'm kidding. I made a noise complaint to the police, and they took care of it."

Because all my concentration has switched from forming words to battling the urge to lean in and sniff Michael's neck, when I try to smile I end up weirdly baring my teeth instead.

"That's probably what you should do," says Michael, eyeing me warily. I'm sure he's wondering if he's going to need something sharp to defend himself with.

Dear Jesus, just take me. Please just kill me now.

"You're right. I know you're right." Overcome with the urge to slam my face over and over onto my desk, I nod like a bobblehead. "But he lives right across the hall from me, and I wouldn't want to have to see him after that. He'd know it was me who snitched on him because I've already confronted him about it."

A small, adorable crease forms between Michael's eyebrows. "Are you worried he'll retaliate? Is this guy some kind of thug?"

I know it's only my imagination that makes Michael's expression and tone of voice seem *concerned*, but my heart doesn't care. It begins to beat wildly against my rib cage like it's attempting to break out of prison.

My rabid badger smile makes a reappearance. "Well, he is a rugby player! Who knows what the guy is capable of!"

Joellen, you're as useless as snake mittens.

But Michael seems to find truth in my ridiculous statement, because his eyes widen in alarm. "Good God, you live next to a rugby man? That's like living next to a silverback gorilla! Definitely don't confront him again, Joellen. Let the authorities handle it."

"Really?"

He nods vigorously. "Believe me, I had my share of run-ins with the daft buggers when I was at Oxford. They're animals. Animals who're in love with themselves. Rugby players take the term *egomaniac* to a whole new level."

I find myself nodding my head, too. "Yeah, that basically describes Cameron McGregor in a nutshell."

Michael's brows shoot up. "Your neighbor is *Cameron McGregor?*"

Why does he look so horrified? "Um, yes?"

"The captain of the Scotland national union team, the Red Devils? *That* Cameron McGregor?"

"Honestly, I have no idea what team he plays for—"

"Six foot six, messy brown hair, built like a skyscraper, covered in tattoos?"

"That sounds like him, yes."

Michael pulls a face. "Christ. You might want to move."

My heart sinks. "Oh God. That sounds bad."

"I don't know how closely you follow sports, but your neighbor is all over the papers, and usually not for his performance on the pitch. Bar fights, sex scandals, being drunk and disorderly in public . . . McGregor's temper is almost as notorious as his women. The UK gossip rags call him Prince Pantydropper because of the sheer number of his conquests."

Michael wrinkles his nose as he says the nickname, proving beyond a doubt that he's a gentleman of the first order. Only a truly fine man of exceptional character would look down on the ability to cause a horde of women to drop their drawers.

"He's well on his way to earning that title on this side of the pond, too," I grumble, thinking of stand-up sex and strip poker parties. I'm afraid of what I'll go home to tonight. The kiddie pool Jell-O wrestling match suddenly doesn't seem so far-fetched. I sigh, shaking my head. "I hope I don't run into him in the hallway again."

"Steer clear of him, Joellen."

Michael says that with thrilling firmness, with *dominance*, like it's an order he expects to be obeyed. Why that should make my ovaries sit up and beg—tongues out, tails wagging—I don't know, but *Lord* I wish he'd use that tone again.

Preferably while I'm bent over his knee with my knickers around my ankles.

Inspecting my face, Michael cocks his head. "Your cheeks just turned bright red. Are you feeling all right?"

"Yep. Peachy keen," I say, my voice strangled.

Jesus? Satan? Aliens from outer space? Anybody who feels like claiming the life of a sad-sack copyeditor can step right up. Bonus points if you hurry.

"Did I say something wrong? I hope I haven't offended you."

Now he looks at me with alarm evident in his baby blues. It's probably only because he's my boss and he doesn't want to get sued for sexual harassment, but for a moment I allow myself to simply bask in the pleasure of being the object of worry from a beautiful, elegant man.

Looking at my feet, I mutter, "Nothing you say could ever be offensive to me. I'm just . . ."

"Out of sorts."

I glance up to find Michael smiling at me. He must've guessed the effect he has on me, because his smile is the gracious, benevolent one a king would send a beggar as he drove by in his gilded carriage, tossing coins out the window.

Can this man do anything wrong?

"Yes. Exactly." I nod, starry eyed. "Out of sorts."

"We both are." His smile falters. He glances away. His eyes darken, and a thundercloud seems to pass over his face. In a different voice, he says, "I wish my only problem were a noisy neighbor."

That's it. Since he's standing here talking to me, treating me like a real human being, and dangling a juicy tidbit about his personal life out there—again—I'm going for it.

"Is everything . . . okay?"

He glances back at me. His jaw works for a moment, then he makes a pronouncement so unexpected it nearly knocks me off my feet.

"I'm getting divorced."

"Oh!" I cover my mouth with my hand. "Michael, I'm so sorry!"

I am *not* sorry, not one tiny bit, and have probably just damned myself to hell for that flat-out lie and how jubilant I feel hearing this poor man's awful news. His marriage is falling apart, and meanwhile I could light up ten city blocks with my joyous glow. I'm incandescent with bliss and have to restrain myself from doing a happy dance around my cubicle.

I'm a terrible, terrible person.

"Thank you," he says solemnly. "Though it wasn't exactly unexpected. We've been having problems for years . . ."

He trails off, lost in thought, while I begin to mentally design my wedding dress and plan our honeymoon. Then he shakes himself out of his fugue and smiles. It looks almost bashful.

"I'm sorry. I don't know why I told you that. Nobody else knows. We haven't even told our families yet."

His eyes plead with me to be discreet with his secret, so of course I rush to set his mind at ease. "You have my word I won't say a *thing* to anyone." That sounds much more convincing than my next sentence, which is another whopping lie. "I'm just so sorry this is happening to you."

Michael looks at me for a beat longer than is comfortable, then murmurs, "Thank you, Joellen. You're always so nice."

Nice? I'm *nice*? Is that nice like a comfortable pair of shoes, or nice like a lap dance?

Michael smoothly changes the subject so I don't have to give myself a brain aneurysm trying to decode the meaning of an innocuous four-letter word. "So, are you coming to the office holiday party?"

The office holiday party is an annual exercise in humiliation for me, akin to having all my skin peeled off and being thrown into a vat of hot salt water. I'm not exactly an extrovert to begin with, but standing around in a group of my peers nursing a glass of bad red wine while dressed in an outfit that looked fine at the store but somehow morphs into a clown costume when out in public is right up there on the Holidays Suck list.

Inevitably, I will spill food down the front of my blouse, blurt something borderline offensive or outright pathetic, and be ignored or pitied by pretty much everyone. Then Portia will come stand next to me with her withering smile, reeking of disdain, and I'll retreat to a dark corner of whatever overpriced ballroom we're in so I can indulge in self-loathing and cram my face with fatty finger foods to my heart's content.

But every year Michael goes, so every year I go. And this year, *he's getting divorced.*

"Yes." I surprise myself at how enthusiastic I sound. "I'll *definitely* be there."

"Good. Will you save me a dance?"

His smile is warm, and so are my nether regions.

Holy moly. Michael Maddox wants to dance with me at the holiday party, *in front of other people*. Hell has officially frozen over.

"Sure," I say casually, as if my digestive tract hasn't just turned into a quaking bowl of jelly.

He smiles at me for a moment longer, then inclines his head in farewell and turns to leave. I watch him stride down the hall, his gait easy and confident, his posture much lighter than before. Then I'm struck by a thunderbolt of terror.

The office holiday party is in less than a month.

I throw myself into my chair, fire up my computer, and google *How to lose forty pounds fast.*

FIVE

By the time I leave work Sunday afternoon, I've finished the edit on the manuscript and worked myself into a lather over exactly *how* I'm going to achieve my new goal of transforming myself into a svelte goddess in the time it normally takes me to go up a dress size.

Okay, "goddess" is a stretch, but I'm trying to think positive. The internet is bursting with examples of the power of mind over matter in achieving your goals, and who am I to question the word of someone named SkinnyGirl69 who claims to have lost half her body weight in a month from following a simple diet of eating nothing but air?

So, basically, I'm going on a crash diet composed of breathing. If I don't drop dead, I'll *definitely* be thin by Christmas. Seems like a reasonable risk to me.

I didn't see Michael again for the rest of the day, and I was way too chicken to go into the executive office area to say good-bye. Plus, I thought our conversation ended on such a fantastic note there was really nothing that could top it. And the danger of me ruining it all was very real, so I slunk out before fate could decide I'd had enough fun and topple the building with a rogue earthquake.

I'm unlocking my apartment door when a booming voice from behind me makes me jump.

"Where's my pie, lass?"

Gah. It's *him*. Over my shoulder, I send Cameron an icy glare that would make Portia proud. "As you can see, I literally just got home. I don't have a magical pie-producing handbag."

"Excuses, excuses! Next you'll be tellin' me they ran out of food at the store!"

I turn around and blast him with the full measure of my dislike, shot from my eyeballs like a hail of bullets. "*Some* people have to work for a living, okay? I haven't had a chance to go to the grocery store to get the stuff for your dang . . ." I'm about to continue, but this is when I notice his latest fashion choice, and I'm left speechless once again.

After a moment during which he simply grins at me, I regain my senses. "Are you wearing . . . *tights*?"

"What, these?" He makes spokesmodel hands at his muscular legs, which are clad in a pair of nuclear yellow, stretchy, shiny things that appear to be sprayed on from ankles to hips, leaving *nothing* to the imagination. Every ripple and bulge are highlighted—especially the bulge in his crotch.

It's inhumanly large. I'm certain he's stuffed an elephant's trunk into his pants.

"Eyes up top, darlin'," he drawls, catching me staring.

I'm so mortified, I'd like to kill myself. Instead, I turn around and unlock my front door. I push it open and am about to slam it shut behind me, but Cameron flattens his big paw over it and pushes it back.

"Now, now, no need to be shy." Laughter warms his voice. "I already know how bad you've got it for me, lass. And no, these aren't tights. They're runner's compression leggings."

Compression? Ha! They're not compressing anything*!*

"Please get your hand off my door." I say that with my gaze pinned on the ceiling so my eyeballs don't do any wandering off on their own. They simply can't be trusted.

"I'll get my hand off your door when you tell me what time supper is. I really want that pie of yours, darlin'."

I growl at the innuendo in his voice, which I'm certain is the way he talks to every female who crosses his path. The pig.

"Don't call me *darling*! And stop talking about my shepherd's pie like it's my *pie* pie!"

From my peripheral vision, I see his brows shoot up. "Your *pie* pie?" He bats his lashes, the picture of innocence. "I have no idea what you mean. I'm just tryin' to find out when I can expect somethin' you promised me." As if on cue, his stomach grumbles. He points to it. "You see? I'm starvin', lass!" Then he grins and slaps his hand on his abdomen, which doesn't budge even the tiniest bit because the man has 0 percent body fat.

"*Rr-ow!*"

We look down to see Mr. Bingley curling himself around Cameron's ankles like a furry little boa constrictor. His purr is so loud it sounds as if someone started an engine.

"Who do we have here?" Cam smiles at Mr. Bingley, who beams up at him and rubs his face on Cam's shiny yellow shin.

I hope he unsheathes his claws and puts a few snags in that stupid fabric. "That's Mr. Bingley."

Cam picks up the cat, flips him onto his back, and cradles him in his arms like a baby. I'm about to protest that he's doing it wrong, but the dumb cat has *closed his eyes* and started to purr even more loudly, his fluffy orange tail swishing in delight against Cam's stomach.

As I stare in astonishment, Cam scratches under Mr. Bingley's chin. "You must've done something really bad to get yourself named after a Jane Austen character, mate."

Now I'm beyond astonished. I'm *floored*. The Mountain knows who Mr. Bingley is? And here I thought hell officially froze over hours ago!

"What?" says Cam to me, not looking up from the cat. "You thought I was all beauty and no brains, darlin'?"

I produce an unladylike snort. "More like all ego and no manners."

He glances up at me from under his lashes and sends me a lazy smile. "So you're not denyin' you think I'm beautiful."

My eye roll is extravagant. "You're depriving some poor village of its idiot. Can I have my cat back now?"

"When I get my pie, you get the cat." He turns around and swaggers back across the hall with Mr. Bingley in his arms, kicking the door shut just as I lunge for it.

"McGregor!" Furious, I pound on his door with my fist. "Give me my cat back right this *minute*!"

From behind the closed door comes a low chuckle and the clack of a dead bolt turning. "Your pie for your pussy, sweetheart." Two seconds later, rap music comes on at full volume, thundering through the walls, cutting off any hope of further conversation.

I stare at his door, fuming, grateful for once that poor Mr. Bingley is deaf so he doesn't have to hear the blistering foul language in the lyrics. A part of me marvels at the audacity of this Cameron McGregor person and how he can work in not one but *two* euphemisms for my vagina in a six-word sentence, while another part of me wants to tear the door clear off its hinges and beat him to a pulp with it.

The bastard stole my cat!

I holler at the top of my lungs, "If he comes back with a single hair out of place, I'll kick your tights-wearing butt!"

I could swear under the boom of bass there's laughter.

Never in the long and storied history of shepherd's pie has one been assembled faster.

I set a land speed record to and from the corner market, my shoes leaving smoke and the sound of peeling rubber in their wake. I chop vegetables like a madwoman, sauté ground lamb as if someone is holding a gun to my head, curse at the pot of water until it finally gives in and comes to a boil from sheer terror. I abuse the potatoes so badly in my hurry to mash them, I almost overdo it and end up with a gluey mess but salvage them just in time by calming myself with a jumbo glass of wine, guzzled with the gusto of an addict at the start of an epic bender.

After that I'm calm—well, *calm* is a relative term when comparing a total mental breakdown to mere crippling anxiety—and am able to finish the dish and get it into the oven without chopping off any of my fingers or suffering a life-threatening cardiac event.

Which is when I realize that in my haste, I never turned the oven on.

"I'm going to kill him," I tell the empty kitchen. "If Mr. Bingley is even a little *miffed* when he comes home, Cameron McGregor is going to die."

I crank up the dial on the oven, then head over to McGregor's and pound on the door. I'm regretting leaving my chef's knife in the kitchen when he opens up.

He's changed from the yellow stretchy leggings into a pair of faded jeans but still isn't wearing anything else. I wonder if the man owns shirts. And why does he have to be so *muscular*? It's distracting!

"Where is he?" I demand, craning my neck to try to look around his broad shoulders.

"Where's my pie?"

"In the oven."

He cocks one eyebrow and stares at me.

"It has to bake! It takes time! You'll have your stupid shepherd's pie in half an hour for God's sake!"

He sends me a saccharine smile. "So that's when you'll have your cat."

He makes a move to shut the door but is unable to as I throw my full weight against it. I knock him out of the way and barge into the apartment, calling Mr. Bingley's name, knowing he won't be able to hear me but unable to stop myself in my panic that I'm two steps away from finding a dead pile of fur on the floor with a beer bottle shoved down its poor throat.

"Mr. Bingley! Mr. Bing—"

I stop short at the bedroom door. There in the middle of the bed is the cat, curled up and sleeping peacefully, the stupid yellow tights wound around him like a security blanket.

"He's a real lover, that one." Cameron stands behind me in the hallway. I can tell from his tone he's trying not to laugh. "Practically had to peel him off me so I could take a shower. Never had a cat take a likin' to me so fast. Takes after his mum, I guess."

I refuse to let him bait me, so I don't answer. Instead, I go to the bed and pick up Mr. Bingley, careful not to touch the yellow tights. When I turn around, Cameron is blocking the doorway, his arms folded over his chest. He shakes his head.

"Now I know you don't think you're leavin' with that cat, lass, seein' as how I don't have a shepherd's pie in my hands."

"Your obsession with that particular food is pathological, you know that?"

"It's just that . . . pie is my favorite thing in the world." He pulls his lips between his teeth, his shoulders shaking with silent laughter.

"Ugh. Keep talking—maybe someday you'll say something intelligent."

He throws his head back and laughs, loud and long, while I stand and stare at him and Mr. Bingley tries to wriggle out of my arms to get back to the bed.

"Okay, comedian," he says, still chuckling. "New deal. We're goin' over to your place while we wait for my pie to finish bakin'." He turns and strolls away, waving a hand dismissively over his shoulder when I holler at him that we *don't* have a deal, and he's *not* welcome in my apartment.

A minute later the point is moot as Cameron lowers his muscular bulk to my sofa, props his bare feet up on my coffee table, laces his fingers together over his stomach, and smiles at me like he's waiting for me to bring him a drink.

"You're unbelievable." I swing the door shut, deposit the cat onto the floor, and flee into the safety of the kitchen. Unfortunately the kitchen is about fifteen feet away from the living room, so I'm not really safe at all.

Then a voice comes through the door. "Ducky? Ducky, are you home?"

Amused, Cameron looks at me. *"Ducky?"*

"Shut up, pie boy," I mutter, headed for the door. When I open it, I find Mrs. Dinwiddle, martini in hand, wearing four-inch heels and a full-length mink coat over a flowered nightgown. The diamond tiara perched on her head is slightly askew.

"*There* you are, dear!" She beams at me as if she's won a game of hide-and-seek.

"Hello, Mrs. Dinwiddle."

She pushes back a wispy gray curl from her forehead, escaped from its proper position under the tiara. "I *just* wanted to *say* that last night was *lovely.* I probably don't tell you *enough*, but I so *appreciate* you making dinner for me every *Satur* . . ."

She trails off right in the middle of her thought, arrested by the sight of a large barechested man smiling at her from the sofa. She instantly switches into coy debutante mode, fluttering her lashes and lifting a shoulder when she says with syrupy sweetness, "Why, *hellooo* there, young man."

Cameron sends her a flirtatious nod, his smile so bright it's practically blinding. Apparently he doesn't care what age the women are who pay him attention, as long as they do.

Her gaze still glued to Cameron, Mrs. Dinwiddle addresses me. "I didn't think you'd have *company*, Ducky. You *never* have—"

"He was just leaving," I say loudly, cutting her off before she can reveal any more details of my pathetic life.

"No, I wasn't." Cameron rises from the sofa and swaggers over, grinning that smug, infuriating grin that tells me in no uncertain terms he's going to give me the business about the "date" I said I had last night.

"Hullo, I'm Cameron McGregor. Pleasure to meet you." He sticks his hand out to Mrs. Dinwiddle. Instead of taking it, she does that limp-wristed thing you see in old movies when the Southern belle wants the courtly gentleman to kiss her hand.

So what does he do? He bends over, lifts her hand to his mouth, and *kisses it*!

Mrs. Dinwiddle giggles like a teenage girl and bats her fake eyelashes so furiously I'm surprised they don't fly off. When Cameron straightens and releases her hand, she wiggles her fingers in his face.

"Well aren't you *dashing*?" she says, eyeballing his chest.

Cameron smiles at her indulgently, enjoying her obvious admiration. "I don't know about that, ma'am, but I do know that a beautiful woman like yourself should always be treated like a queen."

I growl. "And the ugly ones should always be treated like servants?"

Simpering at Cam, Mrs. Dinwiddle chastises me. "He's only paying me a little compliment, Ducky. Leave the poor man alone!"

"Oh, I'd *love* to leave him alone," I mutter. "*All* alone. On a desert island."

When Mrs. Dinwiddle frowns at me, Cam chuckles. "She's just jealous of your style, Mrs. Dinwiddle."

"*No*, I'm jealous of everyone who hasn't met you."

Cam turns the full wattage of his smile toward me. "Oh, c'mon now, lass, meetin' me has gotta be the most excitin' thing to happen to you since your last Pap smear."

Scandalized but trying not to laugh, Mrs. Dinwiddle whips the Chinese silk fan from a pocket of her mink and almost sprains her wrist fanning her face.

"Ha," I say sourly. "You have all the charm of an open grave, McGregor."

"Tch. Just admit it. You're in love with me." He bumps me with his elbow, and I send him a look designed to melt his face.

"Love? Hardly. If you were on a life support machine, I'd unplug it to charge my phone."

Cam laughs, leaving me confused as to why he seems to like it so much when I insult him. My confusion is overtaken by a wave of horror, however, when Mrs. Dinwiddle rejoins the conversation.

"I'm sure she *would* fall in love with you, Cameron, but she's *already* in love with someone *else*."

"That so? Who's the lucky man?" drawls Cam, playing along, thinking she's joking, because obviously no man in his right mind would have anything to do with the likes of me.

I scramble to backtrack, making desperate googly eyes at Mrs. Dinwiddle so she'll take the hint to shut up. "No one! She's kidding. I'm not in love with any—"

"Her married *boss!*" crows Mrs. Dinwiddle, leaning toward Cameron with a conspiratorial twinkle in her eye. Like I'm not even standing right here. Like my deepest, darkest secret is fabulous conversation material with the beefy baller she only just met.

I'm not a violent person, and I especially would never condone violence against the elderly, but Mrs. Dinwiddle is in imminent danger of getting bitch-slapped.

Cam's whole demeanor changes. He looks shocked, his smile falling away and his eyes widening. "You're having an affair with your married boss? And you're judging *me?*"

"I am certainly *not* having an affair!" I huff, indignant. "I'd never do such a thing!"

Mrs. Dinwiddle says sadly, "He doesn't know she *exists*, you see."

"Okay, visiting time at the zoo is over. Good-bye, people." I try to usher them both out the door, but Cam won't be budged, and Mrs. Dinwiddle is too busy downing the rest of her martini to notice my dismay.

"Hold on. Explain this to me." Cam turns to me with new interest. "So you're in love with this guy—who's married—but you've never gotten together with him . . . because he doesn't know you exist?"

I grind my back teeth together. "You make it sound like the only reason I haven't committed adultery is because he hasn't noticed me."

"It's not *adultery* on *your* part if *you're* not married, Ducky," chimes in Mrs. Dinwiddle, who has a rather "educated" opinion on the matter.

"Ugh. Semantics! My point is that even if Michael were all over me, I'd never do anything with a married man! It's just . . . unrequited. He doesn't know how I feel about him. But even if he did, I'd never cross that line."

Cam examines my face with narrowed eyes. After a moment, apparently satisfied I'm telling the truth, he pronounces, "That's a sad story, lass. No wonder you're always in such a bad mood every time I see you."

"I'm in a bad mood every time I see you because I'm *seeing you*," I say sweetly. "And it's not that sad a story, because I found out today that he's getting divorced."

When they stare at me in silence, I feel a little defensive, like they think I'm fibbing. "And he asked me to save him a dance at the office holiday party."

Cam's brows climb so far up his forehead it looks like a party trick. "The plot thickens!"

Mrs. Dinwiddle squeals and bounces on her toes. "In*deed*! *Now* will you let me give you that makeover, Ducky?"

"Just out of curiosity, why do you call her Ducky?"

Mrs. Dinwiddle makes a regal sweeping motion with the fan to indicate my appearance. "Because she *insists* on remaining an ugly *duckling*, my dear, when she could so easily become a *swan*."

Cam turns to me with the biggest shit-eating grin I've seen in my life. "Aw. Ducky."

Wow. If this is Karma, she put on spiked boots before she started kicking my ass.

SIX

A few minutes later, Mrs. Dinwiddle has left to refill her martini, and the Mountain and I are in my kitchen, waiting for the accursed shepherd's pie to finish baking so I can evict him and get back to planning my transformation.

Or hunger strike, in other words.

Cam sits at my kitchen table with Mr. Bingley in his lap, absentmindedly stroking the cat while watching me, taking up far too much space for a single human being. The man has an atmosphere. His gaze has actual weight, like a touch. It's unnerving. Like one of those haunted oil portraits, his eyes follow my every move.

"Stop staring at me—you're freaking me out," I grouse, watching the timer on the oven and willing it to speed up. *Only a few more minutes to freedom.*

"How long have you been in love with your boss?"

"None of your business."

"Oh, c'mon, you can tell me, lass. It's not like I'll ever meet the man. Besides, I go back to Scotland in a month when the new season starts, and you'll never have to see me again. Get it off your chest."

I shoot him a glare, then go back to staring at the oven. "Why you care, anyway?"

I hear the shrug in his voice when he answers. "I don't really, but I guess I can't understand why a woman would waste her time pinin' over a man who doesn't want her when she could be focusin' on findin' one who does. And—forgive me—especially at your age."

I'm too depressed to be insulted. "God, you sound exactly like my mother."

I'm not looking at him, but nonetheless *feel* his gaze sharpen. "So you've talked to your mother about this. Which means it's serious and has probably been going on for years."

Exasperated, I throw my hands in the air. "How on earth would you know what it means?"

"I know women."

I don't have a pithy comeback for that, because it's obviously the truth. He says the words with no bragging or smiles, just a simple statement of fact, backed up by the thousand pairs of panties he probably has stuffed into his closet as souvenirs.

"Fine. Yes, it's serious and has been going on for years."

"How *many* years?"

I stare at him. "Are you writing a book or something?"

He chuckles. "Just gettin' my facts straight. Answer the question."

I can tell by his determined expression that he won't give up until I tell him what he wants to know. So . . . what the hell. I draw a breath and admit, "Ten years. Since the first day I started working at my job. Since the first minute I laid eyes on him." I say it in a muted voice, knowing how pitiful it sounds.

Silence follows. After a moment, I chance a look at Cam. He's gazing back at me with an inscrutable expression, his brows drawn together, his head cocked to one side.

"And what," he asks quietly, his eyes intense, "is so special about him that would make you flush a decade down the toilet?"

I glance away. Heat rises in my face, and I have to swallow around the sudden lump in my throat. "You wouldn't understand."

"Aye, I would, lass. I understand obsession all too well."

When I look at him again, arrested by the new tone in his voice, the darker, more complicated tone, he meets my stare unflinchingly. A flicker of something crosses his face—longing or loneliness, some bottomless despair—but it's gone so quickly I must have imagined it.

I shift my gaze to the oven timer. Three minutes. Then I cross my arms over my chest, close my eyes, and decide on a whim to tell him the truth.

"He's just . . . perfect. In every way."

Cam sounds irritated by my dreamy tone. "Barf. Can you be more specific?"

"He's educated. Cultured. Sophisticated. Kind. Brilliant. Gorgeous."

"Gorgeous?"

I nod, keeping my eyes closed. "He looks exactly like Christopher Reeve in his Superman days. Heroic. Cleft chin and everything. And he's a gentleman. His manners would put the queen of England to shame. And he dresses beautifully. And he knows all about literature, and opera, and ballet, and art—"

"So he's gay."

Outrage flares through me, hot as the surface of the sun. I open my eyes and stab Cam with a look. "He's not gay! He's been married for years!"

"To a man?"

"No! To a *model*, if you must know—some airheaded Amazon with a thigh gap and a twenty-inch waist!"

"Huh." He matches my fierce gaze with one of his own. "So he's superficial."

"What? No!"

"Yes, he is. Just like you are."

I gasp. He might as well have stabbed me in the gut.

"Don't gimme that look," says Cam, slowly shaking his head. "You're in love with some bloke based on nothing more than his résumé and his pretty face."

"That is *not* true!"

The cat jumps off his lap and trots into the living room, sensing the fountain of magma about to explode from the top of my skull. Cam rises and moves toward me.

"No? How many conversations have you had with him?"

"A lot!" That's a lie, but I'll be damned if I'm backing down.

"That don't involve work," he clarifies.

I open my mouth to answer but snap it shut and turn back to the oven. "Forget it. Your pie's almost ready. Take it and get lost."

"The answer's none, right?"

I refuse to answer. Cam correctly takes my silence as a yes and presses on.

"And how much time have you spent with this 'perfect' man away from work? Or work-related functions?" he adds quickly when I turn to speak.

My face throbs with heat. "You don't have to spend years in private conversations with someone to know they're a good person."

"No, but one date would be a good start. It seems to me you don't really know anything about him other than that he's pretty and has rich-boy tastes. Ballet, opera, art . . . sounds like things someone who was tryin' real hard to impress other people would put in a bio."

That bit of insight stings especially badly because under Michael's smiling picture on the company website is his bio, which is where I've discovered most of the fascinating facts of his life. The other places of discovery being Wikipedia, the social pages of newspapers, and over-heard conversations around the office.

And the one holiday party where I hid behind a cluster of potted palms and eavesdropped on his table.

I stare right into Cam's eyes when I answer. *How is he suddenly so close?*

"I've worked at his company for ten years of my life. I've seen how he treats people, how he speaks to them, how he interacts with his employees, vendors, and guests. He's an incredible man. An *exceptional* man. And yes, he's beautiful, but it wouldn't matter if he weren't because he's so *good*. He'd never make someone feel small, or put them down for their beliefs, or heartlessly mock their feelings."

My voice is rising, and my hands begin to shake. Cam and I are somehow now standing almost nose to nose, but I keep going because I'm so damn mad.

"He'd never have sex with a stranger he met in a bar and then throw her out like garbage! He'd never aggravate his neighbors with loud music, or wander around half-dressed like a psychopath, *or steal someone's cat!*"

"But he *would* marry an airheaded model with a thigh gap and a twenty-inch waist."

I scoff in disbelief. "Oh, you're saying you're above marrying a beautiful model, is that it?"

"No," he says quietly, his jaw hard. "I'm sayin' if he were the altruistic, benevolent demigod you make him out to be, he'd marry a woman who more closely reflected his true heart."

I'm momentarily impressed by his use of several big words in that sentence but quickly return to outrage. "Rich men marry women for their beauty every day."

"Aye, they do, and those rich men are the same superficial fuckers who dump those beautiful girls once their looks fade and swap them out for a younger replacement."

My jaw unhinges and lands somewhere in the center of my chest. Cameron McGregor has . . . ethics?

No. I'm hearing him wrong. This is the man whore we're talking about. He's just playing devil's advocate.

The oven timer dings. For seconds that feel like eons, Cam and I stare at each other in bristling silence, neither one willing to back down first. Finally I can't take the tension anymore and turn away, cursing under my breath.

As I don a pair of oven mitts, Cam sits down again, which is the opposite of what I want him to do. "Here." I remove the bubbling dish from the oven and set it on the stove top with a clatter, then rip off the oven mitts and toss them on the counter. "Here's your stupid shepherd's pie. Now go back to Kellen's apartment and leave me in peace with my pathetic one-sided love story."

"Never said it was pathetic, lass."

His voice is gentle, which only pisses me off more. "But that's what you think. It's pretty obvious you think I'm dumb as dirt for feeling the way I do."

"The heart wants what it wants," Cam says, watching me steadily. "But sometimes what you think is love is just a beautiful form of self-destruction. The worst thing in life is to give yourself away in exchange for nothing."

He's surprised me again with his eloquence. I'd have bet my life this swaggering, skirt-chasing beast didn't have it in him.

Then it hits me: this is exactly how he's so successful with women. Pretty speeches and dazzling smiles, parading around in his underwear with his muscles on display, all of it designed with the goal of getting girls on their backs with their feet in the air.

My heart hardens against him like a pond freezing over in a bitter winter frost. The entire population of Manhattan could skate on it, it's so cold.

"Well, my life is mine, and what I do with it is my business," I say stiffly. "Now please leave. I'm exhausted. I worked all weekend, and I have to get up early to go back in the morning."

Why am I explaining anything to him? Why am I not hurling the burning-hot dish at his head? And why, oh why am I letting this blunt instrument of a man upset me? His opinion means nothing!

Cam's face darkens with that strange tension again, but then he breaks into a grin, and the moment passes as if it never happened at all. He rises, stretches his arms overhead, then yawns as if this entire conversation has bored him to tears.

"Tell you what, lass. I'm gonna do you a *huge* favor."

"If the next words out of your mouth have anything to do with your penis, I will kill you where you stand."

"Just hear me out before you go all doo-lally on me now, darlin'."

That growl echoing through the kitchen is emanating from inside my chest. "I don't know what doo-lally means, but what did I tell you about calling me darling?"

"You can tell what it means from the context. And I'll call you whatever I want. Darlin'."

The smug, grinning bastard. I oughta knee him right in his balls.

"You make me feel violent, McGregor. I wish I were a man so I could kick your ass."

He laughs like I'm being silly. "Cute. But there isn't a man alive who could kick my arse." He flexes his arms, causing his ridiculous biceps to pop out and shine.

I pinch the bridge of my nose, feeling a migraine coming on.

"Listen. While you were tellin' your sad story about your unrequited love for pretty boy Michael, a thought crossed my mind."

"Must've been a long and lonely journey," I mutter.

"I'm gonna help you get him."

Startled, I look up at Cam. He's standing there smiling like he's just said the most intelligent, amazing thing ever spoken by a person in the history of humanity.

"You're . . . *what*?"

"I'm an expert at two things, lass." He holds up two fingers for emphasis, as if perhaps I'm unable to count that high. "Rugby, and the art of seduction."

A disbelieving laugh breaks out of me. "Did your parents ever ask you to run away from home?"

"Stop insultin' me for a minute and listen. If you *really* want this bloke, you're gonna have to play your cards right. You can't come at him too hot or too cold. It's like Goldilocks and the three bears."

"Yeah, you lost me there."

"The first bowl of porridge was too salty. That's you, by the way—very salty."

I murder him with my eyes.

"The *second* bowl of porridge was too sweet. Not you."

I sigh and prop my hands on my hips. "Just get on with the damn story, McGregor."

"The third bowl of porridge was *just right*. That's what you have to be for him. Just right."

I stare at him, waiting for further explanation. When it doesn't come, and he only smiles at me like he could stand there doing it for hours, I say, "You're a profoundly strange person."

"I can teach you how to be what he wants."

"Pfft! You don't even know him! How could you *possibly* teach me to be what he—"

"I know men even better than I know women," he interrupts, his voice hard. "And I know exactly what makes pretty rich boys tick."

The vehemence of his words makes me blink. "That sounds a little ominous. Is there a story of dubious sexual consent lurking behind that statement?"

He waves a hand like he's batting away an insect. "Bein' in a fishbowl, living like I do, you're exposed to every kind of person there is. Over the years, I've sorta become a student of humanity."

I laugh, because that's so ridiculous I simply have to. "*You?* A student of humanity? The guy who prances around in yellow tights?"

He gazes at me for a beat, a disappointed expression on his face. "You see? You *are* superficial. You only look at what's right in front of your face."

We look at each other as the seconds tick by, and I grow more and more uncomfortable. "I'm sorry. I didn't mean to be rude."

"Aye, lass," he says softly, "you did." Then he smiles. "But I can take it because I'm not your sensitive pretty boy lover, who'd probably burst into tears if he got a gander at the dragon that hides under that unassuming exterior of yours."

My chagrin evaporates as quickly as it arrived. "Unassuming. That's a polite way of calling me a dog."

Cam looks at the ceiling and sighs. "You're not a dog, darlin'. You're just not doin' yourself any favors."

"Jesus, between you and Mrs. Dinwiddle, my inferiority complex should reach new heights!"

His eyes flash to mine. They have that dark look again, the dangerous one that seems to come and go at will. He growls, "You've nothin' to feel *inferior* about, idiot."

"So we went from darling to idiot in the space of a few minutes. Excuse me while I go get my neck brace. I'm getting whiplash."

A corner of his mouth curls up. He studies me in silence for a moment, then lifts a shoulder. "Suit yourself. Don't take my help. But don't come cryin' to me when pretty boy keeps right on not knowin' you exist."

"Stop calling him that!"

"Stop pretending you're a mouse, dragon lady, and go after what you want. In fifty years, we'll all be dead. Carpe diem."

He moves past me to the stove, picks up the dish from the stove top with the pair of oven mitts, and leaves without another word.

I stand in the kitchen for another ten minutes, going over everything he said, trying to put my finger on what I'm missing. Why would he want to help me? What's in it for him?

I go to bed and fall asleep to his last words stuck on repeat inside my head.

Carpe diem. Seize the day.

For the third night in a row, I dream of Scottish warriors.

Only this time it isn't Mel Gibson who's leading them into battle.

SEVEN

I'm right in the middle of an enormous yawn the next morning at work when Portia soundlessly appears beside my desk like she's been teleported to the surface of the planet from the starship *Enterprise*.

"Good morning, Jillian!"

Startled, I jump, sloshing coffee from the mug I'm holding all over the front of my white blouse. I swear she barks like that just so she can watch me freak out.

"Portia. Hi." *And it's Joellen, you witch.*

She watches with an expression of distaste as I mop up the coffee as best I can with the spare napkins I keep in the top drawer of my desk for emergencies such as these, which occur with depressing regularity. In an ice-blue dress that matches the color of her heart and with her hair swept off her face and tied into a low chignon that showcases her elegant neck, she's immaculate.

Beside her, I feel like a mangy donkey next to a thoroughbred racehorse.

"Have you finished the edit on Maria's manuscript?"

I can tell by her tone she's expecting an excuse, so it gives me satisfaction to hand her the sheaf of banded papers with a smile. Lips pursed, she takes the manuscript from me and thumbs over a few pages, checking my work like a grade school teacher.

If I didn't desperately need the rest of the coffee in my mug, I'd be tempted to hurl it in her face.

"I understand you spoke with Michael this weekend," she says offhandedly.

I freeze.

If she knows I spoke to Michael, it must be because he told her. Why would he tell her we spoke? What could that mean?

"Uh . . . I . . . yes. He was working, too. We said hello."

Her sharp gaze flashes to mine. "You said 'hello'?" she repeats frostily.

I cringe, wondering what on earth she could find so offensive about me speaking to Michael and how she gets her mouth to pinch like that. It looks painful. "Um . . . yes."

She stares at me for a moment, waiting for me to elaborate. When I don't—because I'm too worried about what might fly out of my mouth—she hugs the manuscript to her chest and starts to aggressively tap one manicured fingernail against it.

"Joanna." *Tap. Tap. Tap.* "I'm sure I don't have to remind you that we expect a certain level of . . ." Her gaze travels over my coffee-stained blouse, my unruly hair, my makeup-free face. *Tap. Tap. Tap.* "*Professionalism* here at Maddox Publishing."

A flush of heat crawls up my neck. The words are out before I can stop them. "You mean like calling the employees by their correct names?"

The tapping ceases. She blinks—once, slowly—and it's terrifying.

I'm saved from certain death by a uniformed delivery man carrying an enormous bouquet of long-stemmed red roses. He stops at the cubicle next to mine. "Is there a Joellen Bixby around here?"

"Right there." Shasta, the girl who sits at the next desk, stands and points at me accusingly over the top of the cubicle wall like she's an informant for the Nazis.

The delivery guy ambles past Portia, inadvertently swatting her with foliage, and deposits the vase on my desk with a relieved sigh. It's so huge it takes up almost all the available square footage.

"Man, that sucker's heavy. Sign here, please." He thrusts a clipboard into my face while pointing at a signature line on a routing slip.

My hands shake so badly I'm barely able to manage my signature.

Could it be? Could Michael have sent me flowers?

The delivery guy walks off, whistling, while Portia, Shasta, and I stare in disbelief at the roses.

"Well, who's it from?" demands Shasta.

I swallow, pluck the little white envelope from its plastic holder, and open it, my heartbeat like thunder in my ears.

Your pie is the most delicious thing I've ever tasted.

Sweet. Succulent. Melting on my tongue.

I want more. Tonight.

Oh, that cocky son of a—

"So what does it *say?*" asks Shasta too loudly, making me wonder what her problem is while simultaneously realizing that everyone in the cubicles around me is looking curiously in my direction.

Portia snatches the card from my hand, then reads aloud, "Your pie is the most delicious . . ."

She trails off into silence, her eyes growing wide.

Hearing muffled giggles, I remove the card from her fingers, tear it into bits, and toss it into the wastebasket. I turn stiffly back to Portia and say through gritted teeth, "If you'll excuse me, I have work to do."

I know it's only my fury at Cameron that makes my voice so hard, but Portia seems to think it's directed at her. Her chin lifts. She sniffs, sends me an outraged glare, then turns on her heel and stalks off, trailing smoke from her nostrils.

"Dude," says Shasta, watching her go. "That was awesome." She looks at me and grins. "High five, bitch!"

In a daze, I slap palms with Shasta, who has spoken more words to me in the past three minutes than she has in the past two years since she's been sitting next to me.

My desk phone rings. I snatch it up, grateful for a legitimate escape from my new bestie. "Joellen Bixby speaking."

"Wow, your professional-workin'-lady voice is hot. You ever think of goin' into the phone-sex-operator field? You'd make a killing."

"You!"

The low rumble of a laugh comes over the line. "Aye, it's me, lass, your favorite neighbor."

"The prancer."

"Ha! No, the exquisite physical specimen of a man you've been' dreamin' about since we met."

I balk, shocked that Cam somehow guessed that, but realize he's joking before I blurt something stupid like *How did you know?* "Very funny. What do you want? And how did you know where I work?"

"I asked Mrs. Dinwiddle. Did you get the flowers?"

I glance at the colossal bouquet of roses leering at me from two feet away. "Yes. And your charming note. Shakespeare you're not, my friend."

"Oh ho! So we're friends now!"

"No. I'd still like to push you into traffic. Why're you calling me?"

"To discuss phase one of Operation Pretty Boy."

I collapse into my chair and sigh. "Give me a slight break, would you?"

He breezes right past that request. "I've already kicked things into gear with the flowers. If you're on his radar at all, that'll pique his interest."

"Pique? Did Cameron McGregor just use the word *pique* in a sentence?"

He chuckles. "You'll be happy to know, darlin', that Cameron McGregor has an exceptional vocabulary. Extraordinary, anomalous, remarkable, and preternaturally unprecedented."

I pull the phone away from my ear and make a face at it. When I listen again, he's still talking.

". . . men are competitive by nature. If he likes you even a little, knowin' another man is sniffin' around will arouse his instinct for—"

"*Sniffing around?* How romantic."

"Quit bustin' my balls, lass. I'm helpin' you get your heart's desire. A little gratitude would be nice."

"I still don't understand why you're interested."

He pauses just long enough to make my ears perk up. "I'll tell you later."

"Yikes. That sounds scary."

"Maybe I just want you to keep givin' me that sweet, sweet pie of yours, lass. You ever think of that?"

His voice is warm with teasing laughter, and he's lucky he's not standing in front of me, because I've got a brand-new pair of scissors in my top drawer that would look lovely protruding from his eye socket.

"It's too bad you got stuck in puberty, McGregor—you might've been a productive member of society one day."

"Oh, I'm *plenty* productive, lass."

"Name one way you're productive that doesn't involve the amount of sperm you produce. I'll wait."

He dissolves into gales of laughter that seem to continue forever. I listen, trying not to smile, until he's caught his breath and comes back on the line. "Ach, you're a hoora salty lassie. Pure dead brilliant."

"Thank you. I think."

"Now listen, this is important."

I say drily, "I can hardly stand the anticipation."

"When pretty boy asks you who gave you the flowers, just give him a little Mona Lisa smile and shrug. Don't answer. Be coy as shit. If you can't manage it, pretend you're Mrs. Dinwiddle and do whatever you think she'd do."

"I don't have a mink coat and a silk fan handy. A girl needs props to make that kind of Scarlett O'Hara routine work. He'll think I'm lame!"

Cam sighs. "He'll *think* you're mysterious. The less you say, the better."

"Ouch. I know I'm awkward and weird, McGregor. You don't have to rub it in."

Over the line comes a blistering silence, then Cameron's voice, hard as stone. "I don't ever wanna hear you put yourself down again, Joellen. Don't do it out loud, and don't do it in your head, either. Show yourself some damn respect, woman, or no one else will."

My cheeks heat. I chew the inside of my lip for a while, composing various scathing retorts, but none of them have any teeth because I know he's trying to be supportive. Plus, he's right.

Grr.

"Understood?" he prompts.

"Yes. Fine. Okay."

"Good. Now get back to work. And Joellen?"

He still sounds mad, so I'm hesitant when I answer, "What?"

There's a pause. He exhales, then says softly, "You're not weird. You're unique. There's a difference."

He hangs up before I can reply, leaving me staring at the phone in disbelief. What the hell just happened?

I can't dwell on it, though, because Denny has arrived at my cubicle with a large cardboard box on a dolly. "Hey, kiddo! Special delivery!"

Shasta pops back up over the cubicle wall like a groundhog, eyes bugging out. "Another delivery? What is it?"

Why is this girl suddenly so interested in my business? "I wish I could tell you, but unfortunately my X-ray vision isn't working today."

She's too busy ogling the box to be put off by my sarcasm.

Denny parks the dolly upright and removes a folding work knife from a pocket of his trousers. He slices open the tape on the top of the box. "It's a new chair for you, kiddo. Mr. Maddox put in a requisition over the weekend."

The breath leaves my lungs in a wheeze. Shasta and I gape at each other.

Denny makes a great show of unpacking the box, cutting at the cardboard so the chair is revealed all at once when the sides fall away.

"That's the new ergonomic model," whispers Shasta, agog.

I don't know about ergonomic, but it makes my current chair look derelict.

"Oh, fantastic, you brought it up!" says a male voice to my left, and my heart stops.

It's Michael, watching approvingly as Denny dusts off the chair with a rag taken from his back pocket, even though there's not a speck of dust on the thing.

"Yes, sir! You said first thing Monday, so I made sure to do it before my regular rounds."

Shasta and I share a stunned glance, and I know we're both suffering the same brain meltdown. Michael ordered Denny to bring me a new chair "first thing." Like it was a priority. And then he showed up to make sure it was done!

Don't get ahead of yourself—he's probably just about to tell you you're not getting the raise you requested!

He looks perfect today, so perfect he's almost blindingly beautiful. Smooth hair, gorgeous navy-blue suit, freshly shaven jaw. He obviously didn't spend another night on his office sofa. He turns his gaze to me and dazzles me with a killer smile.

"Good morning, Joellen."

I love you and want to have all your babies. "Uh . . . morning."

He sends a friendly nod to Shasta, who giggles. "Hi, Mr. Maddox!"

"Good morning, Shasta. What a lovely sweater you're wearing. That color suits you."

I can tell Shasta wants to run over to him, throw her arms around his neck, and lay a big wet one on him, but she manages to control herself.

"Thank you. Blue's my favorite color."

"Mine, too," says Michael, causing Shasta to furiously blush.

I'm not surprised. Making females swoon is his superpower.

Then Michael notices the bouquet of roses on my desk. He does a comical double take, blinking in surprise. "That's quite the enormous bouquet. Is it your birthday, Joellen?"

It stings a little that he'd assume the only reason I'd ever get flowers is for a birthday, but who am I kidding? I don't even get them then. "Oh, no, those are just from—"

I bite my tongue just in time. Then, frantically trying to think of how Mrs. Dinwiddle would handle this situation and remembering Cam's suggestion that I should act "coy as shit," I gaze fondly at the roses as if remembering a night of passion.

On a dreamy sigh, I say, "A friend." Then I bat my lashes and look demurely at my feet.

When Michael is silent in the wake of my theatrical performance, I'm convinced I've made a colossal fool of myself. But when I glance up at him, he's staring at the roses with a new expression.

An expression, if I'm not mistaken, like he wants to pick up the bouquet and smash it against the wall.

Michael looks at the roses. I look at Shasta. Shasta retreats into the safety of her cubicle, sinking slowly into her chair, eyeballing me like *What the actual fuck?* until her head disappears beneath the wall.

"I guess it didn't turn out to be such a bad weekend for you after all."

In response to Michael's terse statement, I simply smile. *Mona Lisa. Mona Lisa. Mona-effing-Lisa!*

"Let me get rid of this for you, kiddo." Denny breaks the weird tension as he grabs my old chair and rolls it out of my cubicle. He rolls the new one in with a triumphant, "Ta-da!"

"Thank you. That's great. It looks very . . . ergonomic."

You don't have the brains God gave a flea, Joellen.

Then, right after my own voice in my head, Cam's voice intrudes, full of disappointment under the brogue. *Dinnae tell ye te stop that, lass?*

I smother the thought before it can go any further, because the last thing in the world I need is the Mountain ganging up on me, too.

While Michael and I stand in awkward silence, Denny packs up the old chair in the box, tapes it shut, and loads it back onto the dolly. When he's finished, he turns to me with a grin.

"Did I tell you the one about Bill Gates farting in the Apple store?"

"That will be all, Denny, thank you."

Michael's quiet but firm voice puts the brakes on the next phase of Denny's joke, which I'm sure has something to do with the Apple store having no Windows.

Denny says, "Oh yes, of course. Sorry, Mr. Maddox. I'll be off now."

He's gone with my old chair in seconds flat, leaving Michael and I staring at each other with the stupid bouquet of roses ogling us both. I wonder if McGregor has a listening device or a camera hidden in the foliage and decide I wouldn't put it past him.

"Um, thanks for the chair. I really appreciate it."

"You're welcome. Let me know if there's anything else you need, Joellen. I want to make sure you're well taken care of."

Why does his voice sound so husky?

My eyes flash up to his, our gazes lock, and the heat in his eyes makes me feel like I'm channeling starlight and lightning bolts through my veins. A peep of surprise—maybe hysteria—slips past my lips.

After a rough throat clearing, Michael smooths a hand down the lapel of his jacket. "Well. I'm back to work. Have a good day."

Before I can answer, he turns on his heel and strides away.

I watch him go, hope and confusion and longing churning in my gut, until Shasta says in a stage whisper, "Did someone drug my coffee, or was he *flirting with you?*"

I throw myself over the wall that separates us and stare down at her, crouched in her chair where she has obviously been eavesdropping, and stick out my arm. "Pinch me. I'm dreaming."

Smiling, Shasta shakes her head. "Bitch, I'll do more than pinch you. If Michael Maddox has the hots for you, I'll punch you right in the face."

Today is officially the best day of my life.

EIGHT

I float through the rest of the day on a hormonal high, smiling like a crazy person. I'm not even bothered when I encounter Portia in the ladies' room, washing her hands at the sink, and she gifts me her trademark Glare of Death in the mirror.

Nothing can touch me. I'm invincible. I'm coated in love Teflon.

I'm also not disturbed when I get off the elevator on my floor in my apartment building and rap music blaring from down the hall instantly causes me to lose 5 percent of my hearing.

I pound on the Mountain's door, still smiling.

When he opens up, my smile falters for a moment but then snaps back into place like it's magnetized. "Cool skirt, prancer. You look groovy in plaid. When're you going to invest in some shirts? You do realize it's winter, right?"

He heaves a huge sigh and looks at the ceiling, as if hoping for divine intervention. "It's a *kilt*, lass."

Of course I know that, but I enjoy giving him the business because it obviously irks him to have his kilt disrespected by calling it a skirt. "What's the difference?"

"What you wear underneath."

When I cock a brow, he smiles. "Ask me what I'm wearin' underneath."

"I feel like this is a trick to get me to look at your junk."

He looks insulted. "My 'junk'? Cameron McGregor doesn't have 'junk.' He has family jewels, thank you very much."

I bypass the ridiculous way he refers to himself in the third person. "Yeah, well your family jewels can stay safely under your skirt, buddy, because I'm in too good a mood to deal with a random penis sighting, thank *you* very much."

He lifts the edge of his kilt a few inches and grins, waggling his eyebrows. "You sure? It's a life-changin' event, I promise you, lass."

I snort. "No doubt, but I don't have the cash to bankroll the long and expensive relationship with a psychotherapist that seeing you naked would necessitate."

"Aha! You admit it would blow your mind!"

"I admit that I've seen people like you before, but I've had to pay an entry fee at the circus to do so."

He purses his lips and looks me up and down. "Just make it easier on yourself, darlin', and admit you're wild for me and are dyin' to bring a few dozen little McGregors into the world."

"You're delusional."

"You're massively in love with me."

"I'm massively in dislike with you."

"You've finally figured out I'm the *real* man of your dreams."

"I've finally figured out how you got here. Someone left your cage door open."

We grin at each other while the stupid rap music blares into the hallway, eroding my hearing another few percent.

"You look awful cheery, lass. Did your lingerie store have a sale on beige granny panties?"

Not even that little zinger puts a dent in my good mood. "I just wanted to tell you that you're a genius. I think the roses worked."

The grin wipes from his face like someone took an eraser to it. He steps forward into the hall, forcing me to step back to accommodate him, and stares down at me.

"Aye? What happened?"

I blink up at him. "Whoa. Your ability to go from harmless flirt to serial killer is mutant, you know that?"

"Don't kid yourself. I'm never *harmless*."

He says it while staring me in the eye, a vein throbbing in his temple. A little shiver runs up my spine. It isn't fear, but I'm not sure what it is. Honestly, I don't want to know. This guy is a single shady chromosome away from turning into the Hulk.

"Okeydokey. You're never harmless. Congratulations on being a psychopath. By the way, why's your music so loud? You said, and I quote, 'Your pie for my silence.' That ear-splitting noise is hardly silence."

He folds his arms over his chest and peers at me down his nose. Honestly, the man is pretty intimidating when he does that. Now I understand why biceps are sometimes referred to as "guns." He's got a pair of howitzers on him, locked and loaded.

"That pie you made me yesterday bought my silence *yesterday*. You want more silence today? I want another pie."

I gasp in outrage. "You never said that! You can't change the rules after we made an agreement!"

"Cameron McGregor can do whatever he likes, lass." He steps backward and makes a move to close the door.

"Wait!"

He gazes at me with hooded lids, waiting.

"I don't have the ingredients for another shepherd's pie, but—"

He closes the door in my face.

I pound on the door, shouting, "But I can make you my grandmother's meat loaf, you big jerk! It's even better!"

There's a pause, then the music lowers slightly. The door cracks open, and Cameron eyes me through the space. "Meat loaf?"

"Yes," I say, seething. "Meat loaf. A loaf made of meat. It's friggin' delicious."

The door opens another inch. "What kind of meat?" he asks dubiously.

Oh, for the love of God. "Ground turkey."

He wrinkles his nose like Mrs. Dinwiddle does, and I have to swallow the growl in my throat because I really don't want to hear his sucky rap music all night.

"It's fluffy, juicy, and comes with a side of mashed potatoes and gravy. Do you want the dang thing or not?"

He pretends to think, tapping his chin with his finger, and I'd like to kick him in his blasted family jewels.

"All right." He solemnly nods. "I accept this loaf of meat you offer. But if I discover that you've exaggerated its claims of greatness, our deal is null and void."

My nostrils flare as the urge to commit murder boils in my veins. "I'll show you null and void," I mutter, turning my back to him and stomping across the hall, my happiness evaporated. I dig violently through my purse for my keys. As soon as I get the door open, the music cuts off abruptly, then a door slams and Cameron McGregor pushes past me into my apartment.

I watch helplessly as he lowers himself to my sofa and props his huge bare feet on my coffee table. "No, McGregor. No. Get out." I point to the open door.

His smile is broad and satisfied. He laces his hands behind his head, which shows off all the muscles in his arms and abdomen and makes his tattoos ripple.

"You can tell me all about pretty boy Michael and what a genius I am while you cook."

Then, because the universe hates me, Mr. Bingley jumps up on Cameron's lap, curls up, and promptly goes to sleep. Cameron's smile grows even wider.

I swing the door shut, willing his head to explode like a pumpkin. Unfortunately, I have no such luck, and his big dumb head remains intact.

"If looks could kill, I'd be stone dead, lass," he says mildly, watching as I dump my purse on the console table in the foyer, shrug off my coat, and head toward the kitchen.

I say over my shoulder, "You're the reason God created the middle finger."

He laughs and keeps on laughing, an irritating sound that can be heard over all the clanging of pots and pans as I dig through the cupboard for the loaf pan. Once it's in hand, I slam it on the counter and head to the refrigerator.

"I'm happy you find me so amusing."

He abruptly stops laughing. "That's not exactly the word I'd use."

Oh, sure. Fat is probably the word, right? I try out Portia's Glare of Death on him. "You know, I *was* in a really good mood before I got home."

"Because my roses worked. By the way, you're welcome."

My back teeth are in danger of shattering, I'm grinding them together so hard. But he has a point. "Well . . . yes. And thank you. How much do I owe you for that bouquet?"

"A week of shepherd's pies. And/or loafs of meat, if this one turns out to be acceptable."

He grins at the look of horror on my face, then shrugs. "It's a drop in the ocean compared to what a Manhattan florist charges for one hundred roses, darlin'. But it's up to you."

One hundred roses? I do a quick mental calculation of what a dozen roses might cost retail, multiply it by eight, and wind up with a number so large it makes the blood drain from my face. And that's not including tax and delivery.

But I'm quick to clarify terms because he's a dirty deal changer. "That includes no music for a week, too, though, right?"

"Sure. But it also includes me eatin' over here."

I'm dumbfounded. "Here? Why *here*?"

He takes a moment to answer, then says with a bland expression, "I like your cat."

I narrow my eyes and watch him idly scratch Mr. Bingley behind his ears. "Won't that interfere with your naked poker parties and standing door sex with strangers?"

Amusement flickers in his eyes. "No, I'll just move those to the mornin's."

I can tell he's baiting me, which he seems to really love, so I keep my expression as bland as his and ignore it. "So to clarify, the deal is seven home-cooked meals, which you eat here, in exchange for payment on the roses and no loud music."

He inclines his head, smiling slightly, which makes me suspicious. "And that's it?"

"I can throw in a daily viewin' of the family jewels if you like."

His voice is rich with suppressed laughter, and I want to hurl the meat loaf pan at his head. "No, thank you. But it occurs to me that we should discuss exactly how *long* it will take you to eat your meals here."

He arches his brows. "You want a time limit, lass? That's a trifle insultin'."

"I just want to make sure you don't end up sleeping on my couch."

"What if you invite me to?"

I throw my hands in the air. "McGregor, honestly!"

"It's a legitimate question. I've been told I'm irresistible often enough to believe it. You could very well wind up throwin' yourself at me, darlin', and then where would we be? Just clarifyin', like you said."

I close my eyes, inhale a slow, deep breath, and run my hands over my hair. When I open my eyes again, I find Cameron grinning at me.

I say, "Twenty minutes a night."

The grin doesn't budge. "I'm not a competitive eater, lass, you can't expect me to shovel an entire pie down my throat in less than half an hour."

"Fine. Thirty minutes."

"One hour."

"Forty-five minutes."

He assesses the look on my face, my clenched fists, and my general impersonation of a stick of dynamite with a lit fuse and relents. "Forty-five minutes. Deal."

I feel as if I've just negotiated peace in the Middle East. "Deal. Now sit there, and try not to be annoying while I make dinner."

Low chuckling comes from behind me as I turn and head to the refrigerator again. I'm busy for several minutes—getting the ingredients together, mincing red bell peppers, blending moistened oats with the meat—until I feel a presence behind me and turn.

I let out a scream when I find Cameron standing not two feet away, watching me. "Jesus! You scared me half to death! What're you doing?"

"Did you forget I was here, lass? Is your attention span that short?"

He's laughing at me again, mirth shining in his eyes as his lips curl up at the outer edges. I yank a wooden spoon from a ceramic crock on the counter and slap his shoulder with it. "Get over there! Go sit down at the table, and stop looming!"

"Christ, you're bossy," he grouses, but he says it with warmth in his voice, so I can tell he actually likes it. Which works out well for both of us, because I can see a lot of beatings in his future if he keeps this up.

He lowers himself to a chair at my kitchen table, taking up all the space in the room in that irritating way he has. I throw a dish towel at him, which hits him in the face.

"Can you please cover yourself?"

"With this?" He holds the dish towel up to his broad torso. It covers about a quarter of it. When I frown, he chuckles. "Is the sight of my manly bare chest distracting you, sweetheart?"

I groan, rolling my eyes. "Forty-five minutes of this every night and I'll go insane."

"Aye. With lust."

"Oh. My. *God.*"

"You can just call me Cam, darlin'. Though it's accurate, God seems a wee bit formal."

I make a sound of exasperation that contains a lot of snarling fricatives and go back to assembling the meat loaf.

Cam is quiet until I put the loaf into the oven and set the timer. Then he says, "So. Pretty boy. Tell me."

The thought of Michael's expression when he looked at the roses on my desk brings a smile to my face. I wash my hands in the sink, dry them, then lean against the counter with my arms folded over my chest and meet Cam's gaze. "It was brilliant. He came over first thing in the morning to see about the chair he ordered me, and there's this huge bouquet on my—"

"What chair?"

I'm startled by the force of his question. "Oh. He thought my office chair was broken because I was being my usual clumsy self and . . ." The way Cam's face darkens when I call myself clumsy makes me quickly rewind. "I mean, he thought my chair was broken and ordered me another one."

"This was before he saw the roses?"

"Yeah. This was during the conversation I had with him on Sunday, when I found out he was getting divorced."

"When you say he thought it was broken, that makes it sound like it wasn't actually broken."

"It wasn't. It's hard to explain without getting you mad, because I'll have to describe what happened, and honestly I don't see any way around that without mentioning that I'm clumsy."

Cam gazes at me steadily. "Huh."

"What d'you mean, 'huh'?"

"There's two parts to it."

"There's two parts to a one-syllable word?"

"To the explanation."

"Why do I feel like I should be sitting for this?"

Cam motions to the chair across from him, which I sink into, weirdly nervous about what he might say.

Drumming his fingers on the table, Cam says, "Part one is the interestin' fact that pretty boy ordered you a new office chair."

I chew my lip with worry. "Why is that interesting?"

"Interestin' that he noticed. Interestin' that he took the initiative. Interestin' that he made it happen so fast. Interestin' that he dropped by to make sure it was done. All of it made even *more* interestin' because you're of the opinion he doesn't know you exist."

I lean forward, my eyes wide. "That's what *I* thought!"

"What did he do when he saw the flowers?"

"He sort of . . . glared at them, like he wanted to throw them away."

A muscle flexes in Cam's jaw, but he's silent.

"What's part two?"

"That you care if I get mad when you're too hard on yourself."

I wave that away because I want to get back to Michael. "So, what do you think it all means?"

"I think it means he likes you."

Though I'm thrilled by the possibility that what he's saying might be true, I know it's not reality. "Much as I'd love to believe that, I can't."

"Maybe you should take my word for it, lass."

"This from the man wearing nothing but a plaid skirt who insists I'm desperate to have his babies."

Cam's smile comes on slow and heated. "Aye. And what bonny wee bairns they'd be, too. Pretty little devils with their mum's salty tongue."

"Being around you is slightly exhausting, McGregor."

"Only slightly? I'm takin' that as a compliment, lass."

I can't help it. I start to laugh. Weakly at first, but then I give in to the hysteria I've been holding back all day, brought on by my morning encounter with Michael, and laugh with gusto, my head thrown back, pounding a fist on the table.

"You see?" Cam sounds smug. "You're mad about me. Only a woman in love can laugh like that."

Wiping tears from my eyes, I try to catch my breath. "You were dropped on your head a lot as a baby, weren't you?"

"Not as a baby," he answers softly, the smile fading from his face. "That came later."

That statement shoots my laughter from the air like clay birds. I stare at him—he's suddenly serious, his jaw tense—and wonder if I'm supposed to pretend he didn't say anything or take it as an opening to delve into his personal life. And if I want to open this particular can of worms.

"I can hear the gears turnin', lass," he says, watching my face. "Don't break your brain—just go ahead and ask."

"Um. Sheesh. I don't know where to start." After a moment, I ask tentatively, "You . . . had a rough childhood?"

He lifts an eyebrow. "Don't tell me you haven't googled me."

"Of course I haven't googled you! Why would I do that?"

"Because I'm Cameron McGregor, that's why."

I have to blink at his casual delivery, like he takes it for granted that every person who comes into contact with him rushes to the internet immediately after they meet to discover all the intimate details of his background.

If I thought he had a big ego before, now I think it's positively colossal. "Okay, not to be mean, but I literally had never heard of you until you moved into my building."

He rolls his eyes. "Don't be daft. Everyone's heard of me."

"Dude. You're not Mick Jagger."

"No, I'm much more famous and better-looking."

"No, you're not."

He sits forward, dropping his casual demeanor for a challenging one. He stabs a finger at his chest. "You're saying you think *Mick* bloody *Jagger*, that grizzled old Englishman, is better-looking than *me?*"

"Easy, tiger. Don't get your skirt in a bunch. I'm saying you're not as famous as Mick Jagger."

He leans back in his chair, crosses his arms over his chest, and looks at me down his nose like he so enjoys doing, making a clucking noise with his tongue. "You're sadly misinformed, darlin'. I'm the most famous athlete on the planet."

"Okay, number one, rock stars are more famous than athletes, hands down. And number two, you're not more famous than Michael Jordan."

He laughs like I'm being ridiculous. "I'm *way* more famous than Michael Jordan!"

"Maybe in your own mind, but here in the land of the sane people, you're definitely *not*."

His sigh is a big gust of air, filled with disappointment. "Ach, lassie, you really don't get out enough."

"On a side note to this stupid conversation, McGregor, here in the States, Lassie is a famous television dog. So when I hear you call me *lassie*, I'm hearing you call me a dog."

He considers that for a moment. "What kind of dog?"

"Oh, sweet Jesus."

"I'm bein' serious! Is it a pretty dog? A mangy dog? A pit bull? I've never heard of this Lassie character. You need to clue me in."

"You were kicked out of Scotland because you're so annoying, right? Everyone got together and agreed to throw you out for the greater good of the country?"

He's trying not to laugh, pressing his lips together. "You'd know if you googled me."

"I am *not* googling you, egosaurus."

"C'mon, you know you want to. We can do it together!"

I stare at him, shaking my head. "You have serious mental problems that require professional help."

His hazel eyes sparkle. "All part o' my charm, sweetheart, all part o' my charm."

I look at the timer on the oven, wondering how much longer this torture has to continue, when Mr. Bingley wanders into the kitchen and jumps up into Cameron's lap.

Cam looks at me, smiling triumphantly.

"Oh, shut up, McGregor."

"Never in a million years, lass. I've got too many brilliant ideas to share. Like this one, for instance. Are you ready?" He leans forward, his eyes shining like he's about to dispense some illuminating morsel of galactic wisdom.

"I can *hardly* wait."

"First, a question: When was the last time you kissed a man?"

I'm instantly, totally insulted. "Screw you!"

"I'm not insinuatin' you're a lesbian, if that's what you think. Not that there's anything wrong with bein' a lesbian—that just wasn't where I was headed."

"You're so lucky the knives are in a drawer on the other side of the kitchen, because if I had one in my hand right now, I'd gouge out your eyeballs."

He waves a hand impatiently in my face. "My point is that if it's been a while since you were properly kissed, you'll need a little practice to get yourself up to speed for pretty boy Michael."

I shout, "What the hell are you talking about?"

Cam sits back in his chair and smiles. "I'm talkin' about bein' your coach."

It takes me a moment to understand, but when I do, my ears go hot. "Wait. You're offering to teach me how to *kiss*?"

His smile grows even wider. "Who better than Prince Pantydropper?"

NINE

After I expend an enormous amount of energy glaring torpedoes at Cam and trying to unscramble my brain, a light bulb goes on over my head. "Oh, I get it."

He looks interested. "You get what, exactly?"

"You're one of those guys who can't stand it when a woman isn't into him. Your ego is so inflated with the hot gas everyone blows up your butt, when you cross paths with someone who's indifferent, it drives you crazy. So you have to walk around half-naked showing off your collection of bulges and tattoos, and demand homemade meat loaves, and make outrageous statements like 'I'll be your kissing coach,' all so that your fragile yet ridiculously overblown ego won't implode from lack of attention."

Cam deadpans, "Thank you, Dr. Freud, for that excellent diagnosis."

"You're welcome."

"Too bad it's barmy. But I'm interested in hearin' more about these 'bulges' you speak of. Are there any in particular that're your favorites?"

Hooking a thumb into the waistband of his kilt, he sends me an innocent smile that's like sandpaper scoured over my nerve endings.

"I bet it's even more aggravating to you that the chubby girl is the one who's not all hot and bothered by your flagrant machismo, right?"

There goes his smile, disappearing faster than a bowl of chocolate Häagen-Dazs down my throat. He leans toward me with a low growl.

"Tear yourself down in front of me again, woman, and I'll take you over my knee and make you wish you hadn't."

We stare at each other while the clock ticks on the kitchen wall and Mr. Bingley makes a meal of his hind paw, going at it like I go at a rack of ribs.

"Why're your lips twitchin'?" Cam narrows his eyes at me.

"Because I'm trying to decide if that's sweet, sexist, or so ridiculous I should laugh."

Cam's face clears like the sun breaking through thunderclouds. He leans back into his chair and grins. "That's easy, lass. It's sweet."

Is this guy for real? "Question. Purely for curiosity's sake."

"Shoot."

"Have you ever actually taken a woman over your knee as punishment?"

When his grin turns wicked, I hold up a hand. "Nope. Never mind. I don't want to know." A sudden spike of pain lances through my skull, and I wince, pressing my fingers to my eyes.

"What's wrong?"

"Ugh. Headache."

Cam's brow wrinkles. "I know you think I'm irritatin', but causin' an actual headache is on a whole other level."

"It's not you. I mean it *is* you, but it's mainly because I haven't eaten anything all day."

Cam thunders, "Why the bloody hell not?"

I wince. "Oh, thanks for that. Shouting is great for headaches."

"Don't avoid the question!"

When I sigh heavily and rub my temple, Cam says darkly, "This better not have anythin' to do with pretty boy and the office holiday party."

Okay, so he's smart . . . ish. But he's also on my last nerve, and I know if I admit I'm starving myself to lose weight, he'll have all *kinds* of opinions on the subject, so I decide to tell a teensy white lie.

I inspect a crack on the wall over his left shoulder. "My stomach has just been a little upset."

After a short pause, Cam sighs. "You lie for shit, woman."

He pronounces *shit* like *shyte*. It's kind of adorable, but I hate him, so it's not. "What makes you think I'm lying?"

"Student of humanity, remember?"

I resist the urge to stick out my tongue and simply stare at him instead.

"Okay, your face gets all scrunched up and your whole body does this cringy, foldin'-in-on-itself thing. You might as well be wearin' a sign on your forehead."

"That is inconvenient."

Cam's voice softens, and so do his eyes. "No, lass. It's a good thing." Then his voice gets hard again. "But starvation diets are *not*."

"Could you please be less observant? It's making my headache worse."

"No, and tough. A headache is the price you pay for bein' a bloody idiot. Your body needs fuel, lass, and if it doesn't get it, it'll start to cannibalize your muscles, and then you'll have worse problems than headaches."

I grumble, "What're you, a doctor?"

He stands and braces his hands on his hips, towering over me. Mr. Bingley hops to the floor and waits patiently at his feet.

Cam says, "Look at me, lass. *Look* at this body." He throws out his arms, juts out his chin, and puffs out his chest. "You think I got this perfect physique by starvin' myself? You think I became the world's most famous, beloved athlete by tryin' to be skinny?"

"I'm sorry, could you repeat the question? Your ego is blocking my ears."

"The human body is a complex machine. A temple, as they say. You have to treat it like one!"

"Yeah, well, my temple is more like an abandoned ruin the jungle has taken over and a herd of billy goats is living in."

I can tell Cam wants to laugh, but he's trying hard to keep his serious face because he's not finished with his scolding. He wags a finger at me like Granny Gums does when she's warning that my biological clock is on a death-spiral countdown.

"What you need is a customized diet and exercise program."

"Incorrect. What I need is liposuction."

He shudders, as if the thought repulses him, and drops back into his chair, which creaks in protest under his weight. Mr. Bingley instantly jumps back into his lap. I'm starting to wonder if Cam rubs catnip on his body before coming over.

"*No* lipo. Your body will burn fat efficiently if you feed it properly and work it out."

"Hooray. Unfortunately, I'm addicted to carbs and sugar and allergic to exercise, so the only way *I'm* going to burn fat is if someone comes at me with a blowtorch or if I stop eating altogether. I decided I'd try option two first."

Cam drums his fingers on the table, pinning me in his intense gaze until I'm shifting in my seat because his look makes me so uncomfortable. Then he pronounces, "We start trainin' tomorrow mornin'."

I say archly, "I'm not taking you up on your kissing coaching, pal, no matter *how* many panties you've dropped! Let it go."

He rolls his eyes, as if I'm the one who's being ridiculous. "I'm talkin' about an exercise program."

"Ha! Me adopting an exercise routine is about as likely as you suddenly developing humility and fashion sense." I stand, cross to the oven, and impatiently tap the timer, convinced it's not working.

"How much weight do you wanna lose by the party?" he demands, sweeping his gaze over my figure.

I shoot him a sour look. "A literal ton. And if you can add in glowing skin and a pair of boobs that don't look like something out of *National Geographic*, lengthen my legs by a few inches, and generally reduce my resemblance to the ogress Princess Fiona from *Shrek*, you're on."

I'm too busy assessing the state of the cooking meat loaf through the glass window of the oven to notice the yawning silence, but after a while it dawns on me that Cam isn't saying anything, which can only be bad news.

I glance over at him and find what I know I'll find: Cam doing his best impersonation of Wolverine.

I straighten and sigh, shaking my head. "Please don't bristle at me, McGregor."

He enunciates each word slowly, as if he's biting them off with his teeth. "Who. Told. You. You're. Ugly."

"Every mirror I've ever looked into."

Wrong answer. Wolverine goes full mutant mode. It's lucky he's not wearing a shirt, because it would be ripped to shreds by his sudden angry expansion.

"Stop, McGregor. Just stop. I know how I look."

"Maybe you need new glasses."

That pisses me off. I hate it when well-meaning people try to make me feel better about my looks.

My cheeks flaming with heat, I say quietly, "Don't you dare pity me or patronize me. And don't bullshit me, either. I own mirrors, and a scale, and have a younger sister who's won enough beauty contests that I *know* what pretty is supposed to look like. And I'm not it. Which is fine—I'm not feeling sorry for myself. But when someone like you who's physically gifted tries to be kind about my appearance, it comes off as really disingenuous and honestly kind of cruel."

Because I'm upset and my throat has tightened, my voice breaks over the last word. I hate how vulnerable I sound, how it must be so obvious to him that I'm upset, so I turn away, folding my arms protectively over my chest and hiding my flaming face.

From across the kitchen comes Cam's low voice. "I don't pity you, Joellen. And I'm a lot of things, but a bullshitter isn't one of 'em."

When I shake my head, huffing out a hard breath through my nose, Cam demands, "Look at me."

"I'm too mad to look at you. Now be quiet before I take the meat loaf out of the oven and shove it up your stuck-up butt."

There's a pause, then Cam chuckles. "Y'know, lass, in some cultures when a woman constantly threatens a man with violence, it's a sure sign she likes him."

I'm overcome with sudden fatigue and scrub my hands over my face. "You're relentless. Also that's a totally made-up fact."

"I'm sure I read it somewhere, but here's a fact that isn't made up. If you wanna look different for pretty boy, I'm your best shot."

I slant him a sideways glare.

He meets it with an expression of total confidence, his smile the very definition of smug. "I was a runt as a boy, lass. The incredibly delectable body you see before you is self-made, forged from nothin' but *will*."

Ignoring my exasperated sigh, he makes a motion with his hand to indicate his form. "This majestic display of manhood didn't just *happen*. Cameron McGregor wasn't carved by Michelangelo's hand like the *David*. He was carved by his own. I'm sure you'll agree, the results are even more spectacular."

"Sorry, I think I just vomited a little in my mouth. What were you saying?"

Holding my gaze, Cam rises from his chair and comes to stand right in front of me. "Gimme your hand."

Leery, I back away several inches. "If you're thinking of giving me a tactile tour of other parts of your majestic manhood, you can go jump off a cliff."

He grabs my hand and flattens it over his stomach before I can react. His skin is hot and soft, the muscles beneath are corded and as unyielding as steel, and the blood suffusing my cheeks is in imminent danger of leaking straight through my pores.

Pressing his big hand over mine, he says in a thick voice, "When it comes to the body, I know what I'm doin', lass. Gimme a chance to show you what I mean. I promise you'll be satisfied."

When he gazes deep into my eyes, I discover I'm having trouble breathing.

Here's the thing: I know I have an overactive imagination. I'm prone to flights of fancy, have arguments in my head with people that last for days, could daydream myself into old age if I'm not careful. But I know to the marrow of my bones that the low rumble of heat in Cameron's voice—the absolute conviction behind the words *I promise you'll be satisfied*—is more than his usual Broadway show.

He's telling the truth . . . and he's not talking about an exercise program.

My uterus comes alive like a Fourth of July fireworks extravaganza, exploding with heat and color, the "The Star-Spangled Banner" playing over loudspeakers, bleachers full of screaming fans jumping up and down. Cam's gaze is locked to mine like a tractor beam. I suddenly understand what romance novels are talking about when they refer to the heroine as having weak knees, because mine are rubberized. I'm about to melt into a liquid pool at his feet.

Cam must see something in my eyes, because his own sharpen. He leans closer, his lips parted, a vein throbbing in his neck.

The phone rings.

I jump, sucking in a startled breath, and almost laugh hysterically with relief but manage to swallow it. I jerk away from Cam and fall onto the phone on the kitchen wall like it's a life vest. Into it I bark, "Hello?"

"Hi, honey," says my mother. "Why are you shouting?"

"Oh, sorry, uh . . . I have my music on a little loud."

From behind me, Cam chuckles. Because my mother has super-sonic hearing the X-Men would be proud of, she picks up on the sound right away.

"Who's that? Is someone there with you?"

Avoiding looking at Cam, I stare at the oven, willing my galloping heart to slow down. "Just my neighbor."

"Mrs. Dinwiddle?"

This conversation is about to turn into an FBI interrogation, so I head to the wine rack next to the counter and select a bottle of red. As I'm getting the corkscrew from a drawer, I say, "No, he's a new neighbor."

With the weight of the four thousand unborn grandchildren she so desperately wants, my mother repeats, *"He?"*

I fumble for a few moments with the corkscrew, holding the phone between my ear and shoulder while trying to cut off the foil on the bottle without slicing off a finger, until Cam takes the bottle from me with a look like *Calm down, nutjob.*

He gets the bottle open faster than I can gulp down a calming breath and starts to rummage through my cupboards for a wineglass. I point at the right one and say to my mother, "Don't start knitting baby booties yet, Mother. He's gay."

Cam chuckles again, this time louder. "Tell her my name and see what she says about me bein' gay."

I hiss, "Shut up!"

My mother asks, "What did he say? What's going on over there?"

Why do I feel twelve years old all of a sudden? "My neighbor's just giving me some decorating advice."

"Oh, how nice! Maybe he can help you with your wardrobe, too, sweetie."

Cam holds out the glass of wine he's poured for me, and I guzzle it like it's a competition. Then—bastard!—he wrests the phone from my hand.

"Hullo, Mrs. Bixby. This is Cameron McGregor. Your daughter and I are in love."

Wine sprays from my mouth like a geyser, coating the kitchen counter and my chin.

I leap at him, grabbing for the phone, but he bats me away as easily as if I were a puppy. "Aye," he says into the phone, his eyes sparkling with laughter. "*That* Cameron McGregor." He listens for a moment as I continue to wrestle with him for control of the phone and fail miserably. "Oh, your husband's a big fan?" he drawls, smirking at me. "That's great to hear. Is he home? I'd love to talk to him."

"Give me the phone, you big ape! Give it to me!"

Cam holds me at arm's length with some ninja moves as I twist and turn, desperate to grab the phone from his hand, to no avail. It's like fighting the wind. In a few seconds I'm dizzy from spinning around so much and have to put a hand to my forehead as I try to catch my breath.

Then Cam starts to talk to my father, and I give up. I collapse into a chair at the table and hide my head under my arms, hoping for the best.

"Hullo, sir. Aye, your wife was just telling me—yessir, it's really me."

My groan is long, low, and miserable.

"No, no, nothin' permanent. My cousin and I traded flats for the holidays. I needed a change of scenery, you could say . . ." Cam listens for a while, then his voice darkens. "Don't believe everything you read in the papers, sir."

Curious about his tone, I lift my head and look at him, but he turns his back on me, bending to peer into the oven at the meat loaf. "Aye, it was a bang-up season. No injuries, touch wood." He nods, listening. "You get the matches on cable?" More nodding, a few grunts of acknowledgment. "You can count on it, sir."

Then he laughs at something my father has said and turns to look at me. "So I'm discoverin'." His smile fades as he listens again. "Actually

I know several lads who think she's quite—" Another few moments of listening, then Cam's face turns red. He says stiffly, "I don't know about your other daughter, sir, but this one's a belter." Another pause. "It means 'fantastic.' Have yourself a good night."

He stalks over to me, thrusts the phone in my face, and pins me with a furious glare. "Five o'clock tomorrow mornin', lass," he says through gritted teeth. "Trainin' starts. If you're not ready, I'll kick down the door and drag you out of bed myself."

I watch, mystified, as he strides away, launches himself through the living room, and disappears.

"What about your meat loaf?" I holler after him.

My only answer is the sound of his slammed apartment door.

TEN

"I can't believe that was really *Cameron McGregor*!" my father enthuses as the echo of a slamming door reverberates through my apartment. "Wait'll I tell the guys at the club—they'll totally flip out. Epic."

Because my parents are Los Angeles natives, uttering words like *epic* to describe a two-minute telephone conversation with a stranger is par for the course. Pretty much everyone I grew up with in our small beach community takes great liberties with the English language, as do their parents, who practice yoga and get Botox and eat disgusting things like kale salads and generally act as if aging is something that only happens to people less in tune with the healing energy of the cosmos.

"So he actually *is* famous," I muse, turning off the oven because the meat loaf is finally done.

"Are you kidding?" My father scoffs. "He's like, *the* athlete of all athletes! How do you not know this, honey?"

"Because I hate organized sports and everyone who plays organized sports and would rather burn my eyes out with acid than be forced to watch or read anything to do with organized sports."

My father thinks for a moment. "Yes, I recall when your sister was on the volleyball and swim teams in high school, you refused to go to any of her meets."

Right. Because inevitably I'd be stared at by people comparing me to my beautiful, popular, overachieving sibling and be forced to spend hours suffering through whispered comments behind hands such as, *That can't really be Jacqueline's sister! Was she adopted?*

Pushing away the vile memory, I beg, "Please tell me he's not more famous than Michael Jordan."

My father laughs. "He's *way* more famous than Michael Jordan! He's basically the most famous athlete on the planet."

Mr. Bingley jumps up onto the chair Cam vacated and looks around wistfully, and I need another glass of wine.

Then my father is gone, and my mother is yammering in my ear like a mental patient without even drawing a breath.

"Holy *cow* Joellen how could you not *tell* me Cameron McGregor was living in your building that is *crazy* and you have him in your *apartment* oh my goodness wait till I tell Cindy she'll *die*."

"You're forbidden from telling anyone, Mom, especially that blabbermouth Cindy! It'll be all over Twitter within half an hour!"

She ignores me because her postmenopausal hormones are resurrecting themselves from the dead. "Is he as gorgeous in person as he is in photos? Is he really as muscular as he looks on TV? What about his hair? Does he have good ha—"

"Mother. Focus. He's a person, not a sex object."

The sound of the receiver being tapped against a wall comes over the line, followed by my mother's sarcastic voice. "I'm sorry, we seem to have a bad connection. I thought I just heard my daughter say that Cameron McGregor, the sex object to end all sex objects, is not a sex object."

For some bizarre reason, I feel a little defensive of the Mountain. "He's actually pretty smart, if you want the truth. He's very intuitive, and he's got an amazing vocabulary."

Her silence is thundering. I sigh and relent. "Okay, fine. Yes, he's muscular. And he has good hair. Satisfied?"

"No, I'm not satisfied! Details, sweetie, details!"

"I never thought I'd hear myself speak these words, Mother, but I think you're overdue for some sexy times with Dad."

Her voice drops, and she starts talking to me in that "we're best girlfriends" tone that drives me up a wall. "I'll tell you what, sweetie, your father is in for some big fun tonight, because Mama's hot tamale is *en fuego* at the thought of Cameron McGregor in the flesh!"

"I have to go now. My mental breakdown is calling."

"My God, that Scottish brogue." Her shiver of delight is audible. "And a sense of humor, too!"

"What did he say that was funny?"

"That you two were in love!"

"Oh, that. Yeah, he's a real laugh a minute," I say drily, shaking my head. Then something strikes me. "Why was that funny?"

My mother laughs. "Oh, honey! As if a man like that could fall in love with you!"

That hurts so much it leaves me breathless. When I'm silent too long, my mother realizes her mistake.

"I didn't mean it like that, sweetie—"

"I know exactly how you meant it."

Her voice turns firm. "Joellen, don't do that."

"Do what? Feel insulted when someone insults me?"

"Turn a harmless comment into one of your personal pity parties!"

I stand there with my mouth open, unable to speak because I'm so angry, and so disappointed in myself that I'm letting myself be affected by this ancient family shit once again.

In a steady, quiet voice, I say, "Mom, my dinner's ready. Thanks for the call. I'll talk to you next week."

I hang up before she can reply and spend a few long seconds swallowing down the lump in my throat until I'm sure I can safely speak without crying. Then I take the meat loaf out of the oven, make the mashed potatoes and gravy, and head over to McGregor's with every-thing on a platter.

When he opens the door, neither of us smiles.

I hold out the platter like a consolation prize to the losing team in a bake-off, even though it's me who's the loser. "This is yours."

He looks at it, then back up at me. "I wasn't gonna turn the music on."

"You know what? It's okay if you do. Who am I to tell you how to live your life?"

We stare at each other, the air electric with unspoken words. He makes no move to take the platter from my hands, so I set it on the carpet at his feet, then straighten and look him in the eye.

"Five o'clock," I say firmly. "I'll see you then."

He slowly nods. When I go back across the hall and close my door, he's still standing there, staring at me.

∞

Anyone who'd like to know what hell is like should spend an early morning exercising in freezing temperatures with a professional athlete who has an endless supply of energy and no soul.

"Keep up!" Cam barks over his shoulder at me as I lag behind him on the sidewalk, breath steaming white from my nose and open mouth, sweat pouring into my eyes, my will to live quickly being extinguished.

"Must. Stop. Death. Imminent." My wheezing and staggering frightens a flock of pigeons into screeching flight from their perch on the back of a bus bench.

Cam turns around and trots back to me. He hasn't even broken a sweat, the heartless bastard. "Joellen," he begins patiently. "We're two blocks from the apartment."

"Oh my God! I made it two whole blocks?" I wonder how the heck I'm getting back and decide I'll take a cab. If we don't have to call an ambulance first.

Cam runs a tidy circle around me as I stagger, just to be a prick. "How did this happen? You've got the cardiovascular system of a ninety-year-old!"

I holler, "I told you I was allergic to exercise!"

He trots the other way around me, backward. "I thought you were joking."

I wave an arm at him wildly, hoping to smack him a good one, but miss because the man is the devil and he can't be caught.

"Are you always this ornery in the mornin'?"

"Don't you dare taunt me, devil man." I gasp for air as my gelatinous legs continue their horrific quest to keep me upright and headed forward. I think I might be going blind. "What was in that green goop you forced me to drink before we left? Poison?"

Cam does ten jumping jacks before he answers. "Yep. It's an old Scottish tradition. A draught of poison just after wakin'. If it doesn't kill you, it'll put hair on your chest."

"Oh goody." Gasp. Wheeze. "Just what I need." Wheeze. Cough. "Hair on my chest."

Shadowboxing around me, dancing on his toes so flurries of snow sparkle around his flashing feet, Cam threatens, "If you're about to follow that little speech with somethin' derogatory about your looks, I'll kick your arse six ways to Sunday, lassie."

I make a sound that reminds me of the death rattle bad actors make right before they expire dramatically in the movies. Only mine is authentic. "That dang dog again! I'm really starting to hate that dog!"

Cam chuckles. He looks annoyingly good in his stupid sweats outfit, the picture of health and well-being, while I look like an old armchair someone threw out a window into an alley hoping it would be picked up with the trash but instead was colonized by rodents. Thank

God the sun isn't up yet, because the possibility an alarmed citizen would call animal control to come and collect me as soon as they caught sight of my hideous visage is high.

"I can't believe you voluntarily do this every day. For free. Not at gunpoint."

Cam lifts the waistband of his hoodie, exposing acres of rippling abdominal muscles. "All for a good cause."

I wipe the sweat from my brow with the back of my hand. "Do you hold yourself tightly in bed at night while whispering sweet nothings into your own ear?"

"Think of pretty boy. Visualize his face when you walk into the holiday party in a sexy dress, lookin' all toned and bedazzlin'."

I huff and puff, pondering the image he's put into my head. "Toned is good. Skinny is better."

"Wrong! Strong is the goal, lass, *not* skinny. A man doesn't wanna grab onto a sack of rattlin' bones when he's in the mood. He wants a nice, thick, juicy woman with buttery curves, sizzlin' hot and tasty."

"You literally just described my perfect steak."

"My mum always said you can't trust a skinny woman. Skinny body, skinny heart, skinny love."

"I think I love your mother."

"Aye," says Cam softly. "She was easy to love."

Was. That drains the last bit of energy from my legs. I stagger to a stop, holding my side and panting, and look at Cam. He's refusing to look at me for some reason, keeping his face averted as he jogs in place a few feet away.

"She passed away?"

A curt nod is his only answer.

"I'm sorry."

He swallows, squinting up at a streetlamp. In the cold yellow glow, his face is all stark angles and planes. The sharp cut of his jaw. The razor-straight nose. The dark hollows beneath his full cheekbones.

The pain on his face is another sharp feature, etched there like carvings in glass.

"Hundred years ago. Ancient history. But thanks."

His voice is low and raw, and I've never seen him so naked. Without the usual bravado he wears like a suit of armor, he seems like a stranger all over again, one darker and more complicated, and far more compelling.

But the moment is gone as quickly as it came when Cam turns to me with a brilliant smile. "Quit your lollygaggin', lass, and pick up your feet! We're only just gettin' started!"

He turns and jogs away down the sidewalk into the predawn gloom, his back straight and his head high, his step lively.

But it's too late. I've peeked behind the golden curtain. I've glimpsed the real man behind the Great and Powerful Oz.

"I see you, Cameron McGregor," I whisper to the empty street as a garbage truck rumbles by. I draw a stinging lungful of diesel fumes and force my legs to move once again. Then I'm jogging behind Cam, my will renewed, the pain in my body pushed to the periphery of my awareness by the single thought crowding out everything else in my head.

I see you.

ELEVEN

By two o'clock that afternoon, I've forgotten all about Cam and the interesting moment in the morning cold because I'm in so much agony I'm convinced a trip to urgent care is in my immediate future.

"What's all the groaning over there?" asks Shasta from behind the cubicle wall, in a voice that indicates she's not particularly supportive of my medical condition.

"I started working out. Kill me."

She pops over the wall, resting her chin on the edge and dangling her arms over so she looks like a decapitated marionette. "Pilates? Peloton? Krav Maga? Kundalini? Booty Twerk?"

"What language are you speaking?"

"I'm into capoeira myself."

When I stare at her in pained silence, she explains. "It's a Brazilian martial art combining dance, music, and acrobatic movements."

No wonder she's so lithe and coordinated. Her resemblance to a gazelle is uncanny. "All things I suck at. Remind me never to go."

"So what're you doing?"

I gingerly massage one aching thigh. "Jogging." When Shasta looks unimpressed, I add, "And really aggressive stretching." Her eyebrows lift. "Like, *torture* stretching."

At the mention of torture she looks interested. "Cool. Hard-core stretching is good for sex. My boyfriend is super limber. He likes to hold a backbend while I ride him like a bull."

I nearly swallow my tongue at that piece of TMI but force a smile because I don't want her to think I'm a prude. I will, however, be spending the rest of the afternoon trying to scrub my brain of the image of Shasta in chaps and a cowgirl hat, astride her naked U-shaped boyfriend.

"You're a lucky girl."

She doesn't notice the undertone of sarcasm in my voice and grins. "Totally. D'you want to see a picture of him?"

Before I can be forced to lie about how cute Shasta's bendy boyfriend is, I'm saved by the appearance of Portia, who's wearing a face like someone just executed her cat.

"Joellen," she says, drawing out the syllables in an exaggerated fashion. She's probably mocking me, but I count it as a win because it's the first time she's gotten my name right in the entirety of my employment at Maddox Publishing.

"Portia," I reply, just so she knows she's not the only one who can pronounce a name.

Her lips pinch. "Will you please follow me?"

My heart lurches, and Shasta and I share a worried glance. The only reasons I can fathom that Portia would ask me to follow her anywhere are if I'm about to get fired or she's taking me to the roof so she can push me off.

"Um . . . is everything okay?"

"You have a meeting with human resources."

Panic unfurls inside my chest like a writhing ball of snakes. "I do? Since when?"

"Since *now*," she replies through gritted teeth. She spins on her heel and strides away before I can ask any more questions, like *Does my severance package include ongoing health insurance?* and *How did you get that stick stuck so far up your ass?*

Being the steadfast friend she is, Shasta focuses on the important stuff. "If you're getting fired, I call dibs on your new chair."

I frantically search my memory for any incriminating past behavior that might lead to my termination but come up with zilch. I'm always on time, I never miss a day or a deadline, and if I'm not exactly beloved by my coworkers, at least I'm generally tolerated.

Except by Portia, who would obviously like to suspend me by my ankles over a bed of burning hot coals until I'm dead.

"You better hurry up, Joellen. Portia looked like she was about to bust a nut."

Ignoring Shasta's odd male orgasm reference, I rise from my chair, grimacing as my thigh muscles howl in protest. I hobble through the cubicle maze toward the human resources department, which is on the other side of the floor, past the executive offices. I notice Michael isn't in his office, which is lucky because I'd probably throw myself at his feet and beg for mercy.

I don't have much in the way of savings. If I get fired and can't find a job right away, I'll be sleeping on my parents' sofa by Valentine's Day, contemplating which suicide method would leave the least amount of mess for the coroner to clean up.

"Come in," says Ruth, the HR manager, when I arrive at her open door.

A woman the word *zaftig* was invented for, Ruth is voluminous. Next to her, I look slim. But she dresses in lovely feminine outfits and always has her nails and hair perfectly done, and pulls off the whole Rubenesque look with grand style. If she has any qualms about sitting four feet away from glossy, greyhound-skinny Portia, she doesn't show it.

Skinny body, skinny heart, skinny love.

Cam's words echo inside my head as I take a seat opposite Ruth's desk. I smile at her because if Cam is right, Ruth has enough love inside her heart to heal the world, but Portia's love is as thin and dry as a stale cracker, crumbling to dust when you put it between your hungry teeth.

"Are you all right?" Ruth's brow creases with a frown as she watches me wince when I cross my legs.

"Yes, sorry," I say, embarrassed. "I just started working out, and I'm a little sore."

Ruth beams at me. "Good for you! Regular exercise is the best way to maintain your health!"

Portia, sitting across from us in the small office, makes a small noise in the back of her throat. It's a muted laugh, dripping with disdain. When Ruth glances at her sharply, I know I'm not the only one who isn't a Portia fan.

Opening a manila file on her desk, Ruth thumbs through a stack of papers. "I understand you've just passed your ten-year anniversary with the firm, Joellen." She looks up at me for confirmation. When I nervously nod, she goes back to perusing the file. "And in that time you've missed . . ."

Her index finger skims the length of one page, stopping at a figure at the bottom. She glances up at me again. "One day."

"I had uterine fibroid surgery!" I blurt, freshly panicking that I'm being accused of doing something wrong. "I scheduled it for first thing in the morning because I wanted to come in in the afternoon, but my surgeon wouldn't allow it, so I had . . . to . . ." I look back and forth between Ruth, who has her hand to her throat, and Portia, who has recoiled in disgust. "Um . . . take the rest of the day off."

Behind her glasses, Ruth's brown eyes are owl round. "Of course you had to take the day off," she says, horrified. "Joellen, that's major surgery! I had fibroids removed in my thirties—you should've taken a *week* off!"

I'm relieved I'm not in trouble, but also confused. *Do I have too much accrued sick leave?*

Portia interrupts, her voice as dry as bone. "Let's cut to the chase, shall we?"

When Ruth turns her incredulous gaze to Portia, it's met with an indifferent stare. "I don't have all day."

Ruth takes a little too long to carefully straighten all the papers in my employee file. I imagine she's biting her tongue so hard she tastes blood. She's a woman known for her kindness and tact—excellent traits for her position—but Portia can strain even the most saintly nerves.

"The raise you requested last month has been approved," says Ruth, which is the only thing she manages to get out before I leap from my chair with a whoop of joy.

"Really? That's fantastic! I can't believe it!"

Portia covers her mouth with her hand to stifle a monster yawn, but I'm too ecstatic to care. I try to do a little happy dance, but instead of cooperating, my crippled legs collapse beneath me. I land in Ruth's poor guest chair like a bomb dropped from the sky, horrified to hear a loud crack as the wood frame splits underneath the ugly maroon fabric.

I leap up again and stare at the chair, willing it not to explode into a million pieces, silently begging the universe for a break.

"I think you killed it," observes Portia, just as the damn thing does a slow-motion sideways death dive to the floor.

The three of us are looking at it lying there flat as roadkill, when Michael pokes his head in the door, smiling brightly. "Sorry to barge in. Did we give her the good news?"

Judging by Ruth's expression, it's a breach of protocol for the CEO to show up during an HR meeting with an employee. Either that or she really liked the dead chair.

"We were just getting started with our meeting," says Ruth primly, to which Michael replies, "So you haven't told her about the open position yet?"

Portia makes a retching noise, and everyone looks at her in alarm. Her face is turning an interesting shade of purple, and her eyes are rolling around in her head. She's obviously having a stroke.

"We haven't even p-posted it yet!" sputters Portia, clawing at her skirt like a madwoman. "Bill can take over the extra work for the time being, or Konrad—"

"Nonsense." Michael leans against the doorframe and smiles at me. "Joellen, unfortunately Maria won't be returning to work because—"

Ruth loudly clears her throat. Michael looks at her, startled.

"Oh. Er . . . right." He begins again, more carefully this time. "Maria is no longer an employee of Maddox Publishing."

"Um. Okay?" I'm confused why he'd be telling me this, why Portia is having a meltdown, and what Maria has to do with me. We're both copyeditors. If she's left the company, a copyeditor position will be open. So what?

"Maria had just been promoted to associate editor. We were going to make the announcement this week."

My heart stutters. I look at Ruth, who's smiling gently at me. I look at Portia, who's wishing murder were legal. I look back at Michael, who's waiting patiently for me to respond to what is the most fantastic news I've received in a decade.

"There's an associate editor position open?" I peep, wide eyed.

"Would you be interested?"

The only thing I'm more interested in is tearing off all your clothes and tackling you, sir. I manage to sound like a rational human being when I say, "Yes. I would."

"Obviously the position is at a higher pay grade, Joellen," says Ruth, "so since you've been approved for a raise, if you got the job, you'd get a bump from the starting salary to reflect your raise."

I'm deeply regretting killing the chair, because I really need something to sink into right now. The floor doesn't seem a good choice, so I lean against the wall and try to regulate my breathing so I don't sound like a pug with sinus problems.

"That's amazing news."

Portia snaps, "You have to apply for it, like everyone else!"

Michael frowns at her harsh tone, and I'd like to smear peanut butter all over his naked body and take a weekend licking it off.

Ruth, practiced with alleviating tension in the workplace, intervenes before Portia can beat me to death with the ruined chair. "Of course. All the proper protocols must be followed. But you have seniority, Joellen, and an exceptional work record, and I encourage you *strongly*"—her pointed stare is that of an accomplice—"to apply."

Portia shoots to her feet, and the temperature in the room drops by several degrees. "As the editorial director, the final selection will, of course, be mine."

Then a miracle occurs. The clouds part, a ray of golden light shines down, and a halo appears over Michael's head. He says, "Technically, Portia, the final selection is *mine*."

I hold my breath as they stare at each other. Portia backs down first, her lashes sweeping downward in defeat. "Yes, Mr. Maddox. Of course."

Michael inclines his head, a kingly gesture, and I almost pant with lust.

He's a god. He's a beautiful, benevolent, witch-slaying god.

He turns to me with a smile that could end all wars. "I'd like to see your application by the end of the week." He nods at Ruth and Portia. "Ladies."

Then he turns and leaves, taking my heart with him.

Ruth says brightly, "Well! I think we're done here! Joellen, you can go back to work. I'll bring the application by your desk later today."

She's almost as happy about Portia's comeuppance as I am, and I realize I have a friend in the human resources department. When Portia stalks out of the office with a huff, Ruth grins at me.

I think it says *We big girls have to stick together.*

So of course I grin back, because it's true.

The rest of the day is a blur. I float through it as if on clouds, marveling at my good luck. It's been my aspiration since childhood to be a senior editor at a major publishing house, and with a step up to associate editor, it's finally within reach. Getting to champion outstanding manuscripts, helping new authors be discovered, bringing literature and beauty into a culture-starved world . . .

Some people want to be rich or famous. I want a stable of rock star authors crediting me for their success in the acknowledgments sections of their novels. Books have been my passion since I discovered *Harriet the Spy* when I was a little kid. From there reading became an obsession. I tore through everything from the Nancy Drew mysteries to *Lolita*, which my horrified mother found hidden under my bed.

She wasn't horrified because of the risqué nature of the book—not being a reader herself, she had no idea what it was about—but because it was a year overdue at the library. I checked it out and never returned it, a habit that would one day culminate with an official from the local library knocking on our door and demanding the missing books—by that point there were dozens—or payment of the fines.

I paid the fines with cash I'd saved from babysitting jobs. Even then, books were far more precious to me than money.

When I get home that evening, there's a clean platter and meat loaf pan sitting outside my door, with a note in the Mountain's neat printing.

You were right. It was delicious. Your loaf is even better than your pie.

I'm sure there's nothing that can top it.

I smile, because I know a challenge when I hear one. And even though I won't be taking a bite of anything I make for him, I'll be damned if I'll let the man have the last word.

I cross to his door and knock. He opens so quickly he must've been standing right next to it. "Oh. Hi."

"Hi yourself, lass. Why're you blinkin' like a startled baby bird?"

I look both ways down the hallway. "Were you expecting someone?"

"You mean someone other than you?"

"Well, yeah."

He stares at me for a while with a squinty look, like he can't figure me out. "Y'know, lass, for a bright girl, you're bloody dense."

"Aha. That explains everything, thanks. And by the way, why do you use the word *bloody* to describe things that have nothing to do with blood?"

"Why do you use the word *gorgeous* to describe a man who's had so much plastic surgery he looks like he was created for Madame Tussauds wax museum?"

I rear back in disbelief. "Are you referring to Michael Maddox?"

Nodding, Cam folds his arms over his chest. "Aye. Looked him up on the company website. And I've gotta tell you, lass, that is one odd-lookin' boy."

"He's not a boy. He's a man! And he's not odd-looking in the least! He's classically handsome!"

"He looks like a doll. Only with less to add to a conversation."

I laugh, because he's being funny. "I see. And you think a 'real' man should look like what? A lumberjack? Someone with irregular access to a razor and a bar of soap?"

"I'll bet you fifty dollars he uses a pore-reducing mask and slathers on expensive antiaging skin cream before bed every night."

"Can I just point out at this juncture in the conversation that these observations are ridiculous coming from a man who apparently doesn't believe in clothing himself from the waist up?"

I gesture to his chest, which is—as usual—bare. His legs are clad in a pair of faded blue jeans, slung low on his hips so the V of his abdominal muscles acts like a neon sign pointing toward the bulge in his crotch.

By now I've mastered the art of noticing his bulge without looking directly at it, a Jedi-level skill.

He brushes off my pesky logic with a hand wave and one of his classic Cameron McGregor self-love statements. "It's impossible to find shirts that fit all these muscles."

I shake my head. "Dude, you lift the definition of *egomaniac* to new heights."

He grins at me. "Thank you."

"It wasn't a compliment."

"That's what *you* think."

I laugh again because the only other option is crying. "Moving on. Dinner's in an hour. It *will* be better than my loaf and my pie. And one more thing, Tarzan. Wear a shirt." I turn and head to my apartment, shaking my head at what he says next.

"I could, but you'll probably only end up tearin' it off me at the end of the night, lassie. Waste of a perfectly good shirt."

He closes his door, chuckling. I go inside, smiling because I've had such a fantastic day and I'm about to make the Mountain a meal that will blow his socks off.

I don't take the time to wonder why the second part makes me almost as happy as the first.

TWELVE

The moan coming from across the table would do a porn star proud.

"Sweet Jesus. Oh, for the love of all that's holy. That's so bloody good. Ach, it's like a party in my mouth. Like an *orgy* in my mouth! If I died at this moment, I'd be happy, because I would've finally discovered the meanin' of life."

Trying not to be too pleased by Cam's extravagant praise, I allow myself a small smile. "The meaning of life is rigatoni carbonara?"

"No, lass. The meanin' of life is rigatoni carbonara with homemade garlic bread, black-truffle gnocchi, and a weird fruity salad."

"It's a fennel, orange, mint, red chicory, pomegranate, balsamic, and extra virgin olive oil salad, not a 'weird' salad."

Eyes closed, Cam waves his fork in the air like he's the pope performing a blessing at mass. "Details. My point is that it's pure braw. Pedro."

"What's 'braw' and who's Pedro?"

Cam opens his eyes, and they're sparkling with laughter. "It means 'amazin'.'"

"You could've just said that."

"I did!" He shovels another forkful of rigatoni into his mouth and winks at me as he chews.

"I'm glad you like it. But don't expect this for the remainder of your bribery meals, because today we're celebrating."

"Oh yeah?" he says around a mouthful. "What're we celebratin'?"

"I got a raise."

Cam stops chewing.

"*And* there's an associate editor position open, which the HR director encouraged me to apply for." I beam at Cam as he swallows his mouthful of food.

It's a moment before he answers. "Congratulations, lass. You deserve the raise, I'm sure."

There's something funny in his voice that gets my hackles up. "Why does that feel like one of those backhanded compliments I get on blind dates, like 'It's great that you're not obsessed with how you look'?"

Cam takes a swallow of water from his glass before answering. When he does, he keeps his gaze on his plate of food. "Just seems a little coincidental is all."

"How is it coincidental? I applied for the raise a month ago!"

His gaze flashes up to mine. "Uh-huh. And you're gettin' it the week pretty boy replaced your chair and I sent you roses."

"God, you're a buzzkill."

"Just pointin' it out. What's the deal with the position that's open?"

The memory of Ruth's face when Michael stuck his head in her office gives me a moment's pause, as does the odd way she cut him off when he was talking about Maria. At the time I was too busy being thrilled to notice how strange it was, but now . . .

"The girl who had the job left suddenly."

As soon as it's out of my mouth, I know it's a mistake. Cam's brows fly up. He leans back into his chair and pins me with a pointed look.

"McGregor, your imagination is almost as overactive as mine. There's no conspiracy here, you big lug! It's just an open position! People leave their jobs all the time!"

He stares at me without blinking. "*Do* they?"

The urge to smash his plate over his head is strong, but I'm still in too good a mood to go for it. "So this is interesting. I'm discovering new aspects to your personality every day. Giant ego, check. Fetish for tight leg wear and bad music, check. Ingrained suspicion of good luck and active paranoia, check."

"It's not paranoia if you're right."

"Let me get this straight." I sit back in my chair, pushing my glasses up my nose so I can see him better. "Your theory is that Michael Maddox has targeted me . . . for career advancement?"

Cam lifts a shoulder and goes back to shoveling food into his mouth.

"You could make Mother Teresa go on a multistate killing spree, you know that?"

"You give the best compliments, darlin'. Get yourself a plate before I finish all this food."

"I'm not eating."

A wolf's growl fills the kitchen.

"Be quiet, White Fang. You'll frighten the neighbors."

"Did you eat today?" he demands, inflating in that Wolverine way he has.

"Yes."

He glares at me. "Besides the protein drink I gave you this mornin'?"

I purse my lips and inspect my cuticles.

Cursing under his breath, Cam shoves his chair back from the table and stomps over to my cupboards. I let him bang around for a few moments before telling him the plates are in the cupboard above the coffee maker.

More stomping, more banging, some aggravated huffing. It's as if I've got a wildebeest roaming around in my kitchen. Then he's at the stove, spooning pasta onto a plate with more force than necessary. He adds garlic bread and salad and sets the plate on the table in front of me with a clatter.

He points at it. "Eat. Now."

I smile sweetly at him. "I don't have a fork."

Nostrils flared, he stares down at me. "You're pushin' your luck, woman."

"Unlike some people in this kitchen, I'm not a big fan of eating with my fingers."

The look of anger on his face is perversely satisfying. He spins away, stalks over to the drawers, and starts to pull them out one by one, searching for the utensils. I watch him, still smiling.

"If I'd known it sets you off when people skip meals, I'd have gone on a hunger strike the moment I met you."

Cam comes back with a fork in his meaty fist. He holds it out to me, his eyes burning. "It's not the meal skippin'," he says, his voice rough. "It's the reason behind it."

Our gazes hold for a moment. Then I decide it's not worth the argument and take the fork from his hand.

He settles into his chair and glares at me until I relent and take a bite of pasta. Mollified, he goes back to shoveling food into his mouth but keeps a wary eye trained on me while he eats. I have a feeling he'll try to force-feed me like a goose being groomed for a fatty liver if I don't keep up a brisk pace, so I'm careful to look busy.

"Pushin' your food around with your fork and takin' spider bites doesn't count as *eating*," Cam says after a minute.

"Okay, Dad," I mutter, and take a normal forkful of food. I chew, swallow, then stick out my tongue, opening my mouth wide to prove to the Mountain that I'm a good girl and he can stop badgering me.

"Better. Do it again."

I sigh, roll my eyes, and eat more. I'm starving, so my willpower crumbles pretty fast. In a second, I'm plowing through rigatoni like someone's holding a gun to my head.

Cam grunts in approval.

I hate myself for liking that grunt.

"Speakin' of your father," he says casually, looking now at his plate, "what's his deal?"

"My dad? Oh, he's a photographer. I mean he was. He's retired now."

"Yeah? What kind of pictures did he take?"

"He did some work for the movie studios, but his bread and butter was fashion photography. Modeling shoots, magazine spreads, that kind of thing."

"So he worked with a lot of models."

I nod, chewing garlic bread like a farm animal. "And actors. 'The beautiful people,' he called them."

"And your mum?"

"She was a runway model. They met on a shoot in Paris, actually. Now she mostly gets colonics and obsesses over finding the perfect macrobiotic lettuce on her daily trips to the farmers market."

Cam is quiet for a moment. "And your sister's a beauty queen."

"Yup, Jacqueline made it all the way to the Miss America pageant. Got beat out by a farm girl from Kansas. I don't think she's ever recovered. Her and my mom are practically identical twins—your classic leggy California blonde type. My dad, too. He looks like a surfer—very tan and fit." I chuckle. "My sister used to tease me when we were kids that I was adopted, because I look nothing like anyone in the family."

Cam looks up from his plate. His eyes are dark, and his face is serious. "That explains a lot."

I pause with my fork halfway to my mouth. "What are you talking about?"

"Your negative body image, damaged self-esteem, and conflicted relationship with food."

I slowly lower my fork to my plate, my face burning hot and my stomach twisting. "Excuse me?"

Cam says, "You've got a model mother, a beauty queen sister, and a father surrounded by perfect-lookin' people his entire career—"

"You're in no position to criticize my family or psychoanalyze me," I interrupt stiffly, my heart pounding hard inside my chest. "And let's not forget, you're pretty taken by your own looks, too, McGregor."

"Maybe I am, maybe I'm not. But I'd never make someone else feel bad about themselves because they didn't conform to my idea of perfection."

"And that's what you're suggesting my family did to me?"

"Didn't they?"

I'm so mad my whole body shakes. Making things worse is that he's right. "I think your forty-five minutes are up."

I stand, take my plate to the sink, and dump the rest of my food into it. I throw the plate on top of the uneaten food and blink hard, trying to clear my eyes of the water pooling in them.

"Joellen—"

"Stop. Not another word. You can let yourself out."

There's a long, heavy silence behind me. Then Cam sighs. I hear his chair scrape back from the table as he rises. "Are we still on for the mornin'?"

I count to ten before I answer so my voice doesn't shake. "Yes."

"Okay," he says, his voice softer. "Good." He takes a few steps away but pauses before he gets to the door. "For what it's worth, lass . . . they're wrong."

I close my eyes. A lone tear squeezes out beneath an eyelid and tracks down my cheek. Then my front door opens and closes, and I'm alone with Mr. Bingley twining around my ankles and the realization that I'm not the only one who's peeked behind a curtain.

If I've seen the real Cameron McGregor, he's seen right through Joellen Bixby, too.

That night I don't sleep. Cam's words swirl around in my head like a tornado, kicking up all kinds of nasty, ancient dirt. I hate myself for getting so affected by his simple observation and worry that if he can see me so clearly, everyone else must, too.

But when I think about it, I realize he's the only one who's looking.

In the morning, it's awkward.

"Hi," he says in a subdued voice, dwarfing my doorway when I open to his knock. He's got his hands shoved into the front pockets of a black hoodie, the hood drawn down over his forehead, a pair of black sweats and black athletic shoes completing the look.

"Hi. This is the least skin I've ever seen of yours. Are you feeling okay?"

His lips twitch, but he smiles using only his eyes. "If you want, I can take off my shirt. It'll cut at least five minutes off your warm-up time."

"There he is. Good morning, prancer."

"Mornin', dragon lady." He reaches around his waist and produces a plastic bottle of the green goo he fed me yesterday morning. When I take it, he looks relieved, like he was expecting a fight.

"Wait." I stare at the bottle in my hand, then look up at Cam with furrowed brows. "Where did this come from?"

"My blender."

"You have a blender in the back of your pants?"

"It was in my waistband."

That gives me pause. "You thought it was a good idea to carry a bottle of liquid in your waistband for a five-foot walk across a hall? Are both your hands broken?"

He makes jazz hands at me, breaking into the smile he's been try-ing to hold back. "The hands are fully operational, lass. In case you've a mind to give a lad a tactile tour of your majestic lady parts, as you'd put it."

"Please tell me you're wearing underwear and that this bottle wasn't, like, resting on your butt crack."

With a straight face, he says, "Aye, lass, you caught me. It's a bottle of butt crack juice. Drink up, it's full o' vitamins."

"Vitamins?"

My imagination starts to run wild. I once read a cookbook titled *Natural Harvest* written by a man who thought every dish could be improved by adding a certain "natural" ingredient produced only by a pair of male testicles. The photo accompanying the recipe for Slightly Saltier Caviar haunts me to this day.

"Just drink the bloody thing, lass. It's juiced veggies and protein powder!"

I close the apartment door behind me and shove my keys into the little zippered pocket on my fleece vest. "Fine. But if this tastes suspiciously salty, I'm kicking your ass." I open the bottle and sniff the contents, listening to the Mountain chuckle.

"The only salty thing in this hallway is you, darlin'."

His voice is as warm as his gaze when I meet it over the bottle. He shaved today, but somehow his usual scruff suits him better. He's not the kind of guy who should be buffed to a shine, manscaped and manicured, pretty. All his rough edges combine to make something more interesting. More . . .

Masculine.

I guzzle the green goo and wipe my hand across my mouth when I'm finished, looking away because my face is suddenly flaming.

Cam cocks his head. "Uh-oh. You must've had a dirty thought about pretty boy Michael. Your face just turned to beet."

When I answer with only a smile and a stiff nod, Cam chuckles again. "A little early in the mornin' to be feelin' frisky, innit, sweetheart?"

Hearing him call me sweetheart makes my face go even hotter, and now I'd like to kick my own ass for being a dope.

"Let's get started," I tell him, a little too sharply.

He's amused by my sudden shift in manner. "Okay, okay, no need to get testy."

I leave the empty bottle on the floor next to the door and we do warm-up stretches in the hallway while I listen to him ramble about target heart rates and runner's euphoria and all kinds of other healthy things I can't focus on because I'm too busy trying to avoid noticing his rugged good looks again.

It must be the lack of sleep that has me so flustered.

Either that or I just realized that in his own annoying, arrogant way, the Mountain is actually pretty hot.

THIRTEEN

By Friday I've lost five pounds—five!—and Cam and I have settled into our routine of morning runs and nightly dinners. True to his word, he's kept his music off so my ears haven't bled all week. He also designed an eating plan for me focused on lean protein and veggies and ransacked my pantry and fridge in search of food he deemed inappropriate for my new diet. He took what he found to the local homeless shelter in a cardboard box.

An embarrassingly *big* cardboard box.

Then we went grocery shopping together, and I found myself the object of so much envy from other women I thought they'd all get together and make a voodoo doll of me to stick pins into. Their jealousy was palpable, and all I was doing was walking next to him. They probably thought I was his housekeeper, but the looks I got . . . yikes.

The looks *he* got gave me a glimpse into how his ego had inflated to its Godzilla dimensions. Those women looked at him like he was the juiciest filet in the butcher's case. Like they wanted to rip off all his clothes and mount him, right there in the organic vegetable aisle. Like he wasn't even an actual person, really, just a big ol' piece of tasty man meat they wanted to sink their teeth into.

I was embarrassed for my own gender.

He took it all in stride, though. It was hard to tell if he was absorbing the admiration or deflecting it, because in public his smiles were more brittle than when we were alone together. He clearly enjoyed the attention, but my female intuition told me he wasn't as easy with it as he seemed.

Or maybe that was my overactive imagination again. Either way, neither of us mentioned all those hungry eyes at the grocery store when we got home.

I'm standing in the kitchen in the office Friday morning, making myself another cup of coffee, when a male voice says behind me, "What a pretty dress."

I whirl around so fast I almost topple over but steady myself against the counter before I can fall flat on my face. Two feet away stands Michael, wearing a charcoal-gray suit with a pocket square, looking like a movie star.

He smiles at me. "I don't think I've ever seen you wear a dress. Is it new?"

I glance down at myself. "Oh. This? Um."

I struggle to think of some excuse for this dress that doesn't involve the embarrassing truth that I dug through my closet last night looking for something he might like on the off chance we'd run into each other and this was the only thing I came up with. It's blue, which I remembered is his favorite color. Also, due to some ingenious quirk of design, it performs the minor miracle of making my childbearing hips look slimmer.

I open my mouth to answer and hear Cam's mischievous brogue in my head. *Tell him you have a date.*

"I have a date," I blurt so loudly Michael blinks.

"Oh?" His gaze flickers over me, up and down, head to toe, assessing. "Well, whoever he is, I envy him."

My fingers curl so hard into the Formica counter I'm surprised it doesn't shatter. I attempt a coquettish laugh but end up sounding like I'm trying to expel a hair ball.

Michael must sense my impending mental break, because he cocks his head, his smile growing wider. "Do you mind?" he motions to the coffee maker directly behind me.

"Oh! Of course, sorry!" I leap out of the way and stand to the side, where I can admire his beauty from a safe distance.

Michael wordlessly holds out the mug of coffee I left on the machine. I take it with shaking hands, avoiding his eyes because all my nerve endings are pulsing with lust and I'm afraid he'll be able to see it if we make eye contact.

He smells crisp and clean, like fresh linen. Like new one-hundred-dollar bills.

Busying himself with brewing his own cup of coffee, he says casually, "I reviewed your application for the associate editor position."

I stop breathing. It's a good thing I don't have a mouthful of liquid because it would be all over his elegant suit right about now.

He glances at me from beneath thick black lashes. His blue eyes sparkle. A dimple flashes in his cheek. "Sonnets?"

Instantly, my face blazes with the heat of a thousand suns.

On the application was an area that asked for any additional information not included on your résumé that would be pertinent to your job performance. Special skills, relevant hobbies, any experience outside your formal education or work history that might give you an edge. On a whim, I'd listed the only thing I thought might fit, this being the publishing industry and all.

I write sonnets as a hobby. Classically structured, Shakespearean-style sonnets, because I am a pathetic human being with a nonexistent love life who will someday die alone surrounded by my cats.

Looking at my shoes, I mumble, "Um. Yeah."

"It's all right," says Michael with a laugh. "Don't be embarrassed. I think it's quite charming."

Charming? Did the man of my dreams just describe me as *charming*? I'm not sure what a heart attack feels like, but it's probably close to this.

I look up at him, thrilled by the warmth in his eyes, but my thrill quickly turns to horror when he says, "Recite me one."

My blood ceases to circulate through my veins.

"Oh, come on," he urges gently, seeing the look on my face. "I want to hear one of your sonnets, Joellen. Please?"

Oh God. OhGodohGodohGod. My mouth is a desert. My palms start to sweat. I feel a case of the runs coming on, but Michael Maddox is standing two feet away, looking at me with expectation after uttering the word *please*. I'm doomed to obey him, no matter how much I'd prefer to suffer a massive stroke and die on the spot.

I moisten my lips. My voice comes out as a whisper, barely discernible over my thundering heart. "Please don't laugh."

His expression turns deadly serious. "I promise I won't."

"Okay." I inhale a deep breath I hope will give me courage, which utterly fails. "This is called 'Ode to Old Chicks.'"

Michael's brows shoot up.

"I said don't laugh!"

He lifts a hand, shaking his head. "I swear on my mother's grave I'm not laughing. You have my word. Please continue."

After a moment of inspecting his face, I see no hint of amusement, so I swallow my fright and begin.

> When Life's midcrisis has begun
> And the bloom is off the rose,
> We women of a certain age are glum,
> Ignored by men for those
> Young girls of perky breast and thigh

And coy, long-lashed flirtations.
But such pleasures—such delights!—are nigh
For men desiring new sensations,
For we mature ladies (still full of life)
Are seasoned by our complications.
We bring to love a certain spice
Unknown to less experienced maidens.
So look not, you men, to the young for their
    easy charms,
But satisfy your deeper yearnings in an older
    woman's arms.

In the wake of my recitation of "Ode to Old Chicks," Michael's face goes through a series of remarkable transformations. I don't know how many emotions cross his face, but the final one it settles on is indecipherable and, therefore, terrifying.

"What a fascinating sonnet," he says, his voice tight, his eyes blazing blue fire. "And how interesting you chose that particular one to share with me."

My stomach drops. I've made a colossal, unintentional, but nonetheless unforgivable error.

My boss thinks I've just propositioned him. I'm going to be fired for sexual harassment.

My career is over. I might as well go visit the animal shelter now and adopt the rest of my cats.

My hand over my mouth and my eyes saucer wide, I breathe out in horror. "It—no—that's the most recent one I wrote. I didn't mean anything by it . . ."

Michael's blistering gaze drops to my mouth. He murmurs, "No? Pity." He reaches out and brushes his knuckle over the slope of my cheek.

The earth stops spinning on its axis. I become aware of all the cells in my body, of every singing nerve, my ragged breathing, the tremor skittering over my skin. We stand there and stare at each other as a powerful magnetism wipes my mind blank.

My *mind* is frozen, but my body is all sensation, all pounding heartbeat and flying pulse, the faint press of his knuckle on my skin the center of my universe.

His lips part. He leans closer.

Holy shit. He's going to kiss me.

"Mr. Maddox, I need to speak—"

Portia barges into the kitchen, heels clicking, a file under her arm. She sees us and skids to a stop.

Michael spins away and resumes fixing himself a cup of coffee as if nothing has happened, while I stand rooted to the spot, mortified and strangely guilty, unable to speak or move.

Ice forms in long, crackling fingers on the floor and wall around the spot where Portia stands. She stares at me, her gaze hard, her posture rigid, her expression accusatory, then she turns her icy glare to Michael's back. "Excuse me, sir," she says stiffly. "Your secretary told me you were in here. I didn't mean to interrupt."

Michael turns around with a mug in his hand, a casual smile on his handsome face. "You weren't interrupting. Joellen and I were just discussing her application. She's very eager to get the job."

It's the wrong thing to say. If people could spontaneously combust, Portia would be splattered all over the walls and floor right now in little frozen pieces.

She cuts her freezing gaze to me. Her lips thin and her nostrils flare, and I'm afraid she might physically attack me.

"I see," she says softly, burning holes into my head with her eyes.

This is a disaster of Hindenburg proportions. It's clear what Portia thinks Michael meant by *eager* and what she thinks I'm up to.

With one knuckle brush, I've become the office harlot, sleeping my way to a promotion I wouldn't otherwise deserve.

My voice strangled, I say, "I'll just be getting back to work now."

I slink away, tail between my legs, skirting Portia with my gaze on the ground. As soon as I'm out of the kitchen, I break into a breathless run, headed back to my desk where I plan to spend the rest of the day designing myself various size scarlet *A*s to wear on my clothing.

If I didn't have bad luck, I wouldn't have any luck at all.

A few minutes before five o'clock, my desk phone rings.

"Joellen Bixby speaking."

"Joellen, it's Michael."

My heart slams against my rib cage. I look around surreptitiously, as if Portia might be lurking around the corner of my cubicle, then sink into my chair and cover the phone's mouthpiece with my hand. Why I suddenly feel like I'm in a spy movie, I don't know.

"Um. Hello, sir."

He sighs, and even that sounds beautiful. "Please, stop with the sir. Everyone calls me sir. It makes me feel like my grandfather."

"Sorry. Habit. You being the CEO and all."

Michael clears his throat. "Yes. About that." There's a short pause, then he exhales in a gust. "I'm sorry for what happened in the kitchen. That was inappropriate of me. I hope you can accept my sincere apologies. I clearly made you uncomfortable, and it was absolutely out of line—"

"I wasn't uncomfortable."

Silence.

Strangely emboldened by his lack of response, I drop my voice to a whisper. "I mean, I was, but in a *good* way."

Another exhale, this one longer and slower.

121

"You're not saying anything."

"I'm relieved." His voice drops an octave. "And . . . really happy to hear that."

I hold the phone away from my face and scream silently, kicking my feet up and down and bouncing in my chair like a lunatic. When I put the phone back to my ear, I dredge up every ounce of courage I have and ask him the $64,000 question.

"Why?"

After a nerve-wracking pause, his response is even lower than before. "You know exactly why, Joellen."

My panties are curling off me like burning paper. My glasses are fogging like they did the first time I read *Fifty Shades of Grey*. My heart is in danger of exploding inside my chest.

I whisper, "No, I don't. Tell me." *Who is this person? This bold, flirty person?* A body snatcher has apparently consumed me.

I hear some rustling, the squeak of a chair, what sounds like foot-steps echoing off tile. "What are you doing?"

"Pacing."

He's pacing. And his voice is rough. And he's happy that I wasn't uncomfortable in a bad way, but won't answer when I ask why.

"Michael," I whisper.

"Yes, Joellen?"

"What's happening?"

More rustling. He might be sitting down. I imagine him in his office, staring at the floor, looking all sorts of beautiful and tormented.

He begins haltingly, like he's forcing the words out against his will. "You know . . . that I'm . . . getting divorced."

"Yes."

"And . . . also that . . . I'm the CEO of this company."

"Yes."

"And you're . . . my employee . . . who has recently applied for a promotion."

I can't answer because euphoria has frozen my tongue, but my heart is screaming *YES! YES! YES!*

"So this is . . . complicated."

I shoot to my feet, blind to anyone or anything around me, a death grip on the phone, my soul about to rip itself from my body. I listen for what he might say next with the terrified focus of someone waiting for the verdict from a jury in her murder trial.

"Are you still there?"

"I'm here." My voice is shaky, but I don't care. A nuclear bomb could go off in Lower Manhattan and I wouldn't care.

Sounding miserable, Michael sighs again. "I'm sorry. I'm putting you in a terrible position. I'm being an idiot. I never should have opened my mouth."

Too late. He's opened Pandora's box now, and all the devilish little creatures are running amok, screaming in glee throughout my reproductive organs. "You were going to kiss me, weren't you."

It's a statement, not a question, because now I'm sure it's true. I might have been able to convince myself it was my imagination before this conversation, but things have drastically changed.

"I should go."

"Michael. Tell me."

There's a long, cavernous silence, then Michael whispers, "Yes."

He hangs up.

I lift my arms in the air, throw back my head, and let out a victory whoop so loud everyone in the cubicle maze stops what they're doing and stares.

From behind me comes Shasta's irritated voice. "Bitch, what the hell is wrong with you? People are busy doing nothing around here—be quiet!"

I start laughing and can't stop.

Michael Maddox was going to kiss me.

I can't wait to get home to tell Cam.

FOURTEEN

I stop at the corner market on the way home to pick up a good bottle of wine, because I'm celebrating. The signs of Christmas are everywhere. Shop windows twinkle with colored lights, a soft dusting of snow covers the ground, holiday music plays from every loudspeaker, fake Santas panhandle on corners for charity, aggressively ringing bells in people's irritated faces.

It all seems magical. I'm feeling the holiday spirit like I've never felt it before, simply because Michael's lips had the intent to press against mine.

Never mind that they actually failed to do so. It's the thought that counts. If it weren't for that witch Portia, I'd be celebrating tonight with Dom Pérignon instead of a decent Napa cabernet.

I'm opening my apartment door when I hear Cam's voice. It's muffled behind his own door but still easily discernible.

"Because I don't bloody *want* to come back early, that's why!"

I pause, my ears perked, curiosity overwhelming me.

Heavy footsteps stomp across the floor one way, then turn around and go back the other. "My fucking attorney is supposed to be handling that!" he roars. "He said I wouldn't have to appear in court until the seventeenth of next month!"

Oh boy. That doesn't sound good.

Trying to be quiet, I turn the key in the lock and open my door. I don't want Cam to think I was spying on him and get called a Peeping Tom again, so it's my intention to sneak in, mouselike, but Mr. Bingley has other ideas.

"RRROOOOWWW!" he shrieks, caterwauling like I've stepped on his tail.

"Shh!" I hiss, waving a hand at him. "I'll feed you in one second!"

But it's too late. The door across the hall is already opening.

Staring at me, Cam thunders into the phone in his hand, "I've gotta fucking go! I'll call you back later!"

He stabs his finger against the screen to end the call, tosses the phone over his shoulder so it lands with a clatter on the floor, then stands there staring at me, breathing hard, his chest heaving up and down and his eyes wild.

"Hey there, prancer. Bad day?" I let him seethe silently for a few seconds. "You want to talk about it?"

"No!"

"Okay, okay, don't get your panties in a bunch. Have a nice evening."

I assume he won't want to be social tonight due to the severe thunderstorm boiling over his head, but he puts that notion to rest by slamming his door, striding across the hall, and pushing past me into my apartment.

"Sure, c'mon in, make yourself at home," I say drily, watching him drop onto my sofa. "Always a pleasure to have an angry three-hundred-pound gorilla in the house."

He rests his head on the back of the sofa and closes his eyes. When he speaks, his voice is subdued. "Sorry, lass. Just lemme cool off for a second."

Mr. Bingley reminds me in no uncertain terms of his displeasure at being made to wait for his dinner and trots into the kitchen with his tail held high. I close the door, wondering how I became a meal slave to these two high-maintenance males.

I drop my handbag on the console, shuck off my coat and scarf and drape them over a chair, and take the wine into the kitchen, where I feed the cat and then go on a hunt for the bottle opener and a good crystal wineglass. It's hidden behind all the other crappy, mismatched glasses in a cupboard. I spend a while wrestling with the cork until it pops out, then I call over my shoulder, "You want a glass of wine?"

"Cameron McGregor doesn't drink wine."

I scream, because the bastard has appeared from thin air and now stands right beside me.

"McGregor! Quit doing that!"

He looks faintly amused. "It's not my fault you're as deaf as your cat, lass."

"I'm not deaf at all. You're just unnaturally stealthy!"

He chuckles, and I'm relieved to see a few of the thunderclouds are dissipating. "That's true. Ninjalike, I am."

"Don't talk backward like Yoda. You're too muscular to pull it off."

"Aha! You're finally admittin' to yourself what a handsome, burly devil I am!"

"Here we go." I smile and shake my head, then pour myself a glass of cab. I take a nice long swig, swallow, and sigh happily.

Which is when I notice Cam looking me up and down.

"What?"

"You're wearin' a dress. And heels."

"Congratulations on your astonishing powers of observation."

He doesn't laugh. "You look . . ."

When he fails to complete the sentence, my face flushes. "Like a person in a dress? Why thank you, what a spectacular compliment."

His gaze flashes up to mine. "Great, I was gonna say . . . you look really great."

I narrow my eyes at him, but he gives no indication that he's making a joke.

I swear this dress has magical powers. I might wear it every day from now on. "Thanks. So, if you don't drink wine, what do you drink?"

"Beer. But dark beer. Lager, ale, nothin' you can see through."

"Because *real* men don't drink sissy, pale-colored beer."

"Exactly. I knew you thought I was a real man."

"The jury's still out, pal. You wear an awful lot of skirts. I'm afraid I might find you raiding my closet one of these nights. But if you need a friend to talk to about it, I'm down. I'll even let you try on my bras."

We grin at each other. He leans against the counter and crosses his arms over his chest. Today he's wearing an actual outfit, composed of white T-shirt, black boots, and those faded blue jeans slung low on his hips. With all the tattoos on his biceps, his shaggy hair, and the dark scruff on his jaw, he looks like he could be anything from an outlaw biker to a rock star.

I might be able to see the appeal that had all those women in the supermarket drooling.

"What's that look you're wearin', lass? Your face is funny. You havin' an episode of intestinal gas?"

Embarrassed, I go with sarcasm, my usual first line of defense when called out.

"Yes, McGregor. I'm having an episode of intestinal gas. And I'm not wearing my charcoal panties, so stand back or be blasted." I give him a little shove in the chest, which is like trying to shove a brick wall and exactly as effective.

"Ach, I'm sure your farts smell like rose petals, luv."

I burst out laughing. "Please don't talk to me about farts! There's a guy at work who tells me fart jokes 24-7. I don't need anyone else bringing up the subject!"

Something flickers over McGregor's face—a flash of tension, there then quickly gone. "There's *another* guy at work you're interested in?"

"No. Ew. Denny is like seventy years old. And fart jokes aren't exactly the thing to make a girl swoon. But *speaking* of work . . ."

I set my wine on the counter and clap, hopping a little because I'm so excited to share the news. "Michael almost kissed me today in the company kitchen."

After a pause, Cam strolls over to the kitchen table and sits in one of the chairs. From under lowered brows, he levels me with a look. "Don't take this the wrong way."

"Oh my God. You're already ruining it!"

He ignores me and goes straight to the point. "If you had a girl-friend who told you her *still-married boss* almost kissed her *at work*, what would you say?"

Some of the air leaks from my Michael love balloon. "It sounds bad when you say it."

He makes a gesture with his hand, like *Because it is.*

I pour myself more wine. "Okay, but you haven't heard the whole story."

He quirks his lips. "I'm breathless with anticipation."

I launch into the entire explanation of what happened, including all the details, what I said, what Michael said, how Portia walked in on us, then the phone call where Michael admitted he was about to kiss me. When I'm done talking, Cam looks disturbed.

"What?" I chew my thumbnail in anxiety.

"You think you're old?"

Utterly confused, I stare at him.

"You said the sonnet you recited to him was called 'Ode to Old Chicks.' Was that about yourself?"

Heat ascends my neck in a slow, creeping flush. "I'm thirty-six, McGregor."

"And you think that's old?"

"Are you screwing with me right now?"

He shakes his head, runs his hands through his hair, and mutters something under his breath. "Never mind. Back to the big picture. Married boss. Single employee. An almost kiss in the company kitchen. The possibility of flushin' your whole career down the toilet if your friend the wicked witch decides to report you to management."

"Michael *is* management."

"Aye. And you're up for a promotion. How's that gonna look?"

I hesitate, considering what he's suggesting. Cam must not like my expression, because his voice comes out hard.

"Don't be naïve. If that woman wants to, she can make big problems for you at work. There's all sorts o' ways she can make your life hell. Smear your reputation. Turn people against you. Undermine the legitimacy of your hard work by sayin' the promotion is only 'cause you're bangin' the boss. Use your imagination, lass."

I think of Ruth in HR and how she didn't seem to like Michael barging in on our meeting, of how deep Portia's hatred for me appears to go, and my stomach flips with anxiety. I guzzle the rest of my glass of wine. "Bummer. And here I was thinking I'd take you up on that offer to teach me how to kiss." I laugh nervously. "That's the least of my troubles!"

I pour myself more wine. It isn't until I'm about to lift it to my mouth that I notice Cam has appeared noiselessly next to me once again. "Dude. Seriously. That's freaky. Cut it out."

"I just had a thought."

"Another one? This is a record week for you."

Cam takes the glass of wine from my hand and carefully sets it on the counter. Then he looks at me with shuttered eyes and an expressionless face. "Maybe I'm bein' too hard on you, lass. I did offer you my help, after all."

"Yes, you did."

"So. Go ahead, then."

I furrow my brow and stare up at him. "Go ahead and what?"

"Kiss me."

The sound of Mr. Bingley scarfing his food is the only noise in the kitchen for a moment, until Cam prompts, "C'mon, let's see what you've got. I have to know what I'm workin' with if I'm gonna be any help."

Heat spreads over my chest and up my neck, then my ears are burning.

Cam shrugs. "Or don't. It's no sweat off my back if pretty boy tries to kiss you and winds up with a face full o' slobber."

He starts to go back to the table, but I grab his shirt. "Wait!"

He slants me a look.

"Um . . . okay." I take a deep breath. "But you can't touch me."

"I see," he says drily. "So it'll just be our auras kissin', then."

"Stop being sarcastic. This is serious!"

Cam sighs, folding his arms over his chest. "Lass. I don't know how long it's been since you've kissed someone, but there are these things called lips involved? I'm pretty sure that counts as touching."

"I meant with your hands!"

He holds his hands up in a surrendering gesture. "I wouldn't *dream* of it."

When I narrow my eyes at him, he chuckles. "Tell you what. I'll stand here like this"—he strolls to the opposite counter, puts his hands behind his back, and leans his weight against them so they're pinned—"and you can do your thing with no worry about stray hands."

He looks completely nonchalant. I, meanwhile, am a whirling vortex of emotions.

What I haven't told him is that the last time I went on a date—eons ago—the good-night kiss was so disastrous I cried myself to sleep that night. The guy pushed me away by my shoulders, gasping for air, and said, "That was my lung you just licked!"

I guess I was being pretty aggressive. A long enough dry spell can make a girl desperate, and apparently I had my tongue so far down the poor guy's throat I was examining his internal organs with it.

Needless to say, I never saw him again.

My heart pounding, I smooth my hands down the front of my dress. Cam watches me silently, looking bored.

"Promise me it won't be weird after."

"Well, you're obviously gonna fall instantly in love with me, lass, but it won't be weird on *my* end."

I roll my eyes, relieved a little that he's teasing. I take a step toward him, then stop. "Do you have any STDs that can be passed through your saliva?"

He sighs, closing his eyes.

"I'm just being safe."

"No, you're just bein' chicken."

"I'm not a chicken!"

His look of dry disbelief challenges that statement, and now I'm mobilized. I put my shoulders back and lift my chin. "Fine. We're doing this. If you get handsy, I'll crack your skull."

His long exhalation is that of an exasperated parent dealing with a fussing child.

A few more steps and I'm standing right in front of him. In heels, I'm four inches taller, and he's a few inches shorter because he's leaning against the counter with his legs spread, but I still have to tilt my head back to look up at him.

"You have gold flecks in your eyes," I blurt.

He chuckles. "Maybe you should write a sonnet about my beauty."

I slap him on the shoulder. "Shut up."

"C'mon lass, you're makin' too much of a production of this. Just get it over with. I don't have all night."

I scowl at him. "Sorry to be taking up so much of your precious time, prancer!"

"You're forgiven. Now lay one on me so I can give you some helpful tips for your quest to land Mr. Perfect."

Extremely nervous, I blow out a breath and give myself a little mental pep talk. "Okay, but . . . when you give me your tips, please be gentle."

Cam's brows slowly lift, and the heat spreads into my cheeks. "I'm not exactly talented in this area. The last guy I kissed was left with permanent emotional scars."

His voice is soft when he answers. "I promise I'll be nice."

Okay, Joellen. Be brave. It's not like either one of you is going to enjoy it. This is purely educational. And God forbid you screw it up if Michael ever tries to kiss you again.

"Close your eyes."

Cam obediently closes his eyes. There's a faint smile on his lips, which is encouraging because I take it as evidence that he's amused by this whole exercise.

My hands shaking, I take a fortifying breath, then I lean in and press my mouth against his.

His lips are surprisingly soft. Also surprising is how much heat is emanating from his body. He could be running a fever he's so hot. He smells like clean skin and male musk and something indefinable, dark and earthy, secret and magical, like a midnight walk in the woods.

Delicious.

I break away with a gasp and stand there blinking at him, my heart going a million miles an hour.

He opens his eyes and frowns. "Was that it?"

"Yes!" I shout, on the verge of a meltdown. "Why? Was it that bad?"

"No, it was perfectly fine, lass. If I were your grandma."

His lips curl up, and I realize he's laughing at me.

"Oh my God, you're impossible."

I whirl away, but he grabs my arm and gently drags me back. "You were just nervous, lass. It was a good first effort, nothin' to be embarrassed about. But if I could make a suggestion . . ."

I stand in front of him vibrating with embarrassment, my cheeks so hot they're glowing. "What?"

"Don't hold your breath."

"Oh. I was doing that, wasn't I?"

Cam nods. "Just try to relax into it. Also . . ."

His pause terrifies me.

"A real kiss includes tongue."

I grimace. "To be completely honest, I'm afraid my tongue has a mind of its own. You might find yourself in a wrestling match to the death with it."

He tries to suppress the laughter shaking his chest by clapping a hand over his mouth but isn't successful.

"It's not funny!"

"It's *hilarious*, and you know it!"

I look into his sparkling eyes and have to admit he's right. I groan. "Oh God. I'm so pathetic."

Instantly, Cam's laughter vanishes. "No, goddammit, you're not," he growls, his eyes blazing. "Now kiss me again before I change my mind and take you over my knee for bein' such a bloody idiot."

I search his face for a moment, wondering why he gets so mad when I say things like that, then decide it really doesn't matter.

What matters is Michael. So here we go.

I step into the space between Cam's spread legs, remove my glasses and set them on the counter beside him, flatten my hands over his chest, and, with a final exhalation, press my lips to his.

FIFTEEN

If I thought Cameron McGregor tasted good with his mouth shut, he becomes the most succulent, delicious bonanza of flavor when his lips part and my tongue touches his.

His mouth is sweet, hot, and plush. He applies gentle pressure, sucking lightly on my tongue, and makes a low sound in the back of his throat.

That sound—combined with the taste of his mouth and the hard heat of his body pressed against mine—sends an electric current of pleasure shooting through my veins.

"Oh!" I jump, startled by the shock of it, and pull away. I stand in front of him with wide eyes, my heart thumping, my mind a writhing snarl of dangerous thoughts like a box full of snakes.

Cam's eyes drift open. "Easy, lass," he says softly, pulling me back to him. "We're not done yet."

Before I can decide if I want to keep going, he decides for us both by taking my mouth again and easing his tongue between my lips.

Boy, he's being a really good friend.

"Think of pretty boy," he whispers when I stand there stiff as a board, uncomfortable because I'm liking this little experiment a tad too much. "Pretend I'm him. Pretend it's his mouth on yours. His body against yours. His hand in your hair."

Cam's hand is in my hair. When did that happen?

I discover with a twinge of terror that I don't care because I like it so much. He holds my head in place as we kiss with his hand fisted at the scruff of my neck, an action so wholly and unexpectedly erotic my mind blinks off-line. I sag against him, desperately drawing breath through my nose.

Oh God. Oh that. Oh yes, that. Do that again. You're a genius. My nipples could cut glass.

He's so big, and hard, and hot as a furnace, but his mouth is the softest thing in the world. It's a cloud. A sweet, delicious cloud that's impairing my thoughts and kicking up the release of eggs from my ovaries until I'm sure I could make omelets on a hotel brunch's buffet line with all of them.

Somehow my arms have wound around his shoulders. Somehow his other arm has become an iron bar around my waist. Somehow I'm making desperate growly kitten noises and grinding myself against his body.

Somehow he's making desperate growly wolf noises and grinding back.

The doorbell rings.

We break apart like we've been caught plotting the overthrow of the government and stare at each other.

"Someone's at the door." My voice sounds like I've swallowed a toad.

"Are you gonna answer it?" His voice sounds like he's swallowed a handful of gravel.

I wheeze out an asthmatic breath. "It could be important."

Cam's gaze drops to my lips, then flashes back up to my eyes. The heat in his eyes almost incinerates me. "More important than this?"

Whoa. Was that an earthquake? No, we don't have earthquakes in Manhattan. Then why is the ground moving?

Sounding irritated, the doorbell rings twice more. It breaks the weird spell I'm under, and I'm able to jerk away from Cam and draw a breath before I throw myself back into his arms and beg him to do naughty things to me.

I wonder if his ChapStick is drugged?

I grab my glasses and shuffle to the door with a jolting, stiff-kneed gait, like a zombie. When I open it, Mrs. Dinwiddle stands there in a royal-blue lounging robe with peacock-feather trim at the sleeves and hem, a martini in one hand and an unlit cigarette in a long black holder in the other. Her turquoise sequined headband sports a spray of seed pearls on one side that bob as her head moves.

I'm too discombobulated to bother with small talk. "Since when do you smoke, Mrs. Dinwiddle?"

"Good *gracious*, Ducky, I *don't!*"

I look pointedly at the cigarette holder in her hand.

She waves it around like Hermione casting a spell. "Oh, this! Isn't it *elegant*? I found it in a *trunk* yesterday after*noon*, packed away in the back of my closet with some of my old *stage* costumes. I had Blessica run to the *store* for a pack of *cigarettes*, because it looked quite *sad* without one. Ducky, did you *know* a pack of cigarettes costs *thirteen* dollars? *Shocking!*"

She doesn't look shocked. She looks positively giddy. I wonder what number martini she's on. "How can I help you, Mrs. Dinwiddle?"

She sails past me into my apartment on a cloud of Chanel No. 5, shedding peacock feathers. Mr. Bingley scampers over and starts batting at the feathers, his tail bristling with excitement.

"I had a *thought*, my dear, since you've embarked on your program of self-*improvement*."

I close the door behind her. "Who told you I've embarked on a program of self-improvement?"

She spins around, chin lifted at a regal angle, cigarette holder with its ridiculous unlit cigarette held aloft. The cat scurries around her floating feathered hem with insane-o hunter eyes.

"*Cameron* did, my dear." She notices him leaning against the counter in the kitchen. "Oh! Hello, Cameron!"

"Hullo, Mrs. Dinwiddle."

She squints at him. "Are you all right, my dear? Your face looks funny."

At the same time, Cam and I say, "Intestinal gas."

Our gazes meet across the room. I look away first because I'm not sure what my expression might be doing.

"I've got something *for* that, my dear. I'll have Blessica bring it *over*, along with my makeup kit."

"Your makeup kit?" I've got a bad feeling about this.

"We're giving you a *makeover!*" she crows in glee, then turns practical. "Now that Michael is getting *divorced*, we have to move *quickly*. We don't want another girl snapping him *up*. And forgive me, Ducky, but I thought you might need professional *help* with your hair and makeup. It's Friday night, so we'll have *plenty* of time to experiment with different *looks*."

I form a terrifying mental image of me, postmakeover, with scarlet-slashed lips, heavy blue eye shadow, a fake beauty spot glued to my cheek, and false eyelashes so long they arouse Mr. Bingley's hunting instincts when I blink.

"Um. That's really nice of you, Mrs. Dinwiddle, but I'm not sure that's a good idea."

"Pssh! Poppycock!" She waves a hand in the air. The seed pearls on her headband quiver madly. "It's a *capital* idea! Don't you think so, Cameron?"

"Sure. We want her to look her best for Michael, don't we?"

His tone is casual, but his jaw is tight, and his back is stiff. *Is he mocking me?*

Mrs. Dinwiddle is vindicated. *"Exactly!"*

"Well, fine. If Cam thinks it's a good idea." I didn't mean for it to come out sounding like a challenge, but it does, and Mrs. Dinwiddle is befuddled. She looks back and forth between us.

"Why *wouldn't* he, Ducky?"

Cam and I stare at each other. The sudden tension is excruciating. I'm so confused and just want everything to go back to the way it was before that stupid kiss. That incredible, delectable, stupid kiss.

Leave it to me to mess up everything.

"Actually, I was just about to make dinner, Mrs. Dinwiddle—"

"No," says Cam abruptly, pushing away from the counter. "You girls have a good night. I've got things to do."

His tone is like "I've got *better* things to do," and now I'm unreasonably hurt.

Without another word, Cam strides out of the kitchen, pulls open my front door, and disappears through it. In a few seconds, his apartment door slams, and then his godforsaken rap starts up at full volume, like a big musical middle finger in my face.

The cat chasing her hem, Mrs. Dinwiddle minces over to the door and shuts it. She downs the dregs of her martini and turns to me with a mysterious smile. *"Ignore* him, Ducky. Men are *children."*

I mutter, "Some of them are more like juvenile delinquents."

Her smile grows wider. "Now, while we wait for *Blessica*, let's go through your *closet*, shall we?"

The evening was about as pleasurable as having my fingernails pulled off and all my toes smashed with a hammer.

By the time Blessica showed up with the makeup kit and another martini for Mrs. Dinwiddle, I'd finished the rest of the bottle of wine while being subjected to an elderly woman's shock and horror at the contents of my wardrobe. You'd think she'd stumbled across a mass grave the way she carried on. Horrified exclamations of, "Good God, what is *this*?" were regularly heard from the bowels of the closet, along with disgusted clucks and muttered choruses of *My word*.

A confidence booster it wasn't.

Then I was treated to the unforgettable experience of having a makeover by a person who'd consumed approximately half a dozen martinis and didn't have the steadiest hands to begin with. Clowns have more attractive makeup. By nine o'clock, my face looked like a Rorschach test, and I was drunk and miserable.

For the life of me, I couldn't get that kiss out of my head.

"What do you *think*, Ducky?" asked Mrs. Dinwiddle at one point, peering over my shoulder at my reflection in the mirror as she breathed gin fumes into my face.

"I think it's perfect. If I'm starring in a play about a Kabuki warrior."

Eventually, Blessica carted Mrs. Dinwiddle off to bed, and I fell asleep in my blue dress, still in all my makeup.

I'm awakened by pounding on my front door.

"Ow." There's pounding inside my skull, too. I lift a hand to my head, wincing when I touch my forehead because even that slight pressure hurts. The clock on the nightstand reads five minutes after five in the morning. I wonder if there's an emergency and the building is being evacuated.

More pounding, then the doorbell rings. I swat Mr. Bingley's tail away from my face and attempt to sit up. The room swims woozily, and I clutch my stomach, groaning.

"Joellen! Are you in there? Open up!"

Oh God. It's Cam. I'm late for our morning run.

I'd rather die than go on our morning run.

I shuffle out of bed, fighting nausea, and pad out of the bedroom in my bare feet. When the cat meows for his breakfast, it's like steel spikes being driven through my skull. It takes all my strength just to pull the door open.

Cam jerks back when he sees me. "Sweet mother Mary! What the hell happened to you?"

I grumble, "Mrs. Dinwiddle happened to me."

"Did you lose a bet?"

"Ha. Go away—your voice hurts." I try to shut the door, but Cam pushes it open and barges inside because he's a pushy, obnoxious pain in my butt.

I shuffle away from him, waving a hand over my shoulder. "Do me a favor and feed the cat. I'm hungover. I'm going back to bed."

"For how long?"

"Forever."

"What about our workout?"

Bleary eyed, I turn around and stare at him. "In case you hadn't noticed, I'm in no condition to exercise, prancer."

He inspects my appearance, fighting a smile. "You have a point. It might be dangerous to allow you in public—you'll frighten the children."

I can't be insulted, because it's a legitimate observation. "Cat food's on the third shelf in the pantry." Without waiting for an answer, I head to the bedroom and crawl back into bed.

I hear Cam moving around in the kitchen, opening and closing the pantry door, murmuring to Mr. Bingley. Then he's in my bathroom, running the water in the sink.

"What're you doing?" I mumble with my eyes closed, irritated by his presence.

The edge of the mattress dips with his weight. He presses a cool wet cloth to my forehead. "Gettin' this shit off your face."

He starts to gently wipe the makeup off my skin as I lie there wondering if it's weird that I'm enjoying it.

"Stop frownin'. I'm doin' you a solid here, lass. I think your poor cat is traumatized from seein' you like this."

"Mrs. Dinwiddle had good intentions."

"Or she secretly hates you."

That makes me smile. "I'm glad to hear you don't think it was an improvement."

The washcloth pauses, then goes back to work under my jaw. "You don't need makeup."

I snort because he's being ridiculous. "News alert: you need to see an optometrist. I don't normally wear makeup, but I definitely should. My bare skin has caused many a man nightmares."

Cam's sigh is gentle and also disgusted. "You've got a head full o' bullshit, lass. Your skin is beautiful."

Beautiful? No, he can't mean that. He's screwing with me again. He feels pity. I'm so pitiful he's forced to make up a lie to distract me from my pitifulness.

His voice turns dry. "Do you always freak out when someone pays you a compliment?"

"I'm not freaking out."

"Oh, no? Then why did your entire body go stiff? And your eyes are rollin' around under your eyelids. You look like you're gettin' electric shock therapy." He returns to the bathroom and runs the water again, leaving me feeling exposed and vulnerable on the bed.

No one has ever told me I have beautiful skin. No one has ever told me I have beautiful *anything*. Well, there is Dr. Sternberg, my dentist, who always tells me how lucky I am to have such naturally straight teeth, but in the same breath he usually suggests a whitening product, so he can't be counted.

When the mattress dips again, I crack open an eye and look at Cam. "Do you really think I have beautiful skin?"

He makes a face like I'm being an idiot. A *bloody* idiot, I'm sure he'd say. "You don't even have pores."

"But I'm so pasty."

"Ha! You wanna see pasty, come to Scotland."

"Oh. So that explains it."

He looks at me warily. "I don't know what kind of demented BS is about to leave your mouth, lass, but lemme just say this. Your skin isn't the only beautiful thing about you. If you weren't such a wee numpty, you'd realize what a braw bird you are."

My other eye opens, and now I'm gazing up at him, wishing I had a translator handy. "Um . . . thanks?"

"Close your eyes," he demands, sounding mad. "I've gotta get all the goop off your lashes."

"I think you just pull those off. Be gentle—there was glue involved."

He mutters, "Jesus." It sounds like *Jayzus* and makes me giggle.

Cam carefully peels the fake eyelashes from my eyelids, making noises of disgust while he's doing it. When he's done with that and satisfied he's gotten most of the goopy foundation off my skin, he says, "You didn't eat last night, did you?"

I roll away from him onto my side and bury my face in the pillow.

His huge gust of a sigh stirs my hair. "All right, lass. I'm gonna make you somethin' to drink, and then I'll let you sleep."

He rises and leaves. I don't know how long he's gone because I drift back to sleep, but then he's there again, gently shaking me awake by my shoulder. I roll over to find him holding out a glass of poisonous-looking amber liquid.

"What's that?" I ask groggily.

"Homemade hangover cure. Drink it all, sleep for a few hours, and you'll be right as rain."

I lift to an elbow, take the drink from his hand, and chug it, coughing at the end because it's so vile it makes my eyes water. "What the hell is this?"

He winks at me. "Butt crack juice. Sourced fresh this mornin'."

The faint taste of bile rises up in the back of my throat, hot and acidic. I slap my hand over my mouth.

Cam throws his head back and laughs. He takes the glass from my hand and rises from the bed, looking down at me with a huge grin. "I'll see you later, lassie. Sweet dreams."

I fall asleep within moments, smiling.

SIXTEEN

In green and gold and brown they're lit,
Composed of dazzling color,
With sparks and laughter and lively wit
They move me like no other
Eyes in a face I've ever seen.
So starkly seductive they are,
A gaze straight from a lovely dream
With a shine like a brilliant star.
And lashes long and curved and dark
As soot and devils' souls,
All my resistance is a lark,
These knees are weak as a newborn foal's.
I beg of you, my burning Sun,
With this poor heart you'll soon be done.

When I open my eyes, it's light outside, and my head is perfectly clear. I sit up carefully, worried the room is about to spin, but everything stays stable. I feel no trace of headache or nausea.

I run to my desk, pull out my sonnet book, and quickly scribble down the words in my head.

When I'm done, I read it aloud, then frown at the first line. "It should say blue. Michael's eyes are blue." I scratch out the words *green*, *gold*, and *brown*, and insert *cobalt*, *azure*, and *sapphire*.

It feels wrong. And clunky. Too many syllables, too embellished, too much. So I rewrite the original line again, above the one I've scratched out, and stare at it.

Green, gold, and brown equals hazel. In my sleep, I composed a sonnet about hazel eyes. "He put something funny in that drink," I accuse the book.

"What's that?"

I slam the book shut with a strangled little scream because Cam is standing at my bedroom door. "Nothing! What are you doing here?"

He jerks his thumb over his shoulder. "Watchin' ESPN with the cat. Why're you shoutin'?" His gaze drops to my sonnet book.

I shout, "I'm not shouting!" and throw the book into the top drawer of my desk, slamming it closed so hard the whole desk shakes.

"Uh-huh. That didn't look guilty at all."

His smile is like acid on my nerves. I jump up from the chair, smooth my hands over my hair, and try to compose myself. "I thought you left."

"You thought wrong."

He's still looking at the drawer I threw the sonnet book into, so I move in front of it, crossing my arms over my chest. He glances at me, his smile growing wider.

"Okay, I'll let it go. For now. How'd you sleep?"

"Fine. Amazing, actually. I shouldn't feel this good after all that wine. What was in your homemade potion?"

"It's a secret. I could tell you, but then I'd have to kill you."

When I just stand there staring at him, he relents. "Ginger, raw honey, flaxseed, red pepper flakes, lemon juice, B vitamins, other stuff. Whips up in the blender in no time."

"You're quite the blender master, aren't you?"

"It was my mum's recipe. They all are." A cloud passes over his face. He looks away, shifting his weight from foot to foot.

"What time is it?" I ask, to change the obviously unwelcome subject.

He drags a hand through his hair and shakes his head like he's shaking off a bad memory. "Ten. You got anything planned for today?"

"Nope."

"Good. We're goin' shoppin'." He turns around and disappears, and now I'm worried.

"Shopping?" I hurry after him into the living room. "We already bought enough food for a month—"

"Not for food, lass. For a dress for the holiday party."

When I stand there blinking at him in surprise, he shrugs. "Unless you don't want a man's opinion on the matter. I'm sure whatever you pick will be nice."

I think of what I wore to the last holiday party and cringe. I thought ruffles would help hide my girth, but in photos I looked like a demented pirate who'd consumed his entire crew. "I mean, if you don't have anything better to do, that would be great."

His eyes—damn hazel eyes!—burn right through me. "I don't have anything better to do."

Now I'm feeling shy. Also weirdly guilty and ashamed, like he caught me masturbating or something. "Um. Okay. I need to take a shower."

"I'll go change out of my sweats. How much time d'you need?"

"Twenty minutes."

"That's it?"

"Why do you look so surprised?"

"Nothin'. Just in my experience women usually take a lot longer than that to get ready."

Right. In his "experience" with women, which, if made into book form, would encompass several thousand pornographic volumes.

Inspecting my face, Cam says, "You've got that intestinal gas look again, darlin'."

"I'll knock on your door when I'm ready." Scowling, I go back into my bedroom and close the door firmly behind me, pushing aside my curiosity at why I'm suddenly so mad.

It must be because he called me *darling*.

Jerk.

If I thought going with Cameron McGregor to a grocery store was an education in the collective lust of women, going with him to a mall filled with holiday shoppers turns out to be an education in the collective lust of the entire human race.

Everyone stares at him. *Everyone.* Women, men, children, dogs. Heads swivel in his wake like weather vanes in the wind. Mouths hang open. People stop in their tracks and gape.

It's so creepy that after a few hours of it I'm ready to jump out of my skin.

"God, how do you stand it?" I ask under my breath, edging closer to him as a pair of goggle-eyed women move nearer. They've been circling like vultures for the better part of twenty minutes, whispering to each other as they follow us from rack to rack in the dress department of Saks.

"Stand what?" asks Cam, browsing through the rack with an expert eye. Every once in a while he'll pull something out, then put it back after a brief inspection and move on. Apparently he has a very specific idea of what he's looking for.

"The ogling." I nudge him with my elbow.

He looks up and sees the women. When he smiles at them, they freeze. Then they perform a hilarious about-face and dart away, giggling hysterically like a pair of silly teenage girls, though they're obviously both over fifty.

"I hardly notice it anymore," he says with a shrug, then withdraws a red dress from the rack with a little growl of pleasure. "This one." He tosses it at me and keeps going.

I drape the dress over my arm and watch him continue his quest. "Seriously, though, it must get annoying! The amount of attention you get doesn't bother you?"

"Comes with the territory, lass. This kind of rare, extraordinary beauty has a price." He sends me a wink and I roll my eyes.

"God, I'm glad I'm not beautiful. I'd wind up a hermit if I had to deal with this every time I went out."

I'm fingering the neckline of the dress over my arm when I bump right into Cam because he's stopped moving. Startled, I look up into a pair of hazel eyes, intense and unblinking.

"The only reason you don't have to deal with it is because you don't notice it," he says, his voice low. "And the only reason you don't notice it is because you've mind fucked yourself into thinking you're fat and plain."

My lips part, but I'm too shocked to form a sentence. He takes my silence as permission to continue.

"Since we walked into this store, I've seen at least half a dozen men looking at you. Yes, *you*," he repeats when I start to protest. "If you want an example of what I'm talkin' about, look to your right. Three o'clock. Lad in the leather jacket with the red scarf. Look."

He glances up, and I follow the direction of his gaze. Sure enough, there's a guy across the aisle in a leather jacket with a red scarf looking right at me. He's tall, with nice hair, and a nice face. He's actually kind of cute.

When he sees us both looking at him, he glances away, cheeks ruddy. He turns and pretends to browse through a display of stacked sweaters.

"It must be you," I say, astonished. "I'm getting some of your glow. Like the moon reflecting the sun's rays. If the sun didn't shine so brightly, the moon would just sit there in the night sky like a dead lump of rock."

Cam's sigh is aggrieved. "Bloody fucking hell," he mutters, and storms over to another rack. I follow at a safe distance and watch with growing alarm as he tears through the rack, eyes black and lips thinned, his entire body bristling.

A young man in a suit with a gold name tag on his lapel stares at Cam with glowing heart eyes from a nearby register. When he sees me looking at him, he bites his lip and puts his hand to his throat, like *Cowabunga, girlfriend, is that big, glorious beast yours?*

I should introduce him to Cam. They'd make a lovely couple.

Smiling, I approach the Mountain and brave the storm brewing over his head. "What you're failing to take away from my comment is the compliment I paid you."

He glares at me from under lowered brows. "Don't talk to me right now. I'm mad at you." He savagely pulls a dress from the rack, rakes his black gaze over it, and tosses it in my general direction. I have to leap a few feet to catch it before it drops on the ground.

"Oh, okay," I say, acting casual. As casual as one can be, standing on the slopes of an erupting volcano. "So it's no biggie that I called you beautiful."

He freezes, narrowing his eyes at me. "No, you didn't."

"Didn't I?" I drift toward another rack. Cam follows on my heels like I knew he would, because there's nothing more irresistible to his ego than a stroke down its back.

"When?" he demands, cutting me off as I reach for a sparkly silver jacket.

"Use that big brain of yours and think." I move around him and admiringly fondle the sleeve of the jacket, then decide I'd look like a disco ball in it and let it go.

Cam moves in front of me again. "You said you were glad *you* weren't beautiful. How is that a compliment to me?"

"Because it's implied that *you* are."

He purses his lips, looking at me askance. "No. A negative doesn't count. You can't prove a negative."

It's so obvious what he wants me to say, but I know if I come right out and tell him he's beautiful, I'll never hear the end of it. Also, the building could explode if his ego gets any larger, so I just shrug and drift away again.

Cam surprises me by taking my arm and gently pulling me into his chest. "So what you're sayin' is that you think I'm beautiful?"

I aim for a breezy, nonchalant tone that doesn't give away the sudden thumping of my heart. "Well . . . you're not entirely unfortunate looking."

He's serious and intent, gazing at me with laserlike focus, not a hint of a smile in his eyes or on his face. "It's a yes-or-no question, Joellen. So—yes or no?"

Heat begins to creep up my neck. "You know exactly how you look, McGregor."

"Beauty's in the eye of the beholder, lass. I dunno how I look to *you*."

The roughness of his voice surprises me, as does the intensity burning in his eyes. *Has all my ribbing hurt his feelings?*

I'm breathless with shame when I realize that all the times I've been sarcastic with him might have been taken at face value. Not everyone appreciates a sharp tongue, or that its owner is usually just a big scaredy-cat who uses sarcasm as a shield.

Oh my God. I'm such a dick. A spiteful, petty little dick who's made a man feel bad about himself.

Looking into his eyes, I say quietly, "To me you look like a man everyone underestimates, objectifies, and misjudges because of his appearance. To me you look like a man who's thoughtful, insightful, and kind, but hopes no one will notice because it will be mistaken for weakness. To me you look like a man who hides his pain behind smiles and buries it in women and tries everything he can to forget whatever's hurting him but can't because he's got a soft heart that scars easily, but no one has ever looked close enough to see."

A look of anguish crosses his face. His fingers curl into my arm. He swallows, hard, a muscle in his jaw flexing.

A sudden pop of noise and a flash of light make us both turn.

There's a man with a camera standing across the aisle. It's one of those cameras with the long lenses and the big flash box—the kind the paparazzi use.

A growl rumbles through Cam's chest, so violent and animalistic sounding it raises the hair on my arms to gooseflesh.

It scares the crap out of the photographer, too. He leaps into motion, sprinting off down the aisle, bumping into people as he flees.

Cam lets loose a stream of obscenities under his breath that could peel the paint from the walls.

"Was that—"

"Aye. C'mon."

Holding my arm, Cam steers me away from the aisle and through the dress department, to the dressing rooms located in the back. A young female sales associate is there, helping shoppers into rooms. Her eyes widen when she spots us coming.

"She needs a room," Cam growls, "and I need to speak to your manager."

Neither of us dares to disobey him. In his current state, he's too intimidating to refuse. The girl quickly ushers me into a dressing room, then I'm alone with my shaking hands and knotted stomach, wondering what he's going to do.

And what would've happened if the photographer hadn't been there.

Was he about to kiss me?

"Are you going crazy, Joellen?" I whisper to my reflection. In the mirror I'm all wild eyes and flushed cheeks, a startled bird poised for flight. "Get it together. Your imagination is running away with you again."

But I didn't imagine it when I thought Michael was about to kiss me . . .

With a groan of exasperation, I throw my handbag onto the chair in the corner, hang the dresses on the bar on the wall, and tear off my coat. I spend too long wrestling myself out of my clothes because I'm flustered, and by the time I'm standing there in my underwear, I'm out of breath.

"Stupid," I mutter, yanking the red dress off its hanger. "Stupid, stupid, stupid. One man shows you some attention, and now you think they all want you. Cam *was not* going to kiss you! And he probably paid that guy in the leather jacket to stare at you, because he's nice!"

I pull down the zipper that runs the length of one side of the dress, and step into it, noting absently that it's my size. Lucky guess. "Be grateful the poor guy's helping you out, for Pete's sake, and stop acting like such a dimwit!"

I shove my arms into the sleeves of the dress, get my boobs into position in the bodice, then zip everything up and, with a huff, straighten and look at myself.

"Oh." That's pretty much all I can come up with.

I turn slowly left, then right. The dress isn't something I would have ever chosen for myself, but—somehow, miraculously—it works with my figure. It *worships* my figure.

The bodice is cut into a low V, exposing an acre of cleavage. Around the waist, the fabric is shirred to one side, gathered with a small, sparkly thingy like a brooch. The fit is tight but slimming, cut so well there are no gaps or puckers, no unsightly bulges, just a lot of softly draping scarlet fabric that swings attractively as I move.

Even the color is flattering. It makes my pale skin brighter, my mousy hair warmer, lends my green eyes a mysterious, fiery tint.

"You should definitely wear more red," I tell my reflection, who agrees with an enthusiastic nod.

There's a gentle knock on the dressing room door. "Is everything all right in there, miss? Do you need any different sizes?"

I open the door a crack and tentatively look out. "Um, would you happen to have any heels I can try on with this?"

The salesgirl looks me up and down. "Wow, that looks like it was made for you! What shoe size do you wear?"

I tell her, and she's off. Less than a minute later, she's back, bearing a pair of strappy gold heels.

"I'll break my leg in those," I say doubtfully, noting the height of the heel.

"Honey, if you're gonna go for it, go for broke. Metaphorically speaking."

She has a point. I pull off my shoes and socks and step into the heels, then inspect my reflection once again. Then I pull the elastic out of my hair and comb it out with my fingers so it floats over my shoulders and down my back.

"Your boyfriend's gonna *love* it," the salesgirl says, grinning.

"Oh, he's not my—"

But she's already dragging me out of the dressing room, no doubt dreaming of the commission she'll make if she can convince us to take the dress.

Cam's standing right outside the entrance to the dressing rooms, his back turned to us, his arms folded over his chest.

When the salesgirl calls, "Here she is!" he looks over his shoulder. Then he jerks all the way around, his eyes big and his jaw unhinged.

He drags his gaze up and down my body, says faintly, "Holy shit," and sinks into a nearby chair.

SEVENTEEN

My first instinct is to cover myself with my hands. Whatever's causing that stunned look on his face, it must be really bad. But then it dawns on me that his expression isn't one of disgust.

"Is it . . . okay?"

He swallows. His blink seems to last an unnaturally long time. He clears his throat and offers a curt, "Yup."

"Yup? That's it?" I look down at myself, regretting the heels. *Maybe I look slutty. Maybe there's too much boob showing. Oh God, maybe I was wrong about the color—*

"Joellen."

Cam's sharp tone yanks me out of my head and back into reality. "Huh?" I stare at him, wringing my hands.

Slowly and softly, holding my gaze as he enunciates every word, he says, "You. Look. Sexy. As. *Fuck.*"

My face floods with heat. I look bashfully at the floor while the salesgirl claps happily, squealing in delight.

"Right? I told her the same thing! I mean, not exactly the same thing"—she laughs, a braying noise—"but you know what I mean. She looks fantastic!"

I peek up at Cam from under my lashes. His hands are curled around the arms of the chair so hard his knuckles are white.

This is very confusing. "So . . . um . . . you think Michael will like it?"

At the mention of Michael's name, the salesgirl's happy squeals die a quick death. She eyeballs Cam, then makes a hasty retreat when she sees the thunderclouds gathering over his head.

"Excuse me, folks, there's someone who needs my help . . ."

She's gone. After an excruciating moment of silence, Cam says evenly, "Aye. He'll like it."

"Are you mad again?"

"Don't be silly, lass. Why would I be mad?"

He stares at me, his jaw set and his brows lowered, looking like he's about to blow a gasket.

"It's just that . . . you seem a little mad."

He grinds his teeth together and draws a long, slow breath through his nose. "I'm. Not. Bloody. Mad."

Oh boy. He's super mad. I better go change. Without another word, I spin around and flee to the safety of my dressing room, where I slam the door behind me and collapse into the chair, right on top of my handbag.

I sit there for a minute, trying to figure out exactly what just happened, when I hear Cam's low voice right outside the door.

"Lass."

"Yeah?"

"Try the black one, too."

I chew my fingernail. "Maybe we should just go—"

"Try the black one, too, woman!" he snaps. His footsteps stomp off.

"You're not the boss of me," I mutter, frowning at the door.

From the dressing room next to me comes a woman's voice. "I'd sure let him be the boss of me, sister!"

I sigh and give up all hope of understanding anything. Then I change out of the red dress and into the black one and present myself for inspection once again.

One finger tapping a slow staccato rhythm against the arm of his chair, Cam takes his time perusing my figure. His eyes investigate every inch of me, every curve and bump and awkward bulge. It's so embarrassing, I cover my face with my hands.

"Stop hidin', lass. You're not ten years old."

"Ugh."

"Look at me."

I gather my courage and look at him, but I'm still squirming.

"What's wrong?"

"You're making me self-conscious."

"Why?"

"Because you look like you're about to puke!"

He stares at me for a long time in cavernous, terrible silence, his eyes black, his brows drawn together, that spastic muscle in his jaw jumping around like crazy. "Lass."

"What?"

"What you know about men wouldn't fill a teaspoon."

I cross my arms over my chest and stare right back at him, lifting my chin in a fake show of bravery. "I don't know what that's supposed to mean."

He pinches the bridge of his nose and exhales heavily, closing his eyes. He mutters, "For the love of all that's holy, this woman."

"Excuse me, sir, did you ask to see me?"

A smiling man in a suit stands to my right, looking expectantly at Cam. The saleslady hovers nervously a few feet behind him.

Cam rises to his feet. "Aye. Let's talk over there."

They walk away, and I run back into the dressing room, nearly breaking my ankle on the way as I stumble over an invisible imperfection in the carpet.

No, my brain helpfully reminds me, *that's just your big feet.*

Now I remember why I hate shopping.

In the cab on the way home, Cam is silent. I try several times to make conversation, but when he only halfheartedly responds, I give up and take to staring out the window instead.

I ended up buying the red dress. It's folded on the seat between us in a garment bag, probably just as confused as I am as to why everyone's so tense.

On the ride up the elevator, I thank Cam for all his help. He seems to think that's really funny, but I have no idea why.

When I ask him if he'd like to have dinner with Mrs. Dinwiddle and me—because it's our long-standing tradition on Saturday night—he politely declines, saying he's made plans to meet someone in the Village.

I'm stupidly deflated by that news but tell him with a smile that I hope his date is fun.

The look he gives me in response could freeze magma.

When he quietly closes his apartment door after I bid him good-bye, I'm left wondering what I did wrong, replaying the whole day over and over in my mind.

I don't know what happened, but I'm determined whatever it is, I'm going to fix it.

Dinner with Mrs. Dinwiddle is a blur. On my way out the door, she gives me a bag full of beauty products and tells me I *must* use the hot oil conditioner on my hair or she'll make me babysit Fee, Fi, and Fo when she goes to visit her sister in Cornwall in the spring. I agree quickly, because although her dogs are cute, they're also psychotic.

I sleep fitfully and don't dream. I'm awake before the alarm goes off at 4:30 a.m., surprised by how eager I am to get my daily jog in. It's still hell, of course, but even though my body aches afterward, my head is clearer and it's helping me lose weight.

If someone had told me a few weeks ago I'd actually be enjoying exercise, I'd have told him to seek psychiatric help, but here we are.

Thanks to Cam.

But he doesn't knock on my door at five, or five minutes past, or ten minutes past. By quarter past, I'm worried.

"What do you think, Mr. Bingley? Should I go over there?"

Mr. Bingley is mute on the matter, deciding it's more important to groom his tail than provide an answer, so I decide for myself and head over to Cam's.

When I find his apartment door standing ajar, my heart slams into fifth gear.

"Cam?" I knock on the door, which causes it to swing open a few more inches.

Only one light is on, in the kitchen, but it's enough to see that a pair of jeans lies discarded in the entry beside one big black boot. Its companion is several feet away, kicked under a bench. I poke my head inside the apartment and call out his name again but get no reply. I do, however, spot one of the dining room chairs on its side and a glass smashed on the floor beneath the table.

Now I start to freak out. Was he robbed? Kidnapped? Ambushed? Is he lying in a pool of his own blood on the bathroom floor?

Breathless, I barge inside, frantically calling his name. I get no answer. His bedroom door is open. I push through it, throwing it open so hard it hits the wall.

Then I skid to a halt, horrified.

Cam is sprawled on his back on the bed, his arms and legs flung out, his eyes closed, his chest moving up and down in a slow, even rhythm. He's asleep.

He's also naked.

He's naked!

I whirl around with a gasp, clapping my hand over my mouth, so mortified my face burns with heat. I take a moment to breathe, trying desperately to wipe my mind of the image of his big tattooed nude body from my head, without success.

It's all I can see. The image is burned into my retinas and will haunt me until the day I die.

My God. No wonder the man is so popular with women. He should be starring in his own reality show about the life of a colossally well-endowed bachelor.

I take a few steps away on tiptoe, until I'm caught.

"Lass."

His voice is thick with sleep. Paired with the scalding hot image in my head, it nearly trips me. Hormones I didn't even know I have are throwing some kind of rave party in my lady parts, complete with pounding music, flashing lights, and laser beams.

Shaking, I whisper, "Um."

Behind me, sheets rustle. I can't move. I'm frozen. I've become a pillar of salt, like Lot's wife when she looked back at Sodom.

Cam clears his throat. It's the single most masculine sound I've heard in my existence on the planet.

"Lass. You're in my bedroom."

He doesn't sound angry or even particularly surprised. Meanwhile, I'm glowing with humiliation and would trade my soul to erase the last sixty seconds of my life.

"I . . . uh . . . shit. I'm *so* sorry. I thought you were robbed."

"Robbed?"

"Oh God. I'm such an idiot. I'm going now."

He growls, "Stay where you are." When the mattress squeaks, I almost faint.

The picture in my head . . . holy Christmas. I'll need hypnotherapy. I'll need brainwashing. I'll need to join the witness protection program and assume another identity, because there's no way I'll be able to continue with my life as is, pretending I haven't seen What I Have Seen.

I put both hands over my face and emit a miserable groan. Through my fingers, I see bare feet and legs approach, trailing a bed sheet. The feet stop in front of me.

"Why would you think I was robbed?"

The sleep is still in his voice, making it deeper and rumbly. Combined with that accent, it's devastating.

"Your door was open. There was some clothing on the floor . . . a smashed glass . . ."

I can't go on. I simply cannot speak another word. In a life full of embarrassing moments, this one wins Olympic gold.

Now his voice is warm with laughter. "I've got a sheet wrapped around me, lass, you can stop hidin' now."

I shake my head. "I'm too busy plotting my disappearance. Do you think Jane Smith is a good name for an assumed identity?"

He chuckles. I can smell him, dear Lord. Gorgeous, sleepy male in his physical prime—if bottled and marketed to the female population, it would make billions.

"Too obvious," he says. "You should go with somethin' more exotic. Like Beatrix. Or Seraphina. Yeah, Seraphina Snufflebottom." He taps my shoulder.

I peek at him through my fingers. He's smiling, his eyes half-lidded, his hair mussed, a scruff of beard darkening his jaw. That faint sound I hear is my ovaries moaning.

"I wasn't robbed, Seraphina."

"No kidding."

He rubs a fist into one of his eyes, which is both childlike and adorable. "Had too much to drink last night. Must've passed out. It's a bit of a blur."

I notice that his bathroom door is closed, but the light is on inside, and that strikes me as odd. Why would the door be closed? He was so drunk he couldn't be bothered to close the front door . . .

A few things come together at once, adding up to something awful.

Cam had a date last night. He had too much to drink last night. He slept naked . . . because he wasn't alone.

Sweet Jesus, there's a woman in McGregor's bathroom.

I feel sick. I don't know why, but I do. Without another word, I turn and leave the room, my hand over my mouth and my heart pounding.

"Where are you goin' in such a rush, Seraphina?"

"For a run. See you. Sorry again, it was an accident. I'm just a . . . I'm such a . . ."

Idiot. Moron. Fool.

I bolt from his apartment, take the stairs to the first floor two at a time, and run out into the cold, dark morning as fast as I can, not stopping to catch my breath until the building is far, far behind me and the icy wind has leached the last of the heat from my cheeks.

EIGHTEEN

I run until my thigh muscles are screaming, then limp back home in the cold and dark, determined to put this whole silly episode behind me.

I need to be mature about this. I'm thirty-six, not sixteen. Walking in on him sleeping was an accident, not the end of the world. Seeing him naked is not the end of the world. Certainly him having a woman spend the night isn't the end of the world, nor is it any of my business. I'll just apologize sincerely once more, and we'll be done with it. It will never be mentioned again.

By the time I get home, I feel better. Until I see the note taped to my door.

My dear Miss Snufflebottom,

You're upset. Why? I know it's not because you got an eyeful of my majestic manhood, though that would cause any sane woman to lose her marbles.

If you lie to me, I swear I'll make good on my threat to take you over my knee.

Yours until the sun flames out and all life on earth is extinguished,

Prancer

I knew I shouldn't have told him I write sonnets.

I crush the note in my fist and go inside, slamming the door behind me. I hurl the note into the wastebasket under the console and start muttering to myself like a madwoman as I go into the kitchen to feed the cat.

"Oh, you'll take me over your knee, will you? Hmpf. I'm sure it's a popular spot. I hope you've got some industrial-strength sanitizer ready, because there's no way *I'm* going over your knee without it! Good luck with *that*, buddy! Wait. What am I talking about? I'm not going over your knee *at all*! You dang man whore!"

I stop and huff out an aggravated breath, shaking my head at myself for being judgmental. Live and let live, that's my personal motto. It's none of my business what two consenting adults do together, even if it does involve tetanus shots and antibacterial creams.

"Not that I can really blame you," I continue, flustered. "You're single, you're young, you're famous, you're . . . big." My face reddens. "Why *shouldn't* you take advantage of your situation? In all fairness, why *shouldn't* you sleep around? I mean, If I had men throwing themselves into my path every three feet, I'm sure I'd be a whore, too!"

"Oh really?" a voice behind me drawls.

I scream, leap into the air, and spin around, dropping the can of cat food in the process.

Cam sits at my kitchen table with a lazy smile on his face and the cat in his lap.

I thunder, "WHAT THE HELL, MCGREGOR?"

His gaze piercing, he replies calmly, "You thought I had a woman in my bathroom earlier, didn't you?"

My heart gallops so hard I can't catch my breath. I start to splutter and shake, furious but also—again—horrifically embarrassed. "You . . . you *jerk*! You can't just *waltz* in here unannounced any time you like! This is my home! My *private home!*"

"As I recall, you waltzed into my place unannounced only a few hours ago. At least you're clothed."

His smile is smug, and I want to kill him. "Get out!"

"No."

"Yes!" I stamp my foot and point at the door. "Out!"

His brows lift, but he doesn't budge an inch. "A question for you, Miss Snufflebottom: Why would you care if I *did* have a woman in my bathroom?"

"I wouldn't! I didn't! I don't!"

His steady gaze never wavers from mine. He says softly, "What did I tell you about lyin' to me?"

He stands up, and my heart stops. When he takes a step forward, I take one back and put my hand out. As if that will help anything.

"Cam. Stop. Whatever you're thinking—"

"You know *exactly* what I'm thinkin', lass." His eyes are alight, his lips tipped up at the corners.

What happens inside my body when I hear the tone of his voice and see that look in his eyes is indescribable. I want to throw something sharp and heavy at him, but at the same time I'd like that something to be me.

When he takes another step toward me, I skitter away into the corner, panting. "Cut it out! This isn't funny!"

"I'd stop if I thought you were really scared." His eyes burn as he takes another step. "Are you scared, lass? Tell the truth."

Panicking, I make a sound like a door that needs its hinges greased. He chuckles. "That wasn't a yes."

He gets right up into my face, braces his arms on the counter on either side of me, and stares into my eyes. I shrink away as far as I can until the back of my head thunks into the cupboard. He's so close, I'm certain I can hear his heart beating.

After a moment when he doesn't do anything, I whisper, "I actually am pretty scared."

He glances at my mouth before his eyes flick back up to meet mine. "But not one hundred percent scared."

I close my eyes and swallow. "What's your point?"

His warm breath brushes my ear, raising gooseflesh on my arms. "My point is . . . what's the other percentage?"

I bite my lip to catch the groan threatening to break from my chest and swallow again. "Twelve."

"Twelve?"

I hear laughter in his voice, so I open my eyes. When I find him grinning, I snap. "Yes, twelve! Satisfied?"

His grin quickly fades, and his voice turns husky. "No, lass. Not at all. Not yet." He moistens his lips, then sinks his teeth into the bottom one.

Daaaaaammmmmn, says my uterus, fanning itself.

Just when I think my knees will give out and I'll slither to the floor, Cam pushes away from me and strolls out of the kitchen. Over his shoulder, he calls, "I had a meetin' with one o' my attorneys last night, lass. I came home alone. Not that you care, right?"

The front door slams, and he's gone.

It's a good thing Mr. Bingley is deaf, because my scream of frustration would scare the bejesus out of him.

I spend the remainder of the day inside with the door locked. I check it three times just to make sure. I do laundry, clean the apartment, fiddle with some of the beauty products Mrs. Dinwiddle gave me, and try to keep Cameron McGregor out of my head.

Irritating space invader that he is, he doesn't comply, so I'm stuck with a smug, imaginary Cam inside my brain, lounging naked on a mattress with one leg swinging slowly back and forth off the side.

At six o'clock on the nose, rap music blasts through the walls.

Prince Pantydropper is summoning his dinner.

Muttering made-up voodoo curses, I bang around the kitchen until I've got something for him to eat. When I knock on his door, the music lowers instantly.

"Hullo, lassie," he says when he opens up. "What brings you by?" He grins, leaning against the doorframe with his arms folded over his chest so his biceps bulge out everywhere, just as insufferably smug as he is.

Resisting the urge to kick him in the shin, I smile instead. "I haven't forgotten our bargain." I lift the platter I'm holding. "Pasta primavera with a garden salad. Here you go."

He looks at the platter, then back up at me. "Here I go? Here I go where?"

My smile turns brittle. "Take your food, prancer."

"Oh, no. No, no, no. Our deal was that *you* make me food and *I* eat it over at your place. Forty-five minutes, remember?" He swings his door open wider, and the rap music swells out louder into the hall. "Or would you prefer to spend your evenin' with my good friend Ol' Dirty Bastard?"

He stares at me with a challenge in his eyes, his smile growing wider in obverse proportion to how mine shrinks.

Without a word, I turn around and march back to my apartment. I leave the door open behind me because he'll find his way inside whether I want him to or not. The man is insidious, like an infestation of termites.

But he's not the only one with tricks up his sleeve.

I leave the platter of food on the kitchen table. As soon as I hear Cam's music cut off, I retreat into my bedroom with the cat and shut the door.

And lock it.

Then I call my mother. She picks up on the second ring. "Hello?"

"Hey, Mom. It's Joellen." I always feel the need to remind her who I am, in case she's forgotten she has two daughters since we last spoke.

"Oh, hi, honey! I was just thinking about you!"

"Why? What's wrong?"

She laughs. "Nothing's wrong, silly, I was just thinking I'd call you tonight. How are you?"

From beyond my bedroom door, Cam calls, "You better not be skippin' dinner, lass!"

I stick my tongue out at the door. "I'm good. Great, actually. I got a raise at work."

"Oh, honey, that's wonderful!"

She sounds thrilled, which makes me smile. "Plus, I'm up for a promotion."

"A promotion, too?"

"For an associate editor position. I already put the application in. I'm just waiting to hear back."

"That's fantastic! When will you know?"

Cam knocks on the door. "Is that your mother, lass? Tell her I said hullo!"

I stare at the door with slitted eyes, wishing for whatever the superpower is that lets you shoot lasers from your eyeballs so you can blow people to smithereens through solid objects. "Probably soon, maybe next week? I'll call you as soon as I know. How's Dad?"

"Who's that with you?"

Shoot! Mother hearing strikes again. I turn away and walk into the bathroom, closing the door behind me so now there are two doors between me and the Incredibly Irritating Man. "Hmm?"

"I heard someone's voice, honey."

"It's the TV. I've got the news on."

"So it's not Cameron McGregor?"

The hope in her voice makes me want to vomit. "*No*, Mother, it's not Cameron McGregor."

A voice faintly calls, "I can hear you talkin' about me!"

These people should work for the CIA! I turn the shower on full blast, go into the closet, and crouch down beside my dirty-clothes hamper, feeling like a refugee fleeing from a totalitarian regime. Which really isn't too far off the mark.

"Listen, I wanted to apologize for that remark I made about him the last time we spoke."

I sigh, scrubbing a hand over my face. "Forget about it, Mom. I was just being sensitive."

There's a short pause. "I feel like we're talking about two different things."

"I'm talking about when you said a man like him couldn't fall in love with a girl like me."

Her exhalation sounds disappointed. "Oh, honey, let's not go over that again. It's just reality. Everyone has to box in his own weight class, as your father would say. Birds of a feather and whatnot. What *I'm* talking about is when I called him a sex object. That was a little . . ." She laughs uncomfortably. "I can't call myself a feminist if I'm guilty of the same thing men are always doing to women. Namely, objectifying them."

I'm having a hard time following her logic because now I'm steaming mad. She's sorry she called a man she's never met a sex object, but she's *not* sorry she made her daughter feel undeserving of a successful, attractive man's love. *Twice.*

"Mom."

"Yes, honey?"

"I know I'm not beautiful like you and Jacqueline, but sometimes you make me feel really shitty about it."

She sounds surprised. "What on earth are you talking about?"

Is she being willfully *ignorant?* Years of pent-up frustration at being the ugly duckling in a family of swans starts to gather steam.

"I'm talking about boxing in my own weight class! I'm talking about how you like to make 'jokes' about me not being a size two like you guys! Calling me 'plumpy' isn't an affectionate nickname, it's a personal attack! And just because I'm not tall and willowy and blonde doesn't mean I'll never feel the touch of a man—"

"Joellen!"

"—or deserve to be loved—"

"Now wait just a minute!"

"—or get treated with respect by my *family*, the ones who I'm supposed to be able to trust and be myself with. I've had total strangers say nicer things to me than you do! Somebody told me the other day I have beautiful skin, and I almost fainted from shock!"

"Of course you have beautiful skin, sweetie! You get it from me!"

She's defensive. And completely missing the point. I might as well explain my feelings to a brick wall, because I certainly won't be getting any understanding from her.

Same old shit, different day. The emotion I've worked up fizzles out, and I'm left feeling nothing but drained. "Okay. Good talk, Mom. Later."

I hang up the phone, drop my head onto my knees, and sigh. Mr. Bingley rubs his furry face against my leg. "You love me no matter how I look, don't you, Mr. Bingley?"

His deep rumbling purr assures me that he does.

I pet the cat for a few minutes before girding my mental loins to go out and face Cam. I leave the closet and turn off the shower, then head into the living room with the cat trotting at my heels.

Sitting at the kitchen table in the middle of his meal, Cam takes one look at my face and sets his fork down. "What's wrong?"

I take a seat across from him, trying not to feel rejected when Mr. Bingley jumps into Cam's lap instead of mine. "Can I ask you a serious question?"

"Of course, lass. Ask me anything."

"Is life easier, being beautiful?"

He stares at me in silence for so long I grow uncomfortable.

"Yes, fine, I'm admitting I think you're beautiful." I wave a hand at his body, a gesture of disgust. "You look like you were carved from a perfect piece of marble by a master sculptor. Happy?"

He's so still it's unnerving. Finally he says quietly, "Who were you talkin' to on the phone?"

"My mother. Are you going to answer my question?"

A muscle in his jaw flexes. I sense he's angry, but I don't think it's directed at me.

"All right. Here's your answer: my life has never been easy."

My laugh sounds like a noise someone would make at a funeral. "Really? Because from where I'm sitting, it looks pretty good."

His eyes flare. "Aye? How so?"

"C'mon, McGregor. You're famous. You're good-looking. You're probably super rich. You've got your pick of women—and men, by the looks of it. For you the world is just one big banquet of choices."

"Is it?"

"Isn't it?"

We stare at each other. The temperature in the room seems to warm by several degrees. Holding my gaze, he says, "What did she say that hurt your feelin's this time?"

He puts a slight emphasis on "this." I hate that emphasis and everything it implies. I hate it more that the implications are spot-on. But I hate it most of all that he can so easily guess what this whole conversation is about because the damn man has X-ray vision and can see right through me.

I look away, ashamed at being caught.

"Joellen."

I close my eyes, squeezing them against the hot prick of tears the tenderness in his voice evokes. *He feels sorry for me. God, I'm pathetic.*

Then he's on his feet and pulling me up with his hands around my wrists. Before I can react, he's engulfed me in a bear hug.

With his strong arms wrapped around my back and his head bent next to mine, he says, "People can be arseholes. Sometimes those arseholes are family. It sucks, but it doesn't mean you have to take on their bullshit. Your mother's BS is about her, not you. You're perfect just the way you are, lass. Anyone who tells you different is a stupid bloody arsebadger."

My throat closes. My face crumples. A whimper rises from somewhere deep inside my chest, impossible to prevent. *Oh, no. Don't cry. Do* not *cry, for God's sake—*

I burst into tears, bawling into his chest—loud, ugly-cry bawling, complete with sobs and snot, my body shaking, my hands fisted into his shirt.

He exhales slowly, his arms cinching me tighter against him. His next words are spoken low and soft, with the weight of a vow.

"Ah, lassie. If it were anyone else but family who made you cry like this, they'd already be in an ambulance."

I don't know why, but that makes me cry even harder.

NINETEEN

I wring myself out against him, helpless to stop myself from being such a sad spectacle. Years of anger, hurt, and loneliness pour out of me like a tap has been opened. I cry until I'm exhausted, sniffling and hiccupping, trembling with shame.

Then Cam performs a miracle and picks me up in his arms.

I'd protest, but I'm too tired, so I allow him to carry me over to the sofa while I marvel at how effortless he makes lifting the weight of a baby elephant seem.

He settles me onto the sofa, props a pillow behind my head, pulls a blanket up to my chin, and strokes a lock of hair off my damp forehead. "I'll be right back."

When he leaves, I burrow under the blanket, tucking my legs up and hiding my face. My wet, undoubtedly splotchy and swollen face.

Some women can cry prettily, with dainty little feminine tears and elegant noises of distress, but I am not one of those women. I cry the same way I eat: messily, loudly, and with total abandon.

I am unruly in emotion and appetite. I've spent so much of my adult life trying to not be unruly, to be smaller, more contained, more *acceptable*, but underneath it all I'm still myself. All the passions and desires and tempestuous needs, all the wants and hurts and sorrows, all the ugly and wonderful things. I am just unruly, peculiar me, and I'm so tired of pretending otherwise.

At least with Cam I don't have to.

He returns from his apartment after a few minutes, bearing gifts.

He lifts my legs, sits on the sofa, and places my legs over his lap. "C'mon out, lassie. I've got treats."

I flip down an edge of the blanket and peek out. Cam is looking at me expectantly, holding a white ceramic bowl and smiling.

"Treats?" I sit up, already feeling better.

"Chocolate ice cream drizzled with Kahlúa."

My gasp is low and thrilled. I thrust out my arms and wiggle my fingers. "Gimme."

"No, we're sharing." He scoops up a spoonful of ice cream and eats it, watching as I lick my lips. Then he scoops a spoonful for me and holds it out.

I let him feed it to me, feeling awkward but also comforted, like the time I had strep throat when I was ten and my mother fed me soup at my bedside. That was the last time I can recall that she didn't make a disapproving face as she watched me eat.

"S'good," I say around a cold mouthful of deliciousness. "But it's not on my diet."

"That's why it's called a treat." He takes another bite, savoring it, licking the spoon like it's a woman's thigh. Or maybe that's in my imagination. Watching him eat is distinctly sensual. "Food is fuel, but it's also comfort. The trouble happens when it becomes more comfort than fuel. But that's what hugs are for."

He feeds me more ice cream, and I'm feeling better by the second. "You're a very good hugger, by the way."

"I know."

We smile at each other.

"But am I a good kisser? That's the real question, lass." He eats more ice cream, waiting for my response with lifted brows.

"You waited until I was in a vulnerable state to ask that, didn't you?"

"I'm not that stealthy. Here." He holds out the spoon.

I savor the mouthful of creamy goodness, trying to make it last as long as possible as I wrack my brain for a neutral answer that doesn't reveal just how thermonuclear I thought our kiss was. I decide on, "You seem very experienced."

He makes a face. "That's awfully clinical."

"Oh, I'm sorry, is your ego throwing a tantrum because I didn't say it was the hottest kiss I've ever had?"

He's about to put another spoonful of ice cream in his mouth but pauses, holding the spoon to his lips. "Was it?"

Those damn piercing hazel eyes. I look down at the blanket, picking at a frayed bit of yarn. "It might . . . be up there."

When he doesn't say anything, I glance up at him under my lashes and find him grinning at me.

"Oh, shut up, prancer," I mutter.

He wolfs down the bite of ice cream, smacking his lips. "For the record, it might've been up there for me, too."

I'm startled and commence blinking rapidly like a crazed owl. "Really?"

"Really."

I narrow my eyes at him. "You're just trying to make me feel better."

"Am I?" He takes another bite of ice cream, smiling around the spoon.

I flop backward onto the cushions and pull the blanket up over my face.

I hear a chuckle, low and pleased. "I'm tellin' the truth, lass. You're a champion kisser. Very fine. And not fine the way you Yanks use it—fine as in excellent."

I flip the edge of the blanket down and peer at him.

"I don't mean to make it sound like I don't have anything else I could teach you," he says casually, licking the spoon. He glances sideways at me. "For Michael, of course."

I chew the inside of my lip. "Like what?"

"You want a list?"

Now I'm indignant. "A *list*? There's that much to improve on? I thought you said it was fine as in excellent!"

He lifts a shoulder, nonchalant as can be. I'd like to smash my pillow into his face, but that would probably send the bowl of ice cream flying. His stupid face isn't worth a wasted bowl of ice cream.

I sigh and sit up, pulling my legs off his lap. "Okay. Hit me. And don't leave anything out. I want to hear the whole ugly truth."

He looks at the ceiling, lightly tapping the spoon against the side of the bowl. "It's not really one of those things you can talk someone through."

Getting more and more worried, I furrow my brow. "So how am I supposed to improve?"

He turns his gaze to me. His expression is solemn and regretful, like a doctor about to inform me of the inoperable tumor in my brain. "Practice."

Without waiting for a response, he scoops me more ice cream and holds it to my lips. Then he watches with his wolfish eyes as I suck the spoon into my mouth and swallow.

After I work up the nerve, I venture, "So you're saying . . . you want to kiss me again."

"I wanna help you get your heart's desire, lass," he counters briskly. "Which is Michael, right?"

Those wolfish eyes again. I'm getting confused. "Um. Yes. It's . . . Michael."

His eyes flash, but he nods, apparently satisfied he's made his point. "Right. Think of it as trainin'. Like if you were gonna run a marathon, you wouldn't just run twenty-odd miles in one go. You'd work up to it a bit at a time. Day after day, week after week, a wee bit at a time, until you're in prime shape for the *big* event."

When I sit in silence for too long, just looking at him, Cam shakes his head.

"You're right. It's a bad idea. You'll get all attached, and it'll be funny between us. You'll be heartsick. I'll be uncomfortable. You don't know this, but it's not easy for me to break a lass's heart. I can only stand so much beggin'—"

"Oh for fuck's sake, McGregor!"

He looks taken aback at hearing me curse. "I'm just tryin' to spare you a broken heart, lassie. I'm *agreein'* with you, it's a terrible idea."

"I'm *not* going to fall in love with you, McGregor. Not from kissing you or from anything else."

Unmoved by my outburst, he casually consumes more ice cream while looking at me from the corner of his eye. "Oh, aye, now I remember. You said I'm not your type."

"Exactly." I say it emphatically, unsure if it's him I'm trying to convince or myself.

Cam nods. "Exactly. So then there's no problem."

I sigh, remove my glasses, and scrub my hands over my face. I go into the kitchen, run the tap, splash water on my face, dry it with a dish towel. Then I put my glasses back on, turn, and look at McGregor on my sofa with his feet up on my coffee table, eating ice cream like he's on friggin' vacation at a seaside resort, and sigh again.

"Fine. But this is purely . . . educational. And I don't want to talk about it after tonight. Deal?"

Cam doesn't even turn around when he shrugs. "Whatever you say, lass. I'm just here to help."

It's the nonchalance in his aspect and voice, the total indifference, that finally convinces me. "Okay. Let's do this."

"Sure." He doesn't budge from the sofa.

"Are you coming in here or what?"

"I'm comfortable right where I am."

"Oh. Um. Okay." I return to the living room and perch on the edge of the sofa with my hands folded between my thighs. I never know what to do with my hands when kissing a man, so it's safer to have them trapped.

Cam says, "Well, hop on, then."

"What?"

He gestures to his lap with the spoon.

"Dude! No way! I'm not *straddling* you!"

He smirks. "Afraid you'll get too hot and bothered and rip my shirt off, lass?"

"This is ridiculous."

"Oh, so you're worried *I'll* get aroused."

Visions of his monster manhood swim into my brain. I sputter, "W-what? No! Geez!"

"Good, because I won't. Stop stallin'. I've gotta get to bed soon. I'm meetin' someone for a run early in the mornin'."

I'm irrationally hurt, both by the implication I'm not boner worthy and that he's made plans to work out with someone other than me. "Who?"

Cam inspects my expression with one corner of his mouth quirked, a strange look of satisfaction in his gaze. "You."

"Oh. Right. I mean . . . I know."

The other corner of his mouth lifts, and now he's smiling at me. "You're adorable when you're jealous."

I gasp, loudly and with vigor. "I am *not* jealous!"

Cam leans forward, sets the bowl of ice cream on the coffee table, grasps my upper arms, and drags me onto his lap, where I gasp again, because how could I not?

It isn't every day a girl gets to straddle Godzilla.

Cam says gruffly, "Good. It's sorted. You're not jealous, I'm not your type, and you don't have eyes for anyone but pretty boy Michael.

Now quit yammerin', woman, because I've got other plans for that mouth."

And oh God, does he.

He takes my mouth almost angrily, one hand around the back of my neck and the other curled around my upper arm, his lips hot and demanding. When his tongue breaches my lips and touches mine, a shudder of electricity runs through me, like I've stepped on a live wire.

My hands flattened over his broad chest, I shove him away. "Wait!"

He stares at me with a hard jaw, breathing erratically. "What?"

I remove my glasses and set them on the cushion beside us.

This time he comes at me slower. More deliberately, more controlled. He slides his hands into my hair and bends me to him, hesitating with a hair's breadth of space between our mouths.

"Remember to breathe," he whispers.

"Just kiss me already," I whisper back, surprised by how much it sounds like a plea.

"Your eyes are still open."

I immediately shut them.

His soft laugh sends a thrill up my spine. "If only you were that obedient all the time, lass." He lightly nips my lower lip, a dark, delicious little promise.

My hands. What do I do with my hands? They're flattened against his chest again, but that seems lame, so I slide them up around his neck . . . and discover his hair. Good Lord. Thick, glossy strands of hair slide like silk between my fingers. His hair is longer than any of the men's at the office, much longer than Michael's, past the collar of his shirt, dark and waving, exquisitely soft.

As his tongue slowly begins to probe my mouth, I tug on all that gorgeous hair, forgetting I'm not supposed to be enjoying this.

I arch against him, softening, expanding, breathing deeply through my nose as the kiss deepens and begins to burn. I wasn't kidding when I said he was experienced. He knows exactly what to do, how to get my blood sizzling and my heart hammering and all the pornographic images of him nude and splayed out like the best Christmas gift I've ever received pulsing like neon signs inside my head.

My nipples tighten. There's a new heaviness between my legs, but it's not him, it's me, flushed and aching, every pull of his lips sending a spike of heat to that hollow space inside me that I'm becoming acutely aware of, with its muted little howls of need.

I break away to check in before I lose myself completely and choke him with my prehensile tongue. "How'm I doing?" I mumble, flushed and out of breath.

His eyes drift open. Hot and dark, they pin me in place. "Jury's still out," he says, his voice thick. "Need more evidence."

His mouth. I will drown in the pleasure of his mouth. I'll die on this sofa, and Mrs. Dinwiddle will find my body, fingers and toes chewed on by the poor starving cat.

The kiss grows decadent. Sinful. I moan, a desperate sound rising from the back of my throat. It has an interesting effect on Cam.

His entire body goes stiff.

He takes my head in both hands, breaks the kiss, and turns his face away. He breathes raggedly for a few moments, his nostrils flared and his jaw like granite. With his fingers pressed into my scalp, he says roughly, "You can't make noises like that."

Oh God. I sound like a warthog. A donkey. A trained pig, snuffling through the underbrush in search of truffles. "Okay."

The humiliation in my voice makes his eyes slash to mine. "It's not bad. It's just . . . distracting."

Distracting?

He slightly shifts his weight, and things are clarified.

I bite my lip so hard I might have drawn blood. My heart is a hummingbird beating frantically against a cage. I whisper, "You said you wouldn't get aroused."

He looks at my mouth like a warlord looking over a kingdom he's just seized. "I lied."

A kiss again, dangerous, like standing at the edge of a cliff and looking over, shifting dirt and rocks tumbling beneath your feet. My fingers twist in his hair. His hands move my head, left or right, however he wants it, a throbbing pulse like drumbeats in my ears. I'm so turned on I feel frantic, unstable, like I might break out of my own skin.

Caterpillar becoming butterfly. Chrysalis shed, wings outstretched, wind beneath my belly. Caught on an updraft. Beating, beating, flying free.

He breaks the kiss, suddenly, shatteringly, the separation like breaking glass. Dizzy, I whimper at the loss of his mouth.

"Fuck. Joellen. *Fuck.*"

He's panting, his voice a desperate rasp. He radiates heat like a furnace. Even his hands on my head are hot, burning right through my skull.

With his scent in my nose and his heat wrapped around me and his heart pounding against mine, I'm somewhere else. I'm some*one* else. A gypsy, casting spells. A sloe-eyed singer in a smoky jazz club. A femme fatale in a film noir, all knowing smiles and long legs and a throaty voice with an edge like a purr.

"Don't stop," I say in my new voice. "You taste so good."

He stares right at me, his eyes intensely aglow. Tiger eyes. Wolf eyes. The eyes of a predator about to pounce on his meal.

He growls, "You like the way I taste?"

There's a challenge in the question. Other than his ragged breathing, he's so still, every muscle tensed.

What's happening?

I come back to myself abruptly, all at once aware of how far this little experiment has gone, how dangerously close it is to the point of no return, and the cat up on the kitchen table eating the remains of Cam's dinner from his plate.

Oh shit. My face floods with heat.

I'm not a gypsy. I'm not a femme fatale. I'm an awkward, lonely woman sitting on the lap of the most famous athlete on the planet, making an utter fool of myself.

"Sorry," I say faintly, my voice raw. I clear my throat. "I think I got a little carried away."

I grab my glasses and fly off his lap as if I've been launched. I flee into the kitchen, where I busy myself with cleaning the dinner dishes and attempting to stave off a major heart attack. For a long time, I hear nothing from the living room. When I chance a glance over my shoulder, Cam has his elbows propped on his knees and his head in his hands, looking at the floor.

"So I'll see you in the morning?" I try to make my voice normal.

He huffs out a breath, like a husky laugh only harder. He slowly rises to his feet. "Yup. See you in the mornin'."

He leaves, never looking at me, an awkward hitch in his gait.

I try to convince myself that my weight must've cut off the circulation in his legs, but it's a tough sell considering all the evidence. Ultimately I'm forced to face the truth.

Cameron McGregor was as turned on by that kiss as I was.

I can't decide if that's the best development or the worst.

TWENTY

In the morning, we act as if nothing ever happened.

We jog along the snowy streets, chatting about rugby, Scotland, the best places to eat in Manhattan, everything light and safe. I ache to talk to him about the kiss, but I know it's better left alone. Besides, what would I say? "Hey, that was some great kissing last night, eh? Wow, I sure was grinding on that king cobra in your pants! Had to go to bed and rub one out—how 'bout you?"

So not gonna happen.

At work I'm confronted with a corpse. The roses Cam sent me last Monday committed suicide over the weekend and are stinking up my cubicle something fierce. There are withered petals and crispy leaves all over the place. I consider dumping them into the kitchen trash, but the can is only slightly bigger than the one under my desk, unable to accommodate the remains of one hundred roses. Also I'd probably trip and fall on my way, thereby spilling disgusting flower-rot water all over the company carpet and eliciting the ire of Portia, who has already made several ominous passes by my desk like a shark toying with the seal it's planning to eat for dinner.

So I call for help.

Denny arrives with one of those industrial-size garbage cans on a round dolly with wheels. "Yikes!" he says, grinning. "Is that stench the roses, or did you have chili and beans for dinner last night?"

Even when he's not making fart jokes, he's still making fart jokes.

"Do you want me to help you?"

"No, kiddo, I got it. Thanks. You want to keep the vase?"

I demur. He makes quick work of the roses, placing the entire arrangement into the trash can and sweeping up the trail of leaves littered over the floor with a hand broom and dustpan.

Then from behind the wall that separates us, I hear Shasta's voice. "Oh my God. What the . . . Joellen? Is this *you*?"

I pop my head over the wall and find her at her desk, staring at her computer screen. Her eyes are wide with disbelief, and her expression sends a twinge of panic through my stomach.

"Is this me where?"

"On TMZ." She looks up at me, blinking. "You're on TMZ."

"Me?" I laugh in relief. "I don't think so."

She looks at her computer screen, then back up at me, then back at her screen. "Then you've got a twin you don't know about, because this looks exactly like you."

Frowning, I make my way over to her cubicle, then lean over her shoulder to see what she's looking at. There on the screen is a close-up shot of me and Cam, nose to nose in the ladies' dresses department of Saks, gazing at each other.

Neither of us is smiling. His big hand is curled possessively around my upper arm. The dresses on hangers are crushed between us. It's an intimate and intense moment and looks like we're either in the middle of a fight . . . or about to make out.

The headline screams, CAMERON MCGREGOR AND MYSTERY WOMAN SIGHTED SHOPPING!

Son of a bitch. The man with the camera sold the picture of Cam and me to TMZ.

Cold with horror, I whisper the first thing that comes to mind. "Does my hair really look like that?"

Shasta squeals. "It *is* you!"

"Shh!" I peek up over the cubicle wall, but no one else seems to have heard. Crouching back down, I go into full-blown panic mode, complete with sweating palms and heart palpitations. "Oh God. What should I do?"

"Girl!" thunders Shasta, making me wince. "What you should do is tell me what the hell is going on with you and Cameron McGregor!" As I cringe and beg her to keep her voice down, she peppers me with questions, each more invasive than the last.

"How did you *meet* him? How could you keep it a *secret*? Are you two a *thing*? Is he amazing in bed? Oh, cripes, I bet he's *crazy* in bed. Is he hung? You *have* to spill—oh! How long can he last? Is he freaky? I bet he's *super* freaky, right?" She wiggles her eyebrows salaciously, and is about to continue her tirade, until a familiar voice interrupts and we both freeze.

"Ladies. Hard at work, are we?"

Shasta and I gulp and make guppy eyes at each other. Slowly, I straighten and turn to face the music, edging over a few inches in an attempt to block Shasta's computer screen.

"Um. Good morning, Mr. Maddox."

He glances at Shasta, hiding behind me, then at the screen, which I'm sure is still at least partly visible, then looks back at me. "Good morning."

He answers smoothly, not a ripple of emotion in his voice, but his eyes are pinwheeling like a crazy person's, which is how I know I'm totally busted. He already knows about the story.

Shasta offers a weak, "Hi," then goes back to hiding behind my big butt.

"Joellen. I had a question about your application." He looks at Shasta meaningfully, and I understand. "Walk with me."

He turns and leaves without waiting for an answer, because of course he doesn't have to wait. He's the beautiful CEO, and I'm the lowly scullery maid who'd be happy to scrub his floors for all eternity for crumbs of his time and attention.

I lurch after him, sweating profusely.

His legs are long, and he's set a strenuous pace, so it's hard to keep up. It feels like we're running from someone. I'm consumed with guilt for no other reason than it seems like I should be as we stride down the corridor at a breakneck clip.

"So you're in the news."

His voice is terse, his jaw is set, and his eyes are roving back and forth like he's watching for incoming missiles. It makes me feel a little better that he's uncomfortable, too.

"Um . . . yeah. How'd you hear about it?"

"Word gets around fast. Was he the date you said you had?"

"No!" I say, too loudly. "He's my neighbor!"

Several people look at us from their cubicles as we storm past. He nods at one of them, ignores the rest. "So you said."

I have no response to that, not understanding if it's a challenge or what. Does he think I'm lying? "He's just helping me with a . . . um . . . project. There's nothing going on between us."

We turn a corner, almost colliding with someone coming from the other direction, but quickly regain equilibrium and continue our strange walk-run, looking straight ahead.

"So you two made up?"

"Huh?" I am a sparkling fount of intelligence.

"His music. You said he was disturbing you with his music."

"Oh. Right. That. Yes, we made up." That sounds too lovey-dovey, like a lovers' reconciliation, so I quickly amend it. "We called a truce, I mean. And then, uh, he needed help shopping for his, uh, girlfriend. In Scotland. For a Christmas present."

For the love of God, Joellen, just stick your entire leg in your mouth and get it over with!

Michael adjusts his tie, yanking at it as if it's strangling him. He's in a beautifully fitted navy suit, his skin glows with health under the florescent lights, his face is clean shaven, and his hair is perfect. Everything about him is so perfect.

Too perfect?

Disturbed by my betrayal, I stumble on nothing but quickly right myself.

"Meet me after work for a drink."

Now I almost fall flat on my face.

"Six o'clock. The Liquid Kitty on Fifth."

He's oblivious to my sudden catatonia. Not waiting for a response, he makes a right turn abruptly and stalks off down another corridor, leaving me gaping after him.

Is this a date? Did Michael Maddox just ask me on a *date*?

Before I can faint into a gelatinous pile of limbs, I glimpse Portia headed toward me. My heart sinks. It's too late to run away, because we've made eye contact, so I pretend I'm coming back from some non-existent meeting and stride forward with a plastered-on smile and a purposeful walk.

She cuts me off just as I'm turning a corner, stopping in front of me so my path is blocked.

She rests her hand on my forearm and digs her fingers in. "Be careful," she says softly, blue eyes glittering. "Be very careful, Joellen."

Before I can answer, she's gone, clicking away on five-inch heels, leaving me wondering why her words felt less like an enemy's threat and more like a comrade's warning.

I spend the rest of the day in terror, wearing out my antiperspirant and feeling as if I might keel over and die at any moment. My adrenal glands are hysterically pumping stress hormones into my veins, and it takes an enormous amount of self-control not to let loose the lunatic scream throbbing inside my chest.

By the time I get home, I'm a mess.

"I've only got thirty minutes to get ready," I tell the cat breathlessly, slapping cat food into a dish. "What should I wear? Should I shave my legs?" Mr. Bingley stares at me with a judgy face. "You're right, that's just inviting trouble. But wait—I *want* trouble, don't I? This is Michael Maddox we're talking about here. I want all the trouble I can get!" The cat's eyes narrow to slits. "No, you're right, play it cool, don't be overeager, focus on the long run. If I shag him in the bathroom of a bar called the Liquid Kitty the first time we go out, we'll never be able to tell anyone our first date story."

It's a testament to my crazed state of mind that Michael and I are already married with children and giving each other sly glances over dinner as we tell the rehearsed lie we've made up when some nosy relative wants to hear about our first date.

I shower, dress, and attempt to blow-dry my hair but end up winding it into a messy bun because my hands are shaking too hard to keep the dryer steady. I apply a coat of the mascara Mrs. Dinwiddle gifted me in her bag of beauty goodies, then consider applying lipstick but decide it will probably only end up all over my front teeth, making me look like I've eaten a crayon. I put the tube away and slick on a coat of clear lip gloss instead.

Then I look at myself in the mirror.

My color is high. My eyes are wild. Rebellious little tufts of hair have escaped from the bun and float all around my face like fuzzy clouds. I look like I've recently escaped from a mental institution.

"Screw it," I mutter. "This is how I look. If Michael doesn't like it, he can suck an egg."

Cam's positive body image rhetoric must be having some effect, because a few weeks ago those words would've been heresy.

I don't have enough time to take the subway uptown, so I hail a cab. I do deep-breathing exercises during the ride, which does nothing but make the cabbie look worried. By the time he drops me off in front of the Liquid Kitty, I'm teetering on the edge of hysteria.

This is a moment I've dreamed of for a decade. *Ten years* I've been in love with Michael Maddox. Ten years I've pined and daydreamed and longed for him to notice me, and now here I am, standing on the sidewalk in front of the bar where he asked me to meet him for a drink.

Well, technically ordered me to meet him, but this isn't the time to split hairs.

A doorman in hat and tails opens the door for me, nodding solemnly as I pass. I find myself in a dark anteroom lit by a garish red chandelier that throws prisms of scarlet light over the plain black walls. The effect has a startling resemblance to dripping blood.

It seems the Liquid Kitty is, in fact, a portal to hell.

"Good evening," says a voice to my right. I nearly jump out of my skin.

"Oh. Hello."

A tall, bald man with linebacker's shoulders wearing a tuxedo has materialized from behind a black velvet curtain. His gaze flicks over me, quickly assessing. "Are you here to meet a member?"

I looked up the address on my phone but didn't realize this was a membership club. I thought it was just a regular old bar. Silly me. "Um . . . Michael Maddox?"

He inclines his head. "Very good. Please allow me to take your coat." He extends his hand, which is the size of a dinner plate.

"Thank you." I shrug off my coat and hand it over, then hug my handbag to my chest like it's a life preserver.

Tuxedo Man smiles, amused by my obvious discomfort. He disappears behind the curtain for a moment, then returns without my coat. "This way, miss."

He motions for me to follow him. I do, pleased that he called me "miss" instead of "ma'am." It's the little things.

We pass through another black velvet curtain into a large sitting room decorated by someone with a fond nostalgia for nineteenth-century French bordellos. Red velvet divans are scattered about, fringed with tassels. Elaborately carved gilt mirrors decorate the walls. A fire crackles in a fireplace against one wall, lending the room a warm glow.

I try to ignore the oil painting above the fireplace of the voluptuous nude woman lounging on a sofa with a white dog, but it's so large it's impossible. Her sly smile is vaguely disturbing.

We cross the empty sitting room and go through another curtain, and I'm wondering if the interior designer got a bulk discount on velvet drapes.

We pass through a bar and lounge that looks like something right out of an Edith Wharton novel. Everything supple leather, gleaming wood, and polished antiques. It reeks of upper-class privilege. So do the clientele: well-dressed gentlemen and ladies mingling with cocktails in hand, laughing quietly or engrossed in conversations. No one glances at us as we pass, which I'm grateful for, because I'm embarrassed by my outfit.

I'm sure I'm the only one here who shops at The Gap.

Finally we enter a large dining room. The main floor holds dozens of tables and quartets of large leather chairs. On one end of the room is a stage. The other three walls have private booths of tufted carmine leather, set into large niches with curtains on either side held back with gold tassels.

At one of the booths sits Michael, drink in hand, watching the door.

We make eye contact across the room, my heart leaps into my throat, and I'm terrified all over again.

God, if you like me even a little, please don't let me screw this up.

TWENTY-ONE

"Miss," says Tuxedo Man, bowing. When he gestures toward Michael, I understand I'm to make the rest of the walk to his table alone.

"Keep it together," I warn myself through stiff lips as I approach Michael's table. "Don't say anything stupid. Let him do the talking."

He doesn't take his gaze off me as I walk. By the time I reach him, my face is throbbing with heat.

"Hi," I say shyly.

He stands, kisses me on both cheeks, and smiles down at me. "Hi yourself. Sit."

I do, only it's more like collapsing. *He kissed me! On both cheeks!*

"Do you like bourbon?" He pushes his drink across the table toward me.

No. Gross. "Yes! I love it!" Relieved to have something to do other than drool at him, I guzzle the drink. And immediately regret it.

I cough as fumes sear my nose and throat. My grimace of disgust could win an award.

Michael chuckles. "How about a glass of wine instead?"

I'm so embarrassed I could wrap myself in one of the stupid velvet curtains and spend the rest of eternity cocooned under the table, but I nod because a rational answer is expected. "Thanks."

Michael signals for a waiter, who materializes from thin air. "Sir?"

"A bottle of the 2000 Romanée-Conti."

The waiter bows so low it's comical. It looks like a yoga pose. "Right away, sir."

He vanishes as quickly as he arrived, leaving me, Michael, and my raging insecurity alone.

Michael leans against the booth, stretches one arm along the back, and smiles. "You came."

I know it's just me, but that sounded super sexual. "Um. Yes. I c-came."

He stares at me until I want to squirm. Then he reaches out and softly touches my cheek. "Your cheeks are burning, Joellen."

So are my panties, sir. "I'm a little . . . this is all a bit . . . surprising."

I worry that's the wrong thing to say, because his smile fades. He drags a hand through his hair, props both elbows on the table, and looks at the tablecloth. He's wearing a jacket that matches the color of his eyes, a white shirt open at the collar, tan slacks, and a huge chunky gold watch that glitters under the lights. I think it has diamonds.

Cam would probably snicker at a man who wears a watch with diamonds.

Why am I thinking about Cam?

I sit up straighter, push McGregor out of my head, and focus on Michael. Beautiful, elegant Michael, who now looks like he's about to cry. "Michael? Are you all right?"

He clears his throat and turns to me with a smile that looks forced. "I'm sorry. You'll have to forgive me—it's been a rough couple of weeks. This divorce . . ." He makes a dismissive motion with his hand. "Enough about me and my problems. Let's talk about you."

I don't want to talk about me because I'm boring, but mostly because his show of emotion has made me bold. On impulse, I touch his arm. "It's totally normal to be upset when you're going through a divorce. You don't have to pretend everything's okay."

Who am I now, Dr. Phil?

Michael gazes at me with a look of intense concentration, a little furrow between his brows. "Thank you. That's very kind of you. I've always liked that about you, Joellen. You're kind."

He lightly rests his fingers on the back of my hand, and I have to force myself not to suck in a breath at the jolt of lust that zings through me.

We stare at each other in silence until the waiter reappears, then we break apart like we've been caught having sex in public.

I fan myself with my napkin while the waiter opens the bottle and pours two glasses of wine. This is hell on my nerves. If I get out of this club tonight without having a total mental breakdown, I'll count myself lucky.

When the waiter leaves, Michael lifts his glass. "A toast."

I lift my glass, too. "What are we toasting?"

Michael's lips lift into a small, seductive smile. "New beginnings."

A faint wheeze passes my lips. I repeat, "New beginnings," in a strangled voice, and chug my wine in a few short gulps.

He doesn't look at all disturbed by what most people would consider strong evidence of a drinking problem. He simply takes a sip of his own wine and refills my glass.

"You're nervous." He looks at me from the corner of his eye as he pours.

I exhale hard and close my eyes. "It's that obvious?"

"Don't be embarrassed. I'm flattered."

I open my eyes and stare in disbelief at his handsome profile. "*You're* flattered?"

"That," he says with a chuckle, like he's pointing something out. "I really like that."

Now I'm confused. "What?"

He sets the bottle on the table and turns to me, blasting me with the full paralyzing effect of his baby blues. "You're oblivious to how charming you are. It's very appealing."

It's all I can do not to fall over dead. I swallow more wine and whisper shakily, "Thank you."

After a moment where I refuse to look at him because I'm too afraid of what he might see on my face, he asks, "Do you find me attractive?"

I honk out a laugh that would sound at home coming from a goose. "Attractive? Are you kidding? I think you're the most beautiful man I've ever seen!"

Except for Cam.

I'd like to slap whoever that little voice belongs to inside my head, but I don't have time to dwell on it because Michael has settled his hand on my knee, causing my leg to erupt in flames.

I wore a skirt, one of the few I own. It's a simple black thing, but it fits well. I did end up shaving my legs because I thought what the hell, if we end up shagging in the bathroom at the Liquid Kitty, my life will be complete.

But now that Michael has his hand on my bare skin—hopeful slut that I am, I didn't wear panty hose—I think it might have been a bad idea, because the effect of his warm palm on my knee is what I imagine the three wise men felt when they first glimpsed the baby Jesus in the manger.

Namely, rapture.

"Thank you," says Michael, his voice husky, his gaze on my lips. "I find you very attractive, too."

He leans in until he's so close I can smell his breath, sweet and aromatic with the dry spice of wine. *He's going to kiss me. Oh God. Oh shit. It's really going to happen!*

But then it's *not* happening, because I've flattened my hand on his chest and held him back.

He stares at me. I stare at him. We're both not sure what's happening.

"Um . . . you're technically still married, right?"

He blinks. Frowns. Shakes his head. "We've filed for divorce."

Right! He's a free agent! Get in there, girl!

My inner slut seems to have no conscience, but apparently I do. "I mean . . . it only just happened. Like, last week. Maybe you should . . . give yourself a minute to . . . adjust."

His heart thuds hard and fast under my palm. I find it exquisitely erotic. Also I'd like to punch myself in the face.

"You're probably right," he says reluctantly, as if he doesn't think I'm right at all. He pulls away slowly, looking confused.

I'm sure the man has never been denied anything in his life, but for some reason, here we are, in an alternate universe where it makes sense for a girl like me to turn down a man like him.

"No, you're *absolutely* right." He shakes his head as if clearing it, and now he looks appalled. "Good God, I'm so sorry. I don't know what I'm thinking. I keep putting you in these terrible positions. Next you'll probably think I'm some kind of lecherous creep, expecting favors for advancement in the company!"

The thought had never crossed my mind, but now I've got Cam in my head, standing there staring at me with his arms folded over his chest, tapping his foot like *I told you*.

"Don't be ridiculous!" I shout. Michael looks startled by my volume. I decide it's time to guzzle more wine and do so with gusto.

The waiter reappears, asking if we'd like to order something to eat. Michael takes charge. "Yes. We'll each have filets, rare, and we'll share the Caesar. And another bottle of wine."

"Very good, sir."

The waiter bows off, Michael reaches for his glass, and I sit in misery, wondering how this could have gone so wrong so fast.

I hate rare meat. I'm allergic to anchovies. When a man orders food for me without asking what I want, I don't feel taken care of, I feel disrespected and honestly a bit murderous. And I can't stop thinking about Cam, which is making me confused, uncomfortable, and irritated with myself, a trifecta of negative emotions that add up to an overwhelming urge to flee.

Oh, no. I'm about to do something stupid.

I turn to Michael with a brittle smile. "I'm gonna go. Thanks for the wine."

"What? You're going? You just got here!"

I scoot out of the booth before I can change my mind. "Sorry," I mumble. "I'm sorry. See you at work."

"Joellen, wait! Don't go! Please, just sit down and talk to me!"

I hesitate because it's the first time he's used the word *please*. Everything else has been an order. I glance back at him. He's standing at the side of the table, looking contrite, confused, and devastatingly gorgeous.

But something about this still feels wrong.

"Thank you so much for inviting me here, and thank you again for the wine, but I can't stay for dinner. I . . . . I already have dinner plans."

He looks so crestfallen I feel guilty. So I hurry over to him and kiss him on the cheek before I can change my mind. When I pull away, he grabs my wrist and pulls me against his chest. Into my ear he says, "I want to talk more. Can I call you later?"

His warm breath fanning down my neck makes my eyes cross. I mumble a yes and ask if he has a pen so I can write down my number.

"That's not necessary. I already have it."

I frown, looking up at him. "You do?"

He smiles gently at me, still holding on to my wrist like it's a leash. "Well, technically I have all my employees' phone numbers."

"Oh. Right." I produce a nervous little laugh. "Of course you do."

His gaze drops to my mouth, and his smile fades. He leans forward to kiss me, but I turn my face so his lips graze my cheek. His husky chuckle sends a tingle up my spine.

"Okay. I get it. We're giving me time to adjust." He grips my other wrist, pulls me even closer, and bends his head to my neck. He inhales against my skin, his lips skimming the sensitive spot just under my ear.

He whispers, "I hope it won't take too long." He presses the softest of kisses to the pulse pounding in my throat, then releases me so abruptly I stumble back.

His eyes are electric. They sear the space between us so it seems like the air itself will ignite.

Without a word, I turn around and run.

I'm pacing my living room rug when the knock comes on my door. "It's open," I call, already knowing who it is.

I could pick Cameron McGregor's knock out of a police lineup of knocks. Like the man himself, it's very distinctive.

He comes inside with his usual swagger, asking where his dinner is, but stops dead when he sees my face. His brows draw together. "Were you on the phone with your mum again?"

"I went for drinks with Michael. He tried to kiss me. Twice."

Cam stands there for a moment, watching me pace. "Tried?"

I nod, chewing on my thumbnail, and turn around and pace the other direction.

Cam slowly closes the door, moves around me, and sits on the sofa. But he doesn't prop his feet up on the coffee table like usual. He leans forward with his elbows on his knees and his hands clasped, watching me walk. There's a tenseness in the way he holds himself, a coiled readiness, as if at any moment he might spring to his feet. His eyes are like a hawk's.

"You wanna tell me what happened?"

I tell him everything, from our sprint around the office hallways in the morning through the shortest, strangest date in the history of dating. When I'm finished, Cam is silent.

"What do you think?"

He slowly leans back, spreads his hands over his thighs, and exhales a breath through his nose. "I think it was smart."

I stop pacing and look at him. "Smart? Which part?"

"The whole thing. It was well played. Delay will only make him want you more."

"Cam, I wasn't *playing* him!"

He cocks his head, inspecting my face. "So you didn't *want* to kiss him?"

He sounds disbelieving, which pisses me off. "In case you haven't noticed, this isn't a game to me!"

"Don't dodge the question."

I growl in annoyance, tear the elastic out of the bun in my hair, and pace back the way I came. "It just didn't feel right. The whole thing was weird. Like, *sudden*."

Cam's voice is dry. "You've been lustin' after the man for a decade, lass. That's hardly sudden."

"Sudden from *his* side! He never noticed me before a few weeks ago, and now we're drinking wine at his private club the second his wife files for divorce?"

"How d'you know he never noticed you before? Did he tell you that?"

I stop and consider it. "Well . . . no."

"He's been married the entire time you've known each other, right?"

"Yes."

"So he wasn't in a position to tell you if he fancied you. This was his chance."

I drag my hands through my hair, still damp at the nape from my shower, and consider what he's suggesting. Finally I drop onto the sofa next to him and sigh, rubbing my forehead. "Honestly I don't know what to think. I acted like I was having a breakdown. I was a complete wreck. I probably blew it."

"Except he said he wanted to call you."

I shake my head, unconvinced and unsettled.

"What kind of wine did he order?"

I lift my head and stare at him. "Why does that matter?"

"It matters. Do you remember the name?"

I search my memory. "Romany Conty? Something like that?"

Cam looks impressed. "Jesus. He must really like you."

"You recognize it? I thought you didn't drink wine."

"Doesn't mean I don't know the name of one of the most expensive burgundies on earth. They're at least a few thousand dollars a bottle."

My mouth falls open. A wheeze of disbelief slips out.

"Let's get back to you not wantin' to kiss him. What's that all about?"

I consider the question carefully but find I don't have any good answers. "I guess . . . I was just too nervous."

After a moment, Cam says, "Hmm."

Before I can ask him what the hell he means by that cryptic "Hmm," the house phone rings. I freeze in terror.

"Ohmigod. Do you think that's him?"

"Only one way to find out, lass. Go answer it."

I start to panic. "What if I say something really stupid? What if I ruin the whole thing? This might be my last chance with him!"

Cam looks at the ceiling and sighs, but I ignore his irritation because I've got a brilliant idea. I grab his arm and shake it.

"You go pick up the portable extension in my bedroom and walk me through it!"

He crinkles his nose. "Don't be daft. I'm not lurkin' in the background while you and pretty boy have phone sex!"

"We're not going to have phone sex!" The phone continues to ring, and now I'm having heart palpitations. I shove Cam and leap to my feet, jabbing my finger in the direction of my bedroom. "Pick it up! Go, go, go!" I run into the kitchen and rip the phone from the wall, taking a deep breath before saying calmly, "Hello?"

"Joellen, it's Michael."

"Oh. Hi there." I manage to sound nonchalant. Meanwhile I'm silently screaming at Cam and making wild arm motions directing him into my bedroom.

He shakes his head like he can't believe he's getting talked into this, rises from the couch, and disappears into my bedroom. A second later I hear a soft click and I know he's picked up the line.

In a low, husky voice, Michael says, "I'm in the car. I couldn't wait until I got home to call you."

I respond with a lame and thoroughly unnecessary safety reminder. "I hope you have Bluetooth. It's dangerous and illegal to drive while talking on the phone if you're not hands free."

Cam appears in my bedroom door, holding the portable phone receiver to his ear, grimacing in disgust. He mouths, *You're hopeless.*

I frantically motion for him to join me in the kitchen.

Michael says, "I'm not driving. My driver is."

"Oh." *Duh.*

"But thank you for your concern." There's a touch of laughter in his voice. "It's gratifying to know you're worried about my safety."

Cam strolls toward me making a rolling motion with his hand that I think means I should keep the conversation going.

"So, um . . . sorry again about running out on you like that. I think I was just nervous."

Cam enters the kitchen and leans against the counter, looking bored. Until, that is, Michael next speaks.

"No apologies necessary. Though I have to admit when you said you already had plans for dinner, I was a little worried. You said there isn't anything going on with you and that idiot Cameron McGregor character, but I hope I don't have any other competition!"

Cam stiffens. His nostrils flare. His gaze slashes to mine, and in it I see a holocaust.

Maybe this wasn't such a good idea after all.

TWENTY-TWO

Before Mount Vesuvius can erupt, I quickly put a finger over Cam's lips and set Michael straight. "He's not an idiot. He's actually a really great guy."

Michael makes a gentle noise of disbelief. "You only think that because you're nice, Joellen. Believe me, the man is an absolute animal."

Cam's eyes blaze at me. He's got such a gnarly death grip on the phone, I expect it to crumple into dust at any moment.

"How would you know? You've never met him!"

There's a moment of silence on the end of the line, then Michael clears his throat. "No, I haven't. But if even half of what is printed about him is true—"

"Don't believe everything you read in the papers."

Cam looks satisfied that I'm sticking up for him, but I can tell he still wants to break something. I curse myself for this idea and motion that he should hang up. Lips thinned, he shakes his head.

Wonderful.

"You seem rather defensive of him."

I hear the subtext, the not-so-subtle invitation to shove Cam off a cliff and reassure Michael I've only got eyes for him. For some reason it really irritates me.

"I suppose I am. He's my . . . friend."

Cam and I stare at each other with a weird, unspoken tension building between us, while Michael breathes loudly on the other end of the phone.

"Really? You'd befriend a man who got a teenage girl pregnant and denies any responsibility whatsoever?"

My stomach drops. My mouth hangs open. I stare at Cam in horror.

Cam abruptly hits the "End" button on the portable phone. Then he removes the phone from my hand and returns it to the cradle on the wall, disconnecting my call with Michael. He turns back to me with a hard jaw and lowered brows, his eyes black with anger. "Do you believe him?"

"First of all, why the hell did you hang up?"

"He'll call back in ten seconds. Do you?"

I think of the strip poker party the first night we met, of the anonymous woman he picked up in a bar and had sex with standing up against Kellen's apartment door, of Michael telling me Cam's nickname. Prince Pantydropper.

It sickens me to think some of the panties he's dropped have belonged to underage girls.

I fold my arms over my chest and say stiffly, "It's not really any of my business, is it?"

Cam takes one step toward me, so now we're only a foot apart. Seething, he says between gritted teeth, "Then why're you judgin' me for it without even knowin' the truth?"

The phone rings. We both ignore it.

"I'm not judging you."

"Bullshit."

We glare at each other as the phone continues to ring.

"So is it true?"

Cam's no is hard and final, and he doesn't blink when he says it. I'm relieved but don't understand why.

"So what *is* the truth?"

The phone rings on and on.

"Are you gonna get that?"

"I'm talking to you right now. I'll talk to him later."

Cam's jaw works. He's silent until the phone stops ringing, his whole body tense, the cords sticking out in his neck. He draws in a slow breath, flexes his hands open, and releases the breath. I can tell he's trying to calm himself but not having much success.

He's huge and angry, but I'm not the least bit afraid of him. No matter what else might be true, that he'd never hurt me is a truth I'm completely certain of.

After a long time, he asks quietly, "Does it really matter, Joellen?"

There's another question hidden inside that question, but I don't know what it is. "Yes, of course it matters."

His reply is instantaneous. "Why?"

"Because . . ." I flail around for an explanation, not really understanding it myself. "Because we're friends."

His laugh is short and bitter. "Your ability to lie to yourself is remarkable, lass."

I'm hurt, defensive, and angered by his words and his tone, which indicate he thinks I'm a complete idiot. "What's that supposed to mean?"

He leans in closer, so close we're nose to nose. He says with soft vehemence, "It means we'll *never* be friends."

He spins on his heel and stalks away, leaving me red faced with fury and humiliation as my front door slams shut behind him.

That night I don't sleep. While Mr. Bingley snores and twitches on my chest, chasing mice in his dreams, I stare at the ceiling, going over everything that's happened since I met Cam. Every conversation, every morning jog, every stupid dinner.

In the end I decide he's right. We're not friends. I'm a project he's using to amuse himself while he's on holiday, and he's a means to an end for me. The end being Michael, but most likely I've screwed that pooch six ways to Sunday. He didn't call back except the one time after Cam hung up.

In the morning, I rise in the dark and put on my exercise clothes with a new resolve. If Michael truly is interested, one strange phone call shouldn't be able to kill that off. And if he's not, better to find out now than waste any more years of my life. I'll tell him the phone cut off because the power went down in my building and let the chips lie where they may.

When I open my door to head out for a jog, I'm surprised to find Cam in the hallway, already warming up. He didn't knock, so I figured he'd gone without me.

"Oh. Hey."

He silently hands me a bottle of his green goo, then continues stretching. I watch him for a moment, unsure of what to say or do, but ultimately decide I won't be able to do anything if we don't clear the air.

"I get it. What you meant when you said we'd never be friends. And I'm cool with it."

He stops and looks at me. In his usual sweats and hoodie, he still somehow seems unfamiliar. It must be the wall between us that wasn't there before.

"I mean, I'd rather be friends than not, but if you prefer we keep it businesslike, that's fine with me. You're going to be living here for a while longer, and it would be easier if we can be civil to each other. I really don't want to have to deal with your rap music again. Also I'd still like your help with the Michael thing, if you're still up for it."

His silence lasts an uncomfortably long time. "You're sure that's what you want?"

Why is he standing so still? "Which part?"

"Michael. He's what you want?"

His eyes are hooded, inscrutable, just like the expression on his face. "Yes."

He nods, his eyes shuttering like shades over storm windows. "All right, lass, drink up. Let's get goin'."

We jog in silence. It's horrible. All the light bantering is gone, all the easy conversation is dead and buried six feet under. I long to say something to make it better but don't know exactly how it got so bad in the first place.

Back at the apartment, he leaves me at the door with a word of advice.

"If you talk to pretty boy today, don't reassure him."

"About what?"

"About anything. Me, the 'other competition' he mentioned, how your not-date went. Just play it off like none of it matters. It'll drive him crazy. Okay?"

"Okay. And thanks."

He stares at me, unsmiling. "You're welcome." He goes inside his apartment and closes the door.

I shower, dress, and head to work, my thoughts preoccupied with Cam and the look on his face when he asked me if I was sure Michael is what I want.

When I get to work, there's a note on my desk, slipped under my keyboard so only one corner is showing. It's in a sealed envelope with my name printed on the outside. Curious, I tear into it before even removing my coat.

I'm sorry I upset you. Last night didn't go at all how I'd hoped. I hope you can forgive me for being such an ass. It's been so long since I've dated, it seems I've forgotten how.

M.

His cell phone number is written beneath.

Exhaling a slow breath, I slip the note back into its envelope and put it into my handbag. Then I sit in my chair and stare at my dark computer screen, arguing with myself about whether or not to send Michael an email or give him a call.

Ultimately, I decide to follow Cam's advice and play it off like it doesn't matter. I bury myself in work for the next few hours, until my desk phone rings.

"Joellen Bixby speaking."

"This mornin' sucked."

Cam's voice is curt with tension, but I'm instantly relieved. "Last night, too. I couldn't sleep."

There's a fraught pause, then he exhales. "Me neither."

"Are you still mad at me?"

"I was never mad at you, lass," he says quietly. "You bloody hard-headed woman."

Thank God, we're making up. I'm giddy. "Good, because if I had to listen to your music again, I'd throw myself out a window."

He chuckles. "That's a little dramatic, don'tcha think?"

"Plus I owe you two more home-cooked meals."

"Is that right? You've been countin'?"

His voice is classic McGregor I-know-you're-in-love-with-me smug. "So have you," I shoot back playfully, "and don't even try to deny it, prancer. My meat loaf is the best part of your day."

"Aye, lass. Your loaf is almost as good as your pie."

I smile, twirling the phone cord between my fingers. "Speaking of my pie, any requests for your last two meals?"

Cam's voice changes, goes a little rough. "Well of course I want that pie, lassie. I love that pie. Sweetest thing I've ever had in my mouth."

Heat flashes over my entire body. An image of his face when he broke the kiss on the couch floats into my head, and I squirm in my chair. A new subject is in order or I'll need to change my panties.

"There's a picture of us on the internet. A celebrity gossip site."

He curses under his breath. "I'm sorry. Are you okay?"

"Yes, I'm fine, and you don't have to be sorry. I think it's raised my cred around the office. The girl who sits next to me is treating me like I'm Beyoncé. And a couple of the guys in accounting said hi to me on the elevator. I think next they're going to ask me to get your autograph."

Cam sighs. "It's not me the guys from accounting are interested in, you wee daft bugger."

That makes me feel good. If I had a mirror in front of me, I'd be preening into it, petting my hair like a horse's mane. "You're very good for my ego, you know that?"

He snorts. "Well, you're shit for mine, so at least one of us is happy."

He's unhappy? I don't want him to be unhappy, especially not because of me.

"Don't forget I called you beautiful, prancer." When he doesn't respond, I hurry on, worried he's thinking I was lying. "I meant it, too. You're like this big, gorgeous, mountain of a man, who also happens to have a great sense of humor and an excellent vocabulary. You're a catch."

His continued silence terrifies me. Just when I'm about to ask him if he's still there, he says, "Sounds like I deserve a sonnet. We'll call it 'Mountain Man.' What rhymes with *enormous muscles*?"

I laugh, relieved I didn't just stick my foot into my mouth. "I already wrote you one. But it wasn't about your muscles, it was about your eyes."

As soon as it's out, I want to commit seppuku with the metal letter opener in the pen cup next to the computer. I close my eyes and bang my head softly against my desk.

Cam lets me off the hook with an easy laugh. "Sure, lass."

He doesn't believe me. Thank God. Because what possible reason could I have to be writing sonnets about his eyes? There isn't one. Not a rational one, anyway. It just . . . happened. I can't be held responsible for the doings of my muse!

"Why're you breathin' funny?" asks Cam when I don't say anything. "That pesky intestinal gas botherin' you again? You want me to stop by the store and pick you up a few pairs of your charcoal panties?"

"Ha." I swallow loudly, trying to get myself together.

"Wait." He's quiet for a beat. "Don't tell me you really did write me a sonnet."

My groan is the sound of someone watching a casket being lowered into the ground.

"Lassie. You know what happens if you lie to me."

God, that dark promise in his voice. Why the hell do I like that so much? "Yes, I know what happens, prancer. You'll take me over your knee."

"That's right."

"But . . . if I just don't admit something, that's not lying."

"It's a lie of omission. It *is* lyin'."

"God, it's like you're looking for an excuse to spank me!"

"I'd like an excuse to do a lot of bad things to you, darlin'. You have no idea."

The tone of his voice . . . oh my. Low, gruff, and deadly serious, it sets quite a few of my nerve endings atingle. Okay, *all* my nerve endings.

It must be all those stupid tingles that make me say what I say next.

"Like what?" I hold my breath, waiting for his answer, but his mercurial mood switches from dark and smoldering to light and bantering with the blink of an eye.

"Ach, wouldn't you like to know! Don't you have work to be doin', you slacker?"

"Hey, you're the one who called me."

"Aye, I did. And now I'm gonna hang up. Don't forget—pie tonight, darlin'." His voice drops. "And I want it extra hot."

Then he's gone. I set the phone back in the cradle, surprised to see my hand trembling.

TWENTY-THREE

At six o'clock on the nose, Cam strolls into my apartment without knocking. I'm in the kitchen preparing—you guessed it—shepherd's pie.

"Fair warnin' to all the occupants of this house, Cameron McGregor is here!" he booms, closing the door behind him.

Mr. Bingley had been busily grooming himself on a kitchen chair, but when he feels the vibration of the door closing, he freezes, wide eyed, then flies into the living room with his tail poufed in excitement.

"Hullo, you wee ball-less bastard," I hear Cam say affectionately from the living room. "Where's your mum?"

"In here!"

In a few moments, Cam appears from around the corner of the living room with Mr. Bingley draped contentedly like a stole across his shoulders. "Lassie," he declares, his chest puffed out, "what d'you think of my new fur coat?"

I shake my head in disbelief at the picture they make. "I think that animal is almost as in love with you as you are."

"Aye. He's a sensible lad. How was work?" He ambles over to the stove and sniffs at the steam rising from the pan of meat I'm browning.

I wave the cat's tail out of my face. "Good. And weird. Michael left me an apology note on my desk with his cell phone number. Portia keeps glaring at me like she's plotting my kidnapping and murder. And the girl who sits next to me won't stop pestering me about the size of your junk. She's convinced that picture on TMZ is proof that we're boning."

"We already had the talk about you disrespectin' the family jewels by callin' 'em 'junk,' darlin'." He nudges me out of the way with his elbow so he can scoop a bit of meat from the pan with his fingers.

"Hey!" I slap his wrist. "You know I don't like it when you do that!"

"It's my dinner, lass. I'll eat it how I want." He eats the morsel, licks his lips, sighs in pleasure, then offers his hand to Mr. Bingley, who happily cleans the rest of the sauce from Cam's fingers.

I roll my eyes and go back to stirring. "You shouldn't eat undercooked meat, prancer. You'll get salmonella."

"Pfft. As if bacteria would dare to mess with me. I'll have you know I never get sick."

"Make yourself useful and set the table before I dump this pan over the top of your thick skull."

"So you told her, right?"

I look at him. He's smiling back at me, smug as can be. The cat has rested his head on Cam's shoulder and closed his eyes. I could swear he's smiling, too.

"Told who what?"

"Told the girl who sits next to you at work about the majesty and opulence of my family jewels."

My cheeks prickle with heat. I turn my attention back to the pan. "No."

"Why not? It's not as if you don't know."

The heat spreads to my neck. "Are you going to set the table or not?"

Cam leans in and says deliberately into my ear, "Tell her eleven inches."

When he sees my eyes bulge, he adds with a chuckle, "Or you could tell her the truth and see if she faints."

When I glance at him, he makes a motion with his thumb that indicates the actual number is higher.

"Moving on," I say roughly, then stop to clear my throat. *Steady, Joellen. Steady.* "What do you think about Michael's note?"

I can tell Cam's amused by my awkward segue, but he lets it go. "Did you call him?"

"No."

"Did you email him?"

"No."

"Did you see him around the office?"

"No."

"Then I think you're gonna get a phone call tonight."

My stomach twists with anxiety. "Really?"

"Yep. We should talk strategy."

"Strategy? You make it sound like war."

Cam's smile is casual, but his eyes burn with a new intensity. "Love *is* war, darlin'. Only thing in life worth sheddin' blood over."

He turns away and heads to the cupboard for the plates while I stare down at the pan of simmering meat, wondering why that statement sounded so ominous.

In a few minutes, I've got the cooked meat and vegetables poured into a casserole dish and topped it with mashed potatoes. I pop it into the oven and set the timer, then pour myself a glass of wine.

When I set a beer in front of Cam, who's now sitting at the kitchen table with the cat in his lap, he frowns. "That's dark beer."

"I know. I remembered that's what you said you liked."

When he gazes at me without commenting, I feel a little defensive. "It's imported."

Cam says nothing.

"The guy at the store told me it was good. It cost more than the meat!"

"No need to shout, lassie," he says, his voice as soft as his smile. "I hear you loud and clear."

Another statement that sounds loaded, hinting at unseen layers beneath the surface. He's driving me nuts with this stuff! The last thing I need right now is more mystery in my life!

"You're impossible," I grouse.

"Impossibly wonderful, I know. Back to strategy."

I join him at the table, trying not to smile at his relentless self-love because I don't want to encourage him. Although admittedly I'm a little jealous. It must be comforting to go through life convinced you're God's gift to the human race.

"Fine. Strategy. Tell me how I should act when he calls."

"The same way you act with me."

I make a face. "I can't act with him like I act with you!"

"Like yourself, you mean?"

"Exactly! He'll never like me if I act like myself! I'm a disaster!"

Cam glowers, then takes a long drink of his beer. I've never seen someone swallow angrily, but apparently it's a thing.

"Bypassin' how barmy it is that you'd wanna be with a man who won't like you if you act like yourself, what I meant was don't cater to his ego. Don't fall all over yourself to pay him compliments. Treat him like he's your little brother: sometimes cute but mostly annoyin'."

I stare at Cam as if he's insane. "How is treating a man like he's annoying in any way attractive to said man?"

"It doesn't work with all men. But on lads like him—rich and pretty, used to havin' women fall at his feet—it works like a charm. Because you're a challenge, you see? You're different. He has to *chase* you, which is fun but also establishes that you have value. You won't just hand yourself over. When a man has to work hard for somethin' he wants, he values it twice as much when he finally gets it. Then you're a prize that he earned, not a gift he was given."

I ponder that for a moment, reflecting on all my recent interactions with Michael, and have to concede that Cam might have a point. "Okay, that makes sense."

Cam stops in the middle of lifting the beer to his mouth and chuckles. "I'm sorry, could you repeat that? Did you just admit I might be right?"

"Shut up. What else?"

Cam takes another pull from the bottle of beer. I watch his throat as he swallows, his Adam's apple bobbing up and down, admiring how strong his neck is. My gaze drifts to his arms, all those stupid muscles straining the sleeves of his white T-shirt. His thighs, like tree trunks clad in blue jeans. His stomach, washboard abs outlined under thin cotton like an advertisement for the benefits of a gym membership.

Everything about him is strong, from his body to his ego to his teeth . . . which are now on full display because he's smiling at me.

"What?" I'm taken aback by his sudden blinding grin.

"Nothin'. Only you might want to work on developin' a bit more of a poker face, lassie. If you leer at Michael like that, he'll know the jig is up."

"I wasn't leering at you!"

"I can take my shirt off if you like. I'll even let you pet my biceps, but that's as far as it's goin' because I'm not just a beautiful, sonnet-worthy Mountain Man, you know. I'm a human being. I've got *feelings*."

I exhale in disgust. Then I drink some wine to buy time to compose myself, because I was in fact leering at him, and he caught me red-handed.

"You're funny," I finally manage, aiming for a nonchalant tone. "Can we get back to strategy, please?"

I swear Cam's smile could be seen from outer space. "You're adorable when you're embarrassed. Those pink cheeks."

I stand and go to the oven, peering in like I might find a cure for my mortification inside. But there's only the shepherd's pie, which I imagine is laughing at me.

Cam takes pity on me and lets me off the hook. "All right, movin' on. Rule number one—we'll call it the golden rule—is make him chase you. The longer, the better. But there are lots of subrules to this one. They all involve the art of parsin' yourself out."

"That sounds disturbingly prostitutional."

"Think of it like you're leavin' a trail of crumbs. Small, delicious Joellen crumbs. A little bit here, a little bit there, just enough to heighten his hunger but never enough to satisfy it."

I go back to the table and sit, starting to feel dejected. "This is all very complicated."

"It's the easiest thing in the world, darlin'. It's called seduction, and it's a game where everyone wins." After a moment, he adds, "What was that wistful sigh for?"

"Everything would be so much easier if it could just be like it is with us."

Cam is silent for a while. He finishes his beer, then says roughly, "You mean if you could just be friends."

I'm not sure what I mean, because I've surprised myself with that statement. It was unplanned, but I have to admit it's true. I don't have to think when I'm with Cam. I can just be myself because I'm not trying to impress him.

"Oh!" Dazzled by a flash of inspiration, I sit up straight.

"What?"

I look at Cam, convinced I'm a genius. "I'll pretend he's you!"

Cam stares at me. His jaw works. He shifts his weight in his chair, and the cat jumps off his lap, unsettled. "Come again?"

"Like you told me to do when we kissed—pretend you were him!"

"And did you?" he challenges quietly, his gaze steady on mine.

I open my mouth to answer the obvious *yes*. But the word dies on my lips because the obvious answer isn't the real answer. It isn't the truth.

Both times I kissed Cam, I never once thought of Michael.

Immediately, I start to panic, my pulse skyrocketing and my hands beginning to shake. "Um . . ."

"Go ahead," says Cam softly. "Lie to me."

We stare at each other, and my heart decides it's had enough of this beating nonsense and stops dead in my chest. When the phone rings, I almost faint.

Cam moves first. He strides over to the phone, picks up the receiver, then brings it to me, holding it out silently and watching as I lift it to my ear.

I know he sees how my hand shakes. I know he sees the color in my cheeks. I know he sees how irregular my breathing has become, because he's taking all of it in, his gaze roving over my face as I squeak into the phone, "Hello?"

"Joellen. It's Michael."

Of course it is. The universe is having way too much fun at my expense.

"Oh. Hello, Michael."

Cam and I stand a foot apart, our eyes locked. My blood feels like fire.

"Is now a good time for us to talk?"

"Actually, Michael"—I swallow—"I have company."

Cam moves closer, infinitesimally, a slight lean toward me that doesn't involve his feet.

"Company?" Michael's voice is sharp in my ear. Too sharp.

In a turn of events I never would have predicted, and would have scoffed at anyone who dared to suggest, I'm irritated with Michael Maddox.

"Yes," I say firmly, straightening my shoulders. "Company. I'll have to call you back."

Michael sounds irritated with me, too, but tries to cover it with polite words. "Of course. I'm free for the rest of the night. Call me anytime."

"Will do. Thanks."

"Good-bye."

"Bye."

Wordlessly, I hold the phone out to Cam. He takes it from my hand, stares at me for a beat, then returns the phone to its cradle on the wall, his entire body radiating tension.

I don't know what's happening, but it feels momentous.

"That was good," he says to the wall. "Sounded very natural. When you call him back, don't talk for more than ten minutes, and make sure you end the call first."

"I'm not going to call him back."

Cam turns around slowly. Our eyes meet with a click. "No?"

"I have a dinner guest. I'll talk to him tomorrow."

There's a muscle in Cam's jaw that's getting an incredible workout. "You've been waitin' on him for ten years, lassie."

"So one more day won't hurt. Besides, I need practice with the golden rule. I'm dropping crumbs, right?"

"I dunno, Joellen. Is that what you're doin'?"

His voice is gravelly, as rough as my breathing . . . and he has a point.

What *am* I doing?

As if on cue, the timer on the oven dings. *Saved by the bell!* I swallow the hysterical laugh rising from my throat and trip over to the oven. Before I can make it there, I'm grabbed by a big pair of hands.

Then I'm backed flat against the wall, staring up into Cam's face. His dark, dangerously intense face.

Holding me by the shoulders and gazing into my eyes, he says softly, "Whatever it is you're doin', you better be sure. Take your time. Figure it out. But be sure. You owe it to yourself."

He releases me and strolls back to the kitchen table. He sits, props his feet up on another chair, laces his fingers together over his stomach, and smiles. "Now gimme that goddamn pie, woman. I'm starvin'."

His expression and voice are nonchalant, but his eyes. Oh, his eyes. How hotly they burn.

TWENTY-FOUR

Nowhere girl
Such long-standing dysfunction
Heart unfurled
Pain like heavyweight punches
Chaos of wings
Inside my head
Bittersweet things
Sleep beside me in bed
Ten years, one hope, an impossible dream
And then he spoke, but how can it be
The words he said weren't right but wrong
But perhaps after all the problem is me?
My hunger has grown too impossibly huge
I'm a woman with no one and nothing to lose.

It's Wednesday. I'm at my desk at work, doing what I do best.

Obsessing.

I title the sonnet I've just composed "Hunger," save it to the computer's hard drive, and close out of the word processing program. Then

I do the thing I've been wrestling with my conscience about for the past several hours and google Cameron McGregor.

I'm staggered when the search produces more than forty-five million results.

There's his Wikipedia page, his social media feeds, countless news articles, interviews, and photos. It's jarring seeing the photos of him in action on the rugby field because he looks nothing like the man I've come to know.

He looks feral. Ferocious. Frightening. Like he's released from a maximum security prison on short-term leave only for his games. There isn't a single photograph of him smiling.

Off the field, or *pitch*, as I learn it's called, the situation is even worse. He must be followed relentlessly by paparazzi when he's in Europe, because his every move has been documented on film. He scowls into the camera from all angles, whether staggering out of a pub or swaggering into an expensive car.

Then there are the women.

Universally young, buxom, and beautiful, they're draped over him in photo after photo. At parties, news events, the sidelines of a game, he's almost always covered in women like he's a glue trap and they're flies.

It makes me a little ill, until I realize that he's not smiling in any of those photos, either. And he's never photographed with the same woman twice.

One and done, huh, prancer? I browse thoughtfully through the pictures, becoming more certain with each passing minute that I'm viewing a montage of a profoundly unhappy life. Even when surrounded by an adoring crowd, he looks angry and alone. Our conversation in my kitchen comes back to haunt me.

Is life easier, being beautiful?
My life has never been easy.
For you the world is just one big banquet of choices.

Is it?

If I were going on all the photographs as evidence, I'd have to concede what I think is a banquet seems to him like a wake.

I click on his Wikipedia page and read through his list of career achievements and awards and honors, then skip down to the section titled *Early Life.*

> Born into poverty to a teenage single mother in Edinburgh, Scotland, Cameron Christopher McGregor faced grave odds from the start. Nine weeks premature due to a savage beating his mother suffered at the hands of his father, Duncan, he weighed only three pounds, six ounces at birth. As his lungs were immature, he required supplemental oxygen but quickly developed retrolental fibroplasia from the oxygen therapy, resulting in retinal detachment and subsequent surgery to correct the condition.

"Oh my God," I whisper, horrified, my hand to my throat. I read on, growing more upset with every word.

> Sentenced to eight years in prison for the attack on his pregnant girlfriend, Duncan McGregor hung himself in his cell after serving only ten days. For the first few years of Cameron's life, his mother subsisted on only £180 per month from the government. Due to his premature birth and his mother's drug use during pregnancy, Cameron was plagued by health problems during childhood, including slow physical development, difficulty learning and communicating, and attention deficit hyperactivity disorder (also called ADHD).

In interviews he has described how viciously he was
bullied at school for his small size and learning disability. One such event landed him in the hospital with a
broken jaw and severe internal bleeding after being
beaten into unconsciousness by a gang of older boys.

I start blinking hard to clear the water from my vision. It doesn't
work, so I take a few of the napkins from my top drawer and dab at the
corners of my eyes until I can see again.

When he was twelve, Cameron's mother found a
job through a government program aimed at putting able-bodied citizens on the dole back to work.
She obtained a position as a live-in housekeeper for
Sir Francis Gladstone, a member of Parliament. Sir
Gladstone had three sons between the ages of fifteen
and twenty, all of whom were highly regarded ama-
teur rugby players. It was through their influence that
Cameron was first introduced to the sport.

Cameron and his mother lived with Sir Gladstone until
her suicide when Cameron was eighteen, the same
year he was recruited to the Red Devils. Sir Gladstone
and Catherine McGregor were rumored to be romanti-
cally involved at the time of her death, but he denied
the reports.

I stare at the screen in shock.

Both his parents killed themselves. He was an orphan by the age of
eighteen. He was poor, weak, beaten, and bullied, utterly disadvantaged,

yet somehow managed to find the strength to become one of the world's foremost athletes.

I feel as if I've been flattened by a steamroller. Everything I assumed about Cameron McGregor is wrong.

"Joellen."

I start at the sound of Cam's voice, thinking I must be going insane. But when I swing around, he's standing there in the entrance to my cubicle, the receptionist hovering nervously a few feet behind him.

"This gentleman said you were expecting him, Joellen?" says the receptionist, Kim, a sweet girl with a nervous tic in her left eyelid. She always looks like she's sending a conspiratorial wink.

"Don't tell me you forgot our lunch date," Cam drawls when I sit frozen, mystified by his presence.

"Lunch date?" I repeat blankly. When I see Kim's eyes widen in alarm, I quickly backtrack. "Oh! Yes! Sorry, I was just so absorbed in work I lost track of time!"

Cam's gaze cuts to my computer screen.

I leap to my feet like my chair is on fire and hit the power button so hard I almost knock the screen over. Then I turn breathlessly to Cam and Kim. I'm grinning maniacally like a circus clown. "Okay! All set!"

Kim drifts away with a confused smile, while Cam just stands there, taking up all the space in the room.

From my peripheral vision, I see the top of Shasta's head begin to creep over the cubicle wall. Whispers are starting up all around us because Cameron McGregor is huge, handsome, and impossible not to notice. His shoulders are almost as wide as my desk.

With my crazed smile plastered firmly in place, I say between my teeth, "What are you doing here?"

"I could ask you the same thing, lass." His smile is almost as absurd as mine, but while mine is hysterical, his is smug.

He totally caught me googling him. Life as I know it is over.

He's more dressed up than I've ever seen him, which only means he put on a black sport jacket over his jeans and T-shirt. Paired with his scruffy jaw and boots, the overall effect is one of effortless cool. He looks great, and he knows it.

So do all the females on the floor, who are collectively soiling their panties. Shasta's eyes above the lip of the cubicle wall are like saucers.

Then the worst thing that could possibly happen, does.

"Well, this is certainly a surprise. I recognize you from the tabloids. Cameron McGregor, am I correct?"

Cam and I turn our attention to Michael, who's stopped in the hallway a few feet away. He's gazing at Cam like he's a bug he'd like to smash under the sole of his calfskin Hermès loafer.

Cam jerks his chin at Michael and sends him one of his signature shit-eating grins. "Aye. You'll be wantin' an autograph, I'm sure, but you'll have to excuse me, mate. I'm just' leavin' for lunch with Joellen."

Michael—resplendent in a couture Brioni suit the color of Cam's eyes when he's particularly mad—sets his shoulders. "I wasn't asking for an autograph."

They gaze at each other as I fight the urge to dive under my desk and curl into a ball until all the chest beating is over. I can tell Cam recognizes Michael, too, but he's pretending like he has no clue who he is—just another fan dazzled by his presence.

If he wanted to piss Michael off, he picked the perfect way to do it. Michael's neck has flushed a deep, angry red.

I know exactly what makes pretty rich boys tick, Cam told me. Here's an unmistakable bit of proof.

Things take a turn toward the melodramatic when Portia appears behind Michael, slinking up like a fox past the henhouse door. She looks Cam up and down, her foxy nose twitching at the scent of fresh meat. "Oh. Pardon me," she purrs. "Am I interrupting?"

God, between the three of them I feel like I'm in the Bermuda Triangle. I blurt nervously, "We were just leaving for lunch!"

Portia's gaze slides toward me. I'm surprised to see curiosity in her eyes, not the usual hostility. She looks at Michael, then at Cam, then back at me, but doesn't respond.

Michael says stiffly, "It's a bit early for lunch, isn't it? It's barely past eleven o'clock."

Cam responds with a knowing chuckle. "Joellen couldn't wait. Called and asked me to come sooner."

The flush in Michael's neck creeps up toward his ears, but, more interestingly, the curiosity in Portia's gaze turns into something different. Relief? No, that wouldn't make sense. But I don't have time to think on it because she blows me away by smiling.

"How nice! You work so hard, Joellen. You deserve to take a long lunch. I'll speak to you later this afternoon. I just wanted to go over your current workload with you. It can wait. Gentlemen." She nods at Michael, then at Cam, then leaves with a spring in her step.

I gape at her retreating back, convinced I've suffered a recent traumatic brain injury. There's no way that just happened.

"C'mon, lass. I know how you get when you're hungry." Cam's voice holds an undertone of familiarity that makes Michael's mouth take on a ruthless slant. It's an odd reaction and one I don't like. It's the first time I've ever seen his face be anything but beautiful.

Michael catches me looking at him, and the hardness in his mouth disappears as quickly as it came. He smiles. It's so sweet I wonder if I didn't imagine the whole thing.

"Have a great lunch. See you later. Mr. McGregor"—he turns to Cam with the same genteel smile—"it was a real treat to meet you."

I hear the undertone of sarcasm, but if Cam does, he doesn't acknowledge it. His grin is wide and bright. "I get that a lot."

Michael straightens his tie, obviously wishing it were on Cam's neck instead of his own, with the loose end knotted around a tree branch. He turns and strides away.

I release the breath I didn't know I was holding. "Holy hell, McGregor," I say shakily, watching Michael go. "I hope you know what you're doing."

Cam watches Michael go, too. "Sure I do. I'm wagin' war."

When I look at him, he winks. "If that prissy little peacock wasn't in love with you before, he definitely is now. There's nothin' his kind hates more than a lower-class grunt gettin' uppity and poachin' his property."

"Don't be ridiculous, McGregor. Michael doesn't think I'm his property."

"Aye, lass, he does. The question is whether or not you're gonna enjoy it when you find out what bein' the property of a man like him is like."

He grabs my handbag from my desk, slings it over his shoulder, and saunters away down the hall, leaving me no choice but to follow.

I ignore Shasta's desperate hiss of, "Bitch, what the hell?" as I go.

We go to a little Italian place I've been dying to try that's owned by a couple who met on a blind date and fell instantly in love. When we're seated at the table, I sigh in happiness, looking around at the cozy, comfortable interior, a perfect replica of the Italian place the couple went to the night they met.

I find the whole story incredibly romantic. Tales of fated lovers are my Kryptonite.

"I *love* Italian food," I tell Cam, petting the red-and-white-checkered tablecloth.

"I know." He snaps a white linen napkin over his lap. When I look at him in surprise, he adds, "Mrs. Dinwiddle told me it's your favorite."

I laugh. "Yeah, I'm always trying to get her to try my lasagna, but whenever I suggest it, she looks at me as if I've farted in church."

"The British aren't exactly known for being adventurous eaters."

"I'd hardly call noodles and tomato sauce adventurous."

Cam smiles. "You're not British."

"You've got me there."

"But pretty boy certainly is. He'd give the Prince of Wales a run for his money in the silk-pocket-square-and-stuffiness department."

I smile at Cam's dry assessment. "He's just reserved."

"Repressed, you mean."

I roll my eyes and stuff a fluffy piece of bread, still warm from the oven, into my mouth. I moan at how delicious it is. It's the first piece of bread I've had in what feels like forever. "Carbs are proof that God loves us, don't you think?"

"I think Benjamin Franklin said that about wine."

He watches me eat for a moment, until I become uncomfortable. "You're staring."

"I like watchin' you eat. Your enjoyment of food is obvious. It's not often a woman allows herself that pleasure in public."

My cheeks heat. I swallow the bread as daintily as I can, fearing I look like some kind of farm animal at the trough.

Cam laughs at the look on my face. "Don't be embarrassed. It's sexy."

I'm filled with gratitude for the waiter, who appears at our table at that moment, allowing me to escape having to formulate a response to Cameron McGregor calling me sexy again. I doubt my brain has enough cells to tackle that one.

We give the waiter our drink orders. When he's gone, Cam says, "So."

"So."

His smile comes on slow and heated. "D'you wanna talk about your little internet research project first, or pretty boy?"

I stuff another piece of bread into my mouth.

"Okay. Pretty boy it is. No, wait, first tell me who the woman was who stopped by your desk?"

"That was Portia."

He lifts his brows. "She didn't seem nearly as bad as you've made her out to be."

"I know. It's weird. She almost seemed human for a minute there." I shrug, knowing I'll never solve that particular mystery. "She was probably just dazed into acting like a person and not a witch because her brain was taking a nice warm dopamine bath brought on by standing three feet away from you."

Cam's eyes sparkle with laughter. "Oh? Is that what happens to females when I walk into a room?"

I wave a hand at him. "Oh, please, McGregor. You know the effect you have on women. It's like you're one of those magicians who does mass hypnosis tricks, making everyone in the audience crow like roosters."

He gazes at me for a beat. "Not everyone."

The waiter returns with our drinks: a water for me and a beer for Cam. He takes our food order and leaves, then Cam mercifully changes the subject.

"Pretty boy's gonna ask you what the deal is with us, first thing he can."

"I've already told him we're just friends."

"You're gonna have to tell him again. But don't get drawn into a long discussion about it. Wave your hand like you just did at me, and change the subject. If he insists, tell him that I'm not your type." His voice darkens. "It won't take much convincin' for him to believe it."

"Why do you say that?"

Cam takes a long swig of his beer, then looks out the window. "Because no matter how much money I have, I'm still just a jobby to him."

"Jobby?"

"Trash. Unworthy to even be in his presence, much less earn the attention of a woman he fancies."

227

I wonder how much of his opinion of Michael is due to his own experience living in Sir Gladstone's home. I wonder how it was for him, growing up without a father. Knowing his father killed himself, knowing he beat his mother so badly she went into premature labor.

Whatever my parents' faults, I always felt safe. Maybe not understood or completely accepted, but safe. Cared for. Wanted. I can't imagine the kind of demons Cam has had to live with his entire life.

"Spit it out, lass."

I glance up and find Cam watching me closely.

When I squirm a little under his intense gaze, he says softly, "I already told you, you can ask me anything."

I busy myself with fiddling with the edge of the tablecloth because it feels too nosy to look at him. Or maybe I'm just a coward. It's difficult for me to witness other people's pain, and I think the conversation is about to take a very personal turn.

"I owe you an apology for assuming your life was all butterflies and rainbows. It makes me feel crappy that you probably get that a lot. Assumptions about who you are. Judgments."

Cam's fingers drum the tablecloth. "Thank you. But that wasn't a question."

How does he know I want to ask him something? Probably the same way he knows most other things: he's observant.

I want to ask him if he's happy. I want to ask him if he has any real friends. If that's what he meant when he said we'd never be friends—because everyone wants something from him, including me.

How can I honestly claim to want to be his friend? A true friendship isn't based on what you think you can get out of it. It's based on respecting someone enough to let him be who he really is. A true friend is someone who says "I'm here for you" and proves it.

It dawns on me that Cam is probably the best friend I've ever had.

Cam says sharply, "Lass."

My eyes sting. I shake my head, drawing a deep breath in an attempt to calm my emotions. "Give me a minute," I croak, and take a long drink from my water glass. After a few moments of rapid eye blinking and air gulping, I find the strength to meet his worried gaze. If only my voice had the decency not to wobble.

"I think you're an amazing person. I appreciate everything you've done for me. This whole Michael project . . . it means a lot. I don't take your help for granted. And I'm sorry for all the stupid things I've said to you, all the times I've been sarcastic or flippant. I wasn't trying to be mean. I was just . . ."

"You were just bein' yourself," Cam finishes quietly when I struggle to find the right words.

When I nod, miserable to admit it, he smiles at me. "You can quit beatin' yourself up now, lass. I know you appreciate me. And I love that sharp tongue of yours. I love that you feel comfortable enough with me to give me a good dressin' down. I need that, y'know. Someone to stick a pin in my balloon when it gets too inflated."

I produce a shaky laugh. "Your balloon must have a lot more pin-pricks since you met me."

He laughs, too, a soft and satisfied sound. "Aye. But a real friend is someone who stabs you in the front."

"That's Oscar Wilde."

"Don't look so surprised, lass. I've read Oscar Wilde. You didn't think I was just another pretty face, did you?"

We share a smile across the checkered tablecloth. "So, we *are* friends."

He shakes his head, chuckling. "Why is it so important to you this relationship has a title?"

Because the alternative to friends is either enemies or lovers.

I smile tightly but don't answer, knowing in my heart of hearts that I'd rather die than be enemies with this man.

So if we're not friends or enemies, that leaves only one other choice.

229

TWENTY-FIVE

Cam and I enjoy a long lunch, talking nonstop about everything and nothing. He gives me more advice about Michael, I pepper him with questions about Scotland, he informs me we're moving our workouts from strictly cardio to adding strength training, I tell him I've lost another few pounds. We're at the restaurant for almost two hours.

In the back of my head, I tell myself Portia gave me permission to take a long lunch, but the reality is that I'm reluctant to get back to the office. I'm having too good a time. I keep dragging my feet, asking Cam question after question until he laughs at me and asks if I'm writing an unauthorized biography.

"Yes. I'll call it *Mountain Man Unmasked*. It'll be an instant bestseller."

"Okay. I'll approve it. But only if you include the sonnet about my eyes."

Our gazes catch and hold. I look away first, blushing.

Back at the office building, he asks me if I want him to come up, but I tell him no. I've got visions of a mob of salivating females lined up in front of the reception desk, waiting for him to emerge from the elevator so they can pounce.

We hug on the sidewalk, then he's gone. I stand there waving at his taxi until it turns a corner and disappears. Then I trudge into the building and onto the elevator, bracing myself for whatever might await me on the thirty-third floor.

It's a bloodbath.

First, I'm accosted by Kim, the receptionist. She leaps up from her desk the instant the elevator doors open and runs up to me, flapping her hands, the tic in her eye going so fast it looks painful.

"Oh my gosh, Joellen, I didn't know who that was when he came in. I only knew he was big and handsome and oh!" She bites her fist. "*So* hot! But then Shasta told me who he was and showed me the picture of you guys on TMZ and geez, are you *dating* him? How long has this been going on?"

"He's my neighbor," I say wearily, headed back to my desk. Kim follows beside me, skipping every few feet in excitement.

"So you're *not* dating him? Oh gosh, that's a shame, that man is just"—she fans herself—"*scorching*! But he's your neighbor, you say? Maybe I could come over and hang out sometime, you know, like tonight? Are you free?"

Shasta spots me from a distance and bolts from her cubicle like she's been coughed out. She races down the hallway toward me while I brace myself for impact.

"*Joellen!*" she shrieks, grabbing my arm. "Holy fucksicles that man is ten times hotter in person than he is in pictures! And he's *huge*!"

"Don't ask me about his ju—"

"You *have* to tell me what he looks like naked! Please? Pretty please? Just give me a hint how big it is! Like this?" She holds her hands about a foot apart, then adds a few more inches. "*This?*"

Irritated by her lewd questioning, I scowl at her. "You're deranged, Shasta. He's not a piece of meat. Let it go."

I toss my handbag onto the floor, sit in my chair, and start straightening things on my desk in an attempt to look busy, but I've got two females in heat hovering over me who aren't about to let me off the hook until I tell them more about their newfound stud. Their excited clucking and flapping stirs up all the other chickens in the henhouse, until suddenly I've got a crowd of women at my cubicle door, squawking like mad.

Sue Wong, she of the razor-edged bangs and enviable dimples, wants to know how Cam and I met. Another acquisitions editor, Bethany, wants to know if he has a brother. Questions fly at me from every side until my head is spinning.

"You guys!" I shout above the fray. "Chill out! He's just my neighbor!"

"What's going on here?"

Portia's freezing voice cuts through the noise like a samurai sword. The hens scatter in terror until it's only me and Portia left, looking at each other in silence.

Portia's wearing a lovely sheath dress the color of a new penny. With her perfect gold hair and steely silver-blue eyes, she looks like she was recently minted.

"Sorry about that. I, uh, think everyone was a little . . . overexcited by my visitor."

A ghost of a smile softens her normally pinched mouth. "One can hardly blame them. The last time we had a male visitor on the thirty-third floor was when Theodore Scanlon came in to negotiate his new contract."

Theodore Scanlon is one of Maddox Publishing's most infamous authors. He's older than dirt, has halitosis that could kill a grown man at ten paces, and has made ogling cleavage into a spectator sport. His crime novels—all excellent sellers—include a disturbingly high incidence of sex between siblings. Which makes the old publishing maxim "Write what you know" take on a whole disgusting new meaning.

"Did you have a nice lunch?"

I warily eye Portia, not trusting her innocent question and bland, nonwitchy smile. "Yes, thanks."

"I'm glad to hear it. I meant it when I said you deserved it, Joellen. You really do."

This is so weird. Why is she being so nice? What's she up to?

She turns to leave, but I call her back. "Portia, didn't you want to talk to me about my workload?"

She blinks, obviously confused, but then her look clears. She says airily, "Oh, never mind. I found what I was looking for. Just . . . moving things around."

She leaves without explaining what those cryptic words meant. I ponder her strange behavior until something so horrible occurs to me that it steals my breath.

Portia is in love with Michael.

Oh God. That has to be it! She's been an unrelenting bitch to me for ten years, always watching me like a hawk, always appearing suddenly whenever Michael appears, like she's keeping an eye on me. Like she's guessed how I feel about him. It couldn't have been hard—I follow him around like a nursing calf after its mommy. Then the one day a man shows up to take me out to lunch, she does a one-eighty that could cause whiplash and is nice—because I'm no longer a threat if I have a boyfriend.

All these years, Portia has been in love with Michael, has seen that I'm in love with him, too, and has hated me for it.

And now he's getting divorced.

And is pursuing me.

I'm so screwed.

∞

When I get home that night, my house phone is ringing as I'm unlocking my front door. I rush in and pick it up, still in my winter coat and knitted scarf. "Hello?"

"Hello, Joellen."

A little thrill goes through me at the sound of his voice. "Hi, Michael!"

"Is this a good time to talk?"

I look around the kitchen and decide that Mr. Bingley can wait a few minutes for his food, even though he's glaring at me from the corner where his empty dish sits. If he could cross his arms, he would.

"Yes, this is a great time. How are you?" I sit at the kitchen table and unwind the scarf from around my neck.

"I'm well, thank you. I'm glad we're finally getting a chance to talk. It seems my timing is always off."

His voice is warm, so I know he's not complaining. I'm relieved. I thought for sure I'd have to do a fair bit of groveling after what happened today in the office. I didn't see him for the rest of the day and was too chicken to send him an email, but it's somehow safer to talk like this instead of face-to-face.

"I'm sorry I didn't call you back last night. Dinner went a little late, and I wasn't sure how long you usually stay up."

"You can call me anytime. I mean it. Day or night, don't hesitate to call."

"Okay." I feel bashful and pleased and also happy he didn't grill me about who my dinner was with. "Thanks. Um, are you in your own place now?"

"Yes. We agreed she'd stay in the house while the lawyers fight over the details of who gets to keep what. I've rented a place overlooking Central Park. The view is spectacular. You'd love it."

It's a little weird that he avoids saying his wife's name and instead refers to her as "she," but I'm too fixated on trying to figure out if he just invited me over to his place to care. "I'm sure I would. It sounds beautiful."

We're silent for a moment, awkwardly breathing at each other, until Michael says, "Okay, I have to get this off my chest."

Oh God. That sounds bad. "What is it?"

He laughs a small, self-conscious laugh. "I'm jealous of your rugby player."

I know he's looking for reassurance, but instead of being irritated, I find this admission charming. He's basically saying Cam is a man worthy of his jealousy—which proves he's not the snob Cam thinks him to be—while at the same time showing vulnerability. For a man who has everything in the world and is accustomed to everyone bowing and scraping in his presence, it can't be easy to admit another man makes you jealous.

Michael's stock just climbed a few notches in my estimation.

"You don't need to be jealous of him. I was telling you the truth when I said we were friends. There's really nothing going on between us."

Michael exhales a sigh of relief. "That's good to hear. I know I don't have any right to be jealous, but honestly I've thought about you for so long it would probably break my heart if you were taken the moment I was set free."

He talks about getting a divorce like he's been paroled from prison, but I'm distracted by something far more important. "You've thought about me?" I whisper, my heart doing a happy dance inside my chest.

His voice drops, too. "You must've known. My God, the amount of time I've spent staring at you, I was afraid everyone knew."

Feeling faint, I close my eyes. It's happening. It's really happening. All those nights I dreamed of this man saying those words, and it's no longer a dream . . . It's real.

"You're not saying anything."

"Sorry, I'm just . . . soaking it all in." My laugh is breathless because there's no air in my lungs. "I'm having a hard time believing it."

"You shouldn't be. You're a beautiful girl, Joellen. I've always thought so."

If an asteroid smashed through the ceiling and demolished my apartment and me along with it, I would die a happy woman, because my life is now complete.

Michael Maddox called me beautiful. Either he's in his bazillion-dollar condo overlooking Central Park high as shit on mushrooms right now, or he's telling the truth. No one has ever said anything as wonderful to me as what he just said.

You're perfect just the way you are, lass.

My eyes fly open. What the hell is McGregor doing in my head? At a moment like *this*, no less!

"Are you still there?"

I blurt the first thing that comes to mind because I'm so flustered by the Mountain intruding on my lovely moment with Michael. "I was just thinking about Portia."

Michael sounds confused by my odd transition. "Portia? What about her?"

"I think she has a crush on you."

Michael laughs, long and heartily. "You're giving her too much credit. If she had a crush on me, it would mean she had a heart!"

I have to smile at that because it's true. Then Michael says, "Besides, I don't have the right equipment."

I furrow my brow. "Excuse me?"

"Portia's gay."

I gape at the cat, who stares back at me like he's contemplating whether or not to trot over and hork up a hairball on my shoe. "Gay? Portia's *gay*?"

"A lesbian, yes. Don't tell me you didn't know."

Apparently the list of things I don't know is long and illustrious. "I had no idea! How do *you* know?"

"I've met her girlfriend. They've been together for years. Portia and my wife serve together on the board of a national literacy organization. We've seen them socially many times."

I'm glad I'm sitting down, because if I were standing I might have already collapsed and cracked my skull open on the floor.

Portia is gay. Which means she isn't in love with Michael. Which means my theory about why she's always been a bitch to me is so far off the mark, it's not even in the same neighborhood.

"Wow. I honestly had no clue. I wonder why she never brought her girlfriend to any of the holiday parties or summer picnics?"

There's a short pause. "I think she was concerned how it would be viewed by the staff."

"What do you mean, 'viewed'? You think she's worried she'll be discriminated against?"

"Well, naturally."

"I don't understand. Why 'naturally'? I know a dozen gay people at Maddox who are out, and no one gives them grief. The company culture is very inclusive, but even if it weren't, we have written policies against discrimination. And there's federal law—"

"No one in a position of authority is openly gay in the company."

The curtness of his tone gives me pause. "That's true," I say slowly, trying to put my finger on what I'm missing. Why does he sound annoyed?

When Michael speaks again, his voice is back to normal. "I've encouraged her to take a leadership role in that regard, of course, but she doesn't feel comfortable. And it isn't my place to insist. I respect her wishes to keep her private life private."

"Yes, of course, if she's not comfortable—"

"But enough about Portia," Michael interrupts. "Let's talk about you. Have you been working out? Because I noticed you seem to be looking a bit *tighter* of late."

So this is what I have to look forward to when I hit menopause. This hot flash could ignite the entire kitchen. In the space of a few heartbeats, I'm flushed and drenched in sweat.

"Yes, I have been working out," I admit sheepishly. "That's the project I told you Cam was helping me with. I decided to start exercising and eating better, and you know, he's a professional athlete, so."

"That's great, Joellen!" I can't tell if his enthusiasm is because he likes the idea of me working out or because he's relieved to finally discover the basis of my relationship with Cam. "I'm *very* happy for you. I love to work out, too. Maybe we could work out together! Do you like squash?"

"Oh, sure . . . I love squash." *I really hope he's talking about the vegetable.*

"Great! When I get back from London, I'll take you to my club."

"You're going to London?"

"Yes. I leave tomorrow. I've been meaning to tell you, but I haven't had the chance. I've got meetings with some of our European distributors, but I'll be back on Saturday the twenty-third."

Suddenly I'm filled with cold dismay. "That's the day of the office holiday party. Are you still going to make it?"

His voice warms. "I wouldn't miss it for the world."

Oh God. This feels like a sign. "Okay. Um . . . maybe we can email while you're gone? You know, just to keep in touch?"

"I'd like that," he murmurs. "I'd like that very much. And Joellen?"

"Yes?"

"I'm so glad we finally got to talk."

I whisper, "Me too."

Mr. Bingley, tired of waiting for his dinner, makes a noise like he's being skinned alive. I laugh like a crazy person, feeling high and loose and dangerously happy, like Icarus flying too close to the sun.

But I won't think of what happened to that idiot. I end the call and feed my demanding animal, thinking only of how many days until I see Michael again and how many pounds lighter I'll be.

Skinny body, skinny heart, skinny love be damned, I've got a skinny entrance to make into a holiday party, and God help the fool who tries to stand in my way.

TWENTY-SIX

I'm deep into an internet search of how to play squash when Cam bursts through the front door with a big bouquet of sunflowers wrapped in cellophane and tissue paper. He sees me at the coffee table on my laptop and grins.

"You're lookin' me up again, aren't you, lass? Tch. It's becomin' an obsession!"

"Get over yourself, prancer. There's a whole big world out there that doesn't involve you. I'm trying to find out how to play squash. Who're the flowers for?"

He looks left, right, then behind him. "Is there someone else who lives in this apartment?"

Surprised and touched, I stand. "They're for me? Really?"

He shakes his head and sighs dramatically. "Christ on a crutch, Miss Snufflebottom, you're hopeless. Take the bloody things before I smack you upside the head with 'em."

I cross to him and take the huge bouquet from his arms. "These are my favorite." Smiling, I touch the bright-yellow petals. "They always remind me of home. My mom got them fresh from the farmers market every Friday when I was growing up."

"I know."

I look at him, furrowing my brow. "Have you been going through my trash or something?"

He smiles. "Mrs. Dinwiddle enjoys a good gossip."

I laugh. "True. But . . ."

He sees my confusion and takes pity on me. "It's our last supper, lass. The occasion seemed to call for flowers."

"That sounds uncomfortably biblical, but thanks." I examine his face, fresh shaven and shining. "I see you discovered you own a razor."

He runs a hand over his jaw. "Aye. I was startin' to appear a bit cavemannish." His gaze drops to mine. "You fancy the proper pretty boy look, so I thought it bein' a special night and all, I'd make an effort."

"Scruff suits you better," I say without thinking. "You're way too manly to be overgroomed. All your rough edges are much more . . ."

Cam is grinning at me like a cat that just scarfed up a nice fat canary.

I huff out an aggravated breath. "Oh, shut up, prancer," I mutter, and retreat into the kitchen to find a vase.

"No, I don't think I will, lassie," Cam drawls, following me. "At least not until you tell me how that sentence ends." He sits at the kitchen table, threads his fingers behind his head, and beams at me.

"It ends with me jabbing a sharp object into your eye." I bang around in the pantry and the cupboards under the sink until I find a vase tall enough to fit the sunflowers, then busy myself with arranging them, all the while acutely aware of Cam's shit-eating grin aimed in my direction.

"Hot? Sexy? Devastating?" he muses aloud, clearly enjoying my embarrassment. "Hmm. She's mute on the subject. I must be g'tting close."

"You're getting close to serious bodily injury. Be quiet."

His laugh is delighted. I glance over at him and am struck by how different he looks now than he did in all those pictures I saw of him on the internet. He looks happy and at ease, like he doesn't have a care in the world. Like he belongs right there in that chair at my kitchen table.

"How come you never smile in photographs?"

His laugh dies, his smile fades, and his eyes take on a strange hardness. I sense I've stepped into a minefield, but I'm already here. Might as well jump right in.

"I mean, I see you smiling and laughing all the time, like you are right now, but in pictures you always look kind of . . . miserable."

Silent, Cam looks at me for what feels like a long time. Then he says, "You can't really be that naïve."

His gruff tone surprises me, as do his words. "What do you mean?"

"I mean spend a little time thinkin' about what you just asked me, woman, and you'll find your goddamn answer."

I refuse to be intimidated by him, and send the same fuming stare he's sending me right back at him. "Why are you mad at me? You said I could ask you anything!"

Our gazes clash like swords, but he's hurt my feelings, so I won't be the first to look away. I haven't done anything but ask an innocent question. It's not my fault his moods change faster than the weather.

"Ah, lassie." He scrubs his hands over his face. His low chuckle sounds impossibly sad. "You'll be the death of me."

"Yeah, maybe, if you keep acting like a dick. In case you haven't noticed, I've got pruning shears in my hand."

He starts to laugh, low at first, building on that sad chuckle, but then he's into full-blown guffaws, his head thrown back, one fist pounding the table.

"You're so friggin' weird," I grumble, and continue arranging the sunflowers.

"And you can't see past the end of your nose, but here we are anyway."

"You and your ambiguous statements are gonna be the death of *me*, prancer. Speaking of bad vision, I have a question."

When I turn, I find him smiling. "Of course you do."

"Do you think I should ditch the glasses?"

"For what, a monocle?"

"Yes, a monocle," I say sarcastically. "They're so in style. Can you be serious for a second? This is important."

He arranges his face into a semblance of sternness. "Aye. This is me bein' serious. You can tell by my forbidding brow."

When I just stare at him with a sour look, his fake serious expression is killed by another dazzling smile.

"Okay, okay. Don't put a hex on me. The question is if I think you should ditch your glasses?"

"That is the question."

He cocks his head, purses his lips, and takes so long examining my face I begin to blush.

"Take a picture, prancer, it'll last longer," I mutter, embarrassed.

"I'm tryin' to decide how to phrase somethin' so it won't offend your missish nerves."

"*Missish?* Is that even a word?"

Cam looks smug. "Oh, the fancy editor lady hasn't heard of it?"

When I continue to glare at him, he relents. "It means demure. Squeamish. Prudish."

"You're calling me a *prude?*"

Mischief glints in his eyes. "No man who's ever kissed you would call you a prude, darlin'. What I'm sayin' is that you're highly sensitive about your looks. One misplaced word and you'll be locked in your room makin' a list of all the ways you think you're ugly."

I have to take a moment to absorb that.

The first sentence might've been an incredible compliment, or he could've meant there are far worse adjectives than *prude* that men who've kissed me would use to describe me. Like *ghastly* or *sickening*, for example.

Then there's his observation that I'm sensitive about my looks. Though I probably wouldn't lock myself in my room to make a list of all the ways I'm ugly, I can easily see myself doing it at the kitchen table. In fact, I'm sure there's a piece of paper somewhere in my apartment titled *Things to Improve On* that itemizes "cankles" and "weird moles" among my shortcomings.

Which means Cameron McGregor has my number. If I'm being honest with myself, he has from the start.

"Don't break your brain overanalyzin' that, Joellen," says Cam drily.

"I can't help it. My brain is set to think things to death."

He quirks his lips. "You don't say?"

I close my eyes, sigh, and hear him chuckle.

"All right. Here's what I think about you ditchin' your glasses."

I open my eyes and wait for him to continue, chewing my thumbnail in nervousness.

"I don't think you should do it."

Am I relieved? Or disappointed? Annoyed? Lord, the man twists me up like a pretzel. "I have contact lenses, but I never wear them because they make my eyes red."

"Thank you for sharin'," he drawls. "Ask me why I don't think you should get rid of your glasses."

"Why don't you think I should get rid of my glasses?"

"Because they make you look smart, and sexy, and like you don't give a fuck, which is also sexy."

"Oh." I can't think of anything else to say. *He called me sexy again. This is becoming a thing.*

"I wasn't finished."

That sounds fairly ominous, so I start to chew my thumbnail with renewed vigor.

"The main reason I don't think you should get rid of them is because you prefer them. If you didn't, you'd wear your contacts or get laser surgery. But you like your glasses, so that's what you should wear."

"But . . . don't most guys think they're dorky?"

"The number of fucks you should give about what men think of how you look is zero, lass. Every choice you make about your appearance should be about what makes *you* feel good, not what makes some random lad—or your mother—think you're cute. Don't set aside your preferences for anyone."

He's deadly serious, all traces of teasing gone. I'm not sure how to respond to this sudden change of mood, but he's not finished talking.

"And another thing. Learn to stop saying 'Sorry,' and say 'Don't interrupt me.' Learn to say 'No' and 'None of your business.' Learn to be unapologetic for who you are and what you like and the opinions you hold. I know you think that if other people considered you beautiful, all your problems would be solved, but you'd just have different problems. And they'd all still revolve around the fact that deep down, you don't think you're good enough. That's a lie you learned, and you can unlearn it, but it has to start with you. You have to decide to accept yourself. It's cliché, but you really do have to love yourself before you can love anyone else."

He pauses to inhale a slow breath, his eyes burning. When he speaks again, his voice is low.

"My mother was one of the most beautiful women I've ever seen, but she killed herself over a man who wasn't even worthy to breathe the same air she did. Total fucking waste. All because she didn't think she was good enough. A lie life pounded into her that she never unlearned."

"You're talking about Sir Gladstone?"

Now his tone turns brutally bitter. "Aye. That worthless piece of shit. Thought he could run roughshod over anyone because he was rich. He treated his house staff like slaves, allowing them no voices or power, giving them no appreciation. Unless you were pretty, and then you got the kind of attention a broken soul can confuse with love. He used her for years, until a younger housemaid came along. Then he acted like he never knew my mother. She was replaced, just like that." He snaps his fingers. "I saw the whole thing comin', but she'd never hear a word spoken against him. She thought because he came into her room a few nights a week and let me play rugby with his spoiled fucking children, that meant he loved her. But he didn't. And when she found out, it killed her. She went up to the roof and threw herself off without even tellin' me good-bye."

My face is crumpling. I can feel it, along with my heart thumping and my throat squeezing shut. "Oh, Cam. I'm so sorry."

He looks away, drags a hand through his hair, exhales a hard breath. "Aye. Me too."

He looks so wrecked, so sad and lonely, that I abandon the sunflowers and go to him. "Stand up," I demand, tugging on his sleeve. "I'm giving you a hug."

He stands, and I go up on tiptoe, throw my arms around his shoulders, and hide my face in his neck. He winds his arms around my back and straightens, so my feet dangle above the floor.

I resist the impulse to make a crack about how strong he is to lift my weight, and just breathe into his neck with my eyes closed, feeling his heart thumping against my chest and his arms like a vise around me.

"Promise me something," he whispers into my hair.

"What?"

"No matter what happens with Michael, we'll still be friends."

"I thought you didn't want to be friends."

His sigh is a big gust of air. "God, you're an idiot."

"That's probably not something you should say to someone with low self-esteem," I tease.

He rests his temple against mine and sighs again, but this time it sounds impossibly sad. "Aye, but you know I say it with love, lass. Always with love."

My face is starting to crumple again. I nod, unable to speak.

We stand there like that until Mr. Bingley decides it's getting weird and starts batting at my dangling feet. Cam gently sets me down, and we spend the rest of the evening pretending the hug didn't happen, eating dinner and talking and dancing around the word *love* that lingers like a ghost in the air.

TWENTY-SEVEN

From: Michael Maddox
To: Joellen Bixby
Date: December 15
Subject: Squash

In a meeting with the head of our European distributor, a man who makes watching paint dry seem fascinating by comparison. I've already had three cups of coffee just to try to stay awake. The only thing keeping me going is the thought of you in one of those tiny ruffled skirts on the squash court. The word *flounce* comes to mind. Among other things.

M.

From: Joellen Bixby
To: Michael Maddox
Date: December 15
Subject: Re: Squash

Terribly sorry about your meeting, but being the CEO can't be all fun and games or it would be unfair, considering the obscene amount of money you make. I hate to disappoint you, but tiny ruffled skirts and I are not on the best of terms. Leggings, perhaps?

Hope all is well in jolly old England. You left at the right time: Denny has debuted his Christmas-themed fart jokes, to everyone's delight. I had no idea the baby Jesus was so gassy.

From: Michael Maddox
To: Joellen Bixby
Date: December 16
Subject: Leggings

You're intentionally being cruel. Leggings are even more revealing than tiny ruffled skirts. I lost at least five hours of sleep last night picturing your bottom encased in Lycra.

How do you know how much money I make? Maybe I'm only doing this job for the perks. For all you know, I could be donating my time in hopes of catching sight of you in the office. Sharing a smile over the coffee machine. Having you ignore me so aggressively as you've been doing for the past ten years.

M.

From: Joellen Bixby
To: Michael Maddox
Date: December 16
Subject: Re: Leggings

Ha! You, sir, have a good sense of humor. I've attached a picture of my face right after reading your last email. Yes, that is an eye roll you're seeing. It was so robust I might've pulled something. I *don't* know how much you make, but I know your haircut costs more than my monthly grocery bill, and that's a lot.

I haven't been ignoring you. I've been admiring from afar. Go look up the word *unrequited* in the dictionary. You might be surprised to see a picture of me beside the definition.

From: Michael Maddox
To: Joellen Bixby
Date: December 16
Subject: You're killing me

Stop calling me sir. Not only does it make me feel like my grandfather, but also there's a vaguely *Fifty Shades of Grey*/power exchange undertone that's wreaking havoc on my nerves. If you tell me it's intentional, I might have a heart attack. (But I'll be on the next plane home.)

I don't have to look up the definition of *unrequited* to know that it doesn't apply to our situation. The word assumes feelings are unreturned.

"Barely contained" is a more accurate description, at least from my end.

M.

From: Joellen Bixby
To: Michael Maddox
Date: December 17
Subject: Re: You're killing me

This is me responding to your email even though my mind is blank with shock due to your last sentence. And to think all these years I thought this affair was one-sided . . . sir.

From: Michael Maddox
To: Joellen Bixby
Date: December 17
Subject: Re: Re: You're killing me

!!!!!!!!!!!!!!!!!!!!!!!!!
You're lucky I'm more than three thousand miles away. Send me another picture.

M.

From: Michael Maddox
To: Joellen Bixby
Date: December 18
Subject: WHERE IS MY PICTURE?

Don't make me pull rank and threaten to have you written up for disobedience.

M.

From: Joellen Bixby
To: Michael Maddox
Date: December 18
Subject: As you requested

Being inexperienced in the art of sexting, here is a photo of my left foot. I think it's quite flattering. Good lighting, etc. I tried to take a few more "risqué" shots, but the front-facing camera on an iPhone is designed to kill a person's soul. I'm afraid you'll have to wait until you get back to see the goods in the flesh. So to speak.

From: Michael Maddox
To: Joellen Bixby
Date: December 19
Subject: Arrgh

Front-facing cameras are not the only thing that are soul killing. Disobedient copy editors are up there, too. Although your foot is lovely—those arches, you must be very proud—I was hoping for a glimpse of something a bit more intimate. Kneecap? Inner wrist? Hip bone? Even an earlobe would be satisfactory at this point. I had no idea how accustomed I'd grown to seeing you at the office. I'm ashamed to admit I've been gazing longingly at your eye-roll photo at night while I'm lying in bed.

Have you ever thought about getting contact lenses? Your eyes are so beautiful, but they're a bit hidden behind your glasses. I've always wondered what you'd look like without them.
And a few other articles of clothing.

M.

From: Joellen Bixby
To: Michael Maddox
Date: December 19
Subject: Something to tide you over

Attached is a pic of my earlobe. You'll be in a kerfuffle trying to discern if it's the left or right, I'm sure. Ah, the mystery. I am a master of seduction, am I not?

In other news, Portia apparently has a twin who does not breathe fire and snack on little children. I don't know if she's on new meds, but she's been acting human recently. Come to think of it, since you left.

Contacts make my eyes hurt, though I was thinking of wearing them for the holiday party. I've even bought myself a new dress. It's tight and red and makes my boobs look bigger and my waist look smaller. I've asked it to marry me, but it's playing coy and not answering. Such is love.

From: Michael Maddox
To: Joellen Bixby
Date: December 20
Subject: Have I told you you're irresistible?

From: Joellen Bixby
To: Michael Maddox
Date: December 20
Subject: You've used the word *charming*. *Irresistible* has yet to be introduced.

From: Michael Maddox
To: Joellen Bixby
Date: December 21
Subject: Consider it introduced.

And add *captivating*, *delightful*, *adorable*, *funny*, and *bewitching* to the mix. Honestly, there aren't enough superlatives. You're wonderful. And those arches! Those earlobes!

I can't wait to see you again.

M.

From: Joellen Bixby
To: Michael Maddox
Date: December 21
Subject: Speaking of seeing me again . . .

Here's an awkward but important question: we're not really allowed to date, right? I mean according to company policy. I wanted to look it up in the online handbook but thought it might raise a red flag somewhere. Who knows how closely Ruth in HR monitors things. She could have a bot crawling the web for hits on "Can I shag the CEO without getting fired?"

So . . . can I?

From: Michael Maddox
To: Joellen Bixby
Date: December 21
Subject: Re: Speaking of seeing me again . . .

You'll think I'm strange, but your last email gave me an erection. The thought of you sitting at your desk pondering what kind of dirty things we could do together without getting caught . . . dear God, here it is again. I wonder if I can type with one hand? (Sorry, inside thought.)

To answer your question seriously—yes, there is a company policy against romantic or sexual relationships between supervisors and subordinates. Unfortunately, as I'm the CEO, it could be argued that everyone is my subordinate. It's a family company, but I still have to answer to the board.

Long answer short, it's a big risk. I'll be completely honest: we're both looking at losing our jobs if we're discovered. I will completely understand if you're not willing to accept that risk.

I, however, definitely am.

Think about it. I'm back in a few days. I'll see you at the party. You can let me know then. Either way, I've already informed HR that you've been selected for the acquisitions editor position. It won't be formally announced until we're back from after the holiday break between Christmas and New Year, so please keep it under your hat for now.

No matter what you decide about us, I'll always wish you the best and be your friend.

Hopefully yours,

M.

TWENTY-EIGHT

"Holy cow," I whisper, staring at the computer screen in disbelief. "I got the position!"

I leap out of bed where I've been sitting with my laptop, run through my apartment, and throw open the front door. I pound a fist on Cam's apartment door like I'm the landlord and he's three months late with the rent.

"Cam! Are you home? Open up!"

A muffled, "Comin'!" and then he opens the door, barefoot, wearing what appears to be a woman's robe. It's pink terrycloth, about ten sizes too small, edged in white lace at the wrists and collar.

"Um . . ."

"What?" He looks down at himself. "Oh, this? It was in Kellen's closet. Looked comfy." He shrugs. "It is comfy. "

"I admire that for such a big, manly man, you have very open ideas about gender-specific clothing."

He scoffs. "Whoever made that rule that pink is only for girls is dumb. I'll have you know, pink is very flatterin' to my complexion."

It actually is, but I don't have time for this conversation. "Moving on—I got the promotion! You're looking at the newest associate editor at Maddox Publishing!" I jump up and down in glee, doing a little skip-ping dance and waving my hands like a drugged-out mime.

"Really? That's fantastic, lass! Good for you! You just found out?"

"Yes, Michael emailed me the news! I'm not supposed to tell anyone until after the first of the year when they make the formal announce-ment, but I had to tell you. Oh God, wait until my mother hears—she'll freak out!"

"You told me before you told your mum?"

I stop jumping up and down and make a face at him. "Why do I feel like that's going to be followed with a lecture about how much I'm in love with you, but I just don't realize it yet?"

"Because you are, and you don't." He closes his door and ambles past me. "This calls for a celebration. You have any of that dark beer you bought for me left?"

He disappears into my apartment. I follow him, shaking my head at the picture he makes. No matter what he's wearing—or isn't wearing—the man doesn't have an ounce of self-consciousness. "Your ego is your superpower, you know that, prancer?"

Cam flops onto my sofa, lies back, and crosses his legs at the ankle. He looks like an MMA wrestler wearing his daughter's princess robe. "Oh, no, lass, that's not my superpower." He winks at me, grinning.

"You're never gonna let me forget I saw you naked, are you?"

"I'll forget it as soon as you do. So no, never."

Ignoring him, I go into the kitchen, fish a beer from the fridge, pop the top off it, and pour it into a glass. Then I pour myself a glass of wine and head back into the living room. I give Cam his beer, then sit at the end of the sofa near his feet, crossing my legs under me.

"Why aren't you dressed for bed yet?" He eyes my jeans and T-shirt. "It's almost ten o'clock on a school night. You need your sleep."

That makes me smile. "You'll make a good dad someday, you know that? You're bossy in a very sweet way."

When he arches his brows at the compliment, I hold up a hand. "*Not* in love with you. Just making an observation."

"Well, thank you. I've always wanted to be a father."

"You have tons of time. What are you, early thirties?"

"Don't tell me you didn't find out during your investigative research." With an arm under his head, he takes a drink from his beer, watching me.

"Ugh. I only looked you up that one time, and I didn't pay attention to your birth date. So—are you going to tell me, or is it a state secret?"

"I'm twenty-nine."

I'm floored. He seems so much older. More mature. Twenty-nine is practically a baby! Suddenly I feel like Methuselah, nearly a thousand years old and counting.

"Uh-oh," he says drily, examining my pinched expression. "She's thinkin'. No good can come of this."

I blow out a breath too hard, which causes my lips to flap in a truly unattractive way. But I don't care, because it's Cam, and he's seen me at my worst. "I remember twenty-nine. It was actually harder than thirty. Once I was over that hump, I accepted I'd never be young again."

"Everything's relative, lass. There's a sixty-year-old grandma out there who'd give her eyeteeth to be thirty-six again."

"Oh, thank you for that pearl of wisdom. How comforting to know the elderly are jealous of me."

"Sixty isn't elderly!"

"Dude. Seriously. If the average life expectancy is somewhere in the seventies, sixty is practically knocking on death's door."

"One of my grandmothers lived to be one hundred and fourteen."

"What? That's a lie!"

"Nope. And my other grandmother is one hundred and ten. She's still alive."

I narrow my eyes at him. "Now you're just trying to make me feel better."

"I'm not pullin' your leg! The McGregor clan has exceptional genes, lass. Nobody in my family even starts thinkin' about retirin' until well after ninety."

"Really?"

"Really. If you ever visit Scotland, I'll take you to meet Nanny O'Shea. That's my mum's mum. You two would get a kick out of each other—same sharp tongue and lack of respect for the McGregor men."

He smiles, relishing some memory, and drinks more of his beer, while I sit and think how much fun it would be to meet his ancient, sassy Scottish grandmother.

"My dad's mother is eighty. We call her Granny Gums because she loves to horrify people by popping out her dentures during conversations like it's an accident. She has mild dementia, so she repeats herself a lot, but otherwise she's in pretty good shape. My other grandmother is in perfect health, but you wouldn't know it by the way she carries on. She had a Just Buried party when she turned fifty because she was convinced she was about to kick the bucket any minute. She was a model, like my mom."

I take a long drink of my wine, thinking of all the times my mother and grandmother commiserated about getting old, even when I was a kid and they weren't anywhere close to old. Every holiday and family get-together inevitably turned into a Mourning the Glory Days of Our Departed Beauty party.

"Those people do *not* age gracefully, and I'm not talking about wrinkles."

Cam sits up and holds his beer out toward me, like he wants to toast.

"What?"

"Clink your glass with me, lass. That's the first time you've said somethin' sensible about age, looks, or your family."

"Maybe you're rubbing off on me." We toast and drink, then Cam smacks his lips, looking wistfully toward the kitchen.

The man is as subtle as a wrecking ball.

"I have a chicken breast and some veggies left over from dinner I could reheat if you're hungry."

Cam toys with the lace on the sleeve of his robe, his lashes swept demurely downward. "Only if it's no bother, lass. I don't wanna keep you up."

I kick his feet and grin at him. "Oh, shut up, you big baby."

When he smiles bashfully, his lips in a wry little twist because he's too shy to admit he wants me to cook for him, I'm hit with a sudden, unidentifiable emotion. It's weird and tender and powerful and alien and makes my heart skip several beats.

I stand so abruptly I spill wine on the carpet.

Cam looks up at me, but I spin away, unwilling to let his sharp eyes get a glimpse at my face. In a daze, I walk into the kitchen and start putting together a plate for Cam from the leftovers in the fridge.

What was *that? What's wrong with me? Am I getting sick?* I put the back of my hand to my forehead, but it's cool and dry, no sign of fever.

"So what else did pretty boy say in his email?" calls Cam from the living room.

I'm too distracted to give him the details. "My laptop's on the bed if you want to check it out."

In a few moments, he strolls into the kitchen with the laptop, sits at the table, and starts to read. Almost immediately, he's making faces.

"What's wrong?"

"I like him better in email than in person."

That makes me laugh out loud. "Oh ho! So you admit Mr. Repressed has a cute side!"

My laugh makes him grouchy. "I said no such thing. Let's not get carried away, lass. I'm just admittin' he might have a certain charm in electronic communications that doesn't translate into real life." His voice hardens. "Even if he was tryin' to get you to send nudes."

"Yeah, but I remembered what you said about dropping crumbs, so I took your advice and sent him a picture of my earlobe instead."

"Seems like it worked. Pretty boy's fallin' all over himself here." He's quiet for a moment, then says sharply, "Did you read this part about the policy against subordinates and supervisors bein' in a relationship?"

I sigh, putting the plate of food into the microwave to reheat. "Yeah. It's a bummer, but I guess we'll just have to be extra careful."

"Extra careful as in not sendin' emails like this over the company server?"

I freeze in horror. "Oh shit."

"Aye, oh shit is right. Dumb ass."

Outraged, I turn and stare at him. "Did you just call me a dumb ass?"

"I'm callin' *him* a dumb ass, because he is, because he should fucking know better! He's the CEO, for Christ's sake!"

"I should know better, too!"

Cam sighs and drags a hand through his hair. "Aye. But you're a woman in love. They're always blind as fuckin' bats." He glances up at me. "Sorry. Not to lump you in with the rest of your gender, but in my personal experience, a woman loses her damn mind when she falls in love. And most of the time she loses herself in the process, too."

His look is a little too pointed for comfort. I turn away, occupying myself with watching the plate turn on the carousel in the microwave. "I'll go in and delete everything later. I'll make sure he does, too. I don't think there's anything too incriminating. We're not admitting we're in a relationship, we're just talking about the possibilities. Besides, it won't be a problem unless someone is looking for something, which they aren't."

Yet.

Thinking of all the complications an office romance with Michael will most likely entail, I rub my hand over my forehead. Before it was just a lovely dream, but now reality is setting in, and it's a lot less dreamy.

I could lose my job.

He's worth it. He'll protect you.

Will he? If his own job is on the line?

He's a good man. You can trust him. Everything will be fine.

You're too old to be impractical. You have no experience doing anything else. If you get fired from Maddox Publishing, you'll be temping as a receptionist or living with your parents within a few months.

I rest my forehead on the microwave door and groan.

"You havin' a breakdown over there, lassie? Do I need to call the paramedics?"

"No. I'm just beginning to realize this thing with Michael might be more complicated than I thought." My laugh is rueful. "Or *didn't* think. It was never a possibility before, not really. But now . . ."

After a moment, Cam says, "Reality's settin' in."

"I literally thought those exact words not two minutes ago."

"Great minds think alike. Is my dinner ready yet?"

Despite my worry, I have to smile. "Yes, evil overlord, your dinner is ready." I remove his plate from the microwave, check it to make sure there are no cold spots, and set it in front of him with a knife and fork. "Why are you eating so late, anyway? You told me I shouldn't eat after seven p.m."

He digs into his food without preamble, sawing a big chunk of the chicken off and stuffing it into his mouth. We eat the same way, all flashing utensils and sighs of pleasure, savoring every bite like it's our last meal before the electric chair. How he can enjoy watching me eat I'll never know. Although admittedly I'm getting quite a bit of enjoyment watching him tear through that piece of chicken.

That he likes my cooking so much gives me a weird kind of happiness, a fizzy little starburst of sunshine glowing inside my chest.

"Didn't eat today except for lunch," he says around a mouthful, his attention on the plate. "Don't have much in the apartment except stuff for our mornin' shakes and the odd sandwich."

"So go shopping! What have you been doing for dinner since our last supper?"

He lifts a shoulder. "Nothin'."

I'm dismayed. "You haven't been eating? How do you have the energy to do our workouts in the morning?"

He glances up at me and winks. "'Tis the thought of you that keeps me goin', lass."

My eye roll is extravagant. "Okay. That's it. We're going back to our nightly dinners. I can't have my trainer dying on me—I'm almost halfway to my weight-loss goal."

Cam stops chewing and stares at me. He swallows and wipes his mouth with his hand. "You have a specific number in mind?"

"Yeah. Forty pounds. What did you think this was about, my love for kale and early-morning jogs in subzero temperatures?"

"*Forty* pounds? I thought you just wanted to get into shape?"

"I do! I am!"

He sits back in his chair and examines me closely, a furrow forming between his brows.

"What's that look? You're making me nervous."

"It's your body, lass. If you wanna shrink it, that's your decision. But if I could offer an opinion . . ."

"Sure. Go ahead."

He says softly, "You look great. Truly. If you were payin' me to be your trainer, I'd advise you to stop tryin' to lose weight and focus on healthy eatin' habits and gainin' strength, endurance, and flexibility from your workouts. And, most importantly, practicin' gratitude for the body you've got."

"Practicing gratitude," I repeat doubtfully.

He nods. "You're healthy. You're whole. Your body does whatever you ask it to. There are millions of people who live with chronic pain or physical disabilities who would gladly trade places with you."

When I screw my face up following that little speech, he sighs.

"Your body isn't a thing to be looked at and judged against some standard of perfection that doesn't even really exist. It's the vessel that takes you through life, allowin' you to experience all the beautiful things life has to offer. Food. Sex. Sunsets. Music. Hugs. Laughter. A healthy body is a gift. Don't take it for granted. Don't treat it like some cheap one-night stand. Treat it like the love of your life. Treat it with respect and tenderness, but most of all, gratitude.

"And a healthy dose of awe, too. Your body is made of remnants of stars and massive explosions in the galaxies. Every few years, the bulk of your body is newly created by the regeneration of your cells, but you have things in you that are as old as the universe. We're literally stardust. Every one of us is a little miracle. You're a miracle, Joellen. Think about that the next time you're standin' naked in front of the mirror and want to focus on some stray dimple you don't like."

He digs into his meal again, as if he hasn't just completely rocked my world.

I'm a miracle? Who says stuff like that?

"You're thinkin' again, lass," says Cam, chewing. "I can hear the gears turnin'."

"There's no way you're only twenty-nine."

He grins around a mouthful of chicken. "Why, 'cause I'm so enlightened? Maybe I'm the latest reincarnation of the Buddha, you ever think of that?"

"Oh yes. You're *very* enlightened. I can tell from the girly pink robe."

Cam looks up at me, hazel eyes sparkling. "Exactly," he pronounces. "Great title for another sonnet about me, don'tcha think? 'The Man in the Girly Pink Robe.' I can see it now. Full o' tender endearments about my extreme lovability. You can work on it tomorrow and show it to me at dinner."

We smile at each other, Mr. Bingley jumps up onto Cam's lap and curls into a ball, and I push away the little voice in my head whispering how the man in the girly pink robe will soon be gone from my life forever.

TWENTY-NINE

The man in the girly pink robe and I
Sit on a bench in the park discussing the weather.
He speaks of stardust and miracles while I sigh,
Wondering how it's so effortless to be together
With someone so different from me, yet the same,
Over laughter and food our friendship is dawning.
Yet strip away the smiling outer shells—what remains?
Two hearts in darkness, filled with unbearable longing.
Pink robes can mask pain as well as spare flesh
Can be used as somewhere to hide.
Each time we meet I'm moved afresh
By his eloquence, his beauty, his pride.
The man in the girly pink robe is like home
The safest and strongest and best that I've known.

"I must be getting my period," I mutter, angrily wiping the tears from my eyes. "This is ridiculous."

I stand, place my sonnet book back into the top drawer of my desk in my bedroom, and look out the window. It's snowing. Flakes float sideways past the pane, gathering in white drifts like dustings of sugar on the corners of the sill.

It's Saturday the twenty-third. The office holiday party starts in three hours.

I'm officially freaking out.

I didn't sleep at all last night. Or the night before. Or the night before that. Dinner with Cam a few days ago left me raw in ways I didn't expect and didn't feel right away. It wasn't until after he left that night that I got to thinking about what he'd said about having gratitude for my body instead of treating it like a one-night stand.

For some reason that really resonated.

The first time I went on a diet, I was twelve. I hadn't even gotten my period yet. My mother, on the other hand, had recently turned forty and was inconsolable. Her grief at passing that milestone age was like a black shroud that hung over the house. Everyone spoke in muted tones and tiptoed around for almost a month as if someone had died.

One night at dinner when I reached for a roll from the bread basket in the middle of the table, my mother slapped my hand. "You've had enough," she said tonelessly, looking at my waistline. My sister—beautiful even at nine—snickered.

That was all it took. I remember the moment clearly. It was the last time I put anything into my mouth without feeling guilt.

From then on, every billboard, every commercial, the pages of every glossy magazine declared to me in no uncertain terms that I didn't look how I should. There were no images of voluptuous women back then, hardly any of women of color. Everyone was blonde, thin, perfect. Homogeneous. If you were a European supermodel, then you were allowed to be brunette, but you couldn't look too "ethnic," or forget it.

Making matters worse, I lived at the beach in Southern California. Blonde, thin, perfect women are manufactured in that area of the world like widgets. If you didn't have straight teeth, you got braces. If you weren't slender, you starved yourself. If you weren't blonde, you bleached your hair. If you weren't tan, you laid in a machine shaped like a coffin that blasted cancer-causing UV rays at your skin until it complied and turned an acceptable shade of golden brown.

Or burned and freckled, like mine did.

No one ever told me it was okay to be me. All my friends were on diets throughout our teenage years. All of us were drowning in self-loathing.

I wish I was as fat now as I thought I was back then. It makes me sad to think of how long and how hard I tried to be something I wasn't.

The ghost of my reflection gazes back at me from the window. She's pale, unsmiling, her hair a dark cloud around her head. She looks like she's seen things she wishes she hadn't.

Suddenly I'm filled with anger. "You know what? A wise woman once said, 'Fuck this shit' and lived happily ever after."

Ghost me looks impressed. And a little frightened.

With renewed determination, I head into the bathroom to get ready for the party.

Two hours later, my determination has wilted, and I'm wringing my hands in panic inside the closed bedroom door.

"Any day now, lassie. We could be dead by the time you come out!"

Cam and Mrs. Dinwiddle have gathered in the living room for my big reveal. They must've made arrangements between themselves, because I never invited them, but here they are. I'm regretting giving Mrs. Dinwiddle that spare key.

I take one last deep breath, smooth my hands down my waist, and open the door. When I step into the living room, Mrs. Dinwiddle leaps to her feet with a theatrical gasp.

"*Heavens*, Ducky! You're *beautiful!*"

I know I should be flattered, but she doesn't have to sound so dang shocked. "How's the hair?" I pat it nervously. "I used your hot oil treatment."

Mrs. Dinwiddle floats over to me, little sounds of astonishment falling from her lips as she ogles me up and down. "Oh, my *dear*, it's simply perfect. *Perfect!* How did you get it *up* like that? What a lovely, chic *twist!*"

"YouTube," I admit sheepishly. "They have really good tutorials."

Sitting on the sofa with a beer, Cam isn't saying anything. He's just looking at me. *Really* looking at me.

While Mrs. Dinwiddle hovers over me, plucking at nonexistent bits of lint on my dress and sighing in rapture like some hysterical fairy godmother, I let Cam stare until I can't take it anymore. "Well?"

His voice low and husky, he says, "Let's just say I'm glad I'm already sittin' down."

Pleased, I look down at myself. "I'm taking that as a compliment."

"Aye. It's a compliment. But if you knew what I was really thinkin', lass, you'd run back into that bedroom and bolt the door behind you."

When I glance back up at him, he isn't smiling. He lifts his beer in a salute, then guzzles the whole thing in one go. My face flushes with heat.

"But we need to take it *in* a bit, Ducky. It's a little *loose* here!"

Mrs. Dinwiddle is frowning at my waist, pinching an inch of fabric between her fingers.

"You're right. I've lost weight since I bought this. Shoot."

"No *worries*, my dear, just take it *off* for a minute, and I'll fix it *up* for you! I'm an expert seamstress, of *course*. All those years on the *stage*, I accumulated more than just *men*, let me tell you. My skills with a needle and thread are *legendary*. Tut, tut, *in* you go, take it *off*, put on a robe, and I'll bring it right *back!*"

She waves me off into the bedroom like she's shooing a flock of pigeons away from her lunch. I remove the dress, careful not to mess my hair or makeup, put on my fluffy white bathrobe, and reemerge into the living room with the dress in my arms.

"Back in a *jiff*."

Mrs. Dinwiddle sweeps out of the apartment, leaving me and Cam alone.

"You're not wearin' your glasses."

It sounds like an accusation, so instantly I'm on the defense. "I've got my contacts in. I decided to go whole hog with the transformation thing. I want everyone to not recognize me when I walk into the party. I want to *slay*."

"Oh, you'll slay, lass. No doubt about that. But it's really because pretty boy wanted to see you without them, isn't it?"

My heartbeat ticks up a notch. I swallow, feeling nervous and uncomfortable, unsure of why I'd feel either. "Is that bad?"

He draws a breath through his nose, a long one, like he's biting his tongue or trying to cool his temper. Then he stands, leaving his empty beer bottle on the coffee table. He crosses to me and takes my face in his hands.

"No," he says softly, looking into my eyes. "It's not bad. You want to please your man—I get it. Just don't forget who you are. Don't forget *what* you are, Joellen. Not for anyone."

My heartbeat is now the wild, thundering gallop of a pack of stallions flying over the open plains. "What am I?" I whisper, terrified of the answer.

"Perfect."

He bends his head and kisses me, the softest, sweetest brush of his lips against mine. Then he turns and leaves, closing the door quietly behind him.

I sink weak-kneed to the sofa and spend the next fifteen minutes hyperventilating, until Mrs. Dinwiddle reappears with my dress.

In the cab on the way to the party, I don't see the snowy streets passing by. I don't see the traffic or the lights or hear the Christmas jingle playing on the stereo.

All I see is Cam's face. All I hear is his voice telling me I'm perfect.

Well, I also hear the critical voice that's always with me telling me that Cam has obviously ingested a lot of drugs if he thinks I'm anywhere close to perfect, but I force that voice to a dark corner of my mind and allow myself to accept that maybe I don't have to *be* perfect. Maybe having one person who *thinks* I am is enough.

Maybe his belief in me can be the seed that takes root in the stubborn, self-loathing dirt of my mind and grows into a garden of self-acceptance.

Or maybe I'm nuts.

"God, I really need a drink," I say aloud.

In the driver's seat, the cabbie holds up a silver flask. "You like bourbon?"

I have to smile. *Damn, I love New York.* "Not even a little bit."

Maddox Publishing's annual holiday party is being held at the Broad Street Ballroom, a former Bank of America headquarters converted into a luxury event space. This year, the theme of the party is Winter Wonderland, because apparently no one on the event committee possesses a kernel of originality.

I step out of the cab into bitter wind and hurry up the stone steps toward the door, pulling my coat up around my ears and hoping my hair doesn't get too badly damaged. It's still snowing, and there's frost on the ground.

I walk inside into warmth and a confusion of scents—hot wax and lilies and women's perfume. A girl at a desk takes my coat and gives me a ticket, then I make my way down an elegant hallway toward the ballroom, willing my hands to stop shaking. They refuse.

Music and laughter from around a corner. The sound of clinking ice. I pass myself in a mirror but don't look, knowing that critical voice is too ready to pounce.

I arrive at the large double doors leading into the ballroom. I take one final deep breath, then go inside.

THIRTY

As if I'm having an out-of-body experience, I see everything around me all at once, including myself.

Cocktail tables softly glowing with votive candles. Dinner tables surrounding a large white dance floor. Centerpieces of white branches dripping in strands of faux jewels that catch and reflect the light. A ten-piece band in tuxedos on a riser. People mingling, talking, laughing with drinks in their hands.

Me, standing alone at the door, wearing a drop-dead gorgeous red dress that cost half a month's pay, a pair of glittery sky-high heels that make my legs look fantastic, and my cheap everyday glasses with the black plastic frames.

Because I'm fucking perfect, that's why.

On her way toward the bar in the corner, Shasta walks right by me without batting an eye.

"Shasta."

She turns and looks around, then does a double take that might have caused whiplash. "Joellen? Is that you?"

"It's not like I'm wearing a disguise."

She walks nearer, gaping at me. "You might as well be, bitch! You da *bomb*. Who knew you had those titties stashed away under all those ugly sweaters?"

I can't help it: I have to laugh. "Let's get a drink."

I take her arm, and we make our way to the bar as I note who's in attendance and who has yet to show. Portia's deep in conversation with someone from marketing over by a stand of potted palms. Sue Wong is holding court around a cocktail table with a bunch of the junior copy editors who hang on her every word. A group of guys from accounting have commandeered one of the dining tables and are fighting over who's going to sit with his back to the dance floor.

Michael is nowhere to be seen.

"I'll have a glass of red wine, please," I tell the bartender, who looks homeless. When he gives me my drink, I put a twenty into his tip jar even though the drinks are free. He needs it more than I do.

"Vodka rocks," Shasta tells him. With a little smile for me, he pours her a serving of vodka that could tranquilize a bear.

I watch, alarmed, as she chugs it. "Easy, killer! The night's young."

"Broke up with the boyfriend," she says, taking a breather. "Walked in on the son of a bitch with another girl."

"Oh, Shasta, I'm so sorry!"

She shrugs. "I knew it wasn't going to last when we went on vacation to Bermuda over Thanksgiving and he clapped when the plane landed. No self-respecting woman can marry a man like that."

I hold up my glass of wine. "To being single."

"To being single," she echoes. "Next I think I'll become a lesbian."

"I'm pretty sure it doesn't work like that."

She shrugs again, and we both drink. As I'm swallowing, I spot Michael.

He's standing across the dance floor with three people. One of them is his father, who retired as CEO a dozen years ago. One of them is the current chief operating officer. The third is his wife.

His tall, beautiful, elegant wife, who has her hand on his arm and is smiling at him.

My stomach clenches to knots. I set my glass of wine on the bar because I know if I don't, I'll drop it. Shasta is talking, but all I can hear is a high-pitched noise in my ears, like someone is screaming. I wouldn't be surprised if that someone is me.

"I have to go to the bathroom." I don't wait to see if Shasta has heard me—I simply bolt from the room as fast as I can.

Once outside, I run down the hallway in search of a ladies' room. Luckily in places like these, they're always nearby. I fall on the door, panting, and stagger inside. I lock myself into a stall, wrap my arms around myself, and sit on the toilet, staring at the grout between the tiles until the worst of the pain passes and I can breathe again.

"I don't understand," I whisper, shaking. "I don't understand."

He said he was getting divorced. He said we'd talk tonight, that I could let him know what I've decided about us. How can he be here, now, with his *wife*?

Simple, says the pragmatic voice in my head. *He lied.*

The door creaks open. Footsteps echo hollowly off the floor. Then a voice says, "Joellen?"

I leap to my feet, scalded with fury. "In case you haven't noticed, this is the ladies' room, asshole!"

Michael's loud exhale seems even louder as it bounces off the tile walls. "You're angry."

"And you're here with your wife. I wonder how the two could possibly be related?"

"Can you please come out? I don't want to have this conversation through a toilet stall door."

I'm grateful to whatever guardian angels are helping me be more mad than brokenhearted right now, because anger will help me get through the next few minutes, just long enough to save my dignity until I can shatter into a million pieces in the cab on the way home.

I unlock the door, yank it open, and glare daggers at him from inside the stall.

He looks beautiful, of course. Not a hair out of place. The suit is gorgeous. The shoes are buffed to a mirror shine. I'd like to light his face on fire and put it out with a shovel.

"Please." He gestures for me to come out of the stall. Then he watches warily as I emerge, breathing flames from my nostrils.

I stand near the sinks and fold my arms over my chest. "You have exactly ten seconds to say your piece, and then I'm going to kick you in the balls. Go."

A ghost of a smile lifts his lips. "It isn't what it looks like."

I throw my hands in the air. "Seriously? You expect me to believe that?"

"Just hear me out. I told you our divorce was amicable—"

"No. No, you did *not* tell me that. You said she was living in the house and you got a new place while the attorneys were working out the details. That was the extent of your explanation."

He holds up his hands as if in surrender. "I apologize. I should've made it clearer. Our divorce is amicable."

"Yeah, we're past that. Get to the important part where you're attending the company holiday party together, looking all married and happy."

His expression is pained. "My father thought it would be good for morale. You know, for the staff to see that things are calm and friendly between us. Many times in cases like ours, family companies are broken up in bitter divorces."

When I stare at him, still unsure if he's telling the truth but *definitely* sure I'm unimpressed that he's taking daddy's advice about his personal life, he adds wearily, "We don't have a prenup. If Elizabeth wanted to, she could insist on the sale of the company so the proceeds could be evenly split between us."

That punches a good-size hole in my outrage. "But the company's been around for a million years! Way before you two were married!"

Michael nods. "Yes. It has. But since I took over as CEO, we've tripled in size, and so have our profits. She could argue in court that those profits are marital assets. I'd fight it, of course, but if I lost, I'd have to buy her out to the tune of more than one hundred million dollars. I don't have that kind of cash. The only way would be to sell."

I'm not sure how to react to that. I examine his face, but he seems sincere.

He takes a step closer. "Not to change the subject, but you look incredible."

I know I should say something. All I come up with is a morose "Thanks."

"I'm sorry," he says softly, taking another step closer. "I know it must've been a shock, seeing us like that. I honestly didn't know until late this afternoon that she'd be coming."

Plenty of time to pick up the phone. I huff out an aggravated breath.

He reaches out and strokes my arm, then takes another step toward me, so now we're standing close enough that I can smell his cologne. And the bourbon on his breath, which is surprisingly strong.

"You really do look incredible," he murmurs. "This dress is . . . wow. And your hair. My God, Joellen. You're stunning."

I fight a smile because I'm peeved, but his expression is too admiring to stay mad for long. "I'm glad you like it."

He curls his fingers into my arm and pulls me closer. "I don't like it. I *love* it. You've made me your slave." He leans in and runs his nose along my jaw, raising the tiny hairs on the back of my neck. "Now if only you'd get rid of those glasses, you'd be perfect."

That leaves me breathless. Stunned, like he just hit me across the face. I picture us sitting together at a breakfast table on some morning in the distant future. He's reading a newspaper, ignoring me until

I reach for another croissant, and then he slaps my hand, snapping "You've had enough."

He'll never think I'm perfect just the way I am. He'll never tell me I'm a miracle. I'll always have to fake it with him, trying to live up to some impossible standard, never able to relax and be myself.

A switch inside my head flicks from on to off, and just like that, I can't wait to get out of here. "We should go. Someone could walk in any minute."

"That only makes it more exciting, don't you think?"

He sniffs my neck, making a low noise of pleasure in his throat. When he drags me against him, I'm startled to feel a bulge below his waist that probably isn't his wallet.

"Whoa! Okay. Let's cool it—"

"I couldn't stop thinking about you while I was gone," he interrupts, his voice deeper. He trails his lips down my neck, nipping every so often like he's trying to taste me. *Eat* me. He backs me up until my bottom hits the sink and I can't go any farther.

"You enjoyed teasing me over email, didn't you? Sending me that photo of your earlobe." He chuckles like a comic book villain. "Clever. If it was your plan to make me obsessed, it worked."

I start to panic, because he's acting so strange. "No, there was really no plan—"

He digs his hand into my hair, pulls my head back, and clamps his mouth down on my throat like a vampire. It's so sudden, I jump, startled out of my wits, then yelp when his hand latches onto my breast and squeezes.

"Michael! You're hurting me!"

He crushes his mouth over mine.

I shove him away, panting, and raise a hand to my stinging lips. "Dude! Get a grip! I'm not making out with you in a bathroom! In case you didn't hear me, I just said cool it!"

It's like my refusal makes Michael snap. He's there one minute, the familiar, well-mannered man, then he's vanished, replaced by some random psychopath summoned from a séance gone sideways.

He grabs my upper arms, shoves me up onto the sink, and kisses me again, savagely, his teeth sinking into my tender lower lip. He bends me so far back my head slams against the mirror.

I react on pure instinct and bite him.

"Ow!" He pulls away for a second—breathing hard, astonished—and raises his fingers to his mouth. When they come away bloody, he smiles.

He looks up at me with those psycho eyes, and my blood runs cold. I try to jump off the counter, but he holds me in place, his arms strong from all that stupid squash.

"Let me go!"

"She likes to play rough." He wrestles my arms behind my back. "Me too."

He laughs into my ear, and I smell the alcohol on his breath again, searing fumes that make me want to gag. *How much has he had to drink?* "Stop. Michael, stop!"

"Oh, come on, Joellen, don't be coy. We both know what we're doing. You wanted a promotion, right? Did you think those were handed out for free?"

He kisses my neck, pressing his crotch into mine, dragging the hem of my dress up so he can grab a handful of bare thigh. My heart is going like gangbusters with equal parts fear and fury, overlaid by complete disbelief.

"Are you kidding me right now? I said stop!"

"I'll stop when I'm good and goddamn ready." His voice is a growl. He curls his fingers around the elastic of my panties where they ride over my hip.

Just as I'm about to let loose a full-throated scream, the door opens. The sound of music swells. Michael and I freeze, looking over to see who's come in.

It's Portia.

She's stiff as a statue in the doorway, eyes wide, mouth formed into a horrified *O* of shock at the picture Michael and I make on the counter.

My hair is mussed. We're both breathing hard. My lipstick is smeared all over his mouth. My leg is bent at his waist, and my dress is shoved up so my thigh is completely exposed, all the way up to my panties.

I know exactly what it looks like to her, and it makes me want to throw up.

Portia turns without a word and leaves. The door swings closed behind her.

With all my strength, I shove Michael away. Still off-balance from Portia's interruption, he staggers back, blinking. I slide off the counter, straighten my dress, then stride over to where he's standing by the toilet I came out of earlier and slap him as hard as I can across his face.

"You can take your promotion and shove it!"

I run out of the ladies' room, my vision blurry from the water swimming in my eyes. I hurry through the elegant hallways to claim my coat. Out on the sidewalk, I hail a cab, my breath frosting in puffy white clouds in front of my face, my ears too hot to go numb in the cold.

It isn't until I'm safely inside the cab and have given the driver my home address that I break down and start to cry.

THIRTY-ONE

When Cam opens to my knock, I throw my arms around his shoulders and bury my face in his neck.

"Joellen! What happened? Why're you back already?"

Unable to speak without bursting into a fresh round of tears, I shake my head. My whole body trembles. I'm so upset it's like a bomb went off inside my stomach and ripped a huge hole right through me.

Everything I've been fantasizing about for the past ten years has been just that: a fantasy. Michael isn't a knight in shining armor coming to rescue me on his trusty steed. He's the apple the witch offered to Snow White—perfect, shiny, and filled with poison.

"Easy. Take a breath, lass. Come inside and talk to me."

Cam's shushing me with soft words, his arms strong and protective around my back. He kicks the door shut with his bare foot. "What happened to your hair? And why've you been cryin'?"

"Michael," I whisper. "He . . . he . . ."

Cam goes stiff. His voice comes out low and dangerously hard. "He *what*, lass?"

I'm afraid to tell him exactly what happened, because I suspect by his tone, posture, and expression, he'll march right out the door, find

Michael, and make him wish he were never born. I go with a generalization instead. "He's an asshole!"

Cam takes my face in his hands and forces me to look at him. He growls, "If he got fresh with you, I'm gonna break his bloody knees!"

Though I feel like crying, that makes me smile a little. "Got fresh with me? That's cute, grandma."

"I swear to God, woman, you better tell me what he did to get you into this state or I'm gonna assume the worst, hunt that bastard down, and divest him of his testicles. Talk."

In a small voice, I ask, "Why is it so hard for you to wear a shirt, prancer? This conversation would be a lot easier on me if I didn't have to pretend you're not half-naked."

Though his expression is hard with worry, a glint of humor shines in his eyes at my words. He sweeps his thumb over my cheek, probably wiping away smeared mascara. "All these muscles are distractin' you again, aren't they?"

The truth is, they are. He's huge and muscular and covered in tattoos, the exact opposite of Michael in pretty much every way.

And he'd never "get fresh" with me. He'll joke and flirt and tease me mercilessly, but I know this man Michael once described as "an absolute animal" would rather cut off his own hands than do anything to hurt or disrespect me.

Like force himself on me in a ladies' room in return for a promotion.

"Lass," says Cam, watching me think with a furrow between his brows. "I dunno what's goin' on inside that brain of yours, but—"

I rise up on my toes and kiss him.

He sucks in a startled breath, but I steal it back from him and kiss him harder. He allows it, taking my tongue into his mouth with a small groan, but almost immediately takes control back from me, twisting his head to break the kiss. We stand there for a moment, breathing raggedly, the silence yawning wider with every tick of the clock.

"What was that?" he asks, his voice rough edged.

"That was a kiss."

My arms are still around his shoulders. His arms are still around my back. Our chests are pressed so tightly together I feel his heart thudding like mad against my breasts.

"You mean a revenge kiss? Because I don't think that was really about me."

Groaning, I close my eyes and drop my head to his chest.

"Just answer me this: Did he hurt you?"

"Only my ego," I admit, miserable. "And maybe my faith in humanity."

And my poor, stupid heart, of course, which is weeping at the death of a beautiful dream. Not only have I lost Michael, my career is over. Even if Michael doesn't fire me, Portia will report me for fraternizing with the CEO, and that will be that. She's already interrupted us together in the kitchen and probably made written notes of every time she saw us together at the office. Even if I deny any involvement with him, all they'll have to do is a search of my email to find enough evidence to put my head on the chopping block.

My job is toast.

"Your instincts were right about him, Cam. He was at the party with his *wife*. I'm such a fool."

Cam lifts my head with a knuckle under my chin. "You're not a fool," he murmurs. "Have you already forgotten what I told you before you left?"

"No, but you're biased because you're in love with me."

Cam stops breathing. The air goes electric. I was teasing, the way he always teases me about being in love with him, but the look on his face . . . oh God. How many times I wished Michael would stare at me with such reckless desire. Entire cities are burning to the ground behind Cam's eyes.

There's a split second of hesitation, then we move at the same time, with the same need, our hearts drumming the same crazy beat. Our mouths connect with the sense of two puzzle pieces slipping into place with perfect alignment.

The kiss is deep and hot but also impossibly tender. I'm being peeled open, layer by layer, unraveling to my most vulnerable core. I had only a sip of wine at the party, but I feel drunk. Disoriented. Like my entire world has tilted on its axis and I'm tumbling down a dark rabbit hole toward the center of the earth.

This wasn't supposed to happen. Not with him.

Without another word, Cam swings me up into his arms and heads toward the bedroom, his strides long and quick. When we get there, he lays me down on the bed, braces his hands on either side of my head, and looks into my eyes.

"I'm gonna get you naked. Then I'm gonna make love to you. Then you're gonna tell me if you want it sweet and tender again, or if you want it dirty and hard."

His voice is a whisper, thrilling in its intensity and control. There isn't a man alive who could make those words sound so threatening and so exciting all at once. I feel as if I'm standing on the edge of a cliff, looking down into an abyss, wind whipping my hair around my face.

I don't know what's on the other side of this moment. To be honest, I don't care.

He kisses me deeply, his hair tickling my cheeks. Then he moves his mouth to my neck, the scruff on his jaw scraping the sensitive skin under my ear, his lips warm and soft, his breath ragged like mine. I can tell he's trying to go slow, but his hands are shaking where they're pressed against my head.

I realize we've both wanted this too long to start with tenderness.

"Forget about making love to me, Cam," I say, my blood like fire in my veins. "Let's do it dirty and hard."

He breathes, "Thank God," and fists his hands into my hair, kissing me again like he'll die if he doesn't.

He makes a sound deep in the back of his throat, like an animal's growl. That wolf of his, coming out to play. It sends a weird thrill all the way through me, right down between my legs. I drag him on top of me by the loops in his jeans, desperate to feel his weight. My thighs open around his waist. He's already hard for me. I rock against that hardness, desperate like I've never been.

He's up in a whipcrack motion, staring down at me with black eyes. Crazy person eyes, filled with naked lust. He shucks off my shoes, tossing each one over his shoulder to the floor, then slides his open hands from my knees down the inside of my bare thighs, squeezing my flesh as he goes. Then before I can even register what he's doing, he's bent between my legs and pulled my panties aside.

I cry out in shock because his mouth—his hot, wonderful mouth—is *there*.

A shudder runs through my body. I'm aching everywhere. My skin is flushed and burning. "Cam. Oh God. Don't stop, that's amazing, that's—"

I break off with a porn star moan when he slides a finger inside me.

I'm cracking open. My rib cage feels hollowed out, like all my insides have been scraped away and there's only this, the feel of his tongue and the sounds he's making—chest-deep grunts that are sexy and dirty and hot, sounds like he can't get enough of the taste of me, like he's just as greedy for me as I am for him.

When my thighs start to tremble and my breathing is labored because I'm close, so close to where I want to go, Cam is suddenly gone, hovering over me.

His gaze on mine, he unbuttons his jeans and steps out of them, then drops his boxer briefs. I watch them slide down his legs and pool around his ankles, and I make a little involuntary sound of lust. He palms his jutting erection, watching my face.

I sit up, bat his hand out of the way, curl both my hands around his cock, and take it in my mouth.

His moan makes me feel like a goddess.

He digs his hands into my hair as I suckle him and fondle his balls with one hand while stroking his thick shaft with the other, feeling even more like a goddess when he curses under his breath.

"Bloody hell, that sweet fucking mouth," he whispers, flexing his hips. "I love that mouth. I love—"

He gasps when I take him as deep as I can down my throat.

Then I'm on my stomach, flipped over in a lightning-fast move. Cam drags my ass in the air with an arm wrapped under my waist, props me onto my knees, then flips my dress up, exposing my bottom. The next thing I feel is teeth sinking into my backside.

I suck in a surprised breath. My hands curl to fists in the blankets.

His warm breath feathering over my skin, Cam rasps, "Wanted to do that since the second I laid eyes on you, standin' at my door in that ugly green sweater, tellin' me to turn the music down, all curves and sass."

He bites me again, not hard enough to break the skin but hard enough to sting, and growls. I nearly faint. Adrenaline crashes through me. I can barely catch my breath.

He continues to bite me, sliding a hand between my legs to stroke me as he makes his way across one cheek to the other until my entire ass is stinging and I'm rocking against his big hand, panting into the sheets, dying.

I'm dying. He's going to kill me. He's pinching my clit and biting my ass and I'm in absolute heaven.

"I have to get this dress off." He pulls at my zipper, impatient, but I don't have time for that.

"Leave it on," I say, panting. "Just leave it on and fuck me."

I don't have to tell him twice. He yanks open a drawer in the bedside table. I hear crinkling and the rip of foil and open my eyes to enjoy the incredible pleasure of watching him roll a condom down the length of his big, glorious cock.

Then he's on his knees behind me, steadying himself with his hands on my hips. In another second, his erection nudges me, then stretches me open until I'm gasping.

He takes a big handful of my hair, wraps it around his wrist so my head tilts back, then thrusts his hips, driving inside me.

I cry out. He thrusts again. I moan at the feel of him, big and invading, his incredible heat all over me, inside me, the smell of his skin in my nose. Then he's fucking me with long, hard strokes, holding me in place for his pleasure with that one hand wrapped around my hip and my hair like a leash around his wrist.

He slaps my ass, hard. I laugh like a lunatic because I love it so much.

He knows. Of course he knows what I like. He starts to alternate slapping my ass with reaching around and fondling my engorged clit until I'm moaning and thrashing and completely out of my mind, bucking back into his every thrust, right on the razor's edge of orgasm.

He reaches up and pinches my rigid nipple right through the dress, and I convulse around him.

"Fuck," he whispers hoarsely. "You're coming. Oh fuck, Joellen—"

He cuts off with a groan as I come, everything inside me clenching and unclenching in fast, furious waves. *It's good, so good, oh God, so good.* I don't realize I've said that aloud until Cam agrees with me.

"I knew we'd be perfect together."

He flips me over onto my back but stays on his knees, pulling me up so my head and shoulders are on the pillow, but he's holding the rest of me up with his hands gripped under my ass. I brace my hands against the headboard as he starts to thrust into me this way, his breathing labored and his hair falling into his eyes, every muscle in his chest and abdomen tight and straining.

He's so beautiful it's like I'm having sex with a piece of art.

My body is squishy compared to his, but it doesn't matter. It's all in his eyes, which devour every inch of me like it's the first time they've glimpsed the sun.

He lifts one of my legs and props my ankle on his shoulder. Now he's as deep as he can go, and I'm making sounds I've never made before, animal sounds, urging him on. He turns his head and kisses my ankle, a gesture so sweet it sends a piercing pain like an arrow shot straight through my chest.

I squeeze shut my eyes, but I can't stop the inarticulate sound of distress that breaks from me. Even as I'm building toward another orgasm, I'm fighting a sudden onslaught of emotion, because I know that no matter how good it is, this can't go any further than tonight.

I reach out and grab his arms, pulling him down on top of me, then wrap my arms and legs around him and bury my face in his neck, inhaling his smell, trying to burn this moment into my memory. He shudders and softly groans. His thrusts grow faster. Harder. His breathing is as erratic as the beating of my heart.

"Lass," he gasps.

"Please," I whimper, because I'm right there, too.

Then we're over the edge together, stiffening and crying out, my body bowed beneath his, my head thrown back against the pillow. He's bucking, wild and out of control, digging his fingers into my scalp as he loses himself in my body, and the final shred of my denial unravels and breaks free.

I have feelings for Cameron McGregor.

God, this is really going to hurt.

THIRTY-TWO

It's late—or early. I don't know which. I'm snug in bed in the circle of Cam's arms, tracing my fingers over all the tattoos on his chest because I want to remember every detail about him after he's gone.

I'll need something to sustain me through the next fifty celibate years.

"I never asked you why you and Kellen switched apartments," I murmur. My limbs are heavy, and I'm sore in various places, thanks to Cam's remarkable stamina. We've had sex three times in the last two hours—twice in bed and once in the shower.

Cam trails his fingers up my spine and presses a kiss to my temple. "My coach thought a change of scenery would do me good."

I tilt my head and gaze up at him, smiling. "And did it?"

The smile he returns is soft and sweet. "Aye." He pauses for a moment, his smile fading. "And no."

I know what he means. We both hear the clock ticking down to zero in the background.

"What did you need a change of scenery for?"

After another pause, Cam sighs heavily. "My life had become . . . unmanageable."

The pregnant underage girl Michael mentioned immediately comes to mind. I'm loath to bring it up and ruin an otherwise beautiful moment, but if I've got only a few days to find out everything I can about Cameron McGregor, I'm doing it. "That teenager, you mean."

"Aye. Among other things. I was drinkin' way too much. Lashin' out at everyone. I've never been great at dealin' constructively with my anger, even after years of therapy."

"You were in therapy? For years?"

"I worked on my head as hard as I worked on my body. Can't say the effect was as successful, but yeah. Therapy. Seein' how badly my mum was mind fucked by life, I've always been into self-improvement. I also read a lot. Everything, really, biographies to history to politics. I didn't go to college—gettin' through secondary school with a learnin' disability was tough enough—but I do love to read."

He's all that he is, and *he loves books. Why, universe? Why give me this with someone who has a life on the other side of the world?* I snuggle closer to him, breathing in his wonderful, warm scent, swallowing around the lump in my throat. "You don't seem particularly angry to me, prancer."

He chuckles and nuzzles his nose into my hair. "Beauty tames the savage beast, I suppose."

My heart glows at hearing him call me Beauty, but I hate the thought of him being unhappy. My maternal instinct wants to hug him close to my chest and fight off the wolves for him, but another instinct tells me that his wolves are all on the inside, not out.

"Awkward segue alert."

His chest shakes with suppressed laughter. "Okay. Go."

"The lawsuit you're in, the one I overheard you talking with someone on the phone about. Is it related to the pregnant teenager?"

He nods. "She's suin' me for paternity."

When I gasp, he's quick to add, "I'm not the father, lass. I might not be a pillar of morality, but I know enough to steer clear of adolescents."

"I know. I believed you before when you told me it wasn't true. How old is she?"

"Sixteen."

"Oh my God! She's a child!"

His voice turns dry. "You wouldn't say that if you saw her picture. Or got a look inside her mind. She's a cunning little thing. Wants attention, knows how to get it."

"I think you'd better just tell me the story, because I'm cooking up some really scary scenarios in my mind right now, Cam."

He absentmindedly combs his fingers through my hair as he speaks. "The story, to put it in a nutshell, is that I'm a target. A big dumb bulls-eye. I've done myself no favors with the way I act—drunk and disorderly, my 'dating' history, so to speak. My barrister thinks it's a miracle I haven't seen more of these kinds of accusations." His laugh is chillingly dark. "Lucky me."

I wait, holding my breath, until he continues.

"I had a party at my house. I was always havin' parties. Havin' people around makes me feel better. Less . . . antsy. My house was always filled with people. Friends—if you could call them that—teammates, strangers, whoever."

I think of the strip poker party he had the first night we met, the anonymous girl he picked up in a bar, and shudder to think what would've happened if I lived on a different floor and we'd never met. He might have some random woman accusing him of fathering her unborn child here, too.

Maybe truthfully this time.

"One night over the summer, this guy brings his sister. She looks twenty, at least. Full makeup, high heels, the works. The party gets wild. By three a.m., I'm passed out on the lawn in the backyard. When I wake up in the mornin', the place is a wreck and everyone's gone except this girl, who I find cryin' in my kitchen, lookin' a mess. I ask her what's wrong, she says her brother left and she has no way home. So, idiot me,

I offer to drive her. And that's it. That's all I did: drove her home. The next week I got a visit from the police, who wanted to discuss how I'd like to plead to sexual coercion under the Sexual Offences Act."

I'm queasy. Maybe hearing this story wasn't such a good idea after all. "So she claimed the two of you had sex?"

"Aye. I was drunk, but I bloody well wasn't drunk enough to forget that. I never saw her after she first came in. So my legal team interviews everyone from the party, and it turns out no one can corroborate her bein' near me at any time. Because there was no physical evidence, either, and she had no witnesses to back up her story, the charges weren't filed. But by then the news had picked up the story. I was called everything from a child molester to a rapist."

He pauses to draw a breath. The tension in his body radiates off him in waves. "That kind of stink doesn't wash off."

"Oh, Cam. That's awful."

"That's not even the worst part. Two months later, she finds out she's pregnant and files a paternity suit against me."

"But all it would take would be a DNA test to prove you're not the father!"

"Aye. Which she won't submit to, claiming it can hurt the unborn child. So I'm stuck waitin' until she gives birth so we can get the bloody test done and prove I'm innocent. In the meantime, she's all over the news, cryin' about how I took advantage of her."

I'm furious on his behalf. "But that's not fair! She's lying!"

He sounds weary when he replies. "That's the price I have to pay for refusin' to settle the suit. Her barristers offered me a deal to keep her quiet, but I refused because that's blackmail. It'll all come out in the wash once the baby's born, but until then, it's a circus with me in the center ring."

"But can't you countersue her for defamation of character?"

He says gently, "If anyone's to blame for my character assassination, lass, it's me. And she's a child who's obviously messed up in the head. What good would it do in the end?"

This is all very depressing. "I wish there was something I could do to help. I hate that you're going through this."

He turns his face to my hair, inhaling deeply. "You've already helped, lass. You have no idea how much."

His voice is husky with emotion, deep and raw, and it brings the hot prick of tears to the back of my eyes. We lie quietly for a few moments, just breathing, until he starts to speak again.

"This is gonna sound so fucking weird."

"I'm already worried."

He draws a breath, then blurts, "You remind me of my mother."

"Speaking of awkward segues! I'll just be here trying not to be icked out by that, thanks. You couldn't wait to lay that gem on me until we weren't naked in bed?"

He chuckles. "I know. Sorry. What I mean is . . ." He struggles for a moment to find the right words. "How you're a natural caretaker. How you know how to make people feel good about themselves without tryin'. How you're always honest." His voice drops. "How you feel like home."

I close my eyes and breathe deeply in and out, which doesn't help my voice breaking when I say, "You're killing me here, prancer."

He pulls me tighter against him, hugging me hard with those muscle-bound arms. "Are we gonna talk about the elephant in the room?"

I know what he means, but I make a joke to avoid it, because if nothing else, I'm an expert at avoiding tough conversations and uncomfortable emotional moments with bad humor. "Do you have a name for that thing? Because I've secretly been calling it Godzilla."

"I'm not talkin' about my dick, lass, and you know it."

I scrunch down a few inches, hiding my face in his pecs. "Have I ever mentioned that you have beautiful breasts? Because you do. Man breasts are highly underrated."

Cam's deep sigh stirs my hair. "I have to go back to Scotland on the third."

He lets it hang there, a loaded gun pointed at our fledgling relationship, just trying out its shaky newborn legs. When I don't say anything, he adds, "Trainin' for the new season starts on the sixth or I'd stay longer—"

"No," I interrupt, my voice muffled against his skin. "You can't stay. You have to go back to your life."

And I have to figure out mine. What's left of it. *I wonder whether a job at McDonald's or Starbucks would be better suited to my skill set?*

His voice thick, Cam says, "Come with me."

My heart starts to pound frantically, leaving me breathless. I momentarily lose the power of speech, which is a good thing because my mental state at the moment could best be described as "standing out on a ledge."

"I'll buy you a ticket, one with an open-ended return date so you can stay as long as you want. Take some vacation time, see if you like Scotland . . . why're you shakin' your head?"

"You know it's impossible," I whisper, hating how weepy I sound. These kinds of moments call for the type of frontier-woman fortitude I don't have. I'm pretty sure I'll be wiping my snot from his chest any minute.

"Lass—"

"I'm thirty-six, Cam. You're *twenty-nine*. I've got neuroses older than you. You're a glamorous, famous person whose house is always filled with people and parties, and I'm a homebody who only socializes with my cat. You'll end up resenting me. I'll end up homesick, feeling like a burden. We both have pretty significant problems we have to fix in our lives, and using each other as crutches isn't going to do anything but create more messes."

After a long, tense moment, Cam says, "Wow. That was bloody depressin'. Try again. And this time keep it short and just say yes."

I groan and roll over onto my other side. If I thought that would work as a final punctuation on the conversation, Cam puts that idea to rest immediately by winding his arm around my waist and dragging me backward against him.

He puts his lips against my ear and speaks softly and slowly, like you would to a scared wild animal. Or someone really stupid.

"Number one, I don't give a fuck about our age difference. Neither should you. Number two, my house is always filled with people because I'm lonely, not because I love parties. Two B, my life isn't glamorous. Before I met you, it was a car goin' a hundred kilometers an hour straight toward a cliff. Number three, the only thing I'll ever resent about you is your relentless commitment to put yourself down. I don't have an answer to the possibility that you might get homesick, but I bloody sure *would* do my best to make sure you feel as at home in my home as you do here. And number fucking four, whatever problems we have in our lives would be made significantly better by bein' with the only person either one of us can trust.

"You're not a crutch to me, Joellen. You're a gift. If you don't want to come to Scotland because you just don't want to be with me, have the balls to say it, but don't feed me any more excuses. And stop applyin' your worst-case-scenario thinkin' to this thing between us—keep that negative bullshit in check."

There's a long, terrible silence in which I stare out the window at the flurries of snow and try my damnedest to keep myself together even though he just completely broke me apart.

Normally this is where I'd burst into tears and hurry home to stress eat. No—that's incorrect. *Normally* there's no universe where a smokin' hot pink-bathrobe-wearing famous athlete just screwed me silly and invited me to come live with him in Europe, but apparently this is my new normal, so I'm just going to have to suck it up and deal with it the best way I know how.

"I bet you probably only have, like, *vanilla* ice cream at your house, though."

Cam starts to laugh, softly at first, but then he gives over to it and collapses against the bed, shaking the mattress and both of us as the gales overtake him.

"Sheesh, prancer. You're crap with staying mad at someone, you know that?"

"No, lass." He drags me on top of him—manhandling me in that wonderful way he has that makes me feel tiny and feminine and grateful for his dedication to growing his muscles so large—and gazes up at me, smiling. "You're just too weird and wonderful to stay mad at for long."

He kisses me, his hands in my hair and a smile on his mouth. He tucks me in under his arm, and I listen to his breathing grow deeper and more even until I know he's asleep.

I lie next to him and breathe him in one last time, telling myself it's for the best if I slip out before he wakes so we can avoid the inevitable morning-after awkwardness.

Then I gather my dress and shoes from the floor and tiptoe out, closing the door softly behind me.

THIRTY-THREE

It's Christmas Eve, the third most depressing day of the year behind Christmas itself and Valentine's Day. This year is even worse than usual because not only does Michael Maddox still not love me, I couldn't care less because I've gone and fallen for yet *another* man I'll never have a future with.

I guess it's just my thing.

I'm lying in bed with Mr. Bingley, staring at the ceiling, feeling sorry for myself, when I hear a knock on the door. *His* knock. He must've just woken up, because it's still dark outside.

"I'm not going to answer it," I tell the cat, who gives me a disgusted look, which makes me defensive. "What're you being so judgy for?"

His expression says I know *exactly* what I've done wrong and I should be ashamed of myself. Now I feel worse because even a stupid cat is smarter than me.

Cam's knock comes louder and louder, until I hear his voice through the door. "I know you're in there. I don't care how long it takes, I'll be out here knockin' until you open up."

I sigh, give myself a pep talk that it'll be better to get it over with, and get out of bed. I shuffle to the front door with a blanket wrapped around me.

"Joellen!"

"I'm right here, prancer," I say through the door. "Don't wake up the building."

"Open up."

I rest my forehead against the door. "I can't. I'm too busy kicking myself."

"Are you fucking serious? Open the goddamn door."

He sounds mad. I look through the peephole only to find a pair of hazel eyes glaring at me.

"I can see your head, lass. We've already been over this."

I take a few deep calming breaths, then crack open the door. Cam pushes right through it, knocking me out of the way in the process. Halfway to the living room, he spins on his heel and glares at me in person.

"Tell me I'm wrong and you didn't sneak out without saying good-bye after we had sex four times and some intense, soul-baring afterglow. Tell me you just came over to feed the cat and were on your way back when I knocked."

I wince and wrap the blanket tighter around me. "Um."

He looks astonished, offended, and totally angry. "You fucking ghosted me."

"No, I didn't."

"Yes, you did!"

"No, ghosting is when you're dating someone and you break up with them and disappear from their life without any explanation. Me leaving earlier was just . . ." I struggle to find an appropriate word. "Expedient."

A flush creeps up his neck. His eyes glow with anger. *"Expedient?"*

"Practical, I mean."

That only makes him look angrier.

I pinch the bridge of my nose between my fingers. I'm feeling queasy and like I might be getting a migraine. "Cam. We already went over this. You're leaving in a few days. You live in another country. You have a life there, I have a life here."

"Really?" he says, his voice dripping sarcasm. "How's that life goin' for you, Joellen?"

Now he's not the only one who's mad. "Ouch, prancer."

"You're goddamn right, ouch. Now you know how I felt when I woke up alone. I'm surprised you didn't leave money on the dresser for services rendered."

I swallow around the sudden lump in my throat. "I'm sorry. I didn't mean for you to feel bad. It was just a mistake."

He reacts like I've kicked him in the stomach. He steps back, the blood draining from his face, his mouth open and his eyes wide.

"A *mistake?*"

I realize instantly that the real mistake was using that word, which was obviously an incredibly bad choice. "No—Cam, listen, I didn't mean it like that—"

"I know exactly how you meant it, lass," he says bitterly, blowing past me. He's out of my apartment, across the hall, and slamming his door before I even have a chance to get another word in edgewise.

I stand there for a long time, fighting the urge to run across the hall and throw myself into his arms, but eventually I give in to the inevitable reality of the situation and go back to bed, dragging the covers up over my head.

Mr. Bingley jumps down, wanting nothing to do with me.

I'm still in bed at five o'clock that afternoon when the phone rings. I pick it up with a dull "Hello?"

"Hi, honey! Merry Christmas!"

"Hey, Mom. Merry Christmas. Eve."

She laughs. It sounds like California: bright, beautiful, breezy. "I know I'm a day early, but we're going over to your sister's tomorrow morning and staying over. You know how crazy it gets over there with the kids. We probably won't get a chance to call."

I know she doesn't try to be mean, but it's times like this I have to bite my tongue from saying something bitchy like *You mean won't* make the time *to call.*

Jacqueline and her husband, Jack—don't get me started on that alliteration—have two-year-old twins. Their names also start with the letter *J*, because my sister's astrologer told her the energy would be good. You wouldn't think Satan could inhabit two bodies at one time, but boy, would you be wrong. The amount of projectile vomit and green snot those kids produce belongs in an exorcism movie. As do their screams, which could scour paint from the walls. I have no idea why my mother is so desperate to add more of the little monsters to our family, but she's of the opinion I won't truly be happy and fulfilled until I'm a mother.

Or a size two.

"Oh, we got your packages in the mail yesterday, sweetie! Thanks so much for that cute mohair scarf."

Cute is her code word for hideous. We enjoy sending each other gifts that we know the other one won't like, because mother-daughter relationships are minefields and murder scenes and a whole bunch of other super things like that.

"And thanks for the new Grumpy Cat calendar you sent me, Mom. Can't wait to get that sucker up on the wall and spend another year staring at his constipated face."

"That reminds me, honey—have you heard anything about your promotion?"

My stomach sinks because I know she'll freak out when she hears I'm going to be fired. But then, out of nowhere, I have a moment of pure epiphany. Another *fuck this shit* kind of clarity, only way bigger.

It really doesn't matter what my mother thinks about anything.

Wow, I had no idea how heavy that particular piece of baggage was until I dropped it.

"Yeah, bad news on that front," I say. "My boss—you remember Michael, the one I told you I was in love with years ago and you said he'd be perfect for Jacqueline?—turned out to be a major douche canoe and tried to feel me up in the ladies' room at the holiday party. Apparently that promotion was a kind of pay-to-play deal, and I wasn't playing. The office is closed until after New Year's because of the holidays, but I'm pretty sure I'll be fired first thing when I go back."

My mother squawks, *"What?"*

"Bummer, right? You might want to make up the spare bedroom for me. Oh, also? Cameron McGregor invited me to go back to Scotland with him. We're having some kind of confusing sexual relationship I'm really not emotionally qualified to handle, but I knew you'd be interested to know he's *incredible* in bed."

I hear a thud and wonder if I just killed my mother.

Christmas might not be so bad after all.

Only it is, because I spend it entirely alone, eating cold barbecue beans from a can I scrounged from the depths of a cupboard and drinking a bottle of cheap Syrah while staring morosely out my living room window with only a deaf, judgmental cat for company.

The irony isn't lost on me that I named him after my romantic "ideal" of a man. Mr. Bingley was everything Mr. Darcy wasn't: polite, charming, popular. Even after it turned out in the end that Darcy was more than just a brooding alpha-hole—that he was, in fact, a man of incredible character and depth—I always thought the Mr. Bingleys of the world were preferable, because who really wants to deal with all that smoldering machismo when you can have a light and fluffy marshmallow of a man?

An idiot, that's who.

December 26 dawns to a blizzard, which is convenient because it matches my mood. I decide to spend the next few days watching all the holiday movies I hate as punishment for a) wasting ten years loving the idea of Michael Maddox and b) ruining a perfectly good friendship with Cam by having wild, uninhibited sex with him, falling in love with him, and then immediately freaking out. I'm deep into my third rewatch of *It's a Wonderful Life* when the knock comes.

I freeze, a handful of microwave popcorn in my fist.

The knock comes again. It's Cam's knock, but it's different, because it somehow sounds somber.

I put aside the bowl of popcorn and go to the front door, my heart hammering like mad. When I open up, Cam is standing there in jeans and a T-shirt, looking as devastatingly sexy as ever.

We stare at each other. The first thing out of his mouth is, "I can't believe you didn't wish me a merry Christmas, you dick."

"Well, we sort of weren't talking, I thought."

He scowls at me, a lock of hair flopping attractively into his eyes. This goes on for a while, until he sighs and curses under his breath. Then he reaches into the front pocket of his jeans and produces a key. He thrusts it at me. "Here. In case you want to make any more mistakes before I leave."

Filled with trepidation, I look at the key, which is apparently to Kellen's apartment door. *Oh God. Oh no. Don't do it. Don't make this any worse than it already is.*

But of course I take it. I'm stupid, but I'm not insane.

We look at each other in uncomfortable silence for a few moments longer, until Cam says, "Okay. So. See you around. Or not."

He spins around and stalks back to his apartment, slamming the door just so I know that even though he's inviting me to come over whenever I want for more mind-blowing sex, he's still mad.

I stare at the key in my hand, wondering how long it'll take before I use it.

I last an entire *day*, which I think is pretty good. Actually, it's a few hours more than a day, because when I find myself unlocking Cam's apartment door, it's a quarter after nine o'clock the next night.

All the lights are out except for a small reading lamp burning dimly in the living room. For a moment I wonder if he's not home, but then he comes out of the bedroom and heads right toward me, looking angry and scary and hot.

He picks me up in his arms like it's the most natural thing in the world and heads back into the bedroom.

Staring at his profile, I whisper, "Why are you naked?"

"I sleep naked."

"You were asleep?"

"No. Now shut up."

"Are you still mad at me?"

"Yes. Now *shut up.*"

I shut up. He tosses me onto the bed like luggage. I bounce, breathless, and try to sit up, but he isn't having any of my smart ideas. He pushes me down and kisses me, hard, a knee wedged between my legs and his fingers twisted in my hair.

I melt like butter into the mattress.

"I'm kickin' you out after," he says, breathing raggedly and pushing my skirt up my thighs. He drags my panties down my legs. "And don't you *dare* ask me any personal questions."

Oh, he's so mad at me. He's furious. *God, that's a turn-on.*

He doesn't bother taking off my shirt and bra or getting me ready with foreplay—not that I need it, since I drenched my underwear the minute I saw him—he simply sheathes his erection in a condom and angrily shoves it inside me.

I arch and moan and fall in love with him a little bit more.

He fucks me hard. Like he's trying to prove a point. I clamp my fingers into his biceps and wrap my legs around his back and hold on for the ride. When I'm moaning and panting and just about there, he slows, growls "not yet," and kisses my throat.

"Please, Cam," I whimper, grinding my pelvis against his, desperate for release.

Then I'm on top of him, flipped around and straddling his face, manhandled into the position he wants me, his hard cock jutting inches from my mouth.

He commands, "Suck," and buries his face between my legs.

I gasp and buck, shocked when his tongue plunges deep inside me. He spreads both hands over my bottom and makes a meal of me, licking and sucking until I can't catch my breath.

I get a warning smack on my ass when I leave him unattended too long.

I wrap my hand around his shaft but stop before taking him into my mouth. I don't fancy a mouthful of latex, thank you, so I roll the condom up his length and toss it, then take the engorged crown of his cock between my lips.

He sucks in a breath, then lets it out as a moan that vibrates all the way through me. My eyes literally roll back into my head. I lick his erection from base to tip, tonguing over the veins and thrilling when he throbs in my hands. Then I start a rhythm, sucking and stroking, faster and faster, his tongue working between my legs until I think I'll pass out.

Cam digs a hand into my hair and pulls, making his cock pop out of my mouth. "Wait," he pants, gasping for air. "Fuck. *Wait.*"

We're frozen like that for several moments, until he regains control of himself. Then he presses the gentlest kiss right onto my clit. When I shudder, he laughs, a dark, satisfied sound that thrills me like nothing I've ever known. But I'm not about to be outdone, so I swirl my tongue around the head of his cock and am rewarded by a groan that could win a porn Oscar.

Then it becomes a game of who comes first. Also known as a win-win.

We go back and forth, slowly, taking turns. First he licks and suckles me for a moment, then stops as I lick and suckle him. When I cheat and begin to languidly stroke his balls, he cheats by slipping a finger under my bra and tweaking my throbbing nipple. I take him down my throat, all the way to his base, and he slides two fingers inside me and circles them.

When my entire body is shaking and I'm sweating and cross-eyed, I break first.

"I need to come, Cam."

"So come." He goes back to licking.

"Come with me."

"Like this, or . . . ?"

I'm glad he asked, because suddenly I'm needing eye contact. This game is incredibly hot, but I'm craving more—I'm craving *him*. I want to go over the edge looking into his eyes.

Damn. I knew I was gonna regret this.

I climb off him, get another condom from the bedside table, and get him all wrapped up. Feeling satisfied with my technique, I smile at his erection.

Cam grabs my arms and flips me over so I'm on my back, looking up at him. Easing between my legs, he says gruffly, "Is this what you wanted?"

I nod, biting my lip against a moan. He slides inside me, and God, it's good.

But he doesn't go fast and hard again. He goes achingly slow, cupping my bottom in one hand, cradling my head in the other, propped up on an elbow and staring down into my eyes.

Swamped with emotion, I inhale a hitching breath. He smiles, but it's achingly sad.

"Go ahead, luv," he murmurs. "Tell me it doesn't matter. Tell me it's all a mistake."

I have to turn my face away because I don't want him to see the tears gathering in my eyes. When I finally do go over the edge, he's right there with me, groaning my name and twitching inside me, carving his name into my heart the way Michael never did.

So this is love. Man, it's even worse than Christmas.

THIRTY-FOUR

The mechanics of love go something like this:
Birdsong in the air and your heart in his kiss,
Eyes meet, breath catches, a sparkle of lust
A pulse of pure joy and an aching you must
Pursue against logic; that small voice in your mind
Warns of goblins and trapdoors and things you
    might find
Your beloved will do that will irk and grow boring
Like farting and lateness and that god-awful
    snoring.
But your heart insists on its impossible dream
Until one day you wake to find a terrible scream
Trapped in your throat with nowhere to go
And you think back on that time which seems
    so long ago
When your love was a bird, flying high on the
    wing
Not this dry little crust of a shriveled-up thing.

"Well, that's one for the Romance Hall of Fame," I say aloud, examining with alarm the poem I've just completed. It's not even a proper sonnet, just a bunch of depressing rhyming verses that could be handed out as warnings to couples in premarriage counseling. *Here, see what you have to look forward to? Do you really want to sign up for this?*

I scratch a big *X* through the whole thing and slam my sonnet book closed.

It's January 2, the day after New Year's. Tomorrow I go back to work to get fired for being the office slut, which is really unfair considering when it came time to earn my title, I opted out. Only it didn't look like I did, which is all that matters.

Also tomorrow, Cam leaves for Scotland. Every night since he gave me the key, I've been going over to his place for some hot, angry sex and leaving feeling a little worse than the day before.

We're not talking, except to discuss which position we should switch to next. We're not working out together. We're not having dinner together. We've been reduced to the worst of all possible worlds—fuck buddies, without the buddies part.

The sex is incredible, but I really miss my friend. I miss laughing with him. I miss everything.

It's my fault. I know it's all my fault. I slipped and fell on his magical dick and ruined everything.

I'm too depressed to even look through the help wanted ads. Nobody ever finds a job like that, anyway. I spend a number of hours dejectedly browsing through online recruitment sites but inevitably end up opening a bottle of wine and attempting to drown my sorrows. Spoiler: it doesn't work.

At four o'clock in the afternoon, I'm on my third glass of wine when the phone rings. I don't answer it because it's either my mother . . . or it's my mother. Michael hasn't tried to contact me at all. No emailed apology, no "Oops, I was drunk" text, no nothing.

I'll admit it: that hurts. I mean, it *twinges*. It doesn't feel anything like what I feel when I let myself dwell on what will happen to me when Cam is gone and I'm forced to admit my life is a giant stinking poop emoji without him.

I know I'll eventually find another job. But there's not a chance in hell I'll ever find someone else like Cameron McGregor. I just hope it's a few years before I pick up the paper and see a smiling picture of him and his beautiful wife and their perfect babies, because I need a little time between now and then to convince myself I'm not really in love with him.

Like, ten, twenty years.

A few moments after the phone stops ringing, the flashing red light on the machine tells me I have a voice mail. With nothing better to do, I decide to find out who it is.

"Joellen, this is Portia." A delicate throat clearing, then she begins anew. "From Maddox Publishing. I wanted to wait until after Christmas to call. As you know, ah, the staff will all be returning to work tomorrow." Long, ominous pause. "Please meet us in the boardroom as soon as you come in."

Us? The boardroom? Well, I suppose that's as good a place as any to get canned after ten years of dogged loyalty. It has the best view. Though I'm righteously furious I'll be getting fired for something I didn't do, I've been around long enough to know how these things go.

Men are never punished as severely as women for breaking the rules, because men made all the rules in the first place.

I do have one ace in the hole, though. If I don't get a decent severance package and a reference letter, I'll sue for wrongful termination. Sure, no one will believe me and I'll still be out of a job, but a lawsuit might make Michael Maddox think twice about shoving his hand up some other poor sap's holiday dress that she couldn't really afford.

I don't understand why Portia didn't just fire me over voice mail, but I've got personal things at my desk I want to pick up, so I've got to go back in anyway.

But then things take a turn toward the unthinkable when I unlock Cam's door later that night and he's already gone. I know this because he left an envelope for me on the kitchen counter marked with my name. Inside is a note:

I'm shit with good-byes and we're not talking anyway, so I'm skipping that part and staying at a hotel tonight.

My offer was serious. It still is. My door will always be open for you.

Yours until the sun flames out and all life on earth is extinguished,

Prancer

Included with the note is a first-class ticket to Scotland.

I sit right down on the kitchen floor and cry until I'm sobbing like a baby, curled up into a ball with the note clenched in my sweaty fist.

In the morning, I'm a zombie. Or might as well be, for all intents and purposes. My insides are all mush. My brain has rotted. I can't think, I can't eat anything, and I certainly won't be able to string a coherent sentence together in my defense when I get into work.

Cam's gone. He's really *gone*. I feel dead but also like I've been hollowed out by knives, lit on fire, and tossed into a vat of acid. How do people survive this?

I share the elevator up to the thirty-third floor with Denny, who must be spooked by my appearance because he's quiet as a kitchen mouse. All I get is a tepid, "Morning." Which suits me fine, because in my current state of mind, I'm liable to commit murder if confronted with a fart joke.

The cubicle field is exactly the same yet looks completely different. *How did I sit at that desk for ten years of my life? How did I look at those fuzzy gray walls? How did I waste so much time pedaling as fast as I could on a bike that didn't have wheels?*

I head to the boardroom straight off the bat because there's no sense in delaying the inevitable. When I push open the heavy oak door, I'm surprised to find the room full of people.

Everyone stops what they're doing and turns to look at me.

Ruth from HR is here, of course. So is Portia, looking unfairly pretty in a kelly-green dress. Witches shouldn't have such a lovely glow. Also in attendance are Michael's father, the COO, a few other board members I recognize, and a few guys with thick glasses and faces like slabs of meat who look suspiciously like attorneys.

"Joellen." Portia steps forward and gestures toward the chair nearest me. "Thank you for coming. Please, have a seat."

This is when I start to get nervous. All these eyeballs, everyone so serious . . . am I about to be accused of a crime?

I don't sit so much as collapse into the chair. Then I wait.

It's Ruth who speaks first. "These gentlemen are the firm's attorneys."

I assumed I'd be scared to hear it confirmed, but instead I'm filled with a sudden, blistering fury, so hot I'm momentarily struck dumb. Then I find my tongue and let them have it.

"So it's going to be strong-arm tactics and intimidation right off the bat, huh? Nobody even wants to hear *my* side of the story? Nobody's interested in what really happened—you're just going to pin this all on me and throw me out like garbage after ten years of dedicated service?" My voice rises as my anger picks up steam. "After I've busted my ass and played by the rules and given you everything I've got, *I'm* the one getting punished?"

I stand abruptly, knocking the chair back, my cheeks blazing. Around the board table, people begin to look alarmed.

But I don't care. Today is the worst day of my life. Cam is gone, and I *do not* feel like being messed with.

"I've missed one day of work in the past decade. *One!* And that was only because I had to get some of my lady parts chopped up and taken out, which isn't a walk in the park, I'll have you know! I cramped like a mofo and bled out clots the size of important organs for three weeks after that, sitting right out there in that chair!"

One of the attorneys turns faintly green, and the other coughs into his hand.

Ruth says gently, "Joellen."

"No, I'm not finished! I never did *anything* with Michael except be dazzled by all his sparkly bullshit"—I make frantic, sarcastic jazz hands in the air—"gobble up all his phony-baloney lines, and share a few stupid phone conversations that lasted all of about five minutes! I never even kissed him! In spite of what you *think* you saw, Portia"—I swing around and glare at her, causing her to lift her perfectly sculpted brows—"I was trying to fight him off at the holiday party!"

I huff out a breath, flustered and sweaty, taking no small satisfaction in all the looks of horror I'm getting. *That's right, assholes. I am woman, hear me roar!*

"We know," says Ruth.

I blink at her, convinced I'm hearing her wrong. In the following silence, you could hear a pin drop. "Uh . . . what?"

"I was in one of the stalls in the ladies' room that night, Joellen. I heard everything."

For some reason, the room is rising. Then I realize, no, that's not the room rising, that's me sinking back into the chair because my legs are no longer interested in the work of holding my gobsmacked self up.

Portia takes charge. "We had an emergency board meeting after Ruth disclosed what she overheard in the restroom that evening, Joellen.

Obviously I can't disclose the specifics of that meeting, but what I can tell you is that Michael has been removed as chief executive officer of this firm. He will not be returning."

I breathe, "But . . . I don't . . . understand."

Michael's father—a man with gunmetal-gray eyes and an imposing air who I've interacted with only briefly at holiday parties and the random company picnic—says brusquely, "My father started this company. I'll be damned if my son is going to end it."

When the two attorneys shoot him agitated looks, several things dawn on me at once. I think of Maria, the copy editor who left suddenly before her promotion was announced, leaving a spot open for me, and of how Portia has hovered over me for years, watching Michael and me like a hawk, and not because she was in love with him.

And of Sue Wong, youngest associate editor in the history of Maddox Publishing. Pretty, vivacious, ambitious Sue.

"Wait. I'm not the first one he's done this to, am I?"

Sensing his cue, one of the attorneys stands. "Ms. Bixby, I have some documents we'd like you to sign—"

"Ha!" My barked laugh stops the attorney cold. "Yeah, I bet you do, pal! Good luck with that!"

"Your new position as associate editor has been approved by the board, Joellen," says Portia calmly. "All you have to do is sign the paperwork."

I look around the table, and I have to laugh again. "Dudes. I know I'm not the sharpest tool in the shed, but I'm not signing anything without having my attorney review it." My nonexistent attorney, I fail to add, but this is hardly the time for full disclosure. "And if you don't want me to sue *all* your asses to kingdom come"—I make an unnecessarily dramatic gesture, encompassing everyone in the room, the building, and most of the state—"you're going to leave me alone with Portia now so we can talk."

I level Portia with the same cold look she's been giving me for years.

"Unfortunately, that's not possible," starts attorney number one, but Portia stops him.

"Give us five minutes, gentlemen." She sweeps her cool blue gaze around the table. "Ruth. We'll be fine. Please."

The way they all shuffle nervously out the door looks like they're off to the firing squad. When we're alone and the door has closed behind the last person, Portia and I engage in a staring duel.

Of course I break first. The woman could work for the gestapo.

"Why have you always been such a bitch to me?"

She wasn't expecting that. I can tell because she says, "I wasn't expecting that."

"We'll get to the Michael stuff in a sec. But it's always really both-ered me that you were so mean to me. I could never figure out why."

She glances down at her lap, smooths a hand over her perfectly smooth hair, does that prune imitation with her mouth. Then she sighs and meets my gaze. "Because you remind me so much of myself, and I hate it."

My jaw unhinges and lands on the table. "Me? I remind you of *you*? Are you nuts? We're polar opposites!"

She makes a queenly, dismissive gesture with her hand. "How I *used* to be, before I decided to stop letting life kick me in the teeth and grow some balls." A ghost of a smile lifts her lips. "So to speak."

When I just stare at her with my mouth open like a gaping idiot, she looks at the ceiling and shakes her head. "I always hoped one day you'd have enough of me clapping at you and clap back. And you did, eventually. After I'd been through the entire dictionary of names that start with the letter *J*."

I'm floored. "Portia, that's just . . . diabolical."

She laughs at my horrified face. "I had no idea you'd have so much patience, or I would've sat you down ten years ago and told you to stop being so accommodating." Her smile fades. "Being nice is the worst thing a woman can be. Nice means you have to swallow your own feelings and focus on everyone else's. Nice means you don't speak up when you're wronged. Nice means being a people pleaser and a conciliator and worrying yourself to death over others' opinions. Nice means never getting what you really want."

"So we're all just supposed to walk around being giant bitches?"

She lifts a shoulder. "That's one way to do it. At least you'll get respect. But what I really mean is that when you're focused on being nice, you won't tell a truth that needs telling, because the worst thing a nice girl could ever do is hurt someone's feelings. A better thing to focus on is being real."

"Real," I repeat doubtfully.

"Authentic. Genuine. Live your truth. Let others live theirs. Don't kiss anyone's ass, but don't be an asshole, either. It's very simple."

The air whispering through the vents on the walls seems loud in the following silence. I say, "That was interesting. Also weird. I'm not sure how to respond."

Portia smiles a big toothy smile like I've never seen on her face. "That's *exactly* what I mean!"

"Okay, now you've totally lost me."

"Old Joellen would've found some nice, nonoffensive reply. Instead, you were real. Congratulations, there's hope for you yet. I was also impressed by your little speech when you came in. Very real. Strong, angry, impressive. Good for you."

"I feel like I might be dreaming all this right now? Like I'm in a hospital bed somewhere, dopey on morphine and hooked up to a bunch of tubes?"

Portia does the queenly hand wave again and gets down to business, apparently finished with the life lessons portion of the meeting. "The associate editor position is yours if you want it. You will, however, have to sign a nondisclosure agreement and a document releasing the firm from any future claim of sexual or emotional harassment arising from this incident with Michael."

She pierces me with her iceberg eyes. "You won't be able to speak about the incident in the ladies' room or your personal relationship with Michael, or publicly disparage Maddox Publishing in any way. If you do, you'll be terminated, and the firm will pursue all available legal remedies against you."

I blink. "Wow. And here I thought we were bonding."

More gently, Portia says, "Michael won't be back to the office, so you won't have to deal with him again. On a personal note, I'd like to apologize to you." She clears her throat, looking uncomfortable. "I saw this coming. There have been other incidents. It's one of the reasons he was removed so quickly. I'm putting myself at legal risk by telling you that, but I think it's important you know that what happened is in no way your fault."

I'm actually touched by this confession. Coming from her, it means a lot. "Thank you, Portia. That's very civil of you."

Then there's an awkward silence. It lasts until I finally say, "Okay, I'm going to be real now. This has been a lot to digest. I spent the last ten days thinking I was out of a job, and now I've got the promotion I always wanted. I've spent the last ten years thinking I was in love with a guy who, it turns out, is a prick. I've spent the last month living across the hall from a man who dresses like he's auditioning for the circus, has an ego the size of the earth's atmosphere, and screws like a champ."

I look at her, wide eyed. "Sorry, that last part was probably a little too much reality."

Her smile is tranquil. "Do go on. I'm enjoying this."

"I'm sure you don't want to hear about, you know, the sex stuff, though."

She furrows her brows. "Why ever not? I assume you're talking about the big rugged thing who strutted around like a rooster and had all the girls in an estrogen frenzy? He was quite the stud."

"Well, yeah, but . . ." *This is awkward. Okay, just be real. She told you to be real.* "I mean, it's not like that's your cup of tea."

The furrow between her brows grows deeper. "I might seem cold to you, Joellen, but I can assure you, a man like that is *every* woman's cup of tea."

"Even a lesbian's?"

She stares at me for a while, blinking, then says, "It's quite ignorant to assume a strong, no-nonsense, unmarried woman must be a lesbian. That's really antiquated thinking."

"No, I don't think that—Michael told me you were gay. He said your girlfriend was on the board of some charity with his wife."

I'm startled when she bursts into laughter.

"Michael told you I was *gay*? Oh, that's funny. No, Joellen, I'm not a lesbian. I just wasn't interested in Michael, which was a novel experience for him. He's a petty little liar. It just goes to show how small he is that he thinks calling me a lesbian is getting revenge. Idiot."

Overcome with shame at how naïve I was, I prop my head in my hands and groan. "He wasn't even really getting divorced, was he?"

"No. He'll never divorce that dimwitted wife of his. She lets him do whatever he wants. Although now that he's out of a job, she might divorce him."

After a moment, she sighs. "Just sign the papers and put this behind you, Joellen. You deserve the promotion. You've worked hard. Don't let this opportunity pass by because of the way it came about. That would be a mistake."

Go ahead, luv. Tell me it's all a mistake.

I hear Cam's words in my head, and suddenly I'm breathless with pain. What am I doing? What am I *doing*?

I stand abruptly. Portia looks up at me, startled.

I say, "Oh shit."

"What's wrong?"

Everything is coming at me at once. All the memories, all the emotions, all the things I wish I would have said but didn't. My heart thundering, I close my eyes and inhale a deep breath.

What. The. Fuck. Am. I. Doing?

You already know, dummy.

Thank God one of my inner voices has sense.

"Portia, you'll have to excuse me. I've got to go home and pack."

She rises, looking confused. "Pack? What are you talking about? Where are you going?"

I turn and run from the room, hollering over my shoulder, "Scotland!"

THIRTY-FIVE

By the time the taxi drops me off in front of my apartment building, I've nearly wet myself in panic.

The flight leaves in an hour. One hour. A span of sixty minutes to throw a suitcase together, get Mr. Bingley in his carrier with all his stuff, and get to the airport before boarding ends and no more passengers are allowed on the plane. Which is usually about fifteen minutes before the flight leaves, so I've really got only about forty-five minutes.

Which means I'm going to be forced into one of those terrible, cliché romance movie endings where the hero finally realizes his love for the heroine and rushes to the airport in a car with all his friends, fighting crawling traffic and unnecessary street construction, until he arrives at the very last second before the plane takes off and declares his love, and all the friends cheer and get weepy, and then there's a nice montage of romantic reunions in airports while the credits roll.

Except instead of a carload of my friends it'll just be Mr. Bingley.

The elevator ride takes a thousand years. When it reaches my floor, I burst out of it and run smack into Mrs. Dinwiddle. We collide with an audible "Oof!" and go spinning in opposite directions. Even at eighty-something, in heels, she has better coordination than me. She winds up leaning glamorously against the hallway wall, while I end up on my ass on the carpet.

I leap to my feet, shouting, "Mrs. Dinwiddle I'm so sorry I hope you're not hurt I have to go pack I'm leaving right now for Scotland I'm not letting Cam get away!"

I turn around and tear down the hallway without waiting for a response. My hands are so sweaty and shaky it takes about ten tries before I fit the key in the lock, but then the door swings open and I lurch inside, cursing like a drunken sailor.

I sprint to the bedroom, drag the one suitcase I own out of the closet, toss it onto the bed, then start ripping clothes off hangers and hurling them into the suitcase with no regard for what they are or if anything matches. The ugly green coat my mother gave me when I moved to New York goes in, but then I throw it out because I really hate that thing.

Mr. Bingley dozes peacefully between the pillows, unaware of the tornado occurring right in front of his face.

From the open front door, Mrs. Dinwiddle calls, "Ducky? Yoo-hoo!"

"I can't talk right now Mrs. Dinwiddle I'm having a mental breakdown and I have to be at the airport in like ten seconds Cam's flight is leaving can you please pick up my mail for me while I'm gone?"

Everything comes out in one breathless rush as I storm back and forth from the closet to the bathroom to the suitcase, scooping up tampons and toothpaste and shoes and underwear and throwing it all onto the growing mass on the bed. Mrs. Dinwiddle appears at my bedroom door, looking amused.

"So he finally convinced you, did he?"

Something in her expression or her tone makes me stop and look at her. "Convinced me to do what?"

"Fall in love with him."

When I stare at her blankly, she rolls her eyes. "What on *earth* did you think he was doing all this time, Ducky? Going around without *shirts* and offering to teach you how to *kiss* and having you make him *dinner* so he had an excuse to spend time with you?"

I make an unattractive honking sound, my eyes bugging out of my head.

"Oh *yes*, I know all *about* it," she says, very smug. "He was *smitten* with you from the *first*. It was so romantic, I just *had* to help him, my dear!"

"Help?" I repeat, my voice strangled.

"Well," she says regretfully, "you really are quite *hopeless* with men, Ducky."

I decide I'll keel over dead later. Right now, I've got to get my hopeless ass to the airport. I start the packing rampage again.

"Oh! Before I *forget*." Mrs. Dinwiddle removes a small box from the pocket of her lounging robe and places it right on top of the mountain of clothes.

I stare at it like it might be full of anthrax. "What is that?"

"Your Christmas gift."

"Oh, that's so sweet, Mrs. Dinwiddle. You shouldn't have."

"I *didn't*, my dear."

When I blink at her, she sighs, a great gusting sigh that manages to sound affectionate and disgusted and theatrical all at once. "It's from *Cameron*. He gave it to me before he *left* to give to *you*."

I put a hand over my heart, because in addition to pounding it's now painfully twisting, like a rabid squirrel caught inside my ribs. With shaking hands, I open the box.

It's a pair of exquisite emerald earrings, glittering up at me from a bed of black velvet.

"The exact color of your eyes, he said they were." Mrs. Dinwiddle is gazing at the earrings, misty eyed. "He bought them the same day you bought your party dress."

"The manager," I whisper, my eyes swimming with water. "He asked to speak to the manager. I thought he was going to complain about the paparazzi who took our picture, but he . . . bought . . . these . . ."

I'm gasping for air, drowning in emotion, unable to continue because what I'm feeling is so big. Somehow the feeling morphs and swells until it sounds like music. Loud, strangely irritating music.

Rap music?

With wide eyes, I gaze at Mrs. Dinwiddle. "Can you hear that?"

She looks insulted. "I'm not *deaf,* my dear! Of course I can hear it!"

The box of earrings clenched in my fist, I move slowly past Mrs. Dinwiddle into the living room. My apartment door is still open, like I left it, and from the hallway comes the distinct thump of bass, overlaid with truly awful lyrics sung by a man who sounds as if smoking crack and swallowing razor blades are his favorite hobbies.

> Got yo BACK, muthafucka
> I be WITH ya, muthafucka
> We be gangstas, muthafucka, for LIFE!

In a daze, I cross the hallway and try Kellen's apartment door. It's locked. I knock, but there's no answer, so I go back inside my apartment and get the key Cam gave me, which I've been keeping in a little dish on the kitchen counter.

It turns in the lock, the knob twists in my hand, and the door swings open. And there he is, standing right inside like he's been waiting for me. Like he's been waiting for me this entire time.

He's barefoot and barechested, of course, wearing only a kilt and his signature grin. He says, "Can I help you, lass?"

Cannae help ye, lass?

That's the first thing he ever said to me. I remember what I thought, standing exactly where I am now, staring at this beautiful mountain of a man. My mountain. My prancer. The man who made me believe in miracles, and in myself.

Dear God, he's a Scotsman. A huge, half-naked Scotsman in a kilt. Smiling at me like he knows all my secrets, what color my panties are, and that I'm curious what it would be like to have a man pull my hair during sex.

My voice raw and shaking with emotion, I say, "I was just wondering what the difference is between a kilt and a skirt."

Those hazel eyes blazing, he steps forward, takes my wrist, and pulls me against him. Into my ear, he whispers, "What you wear underneath. Ask me what I'm wearin' underneath."

I wind my arms around his shoulders, hug him as tightly as I can, and smile. "I feel like this is a trick to get me to look at your junk."

"Aye," says Cam. He swings me up into his arms. "It is." Over my shoulder, he tips his chin up at Mrs. Dinwiddle, who's watching us from my doorway, vigorously fanning herself with her silk Chinese fan.

Cam kicks the door shut with his foot and heads toward the bedroom. I kiss him all over his face and neck, thrilled and disbelieving that he's here. He's *here.* "You're supposed to be on a flight to Scotland, prancer."

"*We're* supposed to be on a flight to Scotland, lass."

He takes us down to the bed, and I'm still kissing him, holding his face, ignoring the water leaking from the corners of my eyes, because I feel like I'm flying. "I was just packing, I was coming to meet you, I went into work and realized I'm an idiot and I didn't want to be without you, so I rushed home and then Mrs. Dinwiddle told me everything—you're in cahoots with Mrs. Dinwiddle!—but I was rushing to pack and then I heard your stupid music, and oh—"

He stops my breathless babbling with a kiss—deep, hot, and hungry. When we finally come up for air, we're both breathing hard.

His voice is low and gruff when he says, "I told my coach I needed another week to get the woman I love to fall in love with me."

"Oh." *The woman I love.* I feel the beat of my heart in every part of my body. "What did he say?"

"That I was a bloody idiot and if I wasn't back in two days, I was off the team."

He kisses me again, and I'm melting, but I'm also panicking because Cam can't get kicked off his team due to me. "Wait!" I push him away. We stare at each other, nose to nose. "I got the promotion. They fired Michael. Portia isn't a lesbian."

He crinkles his forehead.

"Never mind. Listen—I have a very serious question to ask you. Our entire relationship could hinge on how you answer."

Deeper forehead crinkles. "So no pressure, then. Shoot."

Looking deep into his beautiful hazel eyes, I ask solemnly, "What flavors of ice cream do you have at your house?"

His eyes do this crazy thing where they soften but somehow also get hotter, and they do it now, burning me up with everything he's feeling, all that Mountain Man love.

"I have *all* the flavors, lass," he says, chuckling. "This is Cameron McGregor we're talkin' about. I've got every goddamn flavor you need."

He kisses me to prove it, his mouth declaring his love without words, his body hot and hard over mine.

"We're going to miss the flight," I whisper, arching as he moves his mouth to my neck.

"What about your job?" His hands are opening the buttons on my blouse, and his lips are following.

"I'm in a good bargaining position to get them to let me work from home."

When he lifts his head and looks at me, cocking an eyebrow, I grin at him. "I'll tell you about it later. Now are we going to try to catch this flight or what?"

His grin comes on slow and sexy. "No, lass. We'll get the next one. We've got more important things to do right now."

And oh, do we. We've got so much important stuff to do, we don't catch a flight out until late the next day.

EPILOGUE

Top Ten Reasons Why Rugby Doesn't Suck

1. Incredibly fit men wearing extremely short shorts and extremely tight shirts who bash into each other constantly while getting covered in mud and looking sexy as hell. It's like a giant violent orgy.

2. Incredibly fit men in tight clothing who take every opportunity to grab each other's asses and hug. Shameless bromances abound, the players adorably unselfconscious about their devotion to their teammates. Their extreme machismo apparently has ample room for spontaneous displays of straight-dude affection and brotherly love, all while wearing shorts so tiny and revealing they might as well be Hanes. It's a beautiful thing.

3. Beards.

4. Tattoos.

5.   Muscles. Muscles for *daaaaays*.

6.   This macho war dance called the *haka* performed before the start of the match by certain teams. It's a crazy tribal thing filled with grunts, chants, and a lot of coordinated stomping that works the crowd into a frenzy. Because incredibly fit men in tight clothing, *dancing*.

7.   No cheerleaders.

8.   The fans. Rugby fans are the friendliest, most passionate people in the world. And the most well mannered. I've never sat in a stadium with a huge crowd who acts polite and formal, like they're awaiting a personal audience with the Queen. Cam keeps telling me rugby is a gentleman's game, and he's right. (Except for the giant violent orgies.)

9.   Cameron McGregor, captain of Scotland's beloved Red Devils, the single most virile, handsome, gifted, sexy, smart, kind, and talented beast of a man who ever lived.

10.   See number nine.

"What're you up to, Miss Snufflebottom?"

That low sexy voice comes from the bed behind me, where I left Cam sleeping to get up and make my list. I glance over my shoulder and find him propped up on an elbow, the sheets pooled around his waist, his hair messy, his tattooed chest bare, those hazel eyes warm with desire and unmistakable love.

Pinch me. This is *way* better than any fairy tale.

"Making a list. Though I was about to start on your Valentine's Day present."

"Oh?" He hungrily eyes my nightie, a sheer black wisp of a thing he bought me the first week I moved to Scotland. It was followed by another, and another, until I had so many I had to take over a section of his closet to house them all.

Not that he complained. I think he'd gladly give up all his closet space if it involved my lingerie.

"Does this present include a striptease and strategically placed whipped cream?"

I was thinking more along the lines of a sonnet, but he looks too eager to disappoint. So I send him a Mona Lisa smile, rise from the chair, and stretch my arms overhead. Cam's eyes follow my every move, sharp as a hawk's. "It might. Depends on how soon you say you'll take me to see Nanny O'Shea again. I adore that woman."

Cam instantly pronounces, "As soon as you want."

I laugh, delighted as always by the ease at which he'll agree to anything I ask if he gets some attention in return. The man is a love sponge. He can't soak up enough.

I make my way over to the bed, moving slowly, enjoying his adoring gaze on me, until I'm close enough that he can grab me by the wrist. Then he pulls me down on top of him, rolls me to my back, throws a heavy leg over me, and kisses me with so much passion it takes my breath away.

He comes up for air only long enough to murmur, "Mornin', sweetheart." Then he kisses me again, more tenderly this time, cupping my face in his hand, his hair tickling my cheeks.

I run my hands up his muscular back, feeling like I'm sinking down into the mattress, melting and gooey like a marshmallow left in the sun. "Good morning to *you*, prancer," I say breathlessly when the kiss ends. "Though it's not morning anymore—it's afternoon. I can't believe we stayed up until four a.m."

"You're the one who had to watch just *one more* episode of *Peaky Blinders*."

"Sorry. Netflix is my Kryptonite. How'd you sleep?"

He nuzzles my neck, raising goose bumps all over my arms as he inhales deeply against my skin. In a husky voice, he says, "Best night's sleep of my life."

I smile, tightening my arms around him. "You've said that every morning since I got here."

"That's because every mornin' it's been true." He lifts his head and gazes down at me, smiling when he sees the happy expression on my face. "What's that big grin for?"

"For the most beautiful man in the world, with a heart almost as big as his ego."

He laughs, a low rumble of noise that makes warmth like sunshine spread through my chest.

"I've got things bigger than my heart *or* my ego, darlin'." He flexes his hips to make his point, and now I'm the one laughing.

"I see Godzilla's awake, too."

"Indeed he is. Awake and hungry."

"When *isn't* he awake and hungry? That thing is on steroids!"

"'Thing'?" Cam repeats, insulted.

I roll my eyes. "Oh, excuse me. I forgot I'm supposed to pay the family jewels their proper respect."

Cam's smile comes on slow and sexy. "And most of the time, woman, you do a hoora good job at showin' your respect."

Now it's my turn to be insulted. "*Most* of the time? What exactly are you implying?"

He grins at the sour look on my face and pinches my bottom. "Now who's got the big ego?"

"You're rubbing off on me," I grouse, pretending to be angry with a pout.

"Oh, I'll rub off on you all right," he breathes. He digs his fingers into my bottom and drags me closer against him so his hardness throbs right between my legs. When I gasp, he cuts it off with a kiss—deep, hot, and demanding.

"I've got a conference call in less than ten minutes." I try to stifle a moan by biting my lip when Cam moves his mouth to my neck and starts kissing a trail down to my collarbone. It feels so good. It always feels so damn good.

He nuzzles his nose between my breasts, then oh-so-gently bites my nipple, right through the sheer nightie.

This time I fail to stifle the moan. I arch into his mouth, sucking in a breath when he palms my breast and swirls his tongue around and around my hard nipple.

"Cam."

"Mmm."

He's nibbling. Oh God, he's *nibbling*. "I have a call with work in—"

"I'll be quick," he whispers, moving that hand from my breast down to my stomach, then sliding it between my legs. He rubs the heel of his palm against me because he knows how much I love it. How that simply drives me wild.

"Let's wait until after," I say. Or pant, technically. "I don't want to be quick this morning. I want to go slow. Long and slow and deep and hard and oh—"

I can't talk anymore because Cam is now doing something with his hand that requires all my mental focus.

In the other room, my cell phone rings.

Cam groans. "Bloody hell. She's early."

I try to push him away, but he doesn't budge. "Sweetie. I have to get that."

He flops onto his back with a dramatic sigh and flings an arm over his face. I clamber off the bed, plant a quick kiss on his chest, and head for the phone, saying over my shoulder, "You'd give Mrs. Dinwiddle a run for her money in the theatrics department, honey."

He's still muttering under his breath about the interruption as I leave the room. I snatch my cell from the coffee table in the living room where I left it last night when Cam picked me up from the sofa, threw me over his shoulder, and carried me into the bedroom, bitching that he'd had enough of TV and needed to get his fill of me.

I'm still waiting for him to be filled, but so far it hasn't happened.

"Joellen Bixby speaking."

"Happy Monday, Joellen. It's Portia. How are you?"

Her voice is warm. Over the past month and a half we've forged something that might actually qualify as a friendship, speaking on the phone several times a week, and not always about work. As it turns out, the ice queen has a really wicked sense of humor.

I sit down on the sofa and prop my feet on the coffee table, looking out the floor-to-ceiling windows of Cam's downtown Edinburgh flat to a panoramic view of Edinburgh Castle, the Meadows—a miniature version of Central Park—and the city center. "I'm great, Portia. How's everything at the home office?"

"Nothing interesting to report since we last spoke, except Denny has launched into some new seasonally themed fart jokes."

"Oh God. Valentine's Day fart jokes? I can't even imagine."

Portia laughs. "Yes. Apparently farts are the screams of trapped—"

"Stop!" I say loudly, waving my free hand in the air. "I left the country to escape fart jokes—I don't need you telling them to me over the phone!"

"I know for a fact you left the country for a different reason altogether, Joellen. And how is your Scottish baller?"

I have to laugh at the term and the innuendo in her voice. "Don't let Ruth in HR hear you talking like that or you'll get a black mark on your employment record. And he's great, thanks for asking." I sigh in contentment, dreamily twirling a lock of hair through my fingers. "He's amazing."

Portia says sharply, "If you're about to tell me you need time off for a honeymoon, I'm about to tell you there are *very* few places on earth without Wi-Fi—"

"Nobody's getting married! We're not even talking about that yet!"

There's a brief silence after my outburst, then Portia goes all practical on me. "Forgive the impropriety, but you're almost forty. You've probably got about half a dozen good eggs left."

"Whoa! We went from getting married straight to infertility! Have you been talking to my mother?"

"No," she says, "but I think *you'd* be a wonderful mother. No time like the present. So how's Beth Addison's book coming along? I can't wait to get that sucker to market. She's such a fantastic writer."

"You're giving me whiplash here, Portia."

"Keep up, Joellen. Just because you're not in Manhattan any longer doesn't mean I'll accept any slack in your mental pace." She pauses. "Or has all the haggis gone to your head?"

I watch as Cam ambles into the room, gorgeous in only a pair of white briefs. He strolls over to where I'm sitting, leans over the back of the sofa, sweeps aside my hair, and kisses my neck.

"I wouldn't eat haggis if you paid me a billion dollars. Let's get back to Beth Addison before this conversation completely goes off the rails."

Against the back of my neck, Cam murmurs, "We *should* talk about marriage, though. Considerin' I already talked to your parents about it." He stands and casually walks into the kitchen, as if he hasn't just dropped a grenade into my lap.

He's already talked to my parents about marrying me? Am I having a heart attack? Is this what a heart attack feels like? Oh God, I can't feel my face.

". . . on track with the dev edit?"

"What? Huh? What'd you say?" I twist around on the sofa so I can look at Cam. He's rummaging around in the cupboard for something, his back to me.

Portia's sigh sounds aggrieved. "I'm glad I didn't already patch the rest of the team in—you're hopeless today."

"Portia, I'm so sorry—can I call you back in five minutes? I'm having trouble with the connection. I'm going to get on a landline." Without waiting for her to answer, I hang up. Then I sit staring at Cam's broad back until he turns around and looks at me.

When he sees the expression on my face, he breaks into a grin. "Oh, no. She's thinkin'. I can smell the smoke from all the way over here."

In a small voice, I ask, "You talked to my parents about marrying me?"

"I know," he says, becoming serious. "It's a little ridiculous considerin' your advanced age, but when we tell our kids the story about how we fell in love, got married, and lived happily ever after, I wanna be able to say I asked your father for permission. Even though I really just *told* him I'd be marryin' his daughter, not asked, but that can be our little secret."

Kids. My heart races like a thoroughbred heading into the home stretch at Churchill Downs. I breathe loudly through my mouth, like I do when I have a cold. "But I've . . . I've only been here for six weeks."

Holding two tea bags he got from the cupboard, he saunters over to the stove. "Yep. And how many times during those six weeks have you told me how much you love it here?"

When I don't answer because I'm too busy hyperventilating through my mouth and wondering if instead of a heart attack I'm suffering a stroke, he continues the conversation without me.

"You love my flat. You love the city. You love workin' from home. You love Nanny O'Shea. You love the food—except for haggis—and the people, and the weather, and my mates on the Devils, and sittin' in the stands, watchin' me play. You love that Mr. Bingley has a girlfriend."

He gestures to the cat bed under the dining room table, where Mr. Bingley contentedly snoozes with a sleek black cat half his size named Cleo. Cam adopted her from a shelter when I first arrived because he thought it was time for Mr. Bingley to give up his bachelorhood. The two cats have been inseparable ever since. Even in sleep, they're curled around each other, one dark and one light, yin and yang.

"In fact," he pretends to think, tapping his chin with the tea bag, "I think the only thing you *haven't* yet said you love . . . is me."

He holds my gaze for a few beats, then turns the gas on under the kettle on the stove, gets two mugs from another cupboard, sets them on the counter, and drops the tea bags into them. Then he folds his arms over his chest, leans against the counter, and stares at me.

Me, sitting on the sofa, concentrating all my energy on staying upright. "I . . . I . . ."

Cam arches his brows. He cups a hand around one ear. "Sorry, what was that? Were you trying to say somethin', lass?"

I stand unsteadily, feeling my pulse in my whole body. Then I slowly make my way over to where Cam is standing in the kitchen. It seems as if I'm floating toward him, my feet barely skimming the ground. When I reach him, he takes me in his arms and gazes down at me with a secret little smile, his eyes half-lidded and hot.

"Go ahead," he prompts. "Tell me how you were in love with me from the start, only you mistook that funny feelin' in your stomach for gas. Tell me how I knocked you off your feet from the first moment I opened my mouth and you heard my incredibly sexy voice. Tell me how no other man on earth looks as good in a kilt as I do or makes you laugh like I do." His voice drops. "Or makes you scream like I do. Go on, lass. Tell me."

I'm trembling all over, my heart fluttering frantically like a trapped hummingbird inside my chest. "Yes," I whisper, gazing up into his eyes. "Yes to all that."

His secret smile deepens. He threads his fingers into my hair and combs them through, watching the strands flow over his hand. Then he gently tugs on a lock to bring me closer. "Now tell me how happy I make you."

"Stupidly happy. Amazingly happy. Yes."

He leans in and brushes his lips against my cheek. "And how you want to spend the rest of your life just like this." He gives me a quick, hard squeeze. "In my arms."

My throat is closing in on itself. My voice breaks when I say, "Yes."

Cam presses the softest of kisses on my neck, then looks deep into my eyes. In a husky whisper, he says, "Now tell me you love me, lass. And make it good, 'cause you've made me wait too long."

I exhale a shaky breath, gather myself, and do as he commands.

"I love you the way I love the smell of old books. I love you the way I love a hot bath on a cold day. I love you the way I love sonnets and ice cream and a swimsuit that doesn't make me look like I'm made of burrata. I love you the way I love the sun on my face in winter. The way I love a favorite song playing on the radio when I'm driving home from the beach on a summer day."

He swallows, his eyes shining with emotion. I go up on my toes and press a soft kiss to his lips.

Against his mouth, I murmur, "I love you like I love starry nights, and really crunchy pickles, and discovering an amazing new author, and Sunday mornings in bed with the paper and chocolate croissants. Like I love the way the air smells after it rains. Like I love to laugh."

He drops his face to my neck and presses it there, tightening his arms around me, so I whisper the last part right into his ear.

"But actually I love you more than all those things combined, Cameron McGregor. I love you like I never knew I could love anything. You're more important to me than air itself, and I don't ever want to spend a day without you. Because you believed in me, this little ugly duckling finally became a swan."

A delicate shudder runs through his chest. He inhales deeply, squeezing me so tight I feel every single wild beat of his heart.

"You were always a swan, you bloody idiot," he says in a strangled voice.

I tilt my head back and laugh, though my eyes are filled with tears. They're happy tears, however. Happy-ever-after tears. "Whatever I am, prancer, I'm yours. Now kiss me before you say something stupid and ruin the moment."

"God, you're bossy," he grumbles, but when he lifts his head, he's grinning from ear to ear. His eyes are filled with happy tears, too. He bends his head toward mine but then stops. "Wait."

I crinkle my brow. "What?"

"You haven't said you'll marry me."

"Well . . . technically, you haven't asked."

He pretends to think about it. "You're right. I haven't."

When he doesn't say anything else, I prompt, "So?"

"So I think I should wait until after lunch. I'm pretty hungry."

"Cam!" Outraged, I smack his arm.

He laughs, delighted by my reaction, which is obviously exactly what he was hoping for. "All right, hold your horses, Miss Snufflebottom, gimme a minute to compose myself before I pop the question!"

I stare at him with pursed lips as he clears his throat and adopts a serious expression. When he looks at me, I realize I'm holding my breath.

He declares, "We're gettin' married."

"Ugh! That wasn't a question!"

He presses his lips together to keep from laughing. "*Are* we getting married?"

I growl like a bear, ready to rip his head off. This is the first marriage proposal I've ever received, and the man is making jokes! I look at his smug, smirking face and decide I need to take matters into my own hands.

"Fine. I can see I'm going to have to take control of this situation." I straighten my shoulders, lift my chin, and look him right in the eye. "Cameron McGregor, will you marry me?"

His expression goes all melty, as if he's fighting tears. He takes my face in his hands, whispers vehemently, "I thought you'd never ask," and kisses me like he's starving.

When the kettle starts to whistle, neither one of us pays it any mind.

Once upon a time, in a land not so far away,
A duckling born to a family of swans
Was mistakenly led astray.
It took a prince of beauty and brawn
With a brogue like rich brown sugar
To show the duckling the way back home
So she could grow bigger, better, surer
Of herself so she no longer had to roam
Through the dark forest of lost hearts.
But along the way she fell under his spell
From the prince she never wanted to part,
In the circle of his arms she longed to dwell.
So the duckling said to her princely valentine
"For all time I'll be yours, and forever you'll
     be mine."

ACKNOWLEDGMENTS

This is the fun part of the book, after all the cursing and crying is done and the bleeding has almost completely stopped. Writing a novel has several things in common with childbirth, not the least of which is the overwhelming relief at a successful delivery after many months of uncomfortable gestation. (I don't have kids, but the comparison was irresistible.)

Before I get to the thank-yous, I want to tell you about a close friend I had when I was a teenager. We'll call her Eva (not her real name). Eva was the most beautiful girl I have ever seen, even to this day, some thirty years later. She was of Irish descent, with long, dark hair, enormous crystal-blue eyes, and skin so perfect it glowed. Tall, graceful, and always the most popular girl throughout junior high and high school, she was universally loved.

She was also filled with intense self-loathing.

Convinced her perfect body was fat, she dieted rigorously, eating only saltines, rice cakes, and celery, until she grew so thin her period stopped. She worked out like a machine, running miles every day before school. She was obsessed with how she looked, down to the tiniest detail, and would spend hours in front of the mirror, trying on new outfits, picking at imaginary blemishes, learning new makeup techniques to contour already-hollow cheeks.

Her mother couldn't be bothered to notice. She was too busy drinking chardonnay. Her father—her parents were divorced—liked to tell Eva she better get married quick because she was too dumb for college.

Eva scored a 1510 on the SAT, in the ninety-ninth percentile. When I told her she could get into almost any college with that test score, that she could go to Harvard if she wanted, she laughed.

She was too dumb for college, she said. Everyone knew that. It was a mistake.

The day she turned eighteen, Eva got breast implants. A few months later, after we graduated, she met a man twenty-five years her senior, a wealthy businessman who spotted her crossing a parking lot. He was struck by her beauty and followed her to her car to introduce himself. Within a few weeks of meeting, they'd eloped to Europe. I never heard from her again.

Several years later, I got a phone call from my mother. Sit down, she said. I have terrible news.

Eva had been murdered. Her much-older husband had poisoned her over the course of many months with overdoses of prescription medication. He'd buried her before even telling her parents she was dead.

The tragedy of Eva is one of huge potential lost to neglect and negativity. People can internalize even the most obvious falsehoods if they're repeated often enough. When you're surrounded by negativity, that's what you tend to absorb. You become what you're most often told you are.

I wish I could go back in time and tell Eva how much I loved her, how smart she was, how much she had to offer the world, but I can't. But every time I meet a young girl, I want to hug her close and tell her she's so much more special than she realizes. That her worth as a person and her looks are two entirely different things.

If you have young daughters at home, I hope you'll do the same. They hear every word you say . . . and all the things you don't.

THANK YOU to my team at Montlake Romance, who has nurtured my career since 2011. I love our partnership and hope it continues until I no longer want to write, which will be never. Thanks to Maria Gomez, my editor, who makes me laugh every time I talk to her. Thanks to Melody Guy, my developmental editor, who is a genius, and who knows how to say nice things about my work while pointing out how much it needs to be improved. Thanks also to the copy editors, proofreaders, and PR and marketing teams at Amazon Publishing, who are the best.

To my "old" readers, thanks for sticking with me for fifteen novels. I had no idea I'd be here, either. To my new readers, I hope you'll stick around for the next fifteen. At my current pace of work, that will be approximately four years from when this book was published, so hang in there. I promise I'll keep it interesting.

To my mother, who turned ninety this year, thank you for focusing on building my character and inner strength and for making it perfectly clear that my value as a human being isn't tied to my looks or to anyone else's opinion of me.

And finally, to my best friend, Jay Geissinger, who also happens to be the best human being I've ever met, thank you for loving all my parts, inside and out, even the ugly ones.

ABOUT THE AUTHOR

 A former headhunter, J.T. Geissinger is the author of more than a dozen novels of paranormal romance, romantic suspense, and contemporary romance, including *Melt for You* and *Burn for You* in her Slow Burn series. She is the recipient of a Prism Award for Best First Book and a Golden Quill Award for Best Paranormal/Urban Fantasy. She's a two-time finalist for the RITA Award from the Romance Writers of America, and her works have been finalists for the Booksellers' Best, National Readers' Choice, and Daphne du Maurier Awards. Find her on the web at www.jtgeissinger.com.